The
Lavender Soul

LK WALSH

Shaun & Kim,
Make an adventure of
every day!

[signature]

4-6-18

PelianWords Publishing House

ISBN: 978-0-9997298-0-9
LCCN: 2017963481

PelianWords Publishing House
Lompoc, CA
pelianwordspublishinghouse.com

Cover art by Catherine Walsh

Manufactured in the United States of America

This book is dedicated to my parents, who have always believed in me and pushed me to fight for my dreams. I love you both more than words.

In a time of great darkness,

when the land has been turned cold by blackened hearts,

a warrior will come and awaken Zakiyyah, Deliverer of Arivos' Light.

This poor noble spirit will have to battle a torrent of power,

and must choose a path through explosive light, or seductive dark.

Only by passing through the gate of White Fire

can the Lavender Soul awaken the Golden Dragon,

who will deliver Arivos' Justice and Grace to all of Zerahlinda.

The Lavender Soul

Prologue

The captive's body, covered in cuts and bruises, was thrown on the ground of the dank cave with a sickening, limp crack. He had been beaten almost to death while being dragged away from his homeland and delivered into the dwelling of a monster. He did not scream—not because he was numb to the pain that coursed through his nervous system—but because his body was too weak and swollen to exert the sound of terror running frantic underneath his skin. The Wachiru, slaves of the monster, had tortured this captive past the level of pain he thought possible, and now they stood against the wall by the cave's entrance like dogs waiting for a command.

Through the tiny slots of vision that his swollen eyes allowed, the prisoner saw his captor's face.

This noxious evil presence, a creature that had once been a man, stared at the treat his minions had brought him. Crouching down, his head cocked to the side, the captor looked like a curious and disappointed lion cub that had just killed a bug with one playful swat. His face was angular and sharp, his eyes like a raven's, pure black and viciously apathetic.

The prisoner tried to scramble his beaten limbs to propel himself out of the cave, away from the horror that surely awaited him. "Dra-Dra—"

An incredibly strong hand slapped the captive's battered face. "You dare address me by name? I am Master, or Dark One. Now tell me!" he yelled, unleashing so much anger into the musty cave that his Wachiru ran. The hostage's breath came out in rapid, hot spurts, the sound horribly grated by his freshly broken nose.

The prisoner's chin dripped with the mixture of his salty tears and the crimson flow from his nose. "I haven't seen her in a month. She…she has been barred from leaving the estate. She can't even write me letters." His voice was shaky and weak, the words uttered between lips that could barely open.

The interrogator hooked a finger under the man's chin. "How does that concern me?"

The man's eyes rolled with the searing pain of the tormentor's cold flesh. "The last night I saw her…when she told me all servants were restricted to the estate grounds…in her frustration…" The words came out in frantic, raspy huffs. "She said something…something she wasn't supposed to…" The tears stopped, and there was a flicker of hesitation.

The villain's hand slid around the prisoner's throat.

"She said…she said, 'Only Arivos knows when I can come home again, and all because that girl has lavender eyes!'" The man's eyes dulled with regret the moment he uttered the words.

A smile revealed yellow teeth and dastardly intention as the Dark One took his hand off the man's throat, one finger at a time. He stood, walked over to a table that leaned against the black wall of the cave, and picked up a scalpel made entirely out of a single piece of emerald.

"What…what're you doing?"

With a smile, the fiend turned around, calmly walked back over to the crumpled prisoner, and crouched over him.

The oppressor held the man's head down against the cold black stone, brought the emerald scalpel to the man's eye, and began carving the outline of a raven's head into the soft white of the captive's eyeball.

The visceral screams of unanticipated agony lured the Wachiru back into the cave. Drawn by the allure of watching his pain, they tried to feel the palpable sensation of torture in the air before the man passed out.

The monster lifted the prisoner's eyelid and looked with pride on his carving. "You will never feel pain—or anything else —ever again." He looked up at his slaves. "Get him healed. He will lead us to the Lavender Soul."

Light glinted through the emerald scalpel, beautifully casting flashes of green onto the dull black and bright red, as the

Dark One wiped the blade off on his trench coat. "All Arivos will know once we find *her* is the sight of his whole creation drowning in blood and choking on the ash of their own destruction."

The Wachiru stood with the body of their newly made brother in their arms, their eyes gleaming with blank stares of fearful excitement. They were almost salivating at their master's words.

The evil overlord looked at them in disgust. "Find her, now."

They ran out of the cave with their limp burden—and soon-to-be guide.

The beast of a man ran his finger along the blade edge of his emerald scalpel, a dark drop of blood rolled down the green stone. "I am eager to meet her." His voice was as cold and smooth as the scalpel in his hand, and for a moment, the color of his eyes burst into a black so dark, nature wouldn't dare claim it.

Chapter 1
Unwelcome Validation

"In a time of great darkness, when the land has been turned cold by blackened hearts…" A ray of sunshine came through the window, putting a glare on the page from which Yateem was reading aloud. He readjusted himself in the velvet armchair and continued. "…a warrior will come and awaken Zakiyyah, Deliverer of Arivos' Light…."

"Pssh." Vera leaned her head against the backrest of the chair and rolled her eyes at the ceiling.

"…This poor *noble* spirit will have to battle a torrent of power," Yateem continued, "and must choose a path through explosive light, or seductive dark…"

"Oooh, seductive."

His voice grew louder. "…Only by passing through the gate of White Fire can the Lavender Soul awaken the Golden Dragon, who will deliver Arivos' Justice and Grace to all of Zerahlinda."

"Oh, the world will rejoice!"

"Vera, it is dangerous to belittle Fae wisdom. They have lived since the creation of Zerahlinda—"

"And will live forever. I know. Can we please just not talk about this?"

Yateem Rukan Wulfgar of Xipili had heard this beautiful young woman speak that phrase for the past eight years, but he couldn't blame her for being frustrated. For half her life she had been pushed to think of herself as a sort of warrior for peace. "Vera Xochiquetzal of Adowa…"

"Ooh…my full name, I must be in trouble."

1

"Your sarcasm and attitude will not change what people think of you."

"I have lavender eyes, and because of this, people think I'm part of a story! What does my auburn hair say about me? Am I going to simultaneously catch on fire? I find it infuriating that I have been treated differently my entire life because some fairies got bored and decided to write stupid legends." Vera looked out the window, her hands clenched and unclenched her cotton dress. She wanted so badly to be able to run across the estate grounds to the sea, not to swim, but to escape.

Sitting in the chair opposite her, Yateem ran his fingers over the carvings of dolphins, humpback whales, and other sea creatures in the armrests. Their eyes met as Vera checked whether he was going to continue his lesson, but his attentions were directed toward the sea, and he seemed lost in memory. His square jaw and dark skin told of his island life, a life he had long since given up.

"Yateem?" Vera said gently, keeping in mind the mini-tantrum she just threw.

"What Vera?" He let a sigh escape out of his chest.

"How long has it been since you've been home?"

"This is my home," he said, continuing to gaze at the sea.

Vera smirked and exhaled a breath of resignation. "As much as I hate to admit that the color of someone's eyes has anything to do with their soul, your eyes are the color of the sea and go from dull stones to raging teal tsunamis when you stare out toward Aequitas."

Yateem had a growing grin on his face. "Teal tsunamis? A bit melodramatic."

"It was the first thing I could think of." Vera's broad smile cleared away any frustration lingering between them. "I'm just trying to remember if you've ever left me to go home."

"I will be with you until your last breath. That is my duty as a handler."

"I'm sorry…you must feel trapped." Vera stared at her hands, the knuckles white as they gripped her knees. Her eyes rose slightly to track the progress of an armed guard marching past the rhododendron bushes in the garden, the multiple swords along his belt glinting sunlight.

Despite the thin smile on his handsome face, Yateem's countenance was melancholic when he said, "Not trapped at all. For sixteen years I have lived in a grand villa. Aequitas is nothing too special—an island, surrounded by water, no adventure, no spirited girl to look after and tutor." His eyes betrayed his real age when he talked of his home, which added a haunted element to his youthful, mid-thirties appearance.

"More like impossibly bratty girl," Vera pouted.

"Well, we all have our moments…or years," he said with a sly smile. "Besides, you have not been a girl for a very long time." Yateem looked at Vera as the adolescent looked out over the gardens of Saman, her family's estate. He had wished to distract her from watching the guards during their perimeter check.

Vera crossed her hands in her lap and closed her eyes as she enjoyed the sun soaking into her coastal olive skin. Her curly auburn hair caught the sun's rays, and for a moment, it almost looked like living fire. "If next to no one knows that I exist, then how do we know that this legend is real?"

"People know you exist. Look at all the servants here."

"You mean the ones sworn to secrecy—the ones recently barred from leaving the estate?"

"Yet they still talk. What about the king and queen?"

"They're family, obviously they know I'm real. But how do we know that my eyes mean anything more than that I was born with light-purple eyes?"

"Draven was the first," he said, his voice slightly strained as memories of his hands covered in the blood of his comrades, and that monster's hollow black eyes staring across a battlefield flashed in his mind.

"And he failed. I know how the story goes, but that was what—a hundred years ago? For all we know, Draven was born with black eyes and was always evil and powerful. The facts may have been changed to prove the legend true."

Yateem ran his fingers through his dark-brown, wavy hair. "Why must we always have this conversation after our lessons?"

Vera stood, her bare feet making no noise on the marble tiles. "Because it is a little fantastical that a sixteen year old, with barely any exposure to the outside world, can be expected to suddenly find a White Gate that leads to a snoring Golden Dragon, that will help her vanquish all the evil in the world. Besides the swordsmanship lessons from you, how can this—" Vera gestured to herself, grabbing the sides of her flowing, pear-colored dress, "—be considered a warrior?"

Her stubbornly clenched jaw and high cheekbones were a testament to Vera's ancient royal heritage. As she stood in the shadows of the parlor, her olive skin took on a richer tone. Although moderately short in stature, her athletic musculature gave her curves, which only added to the beauty of the contrast between her loose auburn curls, her tan skin, and her lavender eyes.

Yateem closed the large leather-bound book that was on his lap, walked it over to one of the sitting room's bookshelves, and put it back in its home. "It is time for some fresh air."

"Do you want to make sure the guards are hiding at their posts, or should they be in constant battle mode and follow us?" Vera asked as she strolled past Yateem. Even with her head held high, she couldn't pass the height of his shoulder.

Taking a long step to catch up with Vera, Yateem lightly squeezed her shoulders. "It is for your—"

"Protection…I know. I'm too young. I wouldn't understand what's best for me. I just have to trust you," Vera muttered under her breath as she pressed her cheek to Yateem's right hand before brushing his hands off her shoulders.

The sun warmed the pair nicely as they walked on the bluffs of Ziva, which offered a marvelous view of the Seija Sea, and which were a safe, comfortable distance from the grand villa of Saman while remaining just in sight of the two guards that stood watching Yateem and Vera through a looking glass.

"Vera, we have to quiet some of the things that people are saying. Draven is looking for you." Tall and muscular, Yateem walked alongside Vera with all the grace and fluidity of an alpha lion as his dark waves swayed in the light sea breeze.

"Finally! I have been saying we should tell people they are crazy since the day all this Lavender Soul stuff started!" She closed her eyes to feel the warmth of the sun on her face, but felt a cold blast instead.

Yateem pushed Vera behind him and drew his sword.

"Calm down, Hebian. I come only to see if the rumors are true." The fairy's voice was a river, brisk and forceful, and Vera realized that the fairy's body seemed like a river too, shimmering and languid, like she wasn't really there.

"What rumors?" Yateem asked, maintaining his protective stance.

"Has Arivos given us another Lavender Soul?" The projection's jade eyes pierced everything they looked at, her hair a golden current flowing down to her back, shimmering as it played with the breeze. Where a human had eyebrows, she had markings that looked like small cresting waves that vacillated color as if water rippled beneath them. Her lips were drawn tight; no smiles had visited her in a while. "This projection will not stay long. It is a simple question. Answer it."

"Who sent you?"

"Yeah! Who do you think you are?" Vera's question lacked the respect Yateem's had shown.

The eyes of the projection changed from the jade of a lagoon to the magenta of a spiky urchin. Her image quivered, rippling with her restrained rage. "I am the first Lavender Soul's handler. How dare you talk to me in that tone!"

"Oh, that's right. I read about you…Mahajleeze right?" Vera smirked.

Yateem's hand gripped Vera's arm and his sword hand was outstretched in a passive offering of peace. "I am…She did not…"

Majlis rose up as an intimidating wave. "My name is My-lis. Lady of the seas. Tamer of lakes. Friend and master of water. My-LIS! You arrogant little toad!" As her body ebbed back down, the woven sea grass of her dress swayed in the aftershock of her rage, and the golden strands of her hair slowly descended from the wrathful mane it had formed around Majlis' perfectly sculpted porcelain face.

Vera shook like she had escaped being swept off a ship in a monsoon. Her mouth opened as if she wanted to speak, but all she could do was stare at Majlis.

"I did not project myself here to humble a spoiled young lady, and I cannot hold this much longer since I had to check her insolence." Her jade eyes focused on Yateem, who was trying to be respectful by not staring too long at her alluring face. "Hebian, do not let this girl run wild. If she is the next Lavender Soul, you have to be prepared…" Majlis' projection wobbled.

"I am prepared to protect her." Yateem sheathed his sword, squared his shoulders, and lifted his chin.

"No, you are not prepared for—" Majlis' slender body contracted, condensed to the size of a blowfish, hovered where her head used to be, and then suddenly exploded, leaving a pond the color of jade behind.

Both Vera and Yateem were soaked and standing waist deep in glistening water. The melody of drops falling from their hair was the only sound until the clanking of metal and heavy, rapid footsteps approached the newly made pond.

"Sir! My Lady! Are you alright? We saw a woman suddenly appear and ran as fast as we could." A strain of panic tightened the guard's voice as both of the guards' chests heaved in much needed air, their grip on their ash-wood spears far too tight. "Do you need help out of there?"

Both guards edged toward the water with confused expressions, their spears pointed down toward imagined water creatures.

"No. Return to your post." Yateem did not turn around to look at the anxious guards, afraid that his own confusion would stir a panic across the ranks.

"But sir, there is a pond…"

"Yes, I can see that. Return to your post, and tell the stable master that a small escort will be leaving tomorrow at dawn."

"Yes sir." In unison the guards complied, bowed, and turned on their heels to march back to their posts.

Once the clanking of the guards died off, Vera sucked in an unsteady breath. "Can you possibly…I mean…what just happened?"

"Astral-projection." Yateem wiped the water from his face.

Vera gaped at Yateem.

"Who would have thought our walk would turn into a swim?" Yateem said, a nervous laugh accompanying his attempt to lighten the mood.

"I don't understand. Why are we standing in a pond?"

"Majlis astral-projected. She took herself out of her body and used the groundwater in this area to project her spirit to us."

"So she's as big as a pond in real life?!"

"No, no. The energy that it took to bring her here and hold the water together in her form for that long is equivalent to condensing this medium-size pond into a single drop. So when she left, she released that energy. Thus, we are drenched."

"I don't like her." Vera wrung her hair out and turned to wade toward the bank.

Yateem stayed, thoughtfully tapping the water that lapped against his belt buckle. He glanced over his shoulder at Vera as she trudged out of the water. His face was full of self-doubt as his eyes looked back down at the tiny luminescent waves his movement was making. The sound of Vera's frustrated mumbling as she tried to warm herself in the early autumn sun brought him back to reality.

"She called me a toad! Why am I supposed to respect fairies if they are rude!" Vera plopped herself down on the hillside.

"Because they know things, Vera! And if you had not acted like a spoiled, discourteous little toad, then she could have finished what she came to tell *me*!" Yateem articulated each word clearly over his shoulder at her, not wanting to face her yet.

Vera sat up, her eyes shining from the tears building up behind her lids. "Well, I'm sorry that I didn't know how to pronounce her name! I've only read it in those stupid fairy legends. That's not my fault!"

Yateem slapped the water in front of him and finally turned, his face aflame. "It was the way that you sneered her name! Like you have the right to insult her without hesitation!"

"I am supposedly this Lavender Soul. *My-LIS* even said so herself! You would think that she would have to respect *me* more, not the other way around."

As Yateem strode out of the pond, he did not notice the splashes his steps made as he approached Vera. "I believe I just got a glimpse of what Majlis was going to warn me of." The water sloshed in his leather boots as he stormed past Vera, not looking back to see her wet arms reaching out for him.

"Yateem, I'm..." Vera's whisper blew off with the breeze as goosebumps appeared on her skin. She shook from the cooling touch of the sea breeze, and her lip hurt from the force of her teeth as she tried to choke down the tears in her eyes. "I'm scared."

Chapter 2
False Sense of Security

       Yateem and Vera were both in a state of shock. The surprise visit from one of the most powerful creatures in the whole world made Vera's eyes seem a bit too lavender, the legend of the Lavender Soul too real, and the danger of it all too close. They needed answers.

       Yateem was braiding his gennadius' thick silky mane while humming a soft lullaby, thinking about the appearance of Majlis as the sun began to rise and start the day. Vulcan nuzzled his master, almost knocking Yateem off the stool he was standing on.

       "Whoa there!" Yateem said, wrapping his arms around Vulcan's long neck to keep from falling and making the gennadius purr. "Vulcan, you will get a treat *after* I am done with your mane." He gently pushed Vulcan's face forward so that he could continue braiding.

       Vulcan's back was a full six feet above the ground, and his tiger stripes highlighted his enormous muscles, which were bulky and sleek. The gennadius' body made the animal a natural athlete. Looking like a cross between a Bengal tiger and a Clydesdale workhorse, and with the strength to bound over land at lethal speeds and pounce on their prey with fatal accuracy, these mountain creatures were made to survive and persevere through the greatest of obstacles. Their faces, while resembling a tiger's, were elongated like a horse, giving them a bigger jaw with which to crush their prey.

       Yateem was tying the end of the braid when a metallic thud behind him brought him out of his thoughts. He turned to see a servant stretching his arms after setting down his burden. "Rafa, what is that?"

"Lady Vera's trunk, sir." Rafa, who, bowed deeply toward Yateem.

"I gave her saddlebags to pack in. Where are those?"

"I was about to go back for them. Begging your pardon, sir, but can you put the trunk on the wagon while I go get the saddlebags?"

Yateem let out a heavy, frustrated moan. "No. No. No. No."

Rafa bowed again, so deeply this time it looked like he was going to touch the ground with his nose. "Forgive me, Lord Yateem! It's just that I have to grab the saddlebags, and cinch them on the saddle, and then put the canopy on Minerva before Vera comes down." He was half-bowing and half-begging Yateem with his eyes for help.

Yateem jumped down from the stool, causing Vulcan to huff and Rafa to flinch. "I will not load the trunk because it is not coming with us. Please take it back to Vera and explain to her that I have graciously put all the food rations in my saddlebags, so hers are completely empty for her to put all the clothes she *needs* in them."

"I do not think she is going to like that."

"Oh, and please tell her that she does not get a canopy on Minerva. That will draw too much attention on us."

"Can you please tell her, sir?"

"Thank you, Rafa. You are a strong and brave young man. Now go utilize those qualities."

The servant boy slouched his shoulders, then slapped the handles as he lifted and lugged the rather humungous bamboo trunk with bronze lion feet back to where it came from.

Shaking his head, Yateem watched the boy tromp to his doom then turned back to his gennadius, who also seemed to pity the boy as he shook his head and huffed out a big breath. "Well, Vulcan, we are about to embark on another long journey. Are you ready?"

Vulcan stamped his heavy paws on the cobblestones, lifted his large head, and let out a roar that made a passing maid scream out the second-floor window.

"I will take that as a yes," Yateem chuckled.

Yateem checked his cinches, making sure that Vulcan had not loosened the saddle by holding his breath when Yateem had tightened it, and also making sure that the saddlebags were as secure and comfortable as possible for Vulcan. "Well, at this rate we will not leave until tomorrow morning!" Yateem looked at the horizon and saw that the sun was just above it. "I better check and make sure the stable boys put Minerva's saddle on." Vulcan swatted Yateem with his thick orange tail before he could get out of reach. "Ouch! Fine, fine!"

Yateem went over to one of the stalls and grabbed a handful of thimbleberries from a basket hanging on the wall. Vulcan could smell the sweet juice in the short, plump berries and shifted his weight with excitement, stretching out his front legs and bringing his head closer to the ground. Yateem put his hands together, making them as flat as possible, and offered the berries to his felinesque friend. Vulcan carefully licked the berries out of Yateem's hands as he'd been trained, so that he did not accidentally bite his master. Finished with his treat, he began to purr and seemed content to let Yateem retrieve Vera's gennadius, Minerva.

As Yateem walked over to the other side of the stables, the two guards that witnessed Majlis' appearance came around the corner holding the reins of two large gennadius in their hands and bowed.

"My Lord Yateem, what are our orders?"

"Ride ahead of us. I do not want to be seen together, that would be too suspicious."

"Yes, my lord." The tawny irises of the guard's eyes flashed with a spark of fear. "And if we come across any Wachiru?"

"Kill them." Yateem's tone was as hard and cold as iron.

The guards bowed, brought their gennadius over to the loading ladders, mounted, and left the stable courtyard at a sprint. Yateem followed their progress with a sorrowful smile and then went to retrieve Vera's steed.

"Yateem! Yateem! How am I supposed to pack for a long trip in these tiny bags? Yateem!" Vera entered the courtyard with the saddlebags slung over her right shoulder. "Yateem! My dresses are squashed, and I can only fit four riding outfits with everything else! Where are you?"

"Settle!" Backing out of the stables, Yateem kept his distance from Vera's gennadius, who was agitated and growling, much like her master across the courtyard.

"Mini!" Vera dropped her saddlebags and stretched out her arms toward her loyal pet. In an instant Minerva crossed over the stretch of stones between them and purred as Vera wrapped her arms around the tall animal's black and white chest, while Minerva nuzzled her cheek against Vera's lower back. "Oh Mini, tell Yateem we need a wagon so that you and Vulkey don't have to carry saddlebags."

Minerva looked back at Yateem and huffed.

"Vera, you do not need to wear something different every day. Two saddlebags are more than enough. Besides, when full of real supplies, like the food and water in mine, they should only weigh forty pounds." Yateem picked up the abandoned saddlebags and groaned at the unexpected weight. "But I should have known that you would find a way to condense a trunk load into two stingray leather bags."

"I like options. Besides, we're going to my uncle's palace and I need to look presentable." Vera stroked Mini's face, tracing the black stripes that curved around her sky-blue eyes, and then rubbed the white stripes surrounded by the black ones, to distract Minerva from Yateem strapping on the saddlebags.

"Vera, please just cooperate. I know that you do not like leaving home on short notice, but we need to figure out what is going on."

"Do you know one of the reasons why I love to ride Mini?"

"She is temperamental like you?"

"Ha. Ha. No, she's faster than Vulkey."

"Vulcan."

"Perhaps we should race today!"

"This is not a recreational ride. Please do not do anything that would cause more people to talk."

"Uh huh, I'll try my best. What do you say, Mini? Ready for a ride?" Minerva shook her head and stamped her feet as one of the stable boys brought out a loading ladder for Vera.

Yateem and Vera mounted their gennadius and turned northeast. Yateem lifted his face up to the blushing sky. "Arivos, protect us."

Vera crossed her arms, resting her hands on her shoulders and watching Minerva's shoulder blades as they alternated stabbing into the sky. "Arivos, guide our steps."

"Guide our minds."

"Guide our hearts."

"Please, Arivos, let our destined path be clear."

Vera took in a deep breath. "And give us the strength to tread upon it."

"Amen," they said together, their voices creating a reflective harmony.

"Looks like we will have fine traveling weather." Yateem scanned the horizon with thinly veiled alertness.

The smell of Minerva's paws unsettling the morning dewdrops with every step invigorated Vera. "Yes, the soldiers in front of us should make sure of that. It's a good thing you made us leave so early. I think we can make it to Kuno before nightfall."

"I see you have been studying your geography. Well done, but we are not going into any towns or villages."

"What? We're going to be arriving at dusk...people will be in their homes. No one will see—or care."

"The world is not how you imagine it."

"You worry too much."

"Majlis, a fairy that by all accounts is a recluse in the Ruwaydah mountains, astral-projected to us because of rumors of a new Lavender Soul. I am not taking the chance that one of Draven's spies will see us."

"I never get to leave home, and now that I'm off the grounds of Saman, I still don't get to see any life!"

Yateem took in an exaggerated gasp. "Just look around you. The rolling hills, the sporadic patches of flowers, the critters and birds—oh, the birds! Swooping through the air as if just for you!" Yateem lightly slapped Vera's arm as he spread his arms wide.

Vera knocked away his hand. "You know what I mean… crazy," she said, looking away from Yateem to hide her smile.

He inhaled through his nose, filling his lungs with crisp morning air. "We should enjoy these days of restful traveling before we reach Lolani and have to hold a palace schedule."

"I guess I can try." Vera's pout was hardly convincing.

Yateem shook his head and patted Vera's shoulder. "I appreciate the effort."

They continued on, the gennadius' steps becoming a smooth rhythm accented by the occasional grunt or the playful thud of Vulcan's thick orange tail hitting Minerva's white one. Vera had put together the interlocking redwood ladder that had been strapped on top of her black stingray leather saddlebags and now handed down the smooth deerskin saddle to Yateem. She tried to take off the bags but decided to let Yateem's stronger muscles do the task instead. He softly chuckled as he lifted the overstretched leather and looked over to see that Vulcan was drinking his fill of the light-blue stream they were camping next to, whose banks told of years of drought.

"I am going to set up the tent. Let Minerva get a drink, and see if you can find some firewood under those aspens over there." Yateem unfolded the dirt-colored canvas tent and used a rock to beat in the poles near the insignia that their escort carved into the ground, assuring Yateem that this campsite was secluded and safe. He tied the corners of the canvas to the bottom of every pole, making a seven-foot by four-foot cube.

Climbing back up the ladder, Vera pulled the blanket off Minerva's back and dropped it on top of the saddle, then immediately brought her hand up to her nostrils. "You smell horrible! You already were smelly, but that blanket released the

small-animal-near-here-may-or-may-not-have-died stink!"
Minerva turned her back on Vera and walked over to Vulcan to
join him for a drink after the long day's ride. "Please roll in the
water after you drink, Mini."

"Vera, the sun's going down fast. Will you get the
firewood before it gets dark, please?"

"Yeah, yeah, I got it." Vera galumphed fifty meters to the
small grove of white aspens, mumbling to herself as she
snatched up fallen branches and twigs, "Firewood, stupid, inn
would be nice, but no." The breeze made the trees sing, and Vera
closed her eyes and opened her lips to giggle with the melody.

Then the breeze changed to a cold gust, and Vera's lips
curled into a frown as she opened her eyes and proceeded to
collect branches as quickly as she could, hugging the wood close
to her chest. The sky was turning red as the sun sunk, igniting
the already red and orange leaves of the trees in the growing
darkness.

When the trees stopped singing and started to groan,
Vera hurried her steps and sped her hands. The fiery leaves
rained down and blustered around her, swirling up and down,
blinding her. The torrent of oranges and reds grew and sped up,
like a tornado, suffocating Vera. She tried to scream but had no
air, clinging still to the branches in her arms as if they were the
only thing keeping her afloat in this airless swirling sea of leaves.

Finally, she charged forward, breaking out of the vortex
and running into the smooth bark of a tree, the groaning sound
deafening her, the smell of newly broken soil directing her
attention to the ground. The roots resembled snakes as they slid
up, out, through the soil. The trees were moving in on her. Vera
tried to run, but could barely move for fear and the roots
tangling her feet. She clenched her firewood so tightly that blood
trickled out of small scratches all over her arms. The pale bark
was all she could see in every direction, the space between most
of the trees too small for her to escape.

She caught a glimpse of the grass outside the trees,
which cleared her mind enough to see the wiggle room through
the two trees closest to what looked like freedom to Vera. Her
torso fit through the space, but the roots hooked and looped at

her ankles. Vera fell hard on the moving ground, her hips lodging in between two trees that were still closing in, making her feel that she was about to be snapped in two.

Still clinging to the branches in her arms, Vera used them as leverage as she started to crawl out, kicking her feet free of the roots and dislodging her hips by shifting her weight. Once her feet were clear of the line of trees and roots, Vera jumped up and sprinted away from the grove, finding her voice on the way.

"YATEEM!" Her fright made the 200 feet between her and the camp disappear in three seconds.

He ran out of the tent, his steel curved dagger in hand, while Vulcan and Minerva stopped wrestling in the water. All stood frozen, trying to comprehend what caused the terror in Vera's voice.

"Why didn't you help me?"

Yateem relaxed his grip on the dagger. "With the firewood? You are strong. You can obviously handle carrying branches." He pointed toward the load in her arms and suddenly went pale. "Why are you bleeding? Was someone in the wood? What is wrong?"

"You must have heard it…it was so loud." Vera stared through Yateem with the memory.

"Heard what? Vera, please…" Yateem cautiously stepped toward her.

"The trees!" She threw her armload of aspen branches against the ground, as if that sound could reenact the chaos that just surrounded her.

"The trees? Did some animal scare you?" Yateem's voice was fluid, calm. He sheathed his knife in his boot and slowly approached Vera with his palms up as a sign of comfort, never taking his eyes away from her crazed lavender stare.

Vera's lips were trembling, trying to contain what wanted to spill out. She looked at Yateem and then jumped over the jagged mess of firewood and into his arms, sobbing. "They closed in on me. Roots…moved. How? Why? It was so loud…I couldn't breathe…" Vera shook. "Please don't make me sleep here."

Yateem hugged her and held her head against his heart, as he always did to calm her down. His eyes were on the aspens that were in the same position as before. He had not heard a sound other than the splashing of Vulcan and Minerva playfully wrestling in the stream. Kissing the top of her head, he stroked her hair as a shade of suspicion fell on Yateem's face. "I do not want to stay in villages, Vera. It is too dangerous."

Vera stopped weeping. "You don't believe me?"

He sighed. "I do. It is just…I do. If we make a fire, the trees will not want to come near us, right?"

Vera shoved Yateem away from her in frustration as Minerva shook herself and strode over to Vera, licking her mistress's scratched arms with care. Squatting in the dirt next to the firewood, Yateem used some flint to start a fire. Vera dug her moose-hair brush out of one of her busting bags and climbed up the redwood ladder, where she waited for Minerva to join her. Minerva followed, trying not to move her body too much when she looked back at Vera as she brushed out the water, sweat, and dirt of the road.

"I will protect you," Yateem murmured as he wrung his hands and nurtured the sparks into a flame.

"You smell like dewdrops, Mini! Good girl, almost done with this side, then I'll have you turn around," Vera cooed to her gennadius, ignoring Yateem's attempt to comfort her.

"I can finish brushing Mini before I brush Vulcan, if you want to sit down by the fire."

Minerva turned around, and Vera started brushing her other side. "I'll feel better when we get to Lolani, with big palace walls around me. Then I'll be safe." Vera inhaled the crisp aroma from the drops of stream water that she brushed out of Minerva's coat. Her pet's low purring comforted Vera.

"You are safe with me." Yateem's voice had the strength of an ox, but his eyes were wide open, as if that same ox was surrounded by a pride of gennadius.

Grabbing their rations for the evening—salted elk, Zivan sour bread, and a chunk of smoked goat cheese—Yateem hid his face from Vera, not wanting her to see that he was as terrified as she was.

Chapter 3
A Soothsayer's Greeting

"Oh, there is a fair lady in Dayo, the fairest that I've ever seen…"

The green hills were spotted with large, sweet lavender bushes. Their scent soothed Vera's still-frayed nerves, comforting her enough to enjoy the lovely sunshine on her face and Yateem's rich baritone voice.

"But when I went to sweet Dayo, she'd been married and had three kids." Yateem's playful version of the song lightened Vera's mood and put pep in Vulcan's and Minerva's steps.

"So much for not bringing attention to ourselves, farmers a mile away can probably hear you." Vera looked out across the rolling hills covered in a quilt of crops and grazing land, the beauty of her country bringing a smile that threatened a laugh.

"Now I wander in the hills, the hills of my dear country…" Yateem leaned toward Vera and sung all the louder. "Oh, Ziva, thy beauty will never leave my heart…"

"Please, Ziva, always be faithful, and don't forget me if I must go." Her voice rung out clear, the harmony of their two voices making a beautiful melancholic ending to the wanderer's anthem.

"Very pretty ending." Yateem reached out and squeezed her hand.

"I thought you said you didn't want people to notice us."

"Well, we are riding through grazing land. I thought it would be a good idea to sing a Zivan song so that if any farmers are near, they know we are not foreigners and mean no harm."

Yateem nudged Vulcan's right side with his heel to keep his animal from indulging and making a meal of the sheep that made drool string from his jowls.

"I guess that makes sense. Mini hasn't hunted since the day before we left. Can we camp in a spot where Vulkey and she can find some dinner?" Vera massaged Minerva's muscular neck to try to distract her from the sheep.

"Yes, I was thinking the same thing."

"How far did we go yesterday?"

"Just over fifty-three miles."

"If we push on a few miles farther, we can reach Dayo just before dark. While Yaffa and I were packing, she told me that her cousin lives there—owns the inn—and that they're having the hardest time with deer coming in and eating their garden."

"Vera, you know I do not want to bring you into towns."

"But the innkeeper will probably be delighted to let Mini and Vulkey hunt down those garden-ruining deer. He'll probably give us free dinner and breakfast!" Vera's tone indicated that she wouldn't give up the idea.

"Well, who are we supposed to be then? Vulcan and Minerva are not exactly yoke-bearing farm animals. You insisted on bringing all those fancy clothes, and I doubt that our soldiers will go unnoticed. People will ask questions."

"We are courtiers going to visit the king at the palace. The guards are making sure the path is safe, if they *are* even noticed. There, you feel better?"

"Your eyes."

Vera glared at a nearby lavender bush in full bloom. "I have some hooded cloaks," she said, slamming a fist down on her leg. "Why couldn't I have had lavender hair? At least I could cover it up with a scarf or hat!"

Yateem stared off in the distance as his right hand reached back toward one of the saddlebags. "I may have something that will help."

"What, Vulkey's blinders?"

"No, we have to be closer to town."

There was very little talking between the two of them as the sun continued its journey in the sky. Yateem kept digging his heel into Vulcan's side, and Vera kept massaging Minerva's neck to draw their attention away from the livestock. It was not till the sun had reached its highest point in the sky that the smell of the sweet lavender no longer made Vera glare at the bushes as she passed by them. Yateem's eyes were intently focused on the road, and he snuck a suspicious glance around when he thought Vera wasn't looking—just as Vera would sneak looks at his saddlebags as if she could see through the thick, black stingray leather to discover what could hide her eyes.

"Okay, let's stop at that little creek to get a drink." Yateem led Vulcan toward the tiny stream. It held clear, crisp water, although the banks were muddy from all the grazing animals that refreshed themselves there.

"Are you going to tell me what's going on?" Vera followed and let Minerva drink next to Vulcan.

"As you know, I am Hebian." Yateem's evergreen tunic rustled as he twisted and started to untie the flap of the right saddlebag.

"Yeah, you're going to live for a very long time. I know. So?"

"There is a sacred pool on Aequitas called Sospitas. A Hebian never leaves the island without a canteen of Sospitas water."

"So-spit-us? Well, that makes me thirsty!"

"This water can help a Hebian change their appearance. Your mother was Hebian, thus you are half-Hebian." Yateem pulled out a bronze canteen holder engraved with his family crest, a man with a sword and a rounded shield with a star on it facing a large lone wolf etched in mid-pounce above him. "I am not sure if this could change your entire appearance, but if we put a few drops on your eyes, it might change their color temporarily."

"Are you kidding me? Why have you hidden this from me?"

"As you can see, I have a limited supply." He gently took the canteen out of its holder, as if the polished steel was a glass orchid that could break under the slightest of winds. "Bring Minerva closer."

Minerva huffed and shook her head as Vera drew her and Vulcan so close that their sides touched. Vera stared at the canteen like it was going to attack her, and then she slowly leaned toward Yateem.

"Look up to the sky," he said. "Make your eyes as wide as you can." Yateem's movements were just as cautious as Vera's to ensure that none of the precious liquid spilled.

"Is this going to hurt?"

"Let me concentrate."

All was silent except for the gennadius lapping water. Yateem let a single drop of the turquoise liquid into each of Vera's eyes.

"Oh, it's warm."

Yateem's face cringed as he regretfully let another drop go into each eye.

"It's hot! Yateem make it go away!" Vera tried to blink out the liquid, but that made it roll around her eyes all the more. She bit the sleeve of her cotton riding jacket to suppress her screaming and pounded her leg to distract herself from the excruciating pain. Minerva started to panic as Vera gripped a chunk of her mane and groaned. "Yes! It's going to hurt, Vera!" she growled. "It's going to hurt very *very* much! You could have warned me!"

"I am very sorry." When Yateem leaned over and stroked Minerva's neck to keep her from bolting, she snapped her teeth at him, and Vulcan stamped his feet. "How do you feel now?"

Vera swiped the tears off her cheeks. "They still sting, but I'm not blind if that's what you're asking. Some magical water you have!"

"If it is of any consolation, it worked."

It was a few hours before sundown when Vera and Yateem rode up to the gate of the small hill town of Dayo, drawing wary looks and scowls from the locals loitering around the entrance.

Vera wore an earnest look and an excited smile, anticipating interacting with people who could not see the true color of her eyes.

An older woman, her body bent by time and labor, proudly approached the two strangers, a glare dampening the beauty and sincerity of her brown eyes. "You are not welcome here."

Vera's smile dropped off her face, and she stammered. "Excuse me?" No one had ever spoken to her as if she was anything but a powerful symbol.

Yateem rested his hand on Vera's shoulder to remind her to calm down. "Ma'am, where can we find lodging for the night?"

"What are you hiding behind those eyes, girl?" The woman peered up at Vera with hatred.

Vera whipped her head to look at Yateem, her eyes widened in panic, questioning the effects of the Sospitas water.

"Be gone, woman," Yateem snarled through clenched teeth and curled lips.

"Could she see my—"

Lightly rubbing Vera's back, Yateem leaned in close and whispered, "Not now," indicating with a barely perceptible nod of his head the small group of people that had taken an interest in the scene.

He prompted Vulcan forward, and Vera followed suit, her eyes flitting to and from the faces of locals that were darkened and aged by a deep-set fear.

The streets, paved with rutted cobblestones, wrapped around in a spiral that worked its way to the top of the hill. The whole of Dayo was covered in tight, skinny clay buildings with thatched roofs, and the bottommost ring of the town was the marketplace where the farmers sold their crops. Minerva's and Vulcan's paws fell silently on the dark stones, but sent a shock wave of hushed, frantic murmurs and flighty looks from the townsfolk that pressed against the produce stands to give the gennadius and their riders an absurd amount of room.

Vera tried to smile at people as they passed, but no one dared to hold eye contact with her for more than a moment. "This was a bad idea, wasn't it?"

Yateem gave her the slightest of smiles. "I have let you talk me into better ones."

A burly, middle-aged man in a white linen tunic and loose pants separated himself from an agitated group of men, one of whom carried a scythe, and placed himself directly in the path of Yateem and Vera. "What is your business in Dayo? Come to recruit farmers' sons as soldiers?"

"We seek a night's rest in the inn. That is all. If you will point us in that direction, we will be sure to disturb no one." As he spoke, his tone calm, Yateem's eyes were alert and ready, scanning the crowd.

"And if I don't?" The man squared his shoulders.

"Then we will ride past you and find the inn ourselves. We only want peace." Yateem's hand rested high on his leg, next to his hip—and the hilt of his sword.

"Your weapons speak of other plans."

"Only fools travel unarmed these days."

"Yes, swords make kidnapping our sons so much easier. You may think that you fool us by traveling with the girl, but your grand animals give you away. You would take our strong young to rescue them from becoming Wachiru, only to have them die at the hands of Draven and his minions in war." The man spat the words out in disgust.

"War?" Vera's voice was strained. The growing crowd inching toward them with quiet approval of this man's proclamation was unnerving her.

"We are sorry for your aggravations, but threats are not necessary." Yateem reached over and held Vera's hand to reassure her.

The man's glare softened a little when he saw the genuine fear and shock in Vera's eyes. "Can you pay?"

"Yes, of course," Yateem said as his hand slid away from the hilt of his sword.

"A cousin of the innkeeper told me…um…having trouble with deer in the garden. If it helps, we could let our gennadius hunt them." Vera's voice was meek, but loud enough that she hoped the owner of the inn, if present, would hear and save them from the hostile looks of the crowd.

"What is this cousin's name?"

"Yaffa."

The man stepped closer, looking up at Vera's face in earnest. "My name is Severino, innkeeper of Dayo. Yaffa has not sent my wife a letter in months, but in her last correspondence she spoke of guards coming to the estate where she works... how do you know my cousin?"

"I know her because...well...we both live—I mean work —at Saman..." Vera felt like the man's stare was going to draw the lavender color through the burned-on illusion of the Sospitas water, exposing her to the crowd.

Yateem squeezed her hand and muttered under his breath. "Silence." He stared down the innkeeper with concrete severity. "Enough of this. Where is your establishment?"

Struck by the protective tenor of Yateem's voice, Severino checked his stare and said, "On the other side of the hill, continue on this road, you will see the stables first. Tell the stable boy to brush down your animals and let them out to hunt."

"Thank you." Yateem tapped Vulcan's side, forcing the gruff innkeeper to jump out of the way as the two huge animals continued down the road, parting the disquieted crowd as they went.

Vera's attempts at normal conversation with the shy stable boy were awkward and forced. As Yateem and Vera were getting settled in their room, she tried again to engage the innkeeper's wife in pleasantries that were not reciprocated.

Their dinner was brought up to their room and laid out on the small table that sat next to the single-paned glass window that overlooked the street and let in even the smallest of breezes. It was a simple meal of lamb chops and quinoa, with jicama slices sprinkled with lemon juice for dessert. After the innkeeper's wife came in to quietly clear the dishes, they both sat at the table, each staring out the window silently.

"You didn't tell me war is in the air around here."

"Why did you think the king sent us guards a couple months ago?"

"I don't know. Is my uncle really allowing people to be kidnapped?"

"The king is trying to protect his kingdom from the Wachiru that are flooding the land and turning everyone they can into a mindless minion of Draven," Yateem replied, brushing the hair out of Vera's face so that he could gauge her reaction to their situation.

"You were right," she said, her voice a sad admission.

"And that surprises you?" He wanted so desperately to bring her out of these dark musings.

The edges of her mouth turned upward. "Yeah, yeah. The world isn't what I wanted it to be. Neither are the people."

"They are scared. As they should be."

"Are they scared of me? Scared of another Lavender Soul?"

Yateem kissed Vera on the forehead. "If they are, they are faithless fools." He smiled at her, trying eagerly to convey all the faith he had in her. "We should get some sleep." He stood and drew a curtain to separate the room into two private sleeping areas.

Vera dressed herself for bed and then sat on the hard mattress, staring into her looking glass. "How long will it last?"

From behind the curtain, Yateem said, "Probably a day. Trust me—I keep checking to see if they are fading."

Vera smiled at the mirror, trying different expressions. "Why are they so dark?"

Yateem stopped arranging his covers and sighed as he stared at the floor. "I do not know."

His raspy whisper drew Vera over to the curtain. "May I say good night?"

Pulling back the burgundy drape, Yateem said, "Good night, Vera," his voice still quiet.

"Good night, Yateem," Vera hugged him.

Yateem's thin smile disappeared when Vera let go and looked up into his eyes with a comforted smile on her face…and midnight-blue eyes.

Chapter 4
Rumor's Blade

The abrupt thudding of a heavy fist on the door made Yateem grip the dagger under his pillow and silently walk to the doorway as the fifth curt knock hit it. He opened it, dagger gleaming, ready for the assailant.

The innkeeper's hazel eyes shot open wide as he took a step away from the threshold. "I mean no harm. Your animals have killed. I suggest you leave as soon as you pack." There were dark puffy circles under his eyes, as if he had just stifled down tears.

Yateem lowered his dagger. "I do not understand. You agreed to let our gennadius hunt."

"Is Mini hurt?" Vera's voice was thick with sleep.

Yateem looked back at Vera and saw that her eyes were already a light violet. He sidestepped to block the innkeeper's view of her and raised his eyebrows to nonverbally repeat the question.

"They did hunt. The stable boy woke me when he heard screams. We grabbed our bows and followed the gennadius' paw prints. We passed by a buck and three deer carcasses. They scared off the herd—I thank you for that." The innkeeper's face lost a little of its color, and his hazel eyes flitted in the direction of Vera.

Yateem squared up his shoulders, becoming an immovable barricade between Vera and the innkeeper. "What did you see?" His teal eyes drove into the man like a gale force wind.

"We heard a faint voice on the other side of the hill in front of us and found five bodies that had been struck down. Only one man was still breathing. He heard us approach and tensed. His cold eyes were blind in the darkness." The innkeeper shuddered. "Before he died, he said something filled with such malice that I couldn't understand his words…until now."

"What?" Yateem clenched his jaw. "What did he say?"

The man stepped closer and in a shaky whisper said, "He will find her."

Yateem kept his face as calm as a break in a storm and, ever so slightly, lifted his hand to signal to the bewildered Vera not to move. "Where are our animals?"

The innkeeper furrowed his eyebrows at Yateem's lack of response. "They returned to the stables and drank their fill to slack their thirst—and to wash the blood off their muzzles."

"Are we to face charges for the deaths of the innocent?"

"They weren't innocents."

"What?"

"All five dead men had the outline of a raven's head carved on the outer corner of their eyes. They wore black clothing that fades into the shadows, and their eyes were glossed over with a fear that was much older than their violent end."

Yateem's eyes narrowed into a dangerous glare. "Wachiru."

Vera sucked in a gasp.

"Draven's minions tried to take over our village a month ago but faced an uprising against them. Few have been seen since, but there has been evidence of them on the outskirts of the fields. There will be no charges, but if the public's approval is attention you and your companion don't want, I suggest you leave now. About four hours remain till daybreak, time enough to put distance between yourselves and this place before people start to wake, and rumors start to rise."

"Thank you. Does your stable boy know how to saddle a gennadius?"

"I was a stable boy at Lolani. I will attend to them myself."

"If the white one gets testy, just give her some oats."

The innkeeper nodded his head and briskly walked down the hall.

Yateem closed the door and turned to Vera, whose light violet eyes were wide open. Her fingers shook with the intensity of her grip on the wool blanket that lay over her. "How did they find us? What happened to the guards? What are we supposed to do?"

Yateem rubbed the back of his neck as he drew the dividing curtain in the room. "Get dressed, and get out all your money. Wear a hood—your eyes are rapidly lightening."

Vera moved to her bags quickly, riffling through the useless gowns till she found riding pants, a linen tunic, and her black wool cloak with a sheer silk-wool-blend hood. "All my money? This room only costs five silver pieces. I have fifty pieces in my money bag."

"Pray that is enough for the innkeeper's silence."

Vera fought her feet into her boots and slung her saddlebags over her shoulder, the coursing adrenaline preventing her body from feeling the weight. "What if he talks anyway?"

Yateem drew back the curtain and adjusted the sword on his hip. "Then pray we get to Lolani undetected. The king's army will protect us there."

Walking down the hallway, they found a doorway that led to the stables where Vulcan and Minerva impatiently stomped their paws as Yateem quickly tied on both his and Vera's saddlebags. As Vera pulled up and broke down her redwood ladder, Yateem bent down from his saddle and handed the blonde-leather moneybag to the innkeeper.

He gently bounced the bag once in his palm. "This is too much."

"For the trouble of discreetly dealing with the public's knowledge of what happened tonight."

"What should I say?"

"Say that the visitors went to see if their gennadius had hunted, and that they must have found the dead bodies and fled for fear of criminal charges because when you woke, they were gone. Never repeat the last words of the Wachiru. They were nonsense, but many dark meanings can be found in garbled last words." Yateem prompted Vulcan forward, and Vera directed Minerva to follow.

The innkeeper bowed and trudged back into the inn.

Vera sleepily muttered as Yateem led them away from the main road and into the rolling hills scattered with crops. "Vulkey and Mini haven't slept. How are we supposed to get anywhere while they are exhausted?"

"They ate well and defended well." Yateem patted Vulcan's neck. "That should give them enough fuel and adrenaline to get through a full day's ride."

"A full day's ride!"

"Yes, I figure noon is an opportune time to find shelter and sleep. The most threatening of Draven's underlings dislike sunlight, which gives us about nine hours to get as far away from Dayo as possible."

"Where are our guards?"

"They should have detected those Wachiru. They should have left me some sort of a warning."

"But if they never went into town, if we're taking another path, then we wouldn't have seen it..." Vera's voice trailed off. She swept the hood off her face as they crested a small hill...and found the guards.

They were sprawled out across the dirt trail, lying in dark sticky pools of their own blood, stripped of their armor and weapons. Tracks suggested their steeds had fled.

"He will find *her*." Vera's voice came out as a ghostly whisper.

Yateem gently turned Vera's face toward him. "I will not let that happen."

She fought to look at the guards. "I don't even know their names."

He looked down at the guards' pale faces. Both looked as if they were left to watch themselves bleed out. With a clenched jaw, Yateem looked back at Vera, reached over, and put the hood back over her nearly lavender eyes. "We have to move on. Keep your eyes on me as we pass over them." Yateem kissed Vera's hand as the gennadius carefully stepped over the two dead men. "You are doing great...keep looking at me."

Vera stared through the black hood that covered her eyes. The tiny woven threads that created the sheer fabric framed the face that was her source of comfort since childhood. "Will their families be notified?"

"Their orders were secret. Not even I knew their real names." Yateem glared at the distant horizon, barely visible in the thick darkness of the night. "Where is your sword?"

Vera turned and reached for her left saddlebag, where the hilt of her sword stuck out from under the flap. "Right here." Her answer was a weak inquiry.

"Make sure it is easily accessible, just in case we run across more Wachiru."

Vera absently nodded her head and ran her fingers through Minerva's thick mane, thinking about the two families that would probably never know about the deaths of their loved ones. They rode on through the night, using farmer-walking trails so as not to tread on newly planted crops as well as those that hadn't yet been harvested. Once they cleared the farmlands surrounding Dayo, they stuck to traveling the long, lazy hills of the Zivan countryside.

Vulcan's and Minerva's paws fell heavily, pushing down the tall grass into a clear trail that their swinging tails erased. Yateem's hand never left the hilt of the sword on his side, his fingers feeling the oiled leather of the grip. Methodically crossing through the night and approaching dawn, Yateem constantly scanned the landscape, making sure that the pale rose hues illuminating the world were not hiding any dark creatures in the cheerful light.

The sun continued its arching marathon. At its highest point, it seemed to beam a hot spot on the wearied travelers.

Vera had been gradually slumping down to lean against Minerva's neck, and the gennadius' paws now shuffled along the ground as she continued her forward motion. Yateem's hand lay limp on top of his sword hilt as he fought to keep his eyes open long enough to find shelter.

About 65 fee ahead stood a small stand of cottonwood trees. When Yateem looked over at Vera, he saw that her eyes were closed, and her body swayed precariously.

"Vera, I see shelter. We could sleep. Do you feel up to stopping?"

She snapped her head up and readjusted herself in her saddle, trying to make it seem like she was just resting her eyes. "I was ready to stop a few hours ago, and Minerva can barely lift her feet. I would sleep anywhere..." Vera looked at the spot Yateem was leading them to and added, "except there."

"A cluster of that many trees means water, which Vulcan and Minerva have not had since the spring we crossed three hours ago."

"Have you forgotten what happened the last time I was surrounded by trees?" Her body tensed as she stopped Minerva from following Yateem and Vulcan. "What if *he* made those trees attack me?"

Yateem rubbed his neck and looked back toward her as Vulcan lazily walked amongst the trees. "That could not have been Draven."

"How do you know? You still don't believe it happened, do you?"

Yateem halted Vulcan just past the border of the cottonwoods. "I just know...yes, I believe you, but this is the only place I have seen for miles where we can sleep without the worry of an ambush." Vulcan stepped on a branch, the loud snap of the dry wood spooking both gennadius into alertness. "See? No one can sneak in here."

"What if the trees attack?"

"Then we will feel them, and cut our way out before any harm can be done."

Vera rubbed her eyes with a heavy hand. "We can't go on without rest." Looking at Yateem, she saw the gentle green light that filtered through the leaves, giving the tree stand a placid atmosphere. Vera prompted Minerva onward. "Even though I'm sure I won't sleep at all in here."

Yateem nodded and then gave Vera a faint, tired smile. "You must admit the shade feels nice."

"Yeah, until we're woken by roots around our necks."

"This tree stand looks to be only thirty strong. It will take more than that to defeat us. Just think—that grove that attacked you was at least 100 strong, and aspens as well."

"Why does that matter? These are big."

"That means they are old, stiff even. Aspens share a root system, giving them a clear, strategic advantage of moving as one. In the unlikely event that these trees wake up, each one would act independently. Imagine the sheer arboreal disorder." Yateem widened his smile.

She shook her head at him. "Thank you for trying to cheer me up."

"Always."

They went to the center of the trees, where a natural spring bubbled out of the ground and created a deep puddle from which the gennadius drank while Yateem's and Vera's hands barely fumbled their red cedar ladders together so that they could half-climb, half-fall off the slurping animals' backs.

Yateem, Minerva, and Vulcan lay down in the shape of a triangle so that Vera could sleep in the middle, completely protected. Exhaustion took command of the entire group, and they were undisturbed during their entire rest. Not even the birds that landed above the sleepers dared to utter a curious peep.

The cool night breeze whispered through the leaves, and Vera rolled up against Minerva as Yateem draped his long leather riding-jacket over his sleeping sack. Twelve hours passed before the fatigued sleepers started to wake their heavy bodies. Minerva purred low in her throat as Vera sat up and leaned against her side.

Stars played hide-and-seek behind the spade-shaped cottonwood leaves that lightly swayed back and forth in the breeze. "How long have we been sleeping?"

Yateem cast his jacket to the side and got out of his sleeping sack. As he rolled the sack up, he peered through the branches and leaves till he saw the moon. "It looks to be around midnight. We slept half a day." Clouds brushed over the moon, leaving a phantom circle of light in its place. "Which is good, because until we reach Lolani, we will only stop for water."

Vera kicked her sleeping sack off. "A full day's ride. Can Mini and Vulkey take another long trek?" she asked as she fumbled about in the moonlight, trying to find her boots.

"Their sense for the necessity of our security will give them no choice."

As Vera finished rolling up her sack she walked over to Minerva—who was still lying down, but whose eyes were alert and darting between Vera and Yateem—and lightly kissed between Minerva's round white ears. The ground beneath Vera's feet vibrated ever so slightly with the deep rumbling of Minerva's purring.

With hurried ease, they put together their ladders and quickly saddled their gennadius. As they passed out of the trees, Vera sighed with relief and settled into the steady rhythm of Minerva's gait. The clouds would diminish the moon's light when they occasionally blew in front of it, casting a ghostly gleam, shifting shadows, and a blanket of unease over the land.

They traveled the whole night in silence until pale yellow and orange sunlight coolly radiated on their backs. The clearer illumination of their surroundings, and the new day, lightened the settled tension amongst the traveling party. Vulcan shook his head and nodded at Minerva, brushing his nose against her cheek, and Minerva pushed her head against his nose, playfully shoving him away. The gennadius' playing lightly jostled the riders.

"Well, good morning to you too, Vulcan." Yateem patted the side of his gennadius.

Vera smiled and ran her fingers along one of the long stripes at the base of Minerva's neck. "Just a little longer, Mini. Then you can sleep and graze all you want."

"Yes, in two hours I believe we will all breathe easier."

"Only two hours?"

"Make that three. The road to the private royal entrance is farther north than the road to the main gateway."

"Why don't we just take the main road?"

"Honestly?"

"Honestly! The entrance plaza is so big that we can just slip into the alley that leads to the stables without anyone noticing. Isn't it generally known that all the best gossips stay up late and don't make an appearance till lunch?"

"You have no experience of life at a palace. A hooded figure will spread rumors faster than a hummingbird can beat its wings. After what happened the other night, I will not jeopardize your life in such a reckless way."

"I barely have a life to jeopardize," Vera muttered.

The pastures, crops, and open land turned into spanning vineyards whose leaves winked warm red and pink in the early morning. Yateem and Vera started down a smooth road that led into a blood orange orchard. After riding through the blood oranges for an hour, a thirty foot tall wrought-iron gate blocked the road.

"Pull your hood down to cover your whole face," Yateem whispered urgently, just out of ears-reach from the gate.

Standing at attention across the length of the gate were six soldiers, their uniforms stiff and gray, their rank denoted by navy blue stripes on the shoulders. Each had a broad sword on his belt and a spear in hand, the tip of which looked more like a blade than a small spear point.

The soldier that stood at the center of the iron gate, having the most stripes along his wide shoulders, addressed Yateem and Vera in a stern voice. "This is the king's private gate. Please turn around and make your way to Lolani's public entrance."

"No." Yateem stared at the young guard through the thick gate bars.

"What?" The spear came up in a ready position.

"I am Yateem Rukan Wulfgar of Xipili, handler of King Koios and Queen Prudencia's cousin. They are expecting us tonight, but her ladyship was so excited about seeing her family, we left early, so as to surprise them."

The guard looked behind Yateem at Vera, whose hood was pulled so low that all the man could see was Vera's chin nervously moving side to side. "I have heard nothing about royal family members visiting."

"I am glad to hear it. If you wish to verify our identity, by all means run down the lane and speak to the general of the king's guard. Or," Yateem gave a courtly smile, "you could let us through, lock the gate behind us, and escort her ladyship and me to Lolani. That way, when you have confirmation that we are not villains, you will not be punished for making us wait to rest our animals and stretch our limbs."

The guard unlocked the gate with a huff, and the other soldiers moved out of the way and surrounded Yateem and Vera once the gate was shut and locked. The tips of the spears smelt burnt, like they had just been sharpened.

Vera let out a terrified squeak and immediately pulled the hood down as far as it could go, and then gripped the reins as if she planned to bolt.

"Stand down at once!" Yateem ordered, reaching toward Vera to try to calm her down. His movement was met by a spear blade against his chest.

"No." The commanding officer walked in between Vulcan and Minerva, patting the shoulder of the guard that held the spear in a lethal position against Yateem's chest. "I do not want to explain to my general why I let in two unauthorized travelers—one suspiciously fond of a hood—during a war council." He leaned against Minerva's side, who started growling, to look up at Vera.

She turned her face away from him and tucked her chin to her collarbone.

"Why would a young woman hide her pretty face, if she wasn't a spy?" He took the tip of his spear, hooked it under the edge of the black material, and started to slowly push the hood back.

Vera desperately held onto the other side of the hood as she felt daylight hit the edge of her nose.

All the guards had their attention on Vera, so Yateem drew his sword and, in one fluid motion, knocked the spear away from his chest, giving the spear's owner a new haircut as Yateem swung over the guard's head and bit the edge of the sword into the commanding officer's throat.

The commanding officer froze. He could feel the drop of blood that escaped the small incision. His grip loosened, letting his spear drop away from Vera's hood, and he slowly turned his gaze toward Yateem.

Yateem snarled. "Maybe she is scared and wants to hide her identity from people who would sell information regarding her whereabouts. Maybe the sun is too bright for her eyes. Or maybe she was embarrassed at the unimpressive, unprofessional, and un-intimidating presence of the king's guard."

The soldier moved his lips, wanting to say something, but the cold steel biting further into his skin silenced him. All the soldiers ran over and positioned their spears just inches away from Yateem's throat as Vera pulled down her hood to cover her face completely once more.

"Let me assure you that the reasoning behind the hood has little consequence to me, other than it is what my lady wants. If you—or any of your men—try to go against my lady's wishes again, I will kill you all. Is that clear?" Yateem's voice was as calm, smooth, and sharp as ice.

"I will have your head for this," the commanding officer growled against the blade.

"Not before I have yours. Tell your men to stand down."

The guard looked into Yateem's eyes and saw his immovable conviction. "At ease."

They all looked over at their commanding officer with disbelief.

"I said at ease!" he yelled, causing another drop of blood to trickle down and underneath his collar.

With white-hot anger blatantly spread thin over their obedient stances, the soldiers brought their spears upright and to their sides, and took giant steps backwards.

Yateem withdrew his sword, wiped the tip off on the side of his boot, and sheathed the blade. "If you escort us in a civilized manner, there will be no more trouble."

The commanding officer glared up at Yateem as he wiped the little bit of remaining blood off his throat. "I will bring you to the general myself." He stomped out in front of Yateem and Vera, pointed to some of the soldiers and indicated behind the travelers, and then turned on his heel and marched down the lane toward the palace. The three he had pointed at marched behind Vera and Yateem, and the other two ran to catch up to their commanding officer in the lead.

After a quarter of an hour, they cleared the orchard. The crunching of their escort's steps became a harsh, methodic drumming as they marched off the gravel lane and onto the tan stone slabs of the king's stable yard, an open space with stable attendants running back and forth between the two wings of grand arched stables, some exercising beautiful stallions and majestic gennadius, others cleaning the stone slabs, and yet others getting angry at the off-duty soldiers that were in their way.

"You there!" The commanding officer pointed to the group of off-duty soldiers that were being chastised by the stable master.

The officers perked up and ran over, clicked their heels together and saluted. "Yes, Captain?"

"Help these officers guard my prisoners." The commanding officer turned with a biting smile toward Yateem. "I will suggest beheading. It is quicker than a hanging."

"How considerate. Run along to your general." Yateem bowed his head with sarcastic cordiality.

The captain mumbled curses as he turned and ran off to a side door into the palace. The soldiers circled around the two travelers, their proximity making the exhausted gennadius antsy, and the nervous movement of the huge predators that carried the "prisoners" put the soldiers on edge as well.

"Oh, well, this is ridiculous," Vera exclaimed after staring out through her black hood at the wide-eyed soldiers. The sun was rising farther in the sky, and her breath was getting caught in the sheer fabric in front of her face. Her fingers twitched to rip off the entire cloak and be done with the charade.

"Patience." Yateem sat up straight and regal, as if he were waiting for a friend to join their party, not the executioner.

"How are you so calm?" Vera folded the sides of the cloak back off her shoulders, just to have it fall over them again.

At that moment the captain came out of the same side door with a tall, burly, older man, whose uniform was the blue of the other soldier's stripes and who had metal stars across his strong shoulders. Both had faces as hard and serious as granite as they approached.

"These are the prisoners I have told you about, General." The captain gave Vera a suspicious glare and added an acidic smile when he made eye contact with Yateem.

The general assessed the two of them. "Yateem? I thought you had returned to Aequitas!" he exclaimed as he pushed aside two soldiers and held out his hand to Yateem.

Yateem accepted the salutation enthusiastically. "Hello, Lazaros!"

The captain had indicated for the soldiers to stand down and form a line in front of the two travelers while the general was questioning them, his disgust at the instant familiarity with one of his prisoners apparent. "I beg your pardon, General, but this man threatened my life." He pointed to the freshly scabbed scratch above his collar. "And this young lady refuses to show her face. This is highly suspicious, and at times like these…"

General Lazaros held up his hand to stop his captain's childish report. "Did you not ask for their identities?"

"He introduced himself and said that she is a cousin of the king and queen."

"And you felt this situation warranted me leaving a war council?" The smile that had been on General Lazaros' face when talking to Yateem was gone.

"Because…he refused to go to the public entrance, and the war council…I thought that they were spies…and wasn't made aware of royal relatives coming today…" He looked up at Vera, his demeanor reflecting the panic of a little boy who knew he was about to be punished. "And he had a sword to my throat and threatened all my men if I touched her hood again!"

"You have gone soft in your old age." General Lazaros smiled up at Yateem and then looked at the captain in angry disappointment. "If it had been me in your place, I would have killed this one on principle alone."

The captain took a step back in horror.

"He was only doing his duty." Yateem's voice had the same calm, scolding tone that he used when Vera did something wrong.

"Captain, you will unsaddle, brush, bathe, and muck out these two gennadius' stalls for the duration of their stay," ordered the general.

"I don't think that's a good idea." Vera's feminine voice sounded oddly sweet against the sternness of the general's. "Mini will kill him if he touches her again."

General Lazaros let out a deep baritone laugh and smiled at Vera, trying not to be disturbed by the veil that hid her face. "What would you suggest, My Lady?"

"Whatever gets me into the queen's garden, and Mini and Vulcan unsaddled and grazing at their leisure."

"I will deal with the captain later then." The general bowed to Vera and then snapped his fingers in the direction of some stable boys, who pushed through the line of embarrassed soldiers with ladders in their hands. They assisted Vera down with smiles on their faces and then got to work. In less than a minute, Minerva and Vulcan were free of their saddles and bags and were being brushed down.

General Lazaros offered his arm to Vera, who only accepted after seeing Yateem's nod of approval. He led them to the same door through which he had come and strolled down the servant's corridor toward the open-air hallways of the royal wing.

"I must apologize for my soldiers' behavior."

"I thought it was a bit abrasive, but I guess I can rest assured that we are safe here."

"And why would safety be an issue here?" The general's tone thickened the air with an alert protectiveness that was a professional hazard.

Vera looked at Yateem, who couldn't see her expression of concern through her hood, but who knew her well enough that he could imagine her widened eyes and bit lip.

"There was talk of Wachiru around Dayo. It spooked her." Yateem's eyes were placid, his smile genuine.

"I see." General Lazaros playfully squeezed Vera's arm against his ribs. "Well, My Lady, I am glad to hear you are not one of these young ladies that runs about without a concern for her safety—or the safety of others." He stopped in a spot of sun that shone through an archway. "I present to you the queen's garden." He bowed with great poise, especially for such a large man. "Where you can rest, and where you will have no fear of foolish soldiers harassing you to take off that hood." The general winked and then stood to address Yateem. "I will go and tell their majesties you are here, but I doubt that they will come right away. The war council is divided."

"Thank you, Lazaros. Tell their majesties we are fine in the garden for now. It just feels good to stretch our legs." Yateem shook his hand with a firm grip.

"We will talk later." General Lazaros eyed Vera and leaned in close to Yateem. "Talk of your recent adventures."

"I look forward to it."

The general bowed toward Vera. "My Lady," he said and then quickly turned and walked down the hallway with a stern, efficient gait.

Ripples traveled through the fountain as Vera's long fingers ran back and forth on the surface of the water, making the reflection of her lavender irises falter. She closed her eyes and breathed in the fresh smell of the rosemary hedges that were trimmed into swirls that danced around the poinsettia-shaped fountain. Yateem's steady footsteps came up behind her, taking her focus off her surroundings.

"We are eating in the king and queen's private dining room," Yateem said, upright and all business.

Vera lifted her hand out of the fountain and flicked the water off in Yateem's direction. "Why can't we have dinner in the main hall?"

"Vera, please." Yateem sat down next to her.

"Uncle Koios and Aunt Prudencia love to eat in the big hall. I'll change into one of my gowns, and you can change too…" Vera returned to playing with the shape of her reflection in the water.

"Or we can go get changed and eat with just the king and queen."

"You've known them all my life. Why don't you call them by their names?"

"I have known them longer than you have been alive," Yateem responded, "and they *are* the king and queen. It is a sign of respect."

"Isn't it a sign of disrespect to take them out of their routine for dinner?"

"Will you act your age? Stop playing with the water."

"We can use your spit-us water—my eyes will be normal. I can take the pain…I think…anyway, I used to come here as a kid. People know I exist."

"Yes, but an unfortunate truth of the life of courtiers is 'out of sight, out of mind.' You have not been here for years. Your uncle—I mean the king and queen—feel it would be much safer if we just kept your presence secret." Yateem leaned over to try to look into Vera's eyes.

With a swift flick of her wrist, Vera momentarily erased her watery face. "So what? I'm supposed to stay in my bed chamber and then be escorted to meals, with guards making sure the halls are empty? That's lovely." She stood and paced around one of the rosemary swirls until she reached the center of the curl where she picked off a little sprig and inhaled the rich aroma.

Yateem watched her with a furrowed brow as he rubbed the back of his neck with his left hand. "Not exactly, we are in the royal family's private wing. Your suite even has doors that open into this private garden. You can wander around here free of care."

Absorbed with the rosemary in her hand, Vera smiled as she crushed it in her palm and took another deep breath of the herb's distinctive, tangy smell. "Free of supervision?"

"Oh, that is not fair. What am I supposed to do with myself if I am not keeping you company?"

"That's what I thought." Vera started back through the swirl's curve toward the fountain where Yateem was still sitting.

"Vera, you like to get your way."

"Who doesn't?"

"I just want to make sure that you stick to the private wing."

"Fine, may I go get dressed for dinner, or do you need to get a blindfold so that you can be in the room while I change?"

Yateem stood up and strode over to Vera, wrapping his arm around her shoulders. "Such drastic measures are not necessary. My suite is next to yours."

"Of course."

"Now, now…cheer up. You get to wear one of the many fine gowns you packed and have a meal fit for your uncle Koios!"

Vera looked away from Yateem so that he didn't get the satisfaction of seeing the faint smile on her face. "I wonder if they'll serve us dessert."

"That's the spirit!" Yateem was being quite boisterous, trying to encourage Vera's improving attitude.

"Yateem?"

"Present."

"Stop it. Will I ever be able to interact normally?"

"No. I do wish it could be different, but there is never going to be a time when people look at you without seeing the color of your eyes."

"We could take a trip to Aequitas and get some more Sospitas water."

Yateem stopped her, placed both his hands on her shoulders, and turned her to look into his eyes. "You would go through that pain every day just to talk with people?"

"No. I wouldn't be able to endure that burning every day. I don't even know if I want to go through that ever again, but…" Vera met Yateem's eyes earnestly, "Dayo was the first time I had a real conversation. Sure, it was with an angry old woman, and I stammered most of it. But she didn't look at me and then drop her jaw, or back away in terror, or bow and mumble requests that I, as a child, don't understand. I know you've seen this happen to me all my life, but you don't know what it feels like. If only the process was slightly less excruciating, then almost boiling my eyes every day would be nothing compared to the pain of feeling utterly isolated."

42

Yateem pulled Vera into a warm hug. "I have seen that pain, and I wish I could make it so that people could not see your eyes, but that is not the path that you must walk. With Draven's minions looking for you, and with what you say happened in the forest…the guards…" Yateem rubbed Vera's back to try to ease the shudders that ran down her body. "We need to find out what is going on, and what our next move should be."

"How are we going to do that?"

"We are traveling to Shifra."

Vera lifted her head off Yateem's chest and cocked one eyebrow up at him. "Shifra is a real place? Are humans allowed?"

"I am sending a messenger hawk asking for permission."

"So we're going to be here for a while?"

"Yes, until we get an answer that is."

"And you said I wouldn't need my gowns!" Vera gently pushed Yateem away and sauntered in the direction of her suite, but then turned around quickly with a half-snarl on her face. "Majlis is going to be there, isn't she?"

"No, unfortunately."

"Unfortunately? She's mean!"

Yateem quickly strode up to Vera so that he could express his anger more quietly than he wanted to. "She is trying to help you. It is not her fault that you are accustomed to people doing everything for you with a big smile on their face."

Vera glared at the tiles, hurt and angry. "I'm going to change for dinner, but don't worry—I can use my own hands to put on my gown—no assistance needed—and there will certainly be no smiles tonight."

Yateem rested his head in his right hand as Vera marched to her room, her shoulders squared.

Chapter 5:
Garden Wanderings

After a dinner full of happy and loving interaction with the king and queen—and barely civil attentions toward Yateem —Vera needed fresh air. Lying down on the thick leptinella that took the place of grass in the queen's garden, Vera threw her auburn hair out behind her. The tiny serrated leaves of the leptinella were so thick that they provided a cushy place for her to lie as she stared at the stars. The sky was dark, as dark as her eyes had turned after Yateem's Sospitas water.

"Well, Arivos, what's it to be for me? Am I supposed to be okay with being separated from society for the rest of my life?" She pushed herself up on her elbows, as if getting closer to the stars would help to hear an answer. "And what about Yateem? Is he just supposed to be my babysitter until I die? What if he wanted his own life? Did you ever think about that when you gave me these horrid eyes, Arivos? Well, did you?" She hissed the questions under her breath. After another minute of looking up at the stars, she let her head fall back against the plush leaves. "I don't understand why I had to be given these eyes."

A nightingale landed on the pomapple tree to Vera's right, making the turquoise fruit bounce. He started to sing her a song, as if he knew she wanted to be cheered up. Vera sat up and crossed her legs, slowly smiling as she watched the little bird deliver his private concert.

"Thank you, Mr. Nightingale!" She jumped up and skipped over to the tree, dramatically bowing to the bird, which flew off abruptly, its shock registering in the key change in his music. Vera, her spirits renewed a bit, unenthusiastically started to dance through the queen's garden.

Her movements were small at first—a few steps with her arms reaching out and up like a swan about to take flight. Then, when the giggles from her silliness brightened her mood even more, she grew bold. She leapt past the pomapple tree, sashayed in between the swirl-sculpted column bushes, and did a one-sided waltz around the poinsettia-shaped fountain. The music inside her soul, inspired by the nightingale's song, propelled her through the queen's garden. She lightly kissed the pomapple, kumquat, and mango trees. She inhaled the fragrance of various rose bushes scattered about the garden, and she hugged some of the column-trimmed cypress trees that served as a wall separating the queen's garden from the palace gardens.

Suddenly she stopped. The palace gardens with their many fountains, sculpted landscapes, and graveled pathways were much more extensive, but she had promised Yateem that if she went outdoors, she would restrict herself to the small garden. Looking up to the windows of Yateem's suite, she saw no candlelight. Her foot wiggled its way from the little green leaves of leptinella to the taller green blades…and then immediately withdrew. A song started, soft and sweet, just barely audible from the other side of the wall of cypress trees.

"Mr. Nightingale?" Vera whispered as she squeezed her slender body through a gap in the trees, making sure that her burgundy sheath gown did not get caught.

The melody grew as rich chords from a guitar accompanied the sweet humming. Vera hesitated, frightened by the thought of music coming from another human being, but as the notes floated into her ears, she raised her hands to the sky, surrendered to the song, and started dancing again. The notes drew her in and affected her so much that her very body movements seemed to be more a part of the melody, and less a part of Vera. Before she realized the music was getting louder, she twirled herself into the fountain right next to the star-serenader. The musician stood as a night watchman does when he's been woken from a nap, and he stared at Vera as she untwisted her wet dress from around her feet and brushed her partially dry hair away from her eyes.

She gaped at the man. "Oh!" Vera exclaimed and then pushed herself out of the lukewarm water and ran.

"Wait!" The man caught up with her in a matter of seconds.

"No! Leave me alone!" Vera made sure not to look back, and kept on running.

"*You* interrupted me!" He was side by side with Vera and gently grabbed her arm with his calloused hands to make her stop. "Just wait, okay?"

Vera noticed his eyes, or rather she noticed that they were looking at her face without seeing her. She smiled. "Are you blind?"

He let go of her arm. "What? No. Well, I mean who isn't blind at this time of night?"

Vera giggled. "What color is my dress?"

The man leaned closer to her. "Black? I might as well be looking at your shadow at this point! Why?"

Vera stuck out her hand, her white teeth the only things that could be seen in the dark of the night. "I'm Ver—very glad to meet you. Sorry I interrupted your song, but I have to go now."

He took her hand and kissed it. "I'm Radov. I wanted to apologize if I scared you."

"No, I'm sorry that my klutzy dancing interrupted your beautiful playing."

"Yeah, I want to apologize for that too…"

"Oh, please don't. I've been pretty down lately, and dancing was just what I needed, and your song…I don't know what it was about it, but it just lifted me up and drew me in!"

"No, that's what I'm trying to tell you…"

"Tell me what? That you're an amazing musician? No one likes a bragger, Radov." Vera started to walk backwards in the direction of the queen's garden.

"Will you please let me explain?" Radov did not walk after her. He didn't want Vera to see him as a threat.

"I really shouldn't have come out here, so I don't think I should talk to you. Sorry." Vera said, but then she stopped and looked at Radov. She couldn't see his features clearly. After all, the night was her friend at the moment, but his inviting voice told her everything she needed to know about his looks. She took the five steps back toward him, went up on to her tiptoes, and kissed him on the cheek.

Radov was glad that the night was there to shade his flushed cheeks. "Why did you do that?"

"Oh...I...I'm...I don't know...It's just that your song made me feel so great, and I thought...well...good night!" Vera doubled her steps toward the wall of cypress trees.

"But wait! What's your name?"

"We won't meet again, Radov. Don't ruin the mystery!" Vera called over her shoulder.

Radov followed but didn't attempt to shorten the distance that she was creating between them. "I don't like mystery—"

"Vera!" The shout came from behind the cypress trees.

"Oh no! Good night, Radov." Vera began to run. "I'm here!"

Radov stopped following her when she started to run toward the angry yell. "Good night, Vera." He could barely hear his own voice, but it somehow got to her ears.

Yateem broke out of the wall of trees in a panic. "Vera! What were you thinking? I woke up to check on you, and you were gone! Have you any idea what I thought happened to you? You could have been kidnapped, or hurt by someone, and I do not want to know what would have happened if the trees...Why are you wet?" He took her hand and started to lead her back to her suite in the same way a wolf grabs his pup by the scruff of the neck to bring it back to the den.

"I'm sorry. A nightingale was singing and I had to dance, and I just sort of ended up outside the queen's garden, and fell into one of the fountains. I didn't mean to!"

"Oh well, I did not mean to almost lose my mind in worry, looking for you!"

Gently Vera squeezed his stomach in a side hug and smiled up at his face. "I'm safe. No one hurt me. No one discovered who I was!" Before they crossed through the trees, she looked back toward Radov.

"Please, for my sanity, go to your suite and go to bed." Yateem removed Vera's arms from around him and nudged her between two cypress trees. He made sure Vera was going in the direction of her suite doors and then stepped out from the trees and looked in the direction Vera came from.

Radov watched as Yateem looked out over the garden. "The song was enchanted, Vera," Radov whispered to the night. "That's why you were drawn to me."

Yateem couldn't see anyone or anything out of the ordinary, but all the same he locked all of Vera's doors and slept against the ones that opened up to the garden.

Chapter 6
Rising Water

Yateem thought about Majlis as he sat on one of the six points of the poinsettia-shaped marble fountain in Queen Prudencia's garden. The water was cascading down the three tiers of petals, reminding Yateem of the stream that was next to his and Vera's camp that first night. As he stared into the clear rippling water of the fountain, his mind traveled back.

The fire had warmed his hands and face. Vera had finally fallen asleep after hours of trembling and murmuring about moving roots and violent leaves. He looked toward the tent and listened; she was tossing around, but seemed to be getting some rest. Vulcan's and Minerva's heavy breathing assured Yateem that they too were resting up for the long journey.

He stoked the fire, making sparks fly as the newly revived flames reached out to touch their surroundings. Once the flecks of embers and the dance of the fire calmed, Yateem lay down beside it—just out of reach of the lick of the flames—closed his eyes, and took in the sounds of the night. The creek, though small, was the loudest noise in the relative quiet of the night. The meandering water slapped the small rocks, giving a chaotic soundtrack to the stars, along with the occasional scurrying of animals through the grass and the shrieking of hungry young owls missing their prey.

Silence.

Yateem sat up. Suddenly the night was as silent as a stone on the bottom of a lake. Even the animals could not be heard. As he stood, Yateem drew the curved dagger out of his tall leather riding-boot. He first checked on Vera and then stalked over to the bank of the stream, battle ready.

There was no motion. The water had frozen, but without becoming ice. Yateem straightened his back and waited, every muscle tense in anticipation. Now the water gathered and climbed, arcing and sculpting, with a finishing flash of glacial cold light as Majlis suspended herself in the empty stream bed. Yateem stood on the bank above her, dagger still in hand, but without the power to use it.

"Do you ever relax, Hebian?" Majlis glowered toward the dagger.

"I am in no position to relax." The dagger slowly made its way to Yateem's side. "Vera was attacked today."

"She was not attacked."

"Were you involved?" The dagger rose again, and the teal of Yateem's eyes focused like the fury of the ocean's wind on the aquatic fairy.

Majlis' projection swelled. "The tree nymphs rarely get involved, and most certainly avoid moving their abodes unless it is absolutely necessary. She was not attacked." Her tone was sharp and final.

Yateem's hand went limp, involuntarily dropping the dagger. He took a step down the bank, but hesitated once the wave of Majlis' beauty hit him. "She was horrified! What did they want that was so important?"

"It was a warning."

"I thought you said it was not an attack."

"Vera is going to face worse than moving aspens. It was a test." Majlis crested up so that she was the same height as Yateem.

"Did she fail?"

"As did you." Majlis receded back to the stream bed.

"How can I protect her?" Yateem wanted to be right next to her, but restricted himself and took only one step.

"The only thing you can do is watch her." Majlis looked down to hide her face as ripples reverberated from her heart.

"Watch her? That is your great wisdom for me? Why should I listen to you? You failed the test of being a handler as well!" Yateem's face was hotter than the fire, and his words were sparks seeking something to burn.

Majlis rose up to twice Yateem's height. "I am telling you that the world will be against her, against you—or at least that is what she will feel. She will lose interest in saving it. She will follow and join Draven. Unless you watch her and check her."

"I am trying." Yateem brought his left hand up to rub the back of his neck and stared at Majlis. Her height was starting to ebb, though her swirling rage and rippling sorrow did not affect her haunting beauty. "She is stronger than her disrespectful sass would lead you to believe."

"She needs to be."

"Why did you come here? I already knew this was going to be hard."

"I wanted to see the new Lavender Soul Handler. I wanted to see this mortal that could take on the responsibilities at which an immortal failed. I wanted validation that it was not my fault that Draven turned to evil." The tears melting into her watery body were nearly imperceptible.

Yateem took a step down the bank toward Majlis, his hands slightly shaking with the desire to touch her cheek or run his fingers through her hair. "He had the seed of evil in him, and he chose to let it grow. You did not cause that. Vera will not follow Draven." Yateem took two more steps toward Majlis, his eyes trying to follow and connect with the quivering of her projection's eyes.

She looked into his eyes, which were only a foot away from her projection but hundreds of miles from her. "Be vigilant of her inner darkness. It consumes everything in its path, and will become a monster faster than you think."

"Majlis, you are an extremely powerful and irresistible—I mean inspiring—fairy. It was not your fault." Yateem stretched out his hand and held it just over her shimmering cheek, fearing that physical contact would break the projection.

"If you should need my help, come to Elea. It is in the southern mountains of Ruwaydah. Find the biggest stream that touches Yakootah, and follow it."

"Yateem!" Vera's shout cut the silent night air like a machete.

Yateem let out a breath he had not been aware he was holding, slowly dropped his hand away from the watery illusion, and reluctantly stepped away from Majlis. He bounded up the bank and ran to the tent where Vera was feverishly swatting at the air in her sleep. Yateem rested his forehead on one of the corner posts, panting.

"What are you thinking?" he whispered to himself. "Majlis is…Majlis." He dashed back to the stream bed.

"Be strong." Majlis quivered and then dissolved into the creek, which was now brimming a little over the bank and moving swiftly, the water twice as loud as before, making it harder for Yateem to think and process what just happened.

"Yateem."

The water washed away all that remained of Majlis' sorrow, anger, and beauty.

"Yateem!"

He awoke from his trance at the poinsettia-fountain and found the water still clear, but the ripples were more distinct.

Vera stood waving her hand in front of his face. "Yateeeeem, what are you doing? It's breakfast time."

"I was sitting out here making sure that you do not accidentally wander out of the garden again." He was still dazed, but managed to sound firm with Vera.

She tugged on his elbow, making him stand up, and started walking arm in arm. "I told you, the dancing took over. I had no idea what I was doing. I just ended up there."

As the two of them strolled away, the fountain water started to shiver and quake.

"There is something I have to tell you."

"What's that?" she asked.

Yateem pensively glared at the granite tiles they were walking on.

"Yateem, hello?"

He snapped to attention. "What? Oh, I wanted to tell you…we are having tea with the king and queen tomorrow afternoon."

"Oh, okay. You made it seem like it was something important."

"We have to discuss leaving Lolani."

"So soon? We just got here yesterday! Did you even send the hawk message?"

"Yes, I had a servant deliver my sealed message to the royal falconer yesterday. I attached a note for the falconer. Only he knows where the message was sent. I am disquieted by the war council. I do not want to stay here long."

"Well, when are we leaving?"

"I am hoping no later than a week."

Vera stopped and looked through the white columns at the beautiful garden. "Only a week?"

Yateem leaned on one of the columns flanking Vera. "Until this situation has settled, until we have a better handle on what to expect, we cannot stay in one place for too long."

"This *situation* being me. I can't believe it, but I'm starting to wish for my boring life at Saman, when I stayed in one place and pretended to pay attention to my lessons."

Yateem looked at Vera. "You know you are a very good student. I wish I could approve staying in Lolani longer, but I will agree to not push our departure until a response to the hawk message arrives."

"It's just hard to think about leaving this place."

"Yes, besides sleeping against your doors last night, it has been a relief to rest with the security of an army nearby."

"No, it's not that." Vera continued to walk with Yateem down the open hallway toward their private dining hall. "My father was the firstborn son, the rightful heir to all of this, and I can't help but think that my parents would have had a much better life without me in it."

"Do not say that!"

"I'm sorry, but it's difficult for me to leave a place so quickly that could've been my home—should've been my parents' home. If my eyes had been a different color, if my father hadn't abdicated the throne, then maybe…maybe…" Vera covered her eyes with her hand, and Yateem put his arm around her shoulder. "My eyes are a death sentence, whether they mean anything or not."

Chapter 7
War Council

It was a taciturn breakfast, with everyone staring at their food, lost in their thoughts.

"Were my guards' families notified?" Vera looked up as if woken from a dream.

"What guards, darling?" Queen Prudencia's lost smile shined across the table.

"The two that got slaughtered in the farmlands outside Dayo because of me." Vera's lips were a thin line.

Queen Prudencia instinctively brought her hand to her pregnant belly, and King Koios looked over at Vera, his brow darkened with disquiet.

"Yes. I was the one that wrote their commission. I wrote letters to their loved ones and awarded them the money that the soldiers would have earned." The king reached over and rested his hand on top of Vera's. "They died nobly."

"Yeah, but they still died." Vera pulled her hand out from under her uncle's.

"That is the risk they took becoming soldiers." Yateem didn't look up from his plate.

"Enough of this talk. I want a pleasant visit as long as we have you." The queen gave a light smile as she popped a grape into her mouth.

"We have to be going. That meeting starts soon." The king's tone was strained as he tried to keep it calm.

"Uncle Koios, I'm not a child. Just say 'war council.'"

"Right." He stood and leaned over to kiss the top of Vera's head. "I always forget."

The queen hoisted herself up out of the high-backed dining chair. "I would much rather stay with you, Vera, but without a woman to calm the men down at these things, it would only end in a chaos of yelling." Her shallow smile highlighted the circles under her eyes.

Vera gave a light shrug. "Don't worry about it. I'm just going to read in the garden."

"Have one of the pomapples. They're good for your health." Queen Prudencia walked around the table and kissed the top of Vera's head, her swollen belly squished against Vera's side. "I'm so happy you're here."

She looked up at her aunt and had to force a smile when she saw the layer of anxiety that rested under the queen's beautiful complexion.

Their majesties quitted the private dining room, leaving Yateem and Vera to sit with only the empty sound of utensils tapping against plates.

"I have a meeting with General Lazaros. Will you be fine by yourself?" Yateem's voice sounded different; there was an unexplained weight behind it.

"Of course I will." Vera continued to stare at her mostly empty plate.

"Reading?"

"What else is there for me to do?" Her eyes lit up slightly.

"Explore the main gardens."

"You need to get over that. I told you the dancing took over—there was nothing a girl could do!" Vera looked up with a smile and an exaggerated shrug of her shoulders.

"It is daytime. There will be people out there that could see."

"Then don't leave me! You're the one stressing about my eyes, not me! If you want to talk with the general so much, tell him to come to your suite. I'll stay out of sight. But please, *please* stop reminding me of the inescapable prison that is my eyes!" Vera slammed a fist down on the dark mahogany table.

"I was not trying to...your eyes are a—"

"Gift. I know!" Vera pushed back her chair and stood with exasperation.

"Vera…" Yateem stood, his voice helpless, his spirit and will defenseless against this adolescent.

"Do what you want. I'll be sequestered in my room, reading about the world I'll never know!" Vera stomped out of the dining room as Yateem collapsed into his chair.

Vera perked up her ears. She'd been reading for an hour, waiting to hear footsteps, Yateem's signature triple knock on the door, and his apology. She hopped out of the armchair she had been curled up in and ran over to her armoire where servants had hung up all her clothes, her fingers dragging over the smooth fabrics until she happened upon her white cloak. She yanked it off the cedar hanger, which bounced against the back of the armoire with a loud, hollow thunk.

She tensed and leaned toward the shared wall with Yateem's suite. When she didn't hear anything, Vera padded over to the pine door, cracked it open, and poked her head out, looking from side to side. The hallway was vacant. Yateem's door stayed shut.

With a silent, excited squeal Vera stepped back into her room and secured the silver butterfly clasp of her cloak at the base of her throat, allowing the egg-white cotton to fall over her bare shoulders and light-red dress. Pulling the hood down over her nose, she smiled. She could see perfectly through the sheer white fabric, but it was woven in a way that made it impossible for anyone to make out her features, or see her eye color.

Stepping across the door's threshold, Vera's bare feet were silent on the sandstone tiles of the hallway. She pushed the handle of her door down and shut it slowly, ensuring that the click of the closing door would be as quiet as possible. She froze, waiting for Yateem to come bursting through his door, dagger in hand. A steady breath escaped from her lips as she straightened her body with a cheeky smile. Only the tips of her toes pushed against the tiles as she scurried to the end of the hall.

Vera was only familiar with the royal wing of the Lolani palace, but she was too smart to get lost. She made her way toward the center of the palace, and the moment she felt confused, she sought a guide.

A short distance from where she stood was a guard about her age, standing at his post. She took in a deep breath, made sure her hood was secure, stood up straight, and sauntered over to him.

"Hi," she said, quieter than she'd intended.

The soldier came to attention at the sight of a white-hooded young woman. "Hello."

As Vera rocked back and forth on her bare feet, the soldier's stare alternated from his boots to her feet, but ended up lingering on the hood that obscured her face.

"So..."

"Can I be of service, My Lady?" The soldier made an uncertain bow, his tight grip on his spear keeping him steady.

"Oh, right." Vera straightened up more and cleared her voice, trying to sound more official. "My handler, Yateem."

"Yes, I've heard of him." His voice quaked a little bit.

"Yeah, I figured." Vera pulled on the sides of her cloak. "He told me that King Koios and Queen Prudencia wanted me to observe the war council."

The young man's amber eyes looked at the white fabric, where he thought her eyes were, waiting for a command.

"I don't know where it is, and to be honest, I kind of just want to sneak in the back. I'm late, and my hood isn't that subtle." She pulled the hood down lower to cover her red cheeks.

"Then why wear it?"

"Uh...I have a birthmark," Vera said, fighting to make it sound like a statement, not a question.

The soldier cocked his head to the side, and then after a couple moments of painfully awkward silence, barely shrugged his shoulders and turned to walk down the hallway. "This way."

Vera waited for a full minute to pass with the soldier not looking back at her before she allowed herself to do two skips of joy while pumping her fists in the air.

He turned around to see the last bit of Vera's happy dance before she composed herself. Stifling a smile, he pointed to a door directly in front of them. "That is the servants' entrance into the ballroom in which the council is being held. Once you enter, go to the left, stick to the wall. No one will notice you there, but you'll be close enough to hear."

"Thank you!" Vera went to give him a hug, stopped herself short, patted his shoulders instead, and swiftly opened and closed the indicated door behind her.

The combination of the cool sensation of the light quartz floor and the angry shouts that filled the large room sent a shock through Vera's body. She could see that the servants were occupied with filling water glasses, so she quickly and quietly moved along the wall. The small ballroom was a 160 foot square, bordered with large quartz columns that supported the forty foot tall ceiling and created a path around the center of the room for servants to walk and work in. A large sun window shed light on tables set as a half-circle in front of the thrones upon which their majesties sat.

Vera silently moved along the wall to the middle of the room, away from where the servants would be standing soon, but close enough that she could clearly hear every word. She positioned herself behind a column where no one would notice her.

"But your majesty!" A tall man with gray-black hair stood. "We cannot wait. The Wachiru are killing our crops and livestock! Are we expected to sit and watch that?"

King Koios shook his head with a look of empathy. "Do you not think it hurts me to see these things, to see our country weaken? Defend your lands against the Wachiru as best you can, and when there is a serious threat, I will consider sending some of the guard."

The man slapped the table. "Draven sending his minions to kidnap our loved ones is not a serious threat to you?!"

"No." The king's jaw was set in a frown.

Vera sucked in a gasp with the rest of the room.

Queen Prudencia rested one hand on her belly, and with the other she took her husband's hand.

"It is a tragic strategy." King Koios rubbed his eyes with his free hand and then looked at the man again. "Draven is striking in small forces all over our country to distract us. As a man, as an expectant father, I would love to send out small task forces of my army all over Ziva to wipe out any Wachiru who would dare to hurt my country, but as a king, I have to step back and know that Draven is planning something bigger, and that he is counting on my humanity. *He* wants the army to be spread so that when he attacks with his full force, Ziva will be defenseless, and the devastation that would follow is beyond our comprehension. Look at the deserts of Elspeth, a once prosperous land."

Quiet murmurs traveled amongst the leaders in the room. The tall man sat back down with resigned understanding. Vera watched all of them with an eager interest, these people that lived out in the world in which she was supposedly going to save. They all looked miserable. Unrest leached the hope out of the room.

A man stood from his seat, and a hush went over the council. "What do you say about the rumors of a Lavender Soul?"

The queen looked at Koios with a guarded, pensive look. Excited whispers traveled through the council.

"Times of trouble always bring rumors. I have nothing to say about them." The king's voice was colder than the tile against Vera's feet.

"So you deny them?" The man's voice was defiant.

"I do." The king's knuckles were visibly white where he gripped the right armrest of his throne.

"You lie." The voice cracked with age.

Everyone in the room held their breath as an old woman pushed herself up from her seat. The veins of imperfection in the column pressed into Vera's right cheek. She recognized the woman.

"I have seen her." The woman's voice held no fear in defying a king. "In Dayo, hours before five Wachiru on the outskirts of town were killed."

The room was an eruption of noise. Some were chattering with excited hope, others shouting questions at the woman. The rest were yelling in disbelief, or scoffing at her.

The queen stood. "Everyone, this is not productive, please." Her voice was well projected, yet still gentle.

King Koios was surveying the room, both hands gripping the armrests to his chair as if his throne was the only thing keeping him from being swept into the tornado of hope, bitterness, and anger that swirled through the council. He shot up, his face aflame. "Silence!"

Sound lost meaning and died, like a mutilated carcass sinking to the bottom of the ocean. All eyes were on the king. Queen Prudencia grabbed the king's arm and begged for discretion with her eyes.

Vera had forgotten if she could breathe with a veil over her face.

"You careless fools! Hope is one thing, but to depend solely on a legend, an unconfirmed prophesy, to believe so fast in the soothsaying of an old woman after rejecting the logic of your king just moments earlier." Koios pulled his arm out of Prudencia's tight grasp. "Do you want to save Ziva? Do you want to be under my rule, or Draven's?" His shouts echoed through the columns.

Vera's knees wobbled, and her nails burned from attempting to dig into quartz. She didn't know whether it was the sunlight or her uncle's shouts that drained all color from the already predominately colorless room.

"We are here to form a unified plan to protect Ziva, not to speak about figments of hope. If we do not put an end to this nonsense and start speaking of the true possibilities for Ziva's immediate future, then this has all been folly."

Queen Prudencia calmly sat back down, her face flushed white, and her lips mouthed the words, "Too far."

Vera was a crumpled white heap on the floor.

At the same time Vera was sneaking out of her room, Yateem was making his way through the maze of the palace toward the general's office. He heard Lazaros' familiar voice and rounded a corner to find the open door through which it came.

General Lazaros hunched over his large desk, looking at a map of Ziva, discussing with his lieutenants reports of Wachiru. The general pushed pins shaped like black ravens into the map wherever his officers expressed genuine threats.

Yateem strutted into the office without hesitation, placed himself at Lazaros' side, and began studying the map.

"Lieutenants, salute the man that taught me how to wield a sword," said General Lazaros without bothering to look up.

"Not to mention the only reason you were accepted into The Guard." Yateem elbowed the general in the ribs.

The four lieutenants exchanged confused glances. This stranger before them looked to be the youngest person in the room—at the very least half General Lazaros' age.

When no one moved, General Lazaros lifted his eyes to glare at his officers. "You don't believe me?"

All four clicked their heels together and brought a stiff right hand up to their brow. Yateem smiled and returned the salute.

"No disrespect, but how old are you?" asked a lieutenant with dark hair and blonde eyes. He stared in disbelief at Yateem as his hand dropped back to his side.

"A whole lot older than I look, son." Yateem flashed a smile that flattered his dark complexion and bright teal eyes; he looked every bit of a young thirty-three year old.

"Gentlemen, we'll continue this meeting after I speak with the king. You're dismissed." The General's voice was exhausted.

The officers saluted their general and then promptly left the office, shutting the door behind them.

"There are more than I thought." Yateem ran his fingers over the pin that stuck out of the city of Dayo.

"Yes, they're spreading, and striking with more violence. It reminds me of my childhood." Lazaros walked over to the drink cart and poured a dark, honey-colored liquor into a crystal tumbler. "Drink?"

"It is a bit early."

"Yes, but war is in the air." Lazaros lifted his glass in a silent toast to Yateem before taking a sip.

"The last Wachiru invasion was eight years ago, and that was crushed." Yateem spoke in a vacant tone as he stared at the numerous raven pins in the map. "Before that...Draven came here fifty-five years ago with his first wave of Wachiru. You remember that?"

"Five year olds can have images imprinted in their mind that old age cannot erase." Lazaros turned and poured some liquor into another glass. "Like a young foreign man cutting down ten Wachiru..."

"Why now? Why did Draven wait this long?" Yateem cut off General Lazaros' musing, not wanting to visit that part of his past.

"Why indeed." He turned around and handed the fresh tumbler of alcohol to Yateem. "Who's the girl?"

"Which girl?" Yateem gave a cocky smile before taking a big swallow of the liquor.

"The royal 'cousin' that caused trouble yesterday."

"To be fair to your officers, it was I who caused the trouble."

"Why are you evading the question?" General Lazaros walked up to Yateem.

"Why are you persisting with it?"

"Because I let the king send four of my best soldiers on a private mission seven months ago, and I received word right after your arrival here that two of them are dead. You mentioned Wachiru around Dayo, and one of my lieutenants just reported five Wachiru slaughtered outside that same town. It looked to be the work of a large predator, like a gennadius." Lazaros' breath was hot on Yateem's face. "What did you and *my lady* ride here on?"

"Did they find the soldiers' bodies?" Yateem squared his jaw, their noses almost touching.

"Yes, a farmer found them on one of his walking trails. Lives are nothing to play with, old man. What's your business with elite soldiers and a teenage girl?" Lazaros' gray eyes flashed.

"Are you going to charge me with something?"

"No."

"Then stop interrogating me in this manner." Yateem stepped back and took a drink while keeping his eyes on the tense general.

Lazaros wiped the back of his hand across his tight lips. "There are rumors, old friend, of a new Lavender Soul."

"Yes, I have heard them," he said, finishing his drink with a slight grimace, "since I was a little boy."

Lazaros reached out to take Yateem's empty glass. The two men were the same height, but the general was bulkier. "I never gave much thought to them either." He pulled on the glass, bringing Yateem in close. "Why does she wear a hood?"

Yateem yanked his hand out from under Lazaros' grip, leaving the glass in the general's hand. "She has sensitive skin. What does it matter to you?"

"You almost killed one of my captains for trying to uncover her face!" Lazaros slammed Yateem's empty glass against the far wall of his office, the crystal showering down on stacks of papers.

Yateem's eyes were set in a stormy glare. "He had a spear-blade much too close."

"You refuse to be honest with me. We have fought together. Does that mean nothing?" The rest of Lazaros' alcohol sloshed out of the glass as he opened his arms in frustration.

"Lazaros, you are looking for a deeper meaning where there is none."

"You called her 'My Lady.' She's not your daughter. Why would a Hebian warrior stay in Ziva to protect a teenager if she's not the Lavender Soul?" Lazaros walked over to his desk and tossed his glass onto the map, the last drop of liquor seeping out of the knocked-over tumbler and into the parchment. "You should have said she was an ambassador from Aequitas. The only royal cousin that we're expecting is a man." He looked up at Yateem with an apologetic look. "I cannot stop my men from speaking amongst themselves. If she's not what they say she is, then identify her, and the whisperings will stop."

"I cannot. Everyone believes her dead. The king prefers it remain thus." Yateem's right hand rested on his belt, where his sword would ordinarily be.

"As general of the King's Guard, I demand you identify her, or else she will be arrested as a threat to their majesties and a traitor to the country of Ziva." He stood up straight, his wide shoulders pulled back, his chest pushed out. His tone was that of a commanding officer giving a direct order to a subordinate.

"You would not dare arrest a royal during a visit to their majesties." The wrinkles around Yateem's eyes deepened as he stared at Lazaros with disbelieving suspicion.

"I'll do whatever it takes to ensure that this palace, and this country, are safe."

"And I will do whatever it takes to ensure that my lady is safe."

"Her name, old friend, or I send a dispatch to her suite."

Yateem looked like a warrior statue, his head held high, his face set in prideful resolution. "I require an oath of secrecy, *old friend*." The sentiment had a bitter taste.

"I swear on my oath to protect and serve Ziva, and by the name of Arivos, that your companion's identity and person will never be spoken of, or questioned any further, as long as I am living."

"She is the daughter of Lord Amynthas and Lady Odelia." Even though they were completely alone, Yateem confessed Vera's identity in a low whisper.

The general's furrowed brow and stormy eyes stared at Yateem in bewilderment. "But...Lady Odelia miscarried, the disappointment of which caused Lord Amynthas to abdicate. He told me this himself!"

"Then my companion is a ghost. Treat her as such, and forget about her." Yateem nudged the general's shoulder with his own as he went to leave the office.

"If their daughter is alive, then why did he abdicate?"

Resting his forehead on the smooth, varnished surface of the door, Yateem said, "You took an oath." Taking a deep breath, he looked back over his shoulder at General Lazaros. "Do not break it. Once I step out of this room, this will not— *she* will not—be spoken of again. I will make known to their majesties your knowledge of their niece, and of your oath. They will not challenge it." He thrust open the door.

"But, Yateem…" The general held his mouth open, as if that would help all his questions form into coherent words.

"Please, old friend, do not make me do something that I will regret for the rest of my long life. Keep your oath." Yateem slammed the door closed and paced in front of it with his hands gripping his dark hair, taking in deep breaths through his nose, trying not to vomit in the hallway in front of General Lazaros' office.

His purposeful steps had a forced calm about them as he made his way back to the royal wing. Staring at the light pine door of Vera's suite, he slowed his hectic breaths then raised his fist and hit the door with three curt knocks.

"Vera, I am sorry. Can we talk?"

A maid juggled an absurd stack of sheets at the end of the hall, and Yateem cocked his head to the side, both at the maid and the lack of response from the other side of the door.

"I'm coming in."

The door glided open silently, and Yateem stepped into the room, taking care in case Vera had fallen asleep while reading. He scanned the room and saw a book carelessly thrown onto the seat of an armchair, the armoire doors splayed open, and an empty hanger sticking out above the rest…and no Vera.

Not wanting the distressing conversation he just had to impair his judgment, Yateem ran across Vera's suite and flung open the French doors to the queen's garden.

"Teatime!" The word masked none of the growing panic in Yateem's shout.

Sunlight glistened on the fountain water, and birds wove charming notes into a playful song as they flew in and out of the trees and bushes. Yateem sprinted around every inch of the garden, his panting making him deaf to the calming song being created around him.

As he sprinted back into Vera's suite, Yateem paused when he saw a drawing on the coffee table. It was a charcoal portrait of the two dead guards with the pools of blood drawn in with a dark red pencil. The words "the risk soldiers take" were scratched across the bottom in red.

"War council," Yateem breathed out the words.

He ran into his room, grabbed the small, curved steel dagger on the nightstand, and sprinted out the door and toward the main section of the palace. After the maid with the tower of sheets screamed at the sight of a man running down the hall with a dagger and tried to slow the assailant by throwing the mountain of laundry in his face while she ran away, Yateem decided it would be best to put the dagger in the special sheath inside his boot.

The sound of his running echoed against the walls, causing the young guard that escorted Vera to jump into the middle of the hallway.

"Halt!" His spear was shaking.

Yateem sped up even more, dodged the spear, side-kicked the guard into the stonewall, and kept moving.

He skidded to a stop in front of the ballroom doors and took in three deep breaths, not wanting to burst into the middle of a war council and draw more attention than his rash actions probably already had. His hand wrapped around the cold, leaf-shaped iron handle, the tendons in his hand clearly visible as he gently pulled. It didn't budge. The doors were locked.

"This is not happening," Yateem hissed under his breath, raising his hand to knock on the ballroom door and announce his current shortcoming to the king and queen.

The metal click of a door handle turning caught his attention just before his fist hit the polished pine of the ballroom door. A butler, carrying a tray of dirty glasses, came out of a small door thirty feet down the hall. Yateem sprinted and caught the door just before it closed, immediately sensing the unease in the room.

At the far end of the ballroom, the king and queen sat on thrones in front of a semicircle of tables filled with what looked like leaders from all over the country. Yateem was against the back wall and couldn't hear very well what they were discussing, but he could see that Queen Prudencia looked quite sick. Scrutinizing all the faces, he noticed the old witch from Dayo, and his mind grew feverish. Yateem was in the back left corner of the room and used the light from the large sun window to trace every square of light-gray quartz along the left wall, looking for any movement. He saw only a servant walking toward the tables with a pitcher of water.

Putting his back against the wall, Yateem slid to the right with the grace and speed of a prowling ocelot. He stood in the back right corner, on the edge of silent hyperventilation, when his eyes landed on a strange lump in the shadow of one of the columns halfway down the ballroom. Forgetting his desire to be unseen and unheard, he ran to the shifting lump. Although the servants hushed Yateem with stern looks and pointed fingers, he couldn't see them.

Yateem knelt next to Vera and placed his hand upon her back. She flinched, pulled her hands out from under her collapsed body, and yanked the white hood down to her collarbone.

"It's me." Yateem gently turned Vera over and looked at her hooded figure with an exasperated tight smile.

She pressed her face against the fabric of the hood and then slowly brought her hands up and lifted it so that she could look Yateem in the eye. Vera's eyes were red and puffy but held no tears. She looked haunted. Letting the fabric fall back over her face, she wrapped her arms around Yateem's neck. He picked her up, as he had done so many times in her childhood, smoothly walked past the curious servants, and exited through the door that Vera had used.

Yateem carried Vera back to her room without a word, and without noticing the onlookers in the palace. His one concern, his only concern, was that Vera felt safe.

When he laid her down on the bed, she didn't fight him when he unclasped the silver butterfly, pulled the cloak from under her, and threw it across the room.

Vera stared at Yateem in wonder. *How did he know?* "I don't want to be here anymore. Have you heard back from Shifra?"

Yateem brushed away a lock of hair that had plastered itself to her sweaty forehead. "No response yet. Tell me."

Vera started to trace the lines on Yateem's hand as she told him exactly what happened. He did his best not to react, so as to get the full truth from her.

When she finished her story, Yateem pulled his hand out of hers. "What were you thinking? What if someone had discovered you? If something had happened to you, and I was not there…" Yateem stood up, his paternal anxiety aflame in his eyes.

"I was careful. I wore a hood, and no one cared. No one cares about the Lavender Soul anyway. My own flesh and blood told his people to forget about it, so why can't you!" Her stare was vacant, but her voice had bite.

"When are you going to understand?"

"Never. I will never understand how I could be expected to become some soldier for people that are angry—most of whom laugh at the idea of a Lavender Soul. I have seen the risks of becoming a warrior, no thank you!"

"Those people are angry and scared because of what is happening in this country. You want to talk about risks? How about the risk the king just took? To crush any rumors of you, to keep you safe, he had to look cruel and unbelieving in front of the leaders of his country. Or what about me? At the risk of imprisonment or worse, I had to threaten General Lazaros, whom I mentored as a young man, so that he would not seek you out and confirm your identity. I threatened an old friend today, for you, for your safety. And what were you doing? Gallivanting around the palace with nothing but a piece of fabric for protection!" Yateem was pacing.

"And nothing happened to me! I was just about to get up and leave when you showed up. If being my handler is too much for you, then go. It's not like I need you," Vera mumbled, her tone holding no real conviction. "I'll live by myself and be fine."

Yateem balled up his fists in front of his face, stopped his pacing, and stood at the foot of the bed, shaking his head at Vera. "You still do not understand. Life is full of risks, but what we do—your uncle and aunt and I—it is not because we believe you to be the true Lavender Soul, which we do. It is because we care about you. It would not matter to me if your eyes were the color of grass, blue skies, or blood! I am responsible for your well-being, for your safety and happiness. *Yours*. Not your eyes. And if anything had happened to you today, I would have… words cannot describe…I would never have forgiven myself."

The edges of Vera's mouth turned slightly upwards as Yateem's monologue turned to staccato babbling. "I love you too."

He rubbed his temples. "Never do that to me again."

"Don't worry. I'm not too excited about going out and experiencing reality anymore."

"Well, I will be in my suite."

"Wait," she said, examining her fingernails and looking a bit embarrassed. "Do you want to stay and read to me, like you used to? I don't want to be alone."

Chapter 8
Shifty

"Did you hear that?" The evergreen satin grew quiet as Vera abruptly stopped and lifted her dress up to keep it from catching on her feet.

"What? No, stop stalling," Yateem said, continuing his earnest gait.

"You seriously don't hear that bird?" Vera asked, looking through the white columns as she passed by them.

"No." Yateem stopped at a large oak door. "You wait here. I will go make sure no servants are in there. You know how they gossip."

"Yellow-bellied flycatcher."

"Vera?"

"It's a bird that whistles like a doorbell. My father taught me how to make the sound with my hands before he and mother left." The coolness of the column felt nice on Vera's flushed cheek.

"I can go in and tell them you want a few more days."

"I'll be fine. Go make sure there are no servants in there to talk about my crazy eyes." She wrapped her arms around the white column and stared out at the big palace garden.

Yateem backed up slowly, wanting to observe Vera, to make sure she was really going to be okay. He then opened the heavy oak door, deliberately pulling against its weight and age, and entered the private living room of King Koios and Queen Prudencia.

The yellow-bellied flycatcher showed himself, making the corners of Vera's lips slightly turn up into a flat smile. "Hello, going to catch any flies today?"

The small bird swerved, curled in the air, dove through an opening between two columns, then flew down the hallway and around a corner. Vera involuntarily dashed after the small gray and yellow creature. As she turned the corner, her feet caught on the soft material of the dark green dress, and she would have fallen on the hard, dusty, red granite tiles if two strong arms hadn't grabbed her by the waist and put her on her feet.

"Who taught you how to walk?"

"Radov! I'm sorry. I really didn't mean to come around the corner so fast, but there was a bird, and I had to..." Her words flew as fast as the bird she was pursuing.

"That seems to happen to you a lot—not meaning to end up somewhere." His smile was disarming. Radov's skin was fair, in direct contrast with the shaggy black hair that swept in front of his ice-blue eyes. The dimples of his smile softened his striking features and sharp jawline, and the fit of his tunic and riding pants showed a musculature that could have only been built by years of hard labor.

"Just lately." Fighting against every cell of her being, Vera took a step away from Radov.

"Going somewhere?" His fingers twitched, seeming to want to feel her hair.

"Vera? Your aunt and uncle would love to see you now." Yateem's voice was gentle.

"Yes, I'm having tea with...I'm having tea." Vera's dress seemed to sigh as she turned and glided into the hallway. "I'm coming."

"Your eyes." Radov's whisper slid into Vera's ear with a frosty tingling.

Vera gasped, putting her hand to her mouth. Her hair was a fiery wave as she whipped to her left and looked at Radov. He stared into her eyes without hesitation, and she clenched her eyelids shut.

"Vera? What's happened?" Yateem's voice was getting closer.

"They're absolutely radiant."

Her hand dropped to show a surprised smile.

"Vera?" Yateem's footsteps were purposeful, the sound still echoing off the granite tiles as he came to a stop by her side, placing his hand on her shoulder. "Why are you closing your eyes?"

"I'm sorry. I was talking to…" Her eyebrows scrunched down as she made eye contact with the blue-and-red-speckled gecko clinging to the wall directly in front of her face. "This gecko."

"The gecko?"

"Yeah, a bug was flying near him. I closed my eyes 'cause I didn't want to watch him eat it."

The gecko opened his mouth and bounced his head up and down in agreement.

Yateem linked his arm with Vera's, placing her hand on his forearm as he eyed the gecko's open smile that revealed the remainder of an insect wing in the crook of his mouth. "Come, they are waiting for us."

The gecko made a low chirp as Vera walked away. She glanced over her shoulder, her lips forming a question she could not find words for.

"But why must Vera leave us so soon?" King Koios' vibrant, gray-blue eyes scoped out the perfect plums in the fruit bowl. He leaned forward, plucked up the juiciest-looking one, and handed it over to his wife. "I have enjoyed her company the past two days. She is quite good at dominoes."

"With all due respect, Your Majesty, Vera has been through some extraordinary things in the past week. I really believe we have to go to the Council of Fairies. They wrote the prophecies and will know what our next step should be. I am awaiting a response to a hawk message I sent to Shifra asking for an audience."

"Yateem is right, my dear." Queen Prudencia dropped the plum on her lap, placed her left hand on top of Vera's, and gently squeezed as her right hand rubbed her swollen belly. "We cannot be selfish and keep Vera here. Draven is spreading his poison, even getting a grasp on our land while his minions search for the rumored second Lavender Soul. If Vera is meant to help rid the world of that monster, then we are meant to let her."

Vera had been drinking tea and keeping her lips shut tight the whole time they were there. Even after Yateem had explained to her the emptiness of her uncle's harsh words, she could not look at him like she used to, and she barely trusted the words that would escape from her mouth. She was also certain that Yateem must have told both of them about her presence at the war council because until her aunt's last comment, niceties had been the only topic of discussion. Vera stared at her aunt's right hand as her fingers traced swirls on the fabric over her swollen abdomen. Tears blurred Vera's vision of the loving gesture when she asked, "Did my parents cry when they saw my eyes?"

The whole room seemed to suck in an agonizing breath. Queen Prudencia was speechless. She stopped rubbing her belly and moved close enough on the couch to hold Vera in her arms. Some of the queen's light-brown curls drifted in front of Vera's eyes when her aunt ushered Vera's head to rest on her shoulder.

"My older brother, Amynthas, your father, sprinted to find me. He wanted to tell me personally about his beautiful daughter. Did he ever tell you what he said to me the day you were born?" Koios' eyes were a blanket of comfort.

Vera shook her head and Prudencia brushed her fingers through Vera's auburn hair.

"He said, 'Koios, come see my daughter. Never have I seen something so beautiful! Her eyes looked right through to my soul. I believe I was put here so that she could be born. She will change the world with those eyes, brother.' I thought he was so exhilarated because you were his firstborn, but he was right, Vera. You were made to change the world, and your parents knew that it would be a tough life, but they knew you would somehow be strong enough."

Vera sniffled. "Did he really say that?"

Prudencia took her long sleeve and dried the fresh tears on Vera's cheek. "Yes, my sweet, I was there, and your mother felt unworthy of such a special child. She prayed for the strength to help you accomplish what you were put on this world of Zerahlinda to do." Queen Prudencia's round face looked upon Vera, trying to convey the depth and width of the love she had for her niece.

"Was it my fault they died?" Vera asked, looking directly into her aunt's eggplant eyes. If only her own eyes were a few shades darker, what could her life have been?

"No." Yateem stood and walked around the low pine end table separating his armchair from the velvet couch and knelt down in front of Vera. "Draven sent some of his Wachiru to steal Zivan land. Your parents were on their way to get you a trinket from a festival you desperately wanted to attend. They were the first to see the mercenaries coming and raised the alarm. They saved a lot of lives."

"But lost theirs." Vera sat up stiff as a canyon wall. "Why did you not tell me this before?"

"I did not want you to feel responsible." His hand touched hers.

She pulled her hand away as if his was poisonous. "So letting me wonder for eight years all the different situations that could have killed them somehow makes me not feel responsible? I'm sixteen, Yateem. I deserve to know the truth, especially from you!"

"They would have wanted you to be protected from thoughts of them being cut down by mercenaries."

"I can assure you that my mind has come up with much more terrible ways for them to die—and I'm pretty sure they would've wanted me to be protected from liars who make up stories like my parents 'died peacefully in their sleep because they accidentally ate Lantana flowers'!" She used all her strength to push Yateem out of her way as she retreated for the door.

"Vera, Yateem has always looked out for what's best for you." Koios' voice asked for forgiveness for Yateem, for them all, as the familial high cheekbones and strong jaw set in a grimace of concern.

"Yes, Vera, sweetheart, we *all* just want what's best for you, and everyone." Queen Prudencia raised her arms, giving Vera a loving place to retreat to.

Vera's hand was on the cold swirl of the brass handle. She took in a deep breath, composed herself, and looked at her three elders with her chin up. "Maybe it's time that I start looking out for what's best for me."

She leaned her entire body weight into flinging the door open, picked up the hem of her dress, and stormed out without waiting for a response.

Chapter 9
Servitude

The burnt-orange leopard seal panted on the bank of the Kallisto River in the shade of a baby fern-tree's fanned out branches that tapped the surface of the light-green water.

"Stop stalling! Vill you shift already!"

The faraway voice pounded down on the seal with as little pity as a falling mountainside. The seal dematerialized and vanished among the round stones of the quick river. Then, just as suddenly, Radov's human figure appeared in front of the fairy.

"Couldn't stand to see me resting, Amaury?"

"You're getting slow, Radov." The fairy rapidly flapped his dark-green and orange striped butterfly-like wings as he looked the boy up and down, his upper lip curled in disgust. "Vell?"

"Well what? I'm supposed to speak directly to their majesties Benoit and Emmanuelle."

"You honestly sought I vas going to let a slimy traitor like you in front of zem?"

Radov's breaths were fast and shallow, his knuckles white with crooked red streaks from curling his fingers into a fist. "What did you say, you...you stupid bear!"

Amaury squared up his shoulders and advanced toward Radov, bumping his chest against Radov's face. "I told zem zat a servant like you cannot be trusted, especially after so short a sentence."

"A hundred years! I have been shifting for a hundred dreadful years! And if you didn't trust me, then why was I sent to Vera?" Radov put his full strength into pushing against

Amaury's solid stomach but failed to move the fairy; instead he made himself fall backwards on the smooth, hard, blue river stones.

"*Zey* trust you," Amaury said as he laid his wings flat on his back and leaned over Radov's head laughing, "and asked me to hear if you have any valuable information so as not to vaste zeir time vith meaningless babble."

Radov dropped his forehead against the tops of his knees. "It's her."

"Speak up Radov. I have to report zis as soon as ve get into Feyerabend!"

Radov lifted his head up, and a pair of tears made slow, lonely paths down his cheeks. "Vera's the Lavender Soul."

Chapter 10
Farewell

Yateem and Vera walked together on the outskirts of the queen's garden, Yateem trying to mend Vera's feelings of betrayal that were still fresh.

"My Lord!" a young squire huffed as he ran to catch them.

Yateem placed his hand on Vera's shoulder to keep her from looking back. "Keep walking," he said before he stopped and turned toward the boy.

While Vera slowly walked on, she tried to nonchalantly look through the cypress trees and kept her ears open for Radov's song.

"The…messenger hawk…returned." The squire took in deep breaths as he held out a small scroll toward Yateem. "My master, the royal falconer…bid me to get this to you…as fast as I could."

Yateem grabbed the piece of paper from the winded boy. "Thank you. You have done well."

"I would've been here sooner, but I didn't know where you were, and the private wing is awfully big, My Lord."

"It is alright. Tell me, do you know where this message came from?"

"No, my master didn't tell me…I could run back and ask." He turned and took a deep breath in.

"Wait. Did you read this?"

The squire turned to face Yateem, a look of shock on his face. "I want to be a falconer, My Lord, and I wouldn't jeopardize that. Check the seal if you question my honesty."

Yateem smiled. "I do not question your honesty, or your honor. You serve your master very well. You may go."

"Thank you, My Lord." The squire swiftly turned and walked away.

When Yateem was sure that the squire was out of earshot, he called to Vera. "You can come back now."

"Why did he come running up on us?"

Yateem held up the scroll. "The messenger hawk returned."

"But you only sent it two days ago! What's it say?" Vera's voice was nervous.

"I want you to read it."

Vera gently handled the scroll. The paper had a slight yellow tinge to it and was fibrous, not like the smooth paper she used to write letters to her aunt. It was sealed with small, golden wax suns that ran along the seam. "They're so beautiful. I don't want to break them."

"Vera."

"Fine." She ran her finger under the piece of paper, breaking all twelve golden suns. "It says:

> *Your charge's true identity has been confirmed. One must have lived in Feyerabend for fifty years before an audience with the Council of the Elders can be allowed, but the queen and I will grant you an audience to bequeath what wisdom we can upon you both.*
>
> *Travel to the place on the Cardea River that lies directly across from the mouth of the Kallisto River. A ferry will be waiting for you. Do not be alarmed to see a shark with it. He will tow you across to safety and protect you, should any evil try to detain you. Amaury will escort you into the kingdom.*
>
> *Arivos' blessing upon you both,*
> *King Benoit the Blessed of Shifra."*

Yateem took the letter and rolled it back up before sticking it in his boot. "We have to pack."

"Where's Feyerabend? I thought we were going to Shifra? And what does it mean my true identity has been confirmed?"

"Feyerabend is the community center of the fairy kingdom. From what I have read, it is a kind of city where a large majority of the pixies live. As for your identity, fairies have ways of knowing things that we do not. It is best not to worry about it. Instead, focus on what you are leaving behind here."

"Any semblance of a normal life."

"I meant your clothes—put only practical things in your pack. We will be going into the pixie kingdom on foot. Vulcan and Minerva will live here until we return."

"That letter didn't say I'd have to travel without Mini!"

"The letter said the two of us will be granted entry into Shifra. It said nothing of our animals, and I am afraid that there may be an enchantment that would harm them if we tried to bring them into Shifra."

"I'm liking fairies less and less."

"They will be living in the stables and grazing lands of a royal palace. I think Vulcan and Minerva will cope. Come on, we have to pack, and then tell the king and queen we are leaving at dawn."

Vera left her saddlebags on the floor in her room and packed only her practical clothing in a brown leather hiking pack with her sleeping sack strapped to the bottom of it. She clasped her black cloak around her neck and slung the pack over her right shoulder. As Vera opened the door that led her to the familiar rust-tiled hallway, she was greeted by her pacing aunt.

Linking her arm with Vera's, the queen escorted her to a side entrance in the private royal wing. "I pray you will be safe, my love."

"Thank you for the prayers, Aunt."

"Don't worry about any servants talking. Only the most trustworthy are allowed here, and the man driving the wagon has been instructed not to look back at you."

"Wagon? I thought we were supposed to go unnoticed."

"Well, yes…the wagon regularly goes to market in the village not far from your destination. You will walk from the village."

When they arrived at the side entrance, Yateem put Vera's pack in the back of the wagon, and the king spoke to an older man.

The queen turned Vera and placed the hood of the cloak low over her eyes. "I love you, and my greatest hope is that I will see you again." Prudencia hugged Vera tight and struggled to hold back tears.

"That's an impossible hope, but I wish it too. Minerva is yours now. After all my clinging to her last night, I'm sure she will be glad to have a different master." Vera was thankful for the cover of the hood because her eyes were welling too.

The king shook Yateem's hand and then walked straight to Vera, embracing her in his loving arms. "You were made for greatness. I wish you were older, but you have all the strength you need. Be safe." He stooped down and picked up her hood to look into her watery eyes. "I do believe in you, with all my heart. I love you. May Arivos be with you always."

"Thank you, Uncle."

He kissed her cheek and replaced the hood over her teary lavender eyes. "The baker here has been so generous as to let you both have two freshly baked rolls. I think he's doing it so that you don't eat all the warm bread in the wagon if you get hungry!"

"I love you, Uncle."

"And I love you, little one."

Vera walked over to the wagon, let Yateem help her in, and sat with a warm roll in either hand as she watched her aunt and uncle shrink—an odd sight, a king and queen standing outside their palace, clinging to each other as if they were peasants that just had all their possessions stolen and their house lit on fire.

"Yateem? What's a shark?"

"A type of fish." Yateem shifted, settling in for the two-hour wagon ride, and took one of the warm rolls from Vera.

"A fish?" Vera lifted up her hood and raised her eyebrow at Yateem.

"You will see."

"You will see the power of the fish…" sang the baker, whose singing voice was full of deep barreling bass tones that resonated through the dawning day as clearly as a giant's would. "You will see the glint of his teeth, and a flash of your reflection in his dead black eyes. Yes, you will see, you will see the frailty of life as you sink into your own crimson tide. You will see the fury, you will see the fury before the end, my dear."

"No singing." Yateem growled the command between his teeth as he put his arm around Vera.

Chapter 11
Red Current

The sound of gentle lapping waves rubbing smooth, gray pebbles together made Vera lift her hood to take in the view of the Cardea River from where she and Yateem stood on top of a small bluff looking over the large expanse of water. The Zivan coast of the river was light-green bluffs that led down to thin beaches covered in small gray pebbles, while the land on the other side was only a thin green line on the light-orange horizon. The Cardea River was so wide that it almost seemed like an ocean. The early morning light cast an eerily soft glow on the shallow green water that kissed the gray stones. As Vera looked across the river, she noticed the water changed from light-green to sea-green, and then quickly darken into a brackish-blue that turned nearly black.

She couldn't help but think of the size of marine life that could swim in those depths. "What did that song mean?"

"It was just an old fishermen song, nothing more. A baker is hardly a soothsayer. There's the dock." Yateem started to hike down the bluff toward the beach.

"How can a fish pull a ferry?" Vera scoured the water as she stepped onto the dock.

"It is a big fish." Yateem placed his pack on the wooden ferry and started to untie the thick ropes from the post, pushing against the wooden railing so that the flat boat drifted away from the dock.

Once the boat was a foot away from the dock, a large gray dorsal fin appeared a few yards off the shore, slicing the smooth morning water with ease. The fifteen foot long shark circled the ferry.

"'Big fish?' That thing is huge! What does it eat—cows?!"

Yateem jumped on the ferry while the shark was on the opposite side. "Come on, the fishermen will be coming out soon."

"I'm not jumping over cow-eating-fish water!"

"It is a bull shark, and he was sent to us for protection."

The bull shark paused in its third cycle around the boat and raised its gray head out of the water, exposing the white of its bottom half to Vera, along with a broad smile of two rows of serrated teeth.

"Can sharks smile?"

The shark sunk its body back into the water, dove beneath the ferry, and found a steel bit attached to chains. Its broad nose surfaced five feet from the bow of the ferry, most of its body underneath to propel it.

"He is in position. Please, before someone sees."

Keeping her eyes on the slick back of the shark, she hopped on and sat in the exact middle of the eight-foot by eight-foot flat wooden boat, hugging her pack to her. "I don't know why a fairy couldn't have come and gotten us."

"People would talk."

"Yeah, and a boat propelled by a giant bull shark monster is very subtle."

Yateem just shook his head and stood against the railing on the left side of the ferry to survey the empty, smooth water and assess how many fishermen on the shore could have seen enough to compromise Vera's safety.

After an hour, the mouth of the Kallisto River was about 300 feet away, and little waves from the rivers colliding started to rock the boat. The shark swam steadily against the slight turbulence.

"Almost to safe waters."

"What strange reeds."

"These waters are too deep for reeds."

Vera stood and went up to the railing on the opposite side of the ferry from Yateem. "Then what are those over there?"

Yateem followed the direction of Vera's pointed finger until his eyes landed on bright-red spines breaking the surface of the black water 600 feet away from the boat. His face grew pale. "Impossible. They live off the eastern coast of Elspeth. They can't survive in fresh water."

"What are *they*?"

The red spikes vanished suddenly under the water.

"Yagim!" He screamed the creature's name at the shark, hoping it would understand, and the bull shark swam with a renewed fervor.

"Yateem?" Vera's eyes were wide as she saw the red-spine dorsal fin appear again, this time only 100 feet away from them. The spines created a wake, and then disappeared again.

"Get away from the side!"

The sea monster breached under the ferry, knocking Yateem off his feet and sending Vera over the railing and into the water. The crashing sound of waves in Vera's ears disoriented her. She opened her eyes, trying to find the boat, when she saw the yagim. It was at least thirty feet long and resembled a shark, except it was bright red, and the fins were made of spines connected by a sort of shiny black webbing. Vera looked for the bull shark but couldn't see it. Her arms were reaching for the surface of the water, reaching for the boat, but movement in front of her made her arms useless.

The yagim had started to charge. As it got closer, it unhinged its jaw, revealing four rows of black serrated teeth the size of throwing daggers. Vera screamed, letting out most of the air in her lungs, and then started thrashing her body to swim for the surface.

She was sure that death had come for her in the shape of a sea monster. She gasped and looked down, and saw a gray and white tail whip against her body, propelling her out of the water and back onto the ferry with a panicking Yateem.

"Are you alright?"

"That thing's going to kill us!"

The boat rocked treacherously as the two monstrous fish fought.

"Where's the line in the water to show we're safe? Can we swim to it while they fight?"

"It's at least 65 feet. The yagim could close that in a second."

Vera watched as the bull shark jumped out of the water, its full body exposed as the yagim came up after it, jaw unhinged and ready to kill. The bull shark twisted to avoid the fatal bite, but got caught on the yagim's top teeth that ripped through the shark's right gills and tore down to the fin. As the shark crashed on top of the sea monster's back, it opened its mouth, bit down, and jerked its entire body, breaking the first five large spines on the yagim's dorsal fin.

The water was bloodied, and between the last huge splash of the aquatic fight and the layer of red on the surface of the water, Yateem and Vera had no clue what was happening until the ferry jerked into motion, knocking both its passengers to their knees. The bull shark was swimming as fast as its body would let it, leaving a trail of thick, purple blood. Splashing started behind them, and Yateem and Vera turned around to see the sea monster clumsily swimming.

"Yateem, we're not going to make it!"

The unhinged jaw crookedly raised above the water, waves crashing around it as the yagim breached to take down the ferry. The monster froze in midair, about five feet above the edge of the boat, its broken dorsal fin dragging in the water, dyeing the white splashes of the surf red.

"Yateem?"

The yagim started convulsing in the air, and then resumed its fall. Yateem held tight to the railing with his right hand, clinging Vera to him with his left.

The monster burst into flames just before hitting the boat. Nothing but its skeleton was left when it collided with the ferry. The red-hot remains of the sea monster snapped its knife-like teeth at the two passengers as it sunk into the crimson waters.

With dazed expressions on their faces, Yateem and Vera clung to each other as they stared at the sinking red eyes.

"Velcome to ze Kallisto River."

Chapter 12
Guided Stumbling

The voice from the bank was authoritative and belonged to a fairy who stood tall with strong, broad shoulders. His dark-green wings, with orange stripes much like Vulcan's fur, stood straight and rigid. "Eat zis and go upstream so you don't die," he said as he threw a strange coral-colored meat into the water. The bull shark attacked the meat and swam away as if a whole school of yagim was after it.

"Thank you!" Vera shyly yelled after the shark.

"He doesn't need sanks," Amaury scoffed before flying over to the ferry, grabbing onto the front railing, and flying backwards to propel them toward the shore.

"He's probably going to die because of me." It was hard for Vera to put much force in her voice. Her surroundings were too distracting.

The water of the Kallisto River was a bright green, like new growth on a tree, and clear. Vera could see and count the blue stones and fish on the riverbed. She could see the dark trail of blood that the shark left behind beginning to dissipate amongst the school of fish that parted out of the predator's way. Out of curiosity, Vera went to the back railing of the ferry and saw that the thick blood of the Yagim pooled on the border of the two rivers, crashing into an invisible wall and then slowly sinking into the dark shadows where the skeleton lay.

"Zen so be it. It's a far more honorable death zan he deserves." He looked over his shoulder and through his wing to check their progress.

"You are Amaury?" Yateem asked, securing his pack on his back as they approached the bank.

"I am." He pulled the ferry onto the shore with very little effort.

The wood made a labored grating noise against the round blue stones that composed the riverbank. Luscious greenery spilled out over the stones, as if the forest were trying to take over.

Vera slung her pack over her shoulder and marched off the boat and straight up to Amaury. Because the top of her head barely made it up to the bottom of his chest, she had to take a few steps back to look into his eyes. They were green with orange specks along the edges. Where a human had eyebrows, he had luminescent markings that looked like thick jagged hooks that interconnected and disappeared underneath his blonde curls. "That shark risked its life for our safety, and all you have to say is, 'Then so be it'? Where were you when that yagim monster came? It seems to me you have less honor and courage than a fish!"

The markings above Amaury's eyes grew from a warm orange to a hot red color as his eyes narrowed to slits, the orange specks in his green irises blooming and turning into small spirals. He flapped his large butterfly wings in a few strong strokes that made it hard for Vera to stand. "Zat shark is a prisoner, a murderer. If I had helped, and zat abomination of a sea monster had tried to cross zah border behind me, zere is a chance zat ze opening zee enchantment vould make for me vould still be open for zat monster to get through, and eat you."

"Well, that inspires confidence. Can I possibly catch up with the shark?"

"Vera!" Yateem pulled Vera back to his side, his face hot with embarrassment. "Sorry, Amaury. She has had a long day so far, and the brush with death has strained her respectful nature."

Amaury closed his eyes and gently flapped his wings while taking in deep breaths. The markings above his eyes cooled to the same dark green of his wings and eyes. When Amaury opened his eyelids, they could see that the orange spirals had receded back into specks. "I should be apologizing. Her identity demands respect, even if her personality does not." Amaury made a deep bow at the waist. "Forgive me, Lavender Soul. Please allow me to velcome you to Shifra."

Yateem elbowed Vera in the ribs when he saw her eyes roll. "You're forgiven. Call me Vera, please."

"And?" Yateem squeezed her shoulder.

"I'm sorry for snapping at you. It's not your fault that a huge sea monster attacked us."

A sly smile was revealed as Amaury came out of his deep bow. "Zee most gracious forced apology I have heard since I vas a child. Sank you. Come, I vill show you to your cabin."

"A cabin? Here I was thinking that fairies lived in hollow trees and drank dew from leaves."

Yateem slapped his hand against his forehead as he shook his head. Amaury gave out a deep, robust laugh.

"Zose stories are just fairy folklore. Most fairies zat live in Feyerabend reside in small homes zat are built on ze branches of giant trees, but zere are cabins built on zah ground, made from fallen trees. And dew off a big fern-tree leaf is zah most refreshing sing you vill taste after a long flight in zah voods."

"I'll have to take your word on that one." Vera smiled at the large wings in front of her as she walked into the rainforest of the pixie kingdom.

The ground under their feet was now a thick mud that made Vera unsteady. Her hands gripped the rough bark of the trees on either side as her feet tried to manage the slippery clay trail. Yateem walked close behind and caught her a few times when the ground started getting slick. It wasn't raining, but every now and then a branch from high above would bend down, and a little shower of drops would hit the three below.

Vera glared up at the latest branch that sprinkled the back of her neck with the balmy water and noticed that the sun was at its highest point. They had been walking for a while. Her hips, legs, and feet seemed to be working independently of each other; this hike was making her feel like a toddler taking those first wobbling steps. The soft, fur-like feel of the moss on the trees was a comfort to her now very well exfoliated palms. When she turned her attention back to the trail, Vera noticed the lack of footprints in front of her. Amaury's feet were about a foot above the mucky trail, his wings the source of the breeze that had been refreshing her since they got deep into the rainforest.

"I thought a big guy like you wouldn't be afraid of a little mud."

Amaury turned in the air and smiled at Vera, hovering so that his shoes were level with her face. "Zese are made from softened crab shells zat vere custom formed to my feet before zey hardened again. If mud gets in one of za little cracks, it vill take me hours to clean. And if I keep my vings static, zeh drops vill saturate zem, and I vill not be able to fly until zey dry."

"I never would've guessed you to be a shoe man."

"I am a personal guard for ze king and queen. Zese are practical for my purpose, but I like to make sure I look pristine as vell, so as not to disgrace myself in front of zeir majesties."

Vera looked down at her riding pants and tunic, both soaking wet, and her boots covered in rich brown-green mud. She looked back at Yateem. "Why couldn't I have brought one gown? I have nothing presentable."

"They will provide us with clothing, Vera."

"But their clothing has slits in the back for wings. I'll feel exposed."

"Stop valking."

"Excuse us, we argue sometimes."

"No, not stop talking." Amaury touched down in front of Vera. "Stop valking."

Looking past Amaury, Vera noticed how huge the trees were—ten times bigger than the biggest tree she'd ever seen, and twenty times as tall. She was sure she would look the size of a baby insect next to them. Whereas Vera's fingers sometimes got caught in the deep grooves of tree bark, it looked like her whole hand could fit in the cracks of the giant trees in front of them.

"Velcome to Feyerabend, ze center of za pixie kingdom. Ve are on ze border of Ze Great Enchantment. If eizer of you have malintent tovard zis kingdom, turn around, because zis vill hurt you."

"I thought the border was the thing that turned that sea monster into a burning skeleton." Vera's eyes searched for the top of one of the huge trees, thankful that Yateem was standing so close behind her when she leaned back too far.

"Zat is to keep any obvious evil out of Shifra. Zis detects any dormant evil zat could possibly slip through."

Vera grounded her feet and eagerly looked at Amaury. "Doesn't it open for you? Can't we just pass right after you?"

"No."

"Why not? We were approved to come here."

"I have already passed through it."

Vera looked down to see Amaury's crab shell shoes on a beautiful path of flowering moss. "Why would you do that?"

Yateem stepped up next to Vera. "Why are you so nervous? What do we need to do to cross it?"

"Simple. Take a deep breath, in your mind say your full name and title, and your true purpose for coming here, zen take za step…and you are through."

"See, Vera, nothing to it. I will go first."

Vera grabbed his arm and whispered in his ear. "But I've said bad things about fairies!"

"Do not focus on words you said in moments of anger. Think about why we are here." Yateem closed his eyes, breathed deep, and then took a big step toward Amaury. He turned to face Vera. "A flash of warmth, and the color teal. That was it."

"Alright." Vera closed her eyes and felt the rush of crisp rainforest air in her lungs. *Vera Xochiquetzal of Adowa. I'm supposed to be the Lavender Soul, and I came here for counsel, for advice on what to do, because I don't know if I believe in the prophesy I'm supposed to be, or if I really care about saving everyone else when all they do is tell me who I am and what I can do, or more like what I can't do. All I want is to get a life and have people stop expecting so much.*

She took the step.

A jolt of warmth felt nice against her cold limbs, and in her mind's eye she saw a spark that erupted into a lavender fire. Her hand went up to her eyes to try to snuff out the internal flame, and for a split moment, she felt asphyxiated.

"Vera!" Yateem reached out for her, but could not catch her in time.

Relief came once her head hit the sweet smelling moss, and Vera could open her eyes again to see the men's shocked faces. "I passed, right?"

"Barely." Amaury picked up Vera and put her on her feet, dusting off the tiny white flowers from the moss that clung to her. "Ve are almost zere." Amaury took one more look at the part of The Great Enchantment that Vera had passed through. It glimmered slightly as the smoke settled against it. "Ve must go."

Chapter 13
Ancient Wisdom

Their first morning in Feyerabend was full of the fluttering of young fairies around their redwood cabin as they readied Yateem and Vera to meet the king and queen.

"You mustn't look at zem until you are called by name, and zen you curtsey, put your hands over your heart, and *zen* you may look up," said Daisy, the queen's dress designer. Her sunny disposition reflected in her appearance, starting with her bright yellow wings. Her eyes were a warm yellow with a white trim, and her markings were the tiniest of daisies strewn about like a summer breeze had placed them on her face. The long brown curls that skipped and bounced with Daisy's every move provided a nice contrast with her milky complexion. Her hands worked methodically with Vera's auburn locks, braiding the fairy's namesake in a beautiful design around the top of Vera's head and down the back of her hair.

The gown that had been woven onto Vera an hour ago was made from baby-pink calla lilies that had been cut into thin strips and woven into a corset top, as well as a skirt that fell from Vera's hips into a flowing gown down to the ground. Her fingers ran over the silky texture of the petals that bent in and over each other in a ballet of intricate beauty.

"I'm sorry, what'd you say?" Vera looked up into the reflection of Daisy's face, next to her own polished one. "Wow."

"Yes, ze color of za dress really brings out ze lavender in your eyes."

"Very funny."

"Zose gorgeous flats are made from za leaves of ze calla lilies. Zey are durable, but can be slippery za first time you vear zem, so be careful."

"Great. I can't remember the protocol, and now I'm going to fall on my face."

Daisy helped Vera stand, kissed her hands, and then kissed her on the cheek. "You vill do marvelously. Don't fret."

"Thank you."

A light rapping came on the door. "Are you ready?"

"Yes."

Yateem walked in looking handsome in a light-green, double-breasted suit and tree-bark shoes. "Who knew pressed and sown moss could look this good?"

Daisy and Vera laughed. "Come, you two. I vill escort you to zeir majesties." Daisy flew out the door.

Yateem offered his arm to Vera. "You look breathtaking."

"Thank you, as do you."

Sun rays glittered through the boughs of the trees as they walked on a path composed of the same flowering moss as before. It gave a little under their weight, but then bounced back after each step; the tiny white flowers showed no sign of being crushed. Daisy navigated the intricate walkway system without a care, while Vera tried to follow the pathways they walked past with her eyes, trying to spy all she could of this mythical place. The trees dwarfed everything; even the bushes looked like inconsequential weeds when compared to the giants that surrounded them. Vera was delighted by the overwhelming sense of life in the rainforest. The birds sang to each other and chattered at the pestering monkeys high up in the trees. Daisy shooed a mountain lion that was sunning itself out of the way, and later a herd of deer popped their curious heads up from behind a thicket of bushes to see the humans pass by.

As Yateem squeezed Vera's arm to make sure she knew he wasn't going to let her fall in her newly made dress and shoes, the quiet murmur of water caused Vera to look down as they walked on a fallen tree to cross over a small stream. The atmosphere was awe-inspiring. No matter where Vera looked, she couldn't see a single patch of decay. There were old, crumbled, fallen trees, but from them sprouted ten more baby giants eager to start their climb for the sun. A breeze brushed Vera's cheek, and somewhere a branch snapped as a young, weak tree groaned as the wind pushed it out of its comfort zone.

The painful sound of the stretching tree made Vera cock her head to the side and stare into the forest beyond the path with a piqued fascination. *I wonder how fast this forest will burn when Draven gets here.*

"I like that this place brings you such happiness."

"What?" Vera stopped short and looked up at Yateem.

"You just had the biggest smile on your face."

Vera opened her mouth as if to explain her thought, but was too shocked at herself.

"Ve are here!" Daisy flittered her bright yellow wings and drew herself to the side so that Yateem and Vera could see they had arrived at the base of the biggest tree in all Zerahlinda, the royal tree of Shifra. Its bark was silver and smooth to the touch, and it gave off a fragrance that invigorated the senses and calmed the soul all at once. Vera tried to look all the way up to the top of the tree, but found herself falling backwards in the process and landing on pillows made of woven grass.

Confused, she looked around her and saw she had landed in a litter, much like the ones her uncle and aunt would use when visiting the towns and villages. Yateem helped her sit comfortably, and then he sat himself next to her and pulled a rope across the side. Four large male pixies appeared, and with bright eyes and smiling faces, they grabbed the carrying poles and started to fly straight upwards.

"Oh, this is not pleasant." Vera clutched her stomach.

"Just hold on. We will be there soon." Yateem leaned ever so slightly to watch the pathways below turn into ant trails.

"We couldn't meet them on the ground?" Vera's hands shook as she stretched her neck to get an idea of how high they had gone. When she got her answer, her body snapped back rigid, and her face gained a greenish pallor.

"This is my first time flying as well, and I find it exhilarating." he said, half-sincerely.

"Exhilarating? Pssh, I now know why I wasn't born with wings." She made eye contact with a young pixie in a neighboring tree that was peering out the window of a small cottage that was impossibly balanced on the branch.

"Here we are."

It had taken merely twenty seconds to travel the 1,000 feet to the entrance branch of the royal pixie court. With grace and poise, Yateem stepped off the litter, but when he went to help Vera disembark, she nearly knocked him down, diving into his arms.

"Calm down."

"Sorry, I just needed to feel like I was on solid ground again."

Amaury walked out on the broad branch. "Zier majesties vill see you now."

"I think I'm going to be sick," Vera said as she smoothed her hands down the corseted petals over her stomach.

"Can we have a moment to adjust to the thin air?"

"Of course, valk into ze trunk, and I vill escort you."

"Thank you."

Vera was nearly hyperventilating.

"Take deep breaths. Lift your arms up."

"I can't do this—look at me."

"All I see is a gorgeous young lady who has a newfound distaste for flying. Just keep taking in deep breaths…do you feel better?"

Vera closed her eyes and breathed in shaky breaths while tapping the top of her braided hair with her fingertips. After a minute or two, she exhaled slowly and looked at Yateem. "Yes."

"Ready to see the king and queen?"

"Sure, I guess."

Yateem linked arms with Vera to help steady her legs. Walking through a carved threshold in the trunk, they saw a long hallway, one that reminded Vera of drawings of secret passages in ancient castles. Before they could get lost, Amaury came from a side hall and walked them to a staircase that went up a flight and opened on a grand, open-air royal courtyard in the canopy of the giant tree. The entire floor was made from the upper branches of the tree, which had somehow been made to grow intertwined and yet even, creating a smooth, silvery bark tapestry for a walking surface. At the other end of the courtyard stood two majestic thrones that seemed iridescent. It took about a minute for them to get close enough to make out the features of the persons on the thrones.

"Vera, look at the ground."

"What? Oh yeah." Vera's eyes went to Amaury's feet, so she would know when to stop walking.

"Your majesties King Benoit Ze Blessed Appraiser, and Queen Emmanuelle Ze Faithful Seer, here are za two vich requested an audience vith you." Amaury bowed so deeply that Vera could see his blonde curls next to his crab shoes.

"Vera Xochiquetzal of Adowa, de Lavender Soul."

Vera's head shot up to look at the king and queen. "Yes? I mean—" Vera put her hands over her heart and curtseyed so low she ended up sitting on the ground.

The laughter that filled the air was a harmony of bright sun rays playing with moonbeams. It delighted and confused Vera's senses.

"Me dear girl, rise." The voice had overwhelming warmth.

Vera stood and was struck by the beauty before her. The king was in a golden suit that seemed to glow all on its own. His wings were opalescent and came to sharp corners at the top and bottom. When light hit them, they shimmered gold, as if the sun rays had gotten caught in his wings. The markings above his eyes were tiny suns, identical to the seals on the scroll Vera opened at Lolani. Neither of them wore crowns because their markings joined together high in the center of their foreheads, making a crown of sorts that was ingrained in their skin. King Benoit's face was narrow and very angular, which was only accented by his close-cropped blonde hair that was so sun-bleached it was nearly white. But his gold crown with a large sun and brilliant rays coming off it, and his golden eyes with yellow swirls in the irises gave off such soothing warmth that Vera couldn't help but be comfortable smiling back at him.

Queen Emmanuelle was wearing a formfitting gown that flowed to the ground and looked like it was made from the deep blue of a clear night sky. Her wings were translucent silver, the top and bottom coming not to sharp corners like the king's, but rather to large swirls. Her eyes were a silver that shimmered as if moonbeam dust had been sprinkled in them. Her markings were small stars with twelve points on each, connected by swirls that gradually grew bigger and led to the constellation of five stars high on her forehead; the swirling moonbeams curled in and around them. Her round face was gentle and beautiful, framed by soft black hair that fell down to her waist. Her presence gave all the soothing relief of a soft cool breeze on a hot night.

The impression of both the king and queen of fairies was that of two halves of one magnificent whole. Their ageless youth, the contrast of Benoit's tanned skin and Emmanuelle's pale complexion, the living glow of their engrained crowns, and the realization that these two immortal beings may have witnessed part of the creation of the world dumbfounded anyone in their presence. Vera felt small—and somewhat jealous of their seemingly unlimited wisdom and beauty.

The flawless round face looked at Yateem with a smile. "Yateem Rukan Wulfgar of Xipili, esteemed handler of de Lavender Soul."

Yateem placed his hands over his heart, bowed deeply, and then stood straight and regal.

"What be the help that we may provide?" The king looked intently between the two.

"Is the shark okay?" Vera blurted out.

"Vera, we did not ask for this audience for trifling questions."

"'Tis quite alright. He is fine, dearest, completely healed in fact." The queen cocked her head at Vera, a coy, curious look in her eye.

"A shark can heal from that kind of wound in a day?"

"No indeed, but a lizard can." King Benoit leaned forward and gave Vera a little wink.

Yateem interjected before Vera could ask another question. "Your Majesties, may I ask that which has been troubling me for some years?"

"That is why you be here, is it not?" The king nodded toward Yateem warmly.

"I wanted to ask if, in your infinite wisdom, you could tell us how to find the White Gate, and Zakiyyah."

The king sat back in his throne, his markings turning from gold to copper as he furrowed his brow. King Benoit looked at his queen in silence for about a minute.

Finally, Queen Emmanuelle nodded her head and looked at Vera wistfully. "Amaury."

The guard flew over from his station and knelt in front of the queen. She looked intently into his eyes, her markings getting brighter and brighter, and with a deep bow Amaury rose and flew into the tree.

Queen Emmanuelle looked again to Vera. "Tis only one way to dah White Gate."

"Deep meditation?" Vera quietly chimed in.

"Death."

Vera's face lost its color. She looked as if she were before an executioner at that very moment.

Yateem ran his fingers through his wavy hair. "Is there no other way?"

"There be no other way, Hebian," the king sighed.

"But I'm only sixteen! Am I expected to kill myself for the slight chance that a flaming White Gate will be waiting for me on the other end?"

"Ah, I clearly see now why you almost did not make it through De Great Enchantment. Watch your temper, and try to see dat Arivos made you for a bigger service den catering to your ego." The Queen never took her eyes off Vera as she stretched out her hand for Amaury to place a small velvet bag in her palm. "You are young to be sure, but I know you feel Draven's evil looking for you, or else why would you be so scared? Dah yagim was merely a taste. I am a seer, and believe me when I say dat death will seek you, and snuff your mortal life out."

Vera looked at her calla-lily-leaf shoes, clenching and unclenching her fists. She could feel the blood in her cheeks. As a wind pricked the heat in her face with its coolness, the queen came to stand in front of Vera.

The long slender fingers of the queen lifted Vera's head so that their eyes met. "Take solace that I also see you wrapped in Arivos' arms. You will find dat White Gate, and once you pass through, without causing smoke," Emmanuelle's smile was light and love, "you will know where Zakiyyah sleeps." The queen took both of Vera's hands and placed the small lavender velvet bag in them.

"What's this?"

"Tis something your parents were smart enough to send to me before Draven could get it. Tis ancient and powerful. Twill help protect you from all evil." Queen Emmanuelle brushed Vera's cheek and then flew back to her throne.

Vera opened the bag and let a large golden object roll into her palm. Picking it up so that she could examine it, Vera saw that it was a solid gold dragon with lavender-colored gems for eyes. Its tail was curled beautifully to make it a ring, and its wings were slightly open. When Vera put it on her index finger, it perched watchfully, as if it could fly of its own free will. She thrust her hand at Yateem to show him.

"May I?"

Vera handed the ring to him, noticing the inscription "Ierá Flóga" on the inside of the tail as she did so. "What do the words inscribed on it mean?"

"Ear-ah Flow-gah, that *is* ancient, from a dead language, meaning 'Holy Flame.'" Yateem looked at the king and queen in their thrones for confirmation.

"Yes. A single drop of holy flame from Zakiyyah before he went into sleeping be what created it. Those gems grew out of the dragon's eyes as the ring cooled." The king's eyes were distant, as if watching an old memory.

"How did my parents get it?"

"It used to be heavily guarded, but when there was word of Draven looking for the ring that was rightfully his, even though he chose not to pass through the White Gate, it was moved to a place that was a wee bit less conspicuous, but where it would still be safe. The royal vault of Ziva be that place. Your mother took a liking to it as a child when she was shown through the vault, and it was given to her as a wedding present." King Benoit looked at Vera, his happy disposition shining through his markings.

"But if it is so powerful, why was it given away? Why didn't she keep it, and let it protect her from dying?" Vera asked as a bitter taste rose into her mouth.

"Your mother be made aware after the wedding day that it was not to be flaunted about, and that it should be protected. I believe that the ring made its way to her, so that someday it would be with you. If she had kept it, 't'would not have protected her, and Draven would have spilt much more blood than he already has."

Vera slipped it on her right index finger, and for the slightest of moments, she thought she felt the dragon's tail adjust to fit her finger perfectly. The thought of her mother wearing this brought flashes of loving memories that were too painful to see.

"Be that the only question you had?"

Vera gazed at the ring, and then locked eyes with the king. "Where are we supposed to go from here?"

"At this point, your destination be of little importance," he said, trying not to sound too matter-of-fact with Vera.

"Excuse me, King Benoit, but I don't understand."

"My dear, until you relinquish your attachment to your life, you cannot know where to find dah Gold Dragon." The queen's words offered clarification, with only a tinge of comfort.

"So what Your Majesties are saying is that it doesn't matter where Yateem and I voyage to, as long as I go and get myself killed?"

"Vera!" Yateem growled at her under his breath. "Forgive her, Your Majesties."

"Tis no offense to forgive, Yateem. Vera had no choice in being dah Lavender Soul. Her reaction to a premature death is understandable." The queen wore a thin smile in solidarity.

"It's just that the aspens attacking me was bad enough, and the thought of Wachiru hunting us in the night and killing those guards was just so terrible, but that yagim would've eaten me whole if the shark didn't save me. It's a lot to handle."

"That be something to address. You may think that rushing into death will make this process go faster, but above all, do not destroy your body with your death." The king's warmth grew to an uncomfortable heat to emphasis his point.

"Isn't that what death is?"

"In normal circumstances, yah, but you be coming back."

"I will do my best to die in the cleanest way possible." Vera tried to keep her sarcasm to a respectful level, although her cheeks were aflame.

"I will be there to protect you when it happens." Yateem's eyes were glazed, his voice distant.

"Even though we said it be of little importance, 't'would be in your best interest to have a destination."

"One in which your body may be protected." The queen's voice went back to the quality of a soothing night breeze, her face now intent on Vera's.

"We could go back to Lolani."

"Be aware dat Draven may bring his evil to dah place in which you choose. Your uncle and aunt's palace may be destroyed."

"Then back home? We can send the servants away."

"Elea." Yateem spoke it as a revelation.

"What?"

"Majlis lives within the Ruwaydah mountain range. That would provide fortification."

"How do you know where she lives?"

"She told me."

"When?"

"Indeed, I see dat she has made an impression on you." The queen gave Yateem a sly smile.

"Impression? She came and yelled at me, and then turned into a pond. What impression could be made from that?"

"She also talked to Yateem after testing you. Twas it dah moonlight on her liquid projection dat caught your eye?" Emmanuelle's silver eyes were focused on something far away, as if she were watching the scene between Yateem and Majlis as she talked.

"Testing me?"

"Dah aspens." Her focus snapped back to the present, and to Vera.

"That was Majlis? Yateem, did you know?"

"Yes. When you were asleep, she projected herself in the stream."

"And you didn't say anything? You treated me like I'd gone crazy!"

"I could not risk you harboring anger in your heart, not now that the White Gate is so close."

"Yes, because learning that the one person in my life that I've ever trusted lied repeatedly to me is a great way to deter anger and bitterness!"

"Vera, I—"

"Silence." King Benoit's authority was that of a judge in a courtroom.

Vera and Yateem turned toward the king, cheeks flushed with embarrassment.

"Vera, Daisy will escort you to the home of Manon. He be gifted with nature—trees in particular. You will learn how to sense, and react next time."

"Yes, Your Majesty." Vera bowed.

"You be pardoned." King Benoit's hand gestured for her to leave.

"Go back to dah court entrance from whence you came. I have summoned Daisy." Queen Emmanuelle's dismissal was oddly wistful.

"Thank you, King Benoit, Queen Emmanuelle." She turned and walked away with her head held high, hands wringing, eyes blinking back hot tears.

"Your Supreme Majesties, I assure you that I have always been forthright with Vera. It is just that I am afraid to push her into a rash state of mind. I could not take it if…"

"If she be as evil as Draven." The king made no attempt to soften the sentiment behind the statement.

"Yes. I have been like a father to Vera, and she is good and strong…but that temper…I do believe she is the Lavender Soul that will fulfill the prophesy. I just hope that she will believe soon."

"She must come to accept dah reality of who she is in her own time. Do not burden your mind with dah obligation of making her see dah power she has. You have taught her well. When she receives her powers, she will use dem judiciously."

"Quite right, My Queen. Yateem, what you have to be mindful of is Draven. He will try to win Vera by any means, and if that fails, he will try to destroy her. When her time comes, you must do everything in your power to preserve her."

"I would die to protect her."

The king leaned forward and stared deep into Yateem's eyes. "That be precisely me point—you have to live."

"How can I be expected to let her die?"

"You must live. It is dah only way her body will survive." The queen's voice was stern.

"Vera being out of my line of sight right this moment is making my skin twitch with anxiety."

"I can see dah tie dat you have to her. In your heart you can feel dat she is safe. Am I right in thinking so?"

"Yes, Queen."

"In Shifra, you have no cause for anxiety when it comes to yours or Vera's safety. Dah fact dat she barely got through Dah Great Enchantment should be of some reassurance dat anyone and anything harboring even the smallest amount of ill will toward those in Shifra will be stopped. But hear me when I say dat dah line between you and Vera will be severed by her death, and you need to loosen your grip so dat when dah rope is cut, you can drop dah slackened line to dah ground and prepare for her return."

"Yes, Queen Emmanuelle."

"One more thing. Until Vera awakens Zakiyyah, she could become evil. Be aware." The words fell off King Benoit's tongue with nonchalance.

"Why did you not say that while Vera was present?"

"She be under too much pressure. I feel that the fear and constant stress of not giving into the dark may in fact be what pushes her into it."

"I am supposed to betray her trust, again, by keeping her —excuse the colloquialism, Your Majesties—in the dark about the constant presence of evil even after she gets through the White Gate?"

"You be protecting her by keeping it from her."

Yateem clenched and unclenched his fists.

"I see her goodness. I feel her strength. I taste de sweetness of dah light to come. You will have many a trouble, but keep dah faith. All dat Arivos has planned will come to fruition." Queen Emmanuelle's smile was too sweet and confident for Yateem's liking.

"There be no more wisdom for us to impart on you," said the king before reaching out for the queen's hand and lightly kissing it.

"Go and enjoy a few nights of peace, for there are dangerous roads before you." The queen's voice was full of empathy, her ageless face devoid of any emotion toward Yateem.

"Thank you, King Benoit, Queen Emmanuelle, this has been truly enlightening. Your wisdom and hospitality have brought me a clear vision of what path to take in the future."

Yateem bowed deeply, and the king and queen bowed their heads in return. He turned on his heel and marched back to the staircase.

Chapter 14
Edification

Vera slowly entered the home to which Daisy had brought her. It was made from the root system of a Kapok tree and looked like a giant, dark-brown octopus had been frozen in the middle of a forest with a tree growing out of its head. While it was truly comforting to Vera that she was on the ground, the thought of being directly under the weight of a humungous tree made her knees feel a bit wobbly—particularly since the tentacle-like roots that lifted up to make room for the dwelling had deep crevasses running along them from age and wear. Putting her hand on one of the roots that made the threshold, she found it rough but reassuringly solid. When her presence did not seem to be noticed by the inhabitant, she pushed with all her weight against the root; not only did it not waver in the least to her weight, but it pushed against her resistance.

"Come in, Vera." The fairy was at a desk with his back to her. His wings were dirt-brown with small green swirls cascading down them.

Vera stood up straight, shocked by the root's movement and embarrassed by being caught testing the stability of the fairy's home.

When the fairy turned around, he had a confused look on his face. "I'm not going to hurt you. My name is Manon. Do you like jasmine tea? I just made a kettle of it." Manon's deep-brown eyes had green streaks in them, and his markings looked like tiny brown tree roots spreading over his brow.

"I like tea."

"Good! Now zat you are talking, why don't you come sit down here and tell me why you were sent to me."

Vera took slow steps. Her trust in trees was slowly coming back, particularly since there was no way of avoiding them in a rainforest, but the root's reaction to her push made her feel like sudden movements would bring the whole tree down on them both. "Didn't they tell you?"

The fairy smiled as he put a teacup made from a giant acorn shell in front of Vera and poured her tea from his smoothly carved kauri wood kettle. "Of course I know, but I wanted to hear your side of za story."

"Queen Emmanuelle saw that a grove of aspens attacked me, and she said it was Majlis testing me." Shivering at the memory, she looked at her surroundings with suspicion.

"Was zis so-called attack near a stream to zah east of Kuno?"

"How did you know that?"

"I am so sorry if it came off as an attack. I told zah nymphs to give you a warning, not terrify you." Although Manon's face had the same timeless beauty of the other fairies, he was the first fairy Vera had seen who had light wrinkles. They were very subtle, like the first creases in young tree bark.

"A warning? Yeah, because I'm supposed to understand a warning that comes in the form of choking leaf tornadoes and moving trees!"

Manon took a sip of tea. "Now I see zat disrespect zat Majlis was talking about."

Vera's eyes narrowed. "Majlis?"

"Yes, Majlis. I visit her in Ruwaydah often. I have a deep connection with trees, Vera, so naturally I like to go all over Zerahlinda, checking on zem."

"The aspens were Majlis' idea, weren't they?"

"We both agreed zat it would be good for you."

"Good for me?! Are you insane?" Vera splashed tea out of the acorn teacup when she slammed it on the table.

"You are ze Lavender Soul. You have to get used to ze fact zat Draven can make ze very earth you stand on revolt against you." He mopped up the spilled tea with a patch of moss.

Vera looked away from Manon, picked up the teacup, took a sip of the perfectly brewed concoction, and sighed. "I didn't choose this."

Manon looked at Vera, his brown-green eyes full of sincerity. "Neizer did any of us. But you have ze choice to rise up to zee challenges in front of you, or to live a life zat you sink of as easier, but zat will never fulfill your purpose." He lightly hit the table with his fist, as if to drum in his message. "If you refuse to do zat which you were born to do, Arivos will give us another, but you will never get zat choice back. All I can say is zat you do not want ze kind of regret Majlis carries with her."

"Is that why she's so rude to everyone?"

"To attempt to explain Majlis would be like measuring ze ocean—a daunting task even when waters are smooth as glass, but most of za time you deal with choppy water, or if you are very unfortunate, a hurricane."

"Yeah, I've experienced that stormy water."

"One must be careful with Majlis. She has all ze power of water and is very vengeful."

"I'm glad she isn't my handler."

Manon set down his teacup and folded his hands, leaning toward Vera as if being closer to her would make her understand. "She used to be concerned with ze affairs of za world. She was a sort of ambassador between humans and ze high council. Majlis was very much active in za fairy and human issues. She helped impoverished lands with irrigation systems zat zey could sustain zemselves, and she helped make ze protection enchantment on ze Kallisto River that surrounds Shifra." He wiped his hands on his banana-leaf pants.

"Zen—because of her concern for ze well-being of everyone and because her advice was zah most treasured by zah elder fairies—she was chosen to be ze first Lavender Soul's handler."

"Does she even come to Shifra anymore?"

Manon stared at the table that was made from the same fallen kauri tree as the kettle. "Zah forests on Ruwaydah were always her favorite. She helped zose trees grow strong in ze cool peaks. So when everything happened with Draven—when her husband Sinclair was murdered and Elspeth destroyed—it was not shocking zat she withdrew into ze mountains zat she always loved."

"I didn't know she was married...I didn't know fairies could be killed."

"Neizer did we." Manon pinched the bridge of his nose. "Evil has a talent for unimaginable, inexplicable destruction."

Biting her lip as she ran her thumb over the grooves of the acorn teacup, Vera clenched her eyes closed to ask the next question. "Why did Draven fail?"

He put a fist to his mouth. "Maybe we should talk about how to handle moving trees..."

"Please, I have to know."

Manon sighed and seemed resigned to answer. "Okay. Majlis told me stories of her first experiences with Draven and how he grew up a spoiled boy, mostly due to his parents taking advantage of his status with people. Zey would show him off to za Elspethians and would demand tribute from zem. Majlis took him away from his family and raised him to be an honorable person, one filled with honesty, loyalty, and faith. She was proud of za progress he was making and rewarded him by taking him on a trip through za rugged hills of Yakootah. It was when she took him to ze Athanaric Cliffs to overlook zah sea zat he found zah emeralds. Majlis saw ze earlier greed of his childhood surge back into his eyes, misting over zah smooth lavender. She told him to leave ze emeralds, zat zey belonged to ze Yakootans."

"Did he stop?"

"He didn't care. His ears were deaf to all sense. Minutes after first seeing zah jewels, Draven was in an absolute fit of madness. He grabbed all zah loose gems and slapped zah rooted ones in an attempt to get zose too. Majlis screamed for him to stop, to watch his surroundings and act his age, but when she went to physically reprimand him, he fell out zah opening in ze side of zah cliff. Zat is how he died."

Vera's eyes widened. "I didn't think that passing through the White Gate actually meant death." she said, her voice catching in her throat.

The fairy poured more tea for Vera. "Should I stop?"

"No. No, I need to hear this perspective on it. I've only read this story in books."

"Majlis flew as fast as she could down to zah ground, but it was too late. She moved him into a low cave in ze cliffs and stayed by his side without eating and drinking for two days, praying to Arivos zat he would make it through zat White Gate, but when his eyes opened, zey were as black as a raven's feathers. Despite her famous strength, Majlis broke down and started to cry. Draven saw her tears and laughed."

"She thinks it's her fault, doesn't she?"

"Majlis had dreamed of Draven finding ze Golden Dragon and vanquishing zah existence of evil, and zen he brought a concentrated presence of it into Zerahlinda and spread it like a virus. She was devastated. If you feel like she is rude to you, it is only because she doesn't want to grow attached."

"Does everyone think I'm going to fail?"

Manon stood and gently flapped his wings as he kissed Vera's forehead. "No. We all have great faith in you."

Vera put her hands on either side of Manon's face. "*I* think I'm going to fail."

They spoke for hours as Manon talked Vera through some exercises to access her connection to and awareness of the nature around her. He taught her how to awaken a baby tree nymph and how to move rocks in a mound of dirt that Manon had put in one of the corners of his abode. Vera had gotten the rocks to just peek out of the top of the dirt when a gentle knock on the thick root threshold broke her focus, making the rocks sink back to their places.

Daisy smiled gently as she leaned into Manon's home. "I'm not interrupting, am I?"

"No, no, we are just finishing. Sank you, Vera, for a wonderful day."

"Thank you, Manon. I learned a lot," Vera said, reaching her hand out to the fairy.

Manon eagerly grabbed it and kissed Vera's olive-toned hand. "Remember, have faith."

Vera stood, gave a quick curtsey to Manon, and then turned to join Daisy at the door.

"Vell?" Daisy linked her arm through Vera's as they walked back to the cabin.

"Well what?"

"Did Manon teach you anysing interesting?"

"Yeah, we talked about Majlis and Draven at first, and then he taught me how to feel the link between me and nature around me," Vera told her as she looked at the pinks and oranges of the sunset streaming their way through the trees.

"Isn't learning new sings fun!"

"Sometimes."

"I know just the sing to brighten za rest of your day!"

"Please say it's my bed because I'm not really in the mood for anything but sleep."

Daisy stopped in front of the steps of Vera and Yateem's cabin. "I'll show you tomorrow zen." Looking at Vera's sunken face, she gave her a tight hug and then held her at arm's length to look into Vera's face again. "Zere is stew on ze stove for you. I already set out a bowl and spoon. Yateem has already eaten, so eat as much as you like."

"Thank you, Daisy."

"Of course. I'll come get you tomorrow morning."

"Night."

"Sleep vell, Lavender Soul."

Vera turned and started to climb the few steps to the cabin door as if they were mountains. "Please just call me Vera," she muttered, so exhausted that she doubted the fairy could hear it as she flew away.

The next morning came much too quickly for Vera's encumbered mind, but when she got out of bed, her face brightened when she saw a simple, light-blue silk sundress laid out on a chair for her. Slipping it on, Vera found that the sweetheart neckline suited her well, as did the swoop of the dress' fabric down to the middle of her back, which gave the dress breathability—or maybe room for wings that she didn't have. The dress came to just above her knees, which already made her movement feel freer than the gown the day before.

Vera sauntered out her room and followed a delicious smell to the kitchen. "What are you making?"

Yateem turned around; he was wearing brown leather pants and a silk tunic with a leather vest. His teeth gleamed white in a broad smile. "Good morning. I found sausage and eggs in the icebox, and I have already toasted some bread. I was going to bring it to you in bed, but now we can eat together."

"What kind of sausage?" Vera asked, looking to see the color of the meat in the frying pan.

"I think it's chicken."

"They have chickens here?"

"Yes, why would that be strange? Fairies can farm too."

"I guess I just assumed that they only eat what they forage in nature."

"Chickens are found in nature."

"You know what I mean. With Manon, I only had tea with fruit and nuts for lunch."

Yateem stared at the sausage and eggs he was cooking. "How *was* that?"

"He makes good tea."

"Do you feel like he helped you learn some valuable things?" He asked as he handed a plate of scrambled eggs, sausage, and toast to Vera.

"Yes, actually." Vera sat at the small wooden table in the kitchen and started eating.

Yateem watched her for a moment and then joined her at the table. "How are you feeling? I did not get the chance to talk to you yesterday."

Vera stared at her plate while she lightly tapped her fork on it. "Yesterday was…a lot." She looked up at Yateem and saw the worried expression on his face. "I saw the light behind your door when I got back from Manon's, but I was just so bogged down…I just ate and went to sleep."

"You do not need to explain. We both learned some heavy facts, and your trust in me faltered. I am sorry. Truly. Everything I do, Vera, I do with your protection and well-being in mind. I never want you to doubt that."

Vera spread some mango preserves on her toast. "I know. It's just that…all of *this* is becoming too real."

They finished their breakfast in silence.

"I was going to go on a hike through the rainforest after this. Care to join me?" asked Yateem.

"Oh, thank you, but Daisy wanted to show me something."

"What?"

"I don't know. Something to 'brighten my day'!"

"Good. I hope you have fun. I will see you later on then." Yateem rose, placed his dishes in the washing tub, and started walking toward the front door.

"You're alright with me being out and about? Out of your sight?" Her hair tickled the bottom of her shoulder blades as she turned with a look of shock.

"You are safe in Shifra, and if I feel anything to the contrary, I will find you so fast you would think I had wings." Yateem gave a half-hearted smile.

Vera smiled back at him. "Have a wonderful day."

"You too." Yateem grabbed a canteen of water off a side table next to the door and walked out.

Vera placed her dish in the washing tub on the redwood counter, found a rag in a drawer, and started scrubbing the plates.

"Zere are attendants for zat."

Vera dropped the plate she was washing and jumped away from the counter to avoid the splash. "Daisy, you scared me!"

"I'm sorry. I'll verk on valking loudly around you."

"It's alright. I guess I'm a little jumpy. Did I ruin the dress?"

"No, you look beautiful. I'm glad it fits. I vore it ven I was younger, before I became ze queen's dressmaker."

Vera felt the thin silk hem in between her fingers. "It's so pretty. Did you make this?"

"Yes, I did." Daisy had a prideful smile on her face.

"Where did you find the silk? I thought fairies only wore things from nature?"

"Silkworms, silly. Yateem vas vearing leather, vasn't he? It's cotton zat is difficult to find. It doesn't grow vell here."

"Do fairies farm?" Vera asked, quietly giggling.

"Of course, vhat do you sink, us fairies just flit here and zere, picking nuts and berries?"

Vera blushed. "All I know about fairies is what I've read."

Daisy giggled. "Come on. I vant to show you somesing zat you von't find in any storybooks."

"Okay, let me grab my boots."

"For shame!"

"What?"

"Traveling boots vith zat dress! You are going to be as most fairies—barefoot."

"I love walking barefoot!"

Daisy linked arms with Vera and steered her toward the door. "I sink you vill find you love a lot of sings today."

Walking upon the flowering moss trails that cushioned each step, it felt like they were walking on velvet air. A maze of trails lead into a part of the forest that grew wild, with rose bushes nearly spilling into the pathway. Music, laughter, and chatter floated to Vera's ears. Before she could ask where it was coming from, Daisy lifted a pine branch out of the trail, and with a wide smile and grand arm gesture, she bid Vera walk into a wide-open meadow.

Although the grass was a rainbow of fuzzy blades that curled and recoiled when stepped on, giving pep to everyone's step in the clearing, that was not what made Vera's eyes almost jump out of her skull or her mouth hang open in wonder. There were hundreds of fairies everywhere, some playing music on lutes, harps, mandolins, and drums, and all looking hand carved out of wood. Others danced about to the music, but most circulated around the tables and stalls full of colorful and fantastical merchandise.

"Velcome to zee Pixie Bazaar. Vant to take a closer look?" Daisy put her hand on Vera's back and gently pushed her off the mossy trail and into the colorful meadow.

"It's a dream, right?"

Daisy giggled and skipped past Vera as fairies fluttered overhead, holding strange objects in their hands. As they got closer to the bazaar, Vera saw the tables made of the scraps of fallen trees, and the stalls created by vines that rose straight out of the ground and spread out to create a canopy over the vendor.

There were so many bright, vibrant colors, and all the fairies were treating Vera royally. She was offered fruits of odd shapes and colors, she tasted sweet cane bamboo juice, adogabi spiced meats, warm breads, and delectable sweets made from flower nectar.

The fairies bartered for whatever they wanted, be it fresh fish from a large glassless aquarium, chickens, sheep, cheeses, clothes, flowers, art, home décor, or potions and powders from the bazaar's apothecary. Fairies walked around with their bartering items and new possessions.

Vera saw some that simply walked around enjoying the atmosphere of community, and of course, the chorus of playful shouts, heated negotiations, calling out of orders, friendly collisions, and the charming sales pitches that added to the music that intermingled with the sounds of the bazaar. One fairy strolled around the market, cradling and petting a strange animal that looked like a very robust lizard with furry, cat-like ears and a long, fuzzy tail.

The music that had danced around Vera's ecstatic brain as she strolled along the aisles of stalls and enjoyed all the delicacies of the bazaar now wrapped its arms around Vera's soul and led her to the dance floor. Raising her arms, she let the rhythm of the wooden drum and a duo of harps move her body.

Vera grabbed hold of some fairy children's hands and joined in their giggling as they twirled round.

When Vera looked up to smile at Daisy, her eyes caught on Radov's face, and she froze.

The little fairies crashed into her as they continued to twirl, knocking Vera down onto a patch of violet grass. The little fae were laughing and crawling on Vera as she craned her neck, trying to see past their little wings into the crowd that had formed around the dancers. He was nowhere to be seen, but Vera caught a glimpse of the black and white feathers of a large condor flying away with a wrapped parcel in its talons.

A little boy from the playful bunch noticed Vera's distracted glances at the crowd. His chartreuse eyes and wavy markings darkened slightly as he focused on Vera's face and stood up straight and proper. "Do you vant us not to play vith Lavender Soul? I can get rascals avay from you." The boy had an exaggerated seriousness about him that he must have seen on his father's face. As an afterthought, he gave a clumsy bow.

Vera's teeth gleamed in a wide smile, and with a mock-official voice, she answered the little fae. "Thank you, noble sir, but I was merely wondering if you children know the game we Zivans call Tag'em."

The little boy's face glowed as he smiled and tried to stop his little feet from dancing and his wings from lifting him off the ground. "Is it ze game zat one person is chosen, and ze rest of ze group try not to get tagged by zat person?"

"That's the one."

"Ve call zat Tag-n-flit."

"I'll be the first tagger, but you little rascals have to remember I don't have pretty wings like you, so keep your feet on the ground. Okay?"

"Okay!" The little fairies yelled in excitement as they untangled themselves from their pile and got off Vera and onto their feet.

Vera got up, brushed the violet and indigo blades of grass off her dress, and gave a side glance to the little faces that were bobbing up and down in anticipation. "Well then…Go!"

The jubilant children squealed and left a misting of fairy dust around Vera as they shot into the sky and flew over the adults that had formed a circle around the musicians and little dancers.

"Feet on the ground!" Vera called as she ran after them, her bright smile parting a path in the circle to the open part of the meadow where the laughing little pixies waited for her.

The market resumed its ordinary pace, and the sounds of Tag-n-flit added to the rest of the happy sounds in the meadow. As the sunlight started to fade, Daisy found Vera lounging on a jaguar, eating honeysuckle, and describing to a group of fairies a gennadius.

"Mine is named Minerva. I call her Mini, and she can take down a large elk before the poor animal even knows she's there."

There was a mixture of shocked and impressed gasps from the crowd.

"Not while I'm riding her, of course," Vera hurried to add.

"It seems like an odd way to get around," murmured a little girl with eyes the colors of a ripe nectarine. She looked at the jaguar Vera was using as a pillow, seeming to imagine it stretched out to the size and shape Vera was talking about.

"Vell, humans don't have vings, little one." Daisy stepped out of the crowd and approached Vera. "It's getting dark. Ve should start valking back. Don't vant to be late for dinner."

Vera nodded. She tickled the purring jungle cat's chin once more and then stood up. "Good night, friends. Thank you for showing me my first jaguar."

"Good night, Lavender Soul!" the happy crowd said in unison.

Vera turned to Daisy. "Lead the way."

Once the sunlight left the rainforest, seedpods on short shrubs that were scattered amongst the trees started to glow.

"Daisy..."

"Zey are called illumiem shrubs. I vish it vere a month from now because zen zah seedpods bloom, and it is gorgeous. Zah flowers are big vith rounded petals zat look like sunset, but zey glow in the night. Zey bloom year-round, and ven zah flowers die, it only takes ze plant about a veek to produce a seedpod zat is mature enough to glow. So you see, zere are only five veeks in a whole year zat zee floor of zah rainforest doesn't glow!"

"Fascinating…but I just wanted to say thank you." Her tone was abrupt, but sincere.

"You're velcome. I'm glad you liked it. Of course, I have no clue vhat you must be feeling with all ze pressure you have been under your entire life," Daisy said, grabbing Vera's hand and squeezing it tight. "But any human who can play vith fairy littl'ns all afternoon and still have ze strength to dance for hours vith strapping pixie adolescents has za strength to face anysing!"

Their laughter burst through the thick quiet of the night as they stopped in front of the cabin steps. "I don't have any siblings, but our day together gave me an idea of how wonderful it must be to have an older sister."

Daisy laughed. "Four hundred years older. As much as I may vish it, ve could not be related. My family has round faces. Zere are no high cheekbones like yours."

Vera smiled at her. "I think my lack of wings and face markings already hinted to us not being blood-related."

"But I vould cherish your friendship."

"Friends it is. Do you want to join Yateem and me for dinner?"

"Sank you, truly, but I am being courted and have an engagement for dinner tonight." Daisy replied as the outdoor cabin lanterns shed light on her red cheeks.

A sly smile came onto Vera's face. "I thought I saw you flirting with a dashing man today! He is lucky to have you."

Her cheeks deepened in color. "He doesn't have me yet, but sanks for zah compliment."

"You're welcome. Go have fun."

Daisy quickly hugged Vera and then flitted off into the trees.

Vera smiled and went into the warm cabin. She closed her eyes and inhaled a tangy, spice-infused, savory scent that wafted out of the kitchen. "Mmm. What's that smell?"

"Your dinner."

Vera strutted into the kitchen. "Well, I figured that."

Yateem smiled at her as he started to plate both their dinners from a sizzling pan. "It is pan-seared, hazelnut-encrusted piranha on top of mashed yucca root, with a cold salad of pomapples, mangos, and wild strawberries on the side." He placed the plate in front of Vera and gave a theatrical bow.

She applauded enthusiastically. "Bravo! Since when have you been a master chef?"

"I did not always live in a place with a full kitchen staff."

"Well, this is a meal fit for a royal banquet. Thank you."

"You are welcome. How was your day with Daisy?"

"It was just what I needed. She took me to the Pixie Bazaar!"

"I am glad to hear it. See anything interesting?"

"Everything! There was music and dancing and all these stalls made out of vertical growing vines and full of things I never even knew existed!" Vera savored a bite of piranha and mashed yucca, the light flesh of the fish complementing the rich flavor of the root. "Delicious. Oh, and there was a stall selling fresh fish in glassless aquariums. The water was holding its shape!"

"Well, Majlis is not the only fairy that can control water, but I do think she is the oldest and most powerful."

Vera fell silent, continuing to eat her dinner. After a few minutes she looked up and watched Yateem run his fingers through his hair while taking small bites of his food. "How was your hike?"

"It was great. The rainforest is overwhelmingly beautiful. I came across a stream and found Manon fishing."

"Really?"

"Yes. He invited me to join him, and we fished for most of the afternoon. I caught this piranha myself!"

"Wait…attendants didn't put this food in the icebox?"

"No. I gathered it."

"The yucca root, pomapples, mangos, strawberries… how did you carry it all?"

"Manon had a basket he let me borrow. He was the one that showed me where to find hazelnuts for the rub. I found the rest on my hike back."

"Sounds like we both had a full day."

"Yes, we did. It was nice to just wonder about."

"Without having to worry about me."

"I will never stop worrying about you, Vera. That is my part in your life…Manon had nice things to say about you. Said you have more power than you realize, and that you will have no troubles getting through the White Gate."

Vera stared at her empty plate. She'd thought about asking for seconds, but now had a bad taste in her mouth. "Yeah, I'll just have trouble dying first."

Yateem winced.

"You know what? This was scrumptious, but I'm going to get some air." Vera dropped her plate in the wash bin and walked toward the door.

"Vera, I thought there was another way."

She stopped and leaned against the kitchen entrance. Her eyes were focused on the cabin's front door, five paces away, and her voice came out crisp and clear. "You know what the only damper on my day was?"

Yateem's brow furrowed as he looked up at her.

"Everyone called me Lavender Soul. They refused to call me by name. Every time a pixie called me by that title—like it was an honor just to utter it—I flinched on the inside. Do they know, Yateem? Are they taught as children exactly what 'battling a torrent of power' and 'passing through the White Gate' means? If so, why do they smile and treat me like I'm a princess, when they should be eyeing me like a cow picked for slaughter? And why is it that a fairy, with all their wisdom and gifts, has never been a Lavender Soul? Why is it that humans, with the shortest life span, are chosen?"

Yateem walked over to her and placed his hand on her shoulder. "You were chosen because of your courage and incredible strength, and your amazing capacity for love."

"I need a walk." Vera marched to the door without looking back at Yateem.

"Vera, do *not* get lost in the dark."

Vera opened the door and looked back with a dry smile on her face. "Don't worry. They have glowing plants here."

The door closed behind her, and Yateem listened to her heavy footsteps down the stairs.

"That is not what I meant."

Chapter 15
Vacillated Confession

Her fingers ran over the rough wrinkles of the pine tree behind the cabin as she pet it as she would Minerva, feeling the soft coat of light green moss that clung to the tree, seeing the age through the many dimples and creases of the bark.

Whoo whoo.

Vera's head whipped up, her eyes searching for the somehow familiar bird, but she underestimated the height of the tree's branches and became disoriented. Her head swam, and her arms reached for a steady tree hug, but her body felt the full force of gravity as it was pulled down to the ground.

"Vera, are you okay?"

She woke slowly to ice-blue eyes and shaggy black hair. "Radov?"

"I'm sorry. I didn't think you would try to look up there."

"I don't understand…How are you here?"

Radov stroked the auburn hair away from Vera's lavender eyes. "I serve here."

Vera sat up and rubbed the back of her head. "But, wait…what?"

"I'm a prisoner."

"A prisoner?" Vera started to back away from him.

"More like a servant."

Vera's eyes narrowed. "So I did see you at the bazaar today."

"I was sent to get some food for the royal cook. I'm sorry if seeing me startled you." Radov's calm voice melted away any suspicion that lingered on Vera's face.

"Startled me?" Vera crawled back to Radov, gave him an awkwardly warm hug, and then immediately pulled herself off him, her cheeks hot with embarrassment. "I was surprised— thought I was seeing things."

Radov pulled her up to her feet and then put Vera at arm's length. "We can't talk long. I'm probably going to be punished for speaking to you at all, but I had to see you."

The glow from the illumiem shrubs shone on the raw pink skin of newly made scars along Radov's neck, drawing Vera's attention. Bringing her hand up slowly, she just barely touched the smooth scar tissue with the tips of her fingers. The wound ran deep. It looked as if someone had taken a steak knife and drug it through his flesh, making five columns that ran from the base of his jawbone and continued under the collar of his cotton work shirt. Radov watched Vera's reaction carefully.

"How?"

"Oh…well, when I was released for a short time in Ziva, I picked up some cotton shirts in a market." His voice was light and matter of fact.

"That's not what I meant." Vera was giving him a scolding smile that snapped to a frown when a memory flashed before her eyes. "The shark. You were the shark?"

"Yes. Queen Emmanuelle saw evil was waiting for you in the Cardea River, so she got a message to me to shift into a creature that would make sure you got across the water safe."

"I don't understand. Why are you a prisoner, and if you're a prisoner, then why were you at Lolani, and how do you change…what are you?"

Radov's eyes were full of regret and sadness. He leaned his back against the big pine tree, slid down to a crouched seated position, and looked up at the stars. "I'm human. That's what got me in trouble, being human. Because our lives are ordinarily so short, we have no perspective on the impact our actions can have in the future."

"What are you saying?" Vera kneeled next to him, grabbing Radov's hand that was nervously fiddling with the clovers that blanketed the ground.

"I feel like I can trust you." His voice had a shaky quality that was almost imperceptible, but it got Vera's attention.

"I feel the same way about you," she said, her eyes focused on the scars he received for her safety.

Radov pulled his hand away from hers. "I was young, Vera, and stupid. Draven saw how strong I was, said he would spare my family and our ranch, if I did one thing for him in return. You have to know I thought it was going to be manual labor, something horrible like digging mass graves for all the Elspethians he killed in cold blood. I had no idea he would be so…evil." Radov closed his eyes and took in deep, shaky breaths.

"What did you do?"

"Draven told me to go down to the great lake Kassiopeia. On the bank I found the fairy named Sinclair. I was to go and talk with him, distract him, while Draven came up and plunged a black stone dagger through his left wing into his back, through his heart. A great light came out of him and swirled up into the sky, carrying the dagger with it. Draven screamed at me, saying I made a deal with the fairy, that I somehow knew the energy would steal the dagger." Radov took in a deep breath and glared at the ground.

"When he stopped screaming words I didn't understand, a sadistic smile spread across his face, and he calmly said, 'You have failed. Your family is dead.' After he uttered the word 'dead,' my blood went cold. I heard the screams of my family, even though they were miles away, and I knew."

"Knew what?" Vera whispered the question.

"Knew that I had killed my family by making a deal with Draven…He knocked me unconscious next to Sinclair and left. When I woke up, I was in Shifra, and I told my story to those that had arrested me. For my part in the first—and only—fairy murder, I was sentenced to be a shape shifter until the fairy elders decide I have learned from my mistake."

They sat in silence for a while as Vera stared at the trees and the glowing shrubs, trying to process all that she had heard. "How long?"

"One hundred years. Draven had only been an evil plague to the earth for a couple months."

"How old were you?"

"Nineteen."

"But you look like you're nineteen now."

"Because we constantly have to change shape, shape shifters don't age."

"And they don't think you've learned after one hundred years?!"

"I was lucky they didn't hand me over to Majlis to be tortured."

"Why would they have allowed that?"

"Justice. Sinclair was the writer of the book of fairy tales. He was the most connected to Arivos, could hear exactly what he was supposed to write. He was also Majlis' husband. For both those reasons Draven wanted him dead, and he tried to take his inner light energy in the process."

Vera looked at Radov's face, but his eyes were focused on something far out of his reach. "I don't know what to say," she told him.

Radov turned and focused his ice-blue eyes on Vera. "Say you won't let anyone corrupt you. Vera, you are my only hope of freedom from the pain of this life."

Vera glared at Radov. She thought he was opening up to her, not giving her a lecture. "Do you know I have to die to get to the White Gate?"

"Yes."

"Then why are you so eager for me to find it, to make that *big* decision?" Vera stood up and brushed herself off.

"I'm not—trust me…I just want you to be happy." Radov stood and held Vera in his arms.

Vera breathed in his slightly musky scent and tried to escape his strong embrace. "Then can we please talk about anything else? *That* would make me happy." She looked up at him and relaxed her body with a huff.

He smiled and kissed her forehead tenderly. "Can I know your story? Where did you grow up? What do you like?"

"After the last week and a half, I feel like I barely know myself anymore."

"Will you dance with me then?" There was a look in his eyes that made Vera's stomach knot.

She flashed a bright smile at him. "Yes."

Radov took Vera's left hand and placed it on his right shoulder, his debonair smile reassuring Vera that her hand on top of his new scars caused no pain. His left hand squeezed her right. His fingers felt the silk that swept across the middle of Vera's back, sending a shiver up her spine. He rested his hand on her bare skin and drew her in close. "Are you cold?"

"No." Vera's heart jumped around her chest.

Radov smiled, the same disarming smile Vera had seen in the halls of Lolani before he turned into a gecko. He started to hum a slow melody that carried their feet in unison, twirling around trees and glowing shrubs.

After what seemed like forever, but what felt like a second, Radov stopped dancing and stared into Vera's lavender eyes that were only inches away from his. Vera bit her lip, causing Radov to smile. He cupped the side of her face in his hand and brushed his thumb across her soft lips then pulled Vera toward him and passionately pressed his lips against hers. She pulled away from Radov, an alarmed look on her face. He looked over her face with concern, and she shyly smiled up at him, and then kissed his lips with a returned passion. Her fingers played in his dark hair, and his hands held her close. Their chests heaved as they pulled apart, and Vera giggled nervously.

"I have wanted to do that since the first time I saw you dance, when I was that nightingale."

Vera's glowing face darkened with confusion. "You were Mr. Nightingale?"

Radov bit his lip. "Yes, I had to—I mean, I wanted to sing to you."

Vera pulled her arms away from Radov's grasp and took a step back. "You said 'had to.'"

Radov let out a resigned sigh. "I'm sorry. I didn't mean to draw you in...or anything, really. They made me and..."

Her eyes narrowed as she looked at him. "Draw me in? Who made you do what?"

"I can't. I have to go. I've been here too long." Radov looked right and left as if lost.

"No!" Vera grabbed his wrist. "No, you tell me what is going on right now!"

"I can't..."

"I don't care."

Radov sighed and took her other hand in his own. "I was sent by King Benoit and Queen Emmanuelle to see if your handler's hawk message was legitimate. I was given an enchanted song to play that would act as a magnet to a true Lavender Soul."

"I thought I was drawn to you because...because we were supposed to be..."

"I want us to be something, more than I can explain. But we can't." Radov stared into Vera's eyes, his look holding the sorrow of a hundred years.

"I don't understand. Why are you always around me? Are you some kind of spy?"

"Yes." Radov brushed his thumb lightly across her cheek. "Life is just. It doesn't mean it's fair."

Vera hit Radov's hand away from her face. "Who do you think you're talking to? I am not a child! Life is just? Yes, it is just that I have been hidden from the world since childhood. It is just that everyone thinks that I am some warrior savior that has to juggle the world in my hands!" Her voice was hushed, but it cut the air between them like an axe. "Well, maybe I am a child in your eyes, since obviously your interest in me is equivalent to a hound retrieving a shot bird and bringing it back to his master!"

Radov's eyes were wide like an owl's, and they started to glisten. "Vera, I do—"

"Any feathers stuck in your teeth?" Her eyes flamed.

"I wish that..."

"I wish that I never heard your stupid song!" Vera took one more look at Radov. As the anger in her eyes quelled, she slowly shook her head, opened her mouth to speak, but instead turned on her heel and stomped back toward her cabin.

"...Life could be different for both of us." His whisper could not reach Vera's ear this time, but Vera heard the howls all night—the wolf that only ever has the moon as company.

Chapter 16
Haunted Relaxation

Vera lay in the spot where Radov kissed her, running a daisy over her lips and fighting the urge to cry or yell—she couldn't decide which would feel better.

"Want an egg-stuffed crepe?" Yateem's voice was soft.

She lifted her head from the clover-covered ground and looked at Yateem standing in front of her with a platter stacked high with breakfast. When she reached out her hand, he placed a warm egg-stuffed crepe in it. As she took a bite, Yateem sat down next to her.

"I think you missed your calling." Vera said, reaching for another delicious wrapped morsel while she shoved the rest of her first one in her mouth.

"Oh, I cannot make crepes. These were delivered to us. I think by someone you danced with at the bazaar."

"What?"

"Yes, a large eagle—with a weird scar, I might add—dropped a basket on the porch with a note that said, 'Sorry for the song.' Does that mean anything to you?"

Vera threw the crepe in her hand at a nearby tree, sending scrambled eggs all around the base of it. "No, nothing comes to mind." Vera pinched the bridge of her nose.

Yateem put his arm around Vera's shoulder. "Do I need to kill anyone?"

"No."

He squeezed her shoulder and waited.

Vera huffed out the breath she'd been holding. "He was sent to Lolani to see if I was really the Lavender Soul."

"Who?" Yateem's face set in a protective glare.

"He changed into a gecko when you came around. His name is Radov. He was also the bull shark."

"A shape shifter." His mutter was self-scolding.

"Yeah." She curled her knees up to her chest. "It's just… I was…urg…I was so dumb."

Yateem set the plate on the ground and leaned over to look Vera in the face.

She avoided eye contact. "I read too many books. I thought he liked me. I thought he was around me because one day we could be…but he's a spy for King Benoit and Queen Emmanuelle. Just another person to tell me what I'm destined to become." She rested her head on her knee. "All he wanted was…" Her voice cut off.

"What did he want?" The words were abrupt and sharp.

"He said…he said I was his only hope for freedom." Her exasperation was muffled as she talked into her leg.

Yateem rubbed his hand in circles on her back. "You are a source of hope for all of us, surely you know that. I assume you saw him on your walk last night, and that is the reason a wolf was in the rainforest?"

Vera nodded her head up and down.

"This Radov did not make himself known to me, which I do not like, but he is considerate enough to not want to distract you. If it seems like he has ulterior motives, then I would suggest trying to forget about him. Maybe in the future you two will meet again, but until then, we have to focus on the quest in front of us." Yateem leaned down and kissed the back of Vera's head.

She lifted her head to glare at Yateem. "What future? Our *quest* is to wonder around till I die."

"You will return triumphant!" He bit down on the words with a bitter stubbornness.

"And then what? I become a warrior against evil until I die a second time?"

"We will walk across that bridge when it presents itself."

Vera wiped her nose. "And what bridge do we have to cross right now?"

"Leaving Shifra."

"Today?"

"No, today we enjoy peace. I think a hike would do you good."

"After last night, I'm not going to fight you to stay here longer," Vera said, leaning over and resting her head on Yateem's chest.

A chuckle burst from his lips. "Oh, my dear Vera, I am certain that no matter what, you will always fight." Yateem grabbed the plate of crepes from the ground, stood up, and held out his hand to Vera.

She let him help her stand, grabbed another crepe off the plate, and sauntered toward the cabin. Vera went to her room and started to go through the pile of her dirtied traveling clothes.

There were no footsteps, but Vera heard the door to her room open and felt a light breeze. "Do you think it's okay to leave clothes here? My outfit from that first day was torn by the trees, and I assume we're going to get muddy on our hike…" She turned around and dropped the tan riding pants she'd been inspecting.

A young fairy stood in the doorway like a child who knows they should be punished. Her straight black hair framed her fair face beautifully, and her deep-purple, angular markings above her sea-foam colored eyes were so striking that the look of shock on the fairy's face reflected on Vera's as well. "Pardon me, Lavender Soul. I did not mean to startle. Your handler said you both needed soap for vashing. I sought it vould be easier if I did it." She politely smiled and slowly entered the room as her round wings fluttered lightly. The top half of them was a purple so deep it almost looked black, and the bottom vibrant sea foam.

"You don't have to really. I just need two bins and soap. I know how."

The fairy flew to the door and hovered with her armload. "I do not doubt your abilities, Laven—Vera—but I vant to be able to say zat I did a service for you once." With a smile and a girly giggle, she flew out of sight with Vera's grungy clothes.

"Thanks!" Vera called after her.

She changed out of a light-orange linen frock that had been left for her that morning, and into the tan riding pants and maroon cotton shirt she'd been wearing when the trees attacked. Her fingers fiddled with some of the tears in the fabric. *They weren't trying to hurt me.* In her musings she scratched at the dried blood that was encrusted on her sleeve. *Only hope for freedom… what does freedom even mean?*

Yateem knocked on the door. "Ready?"

"No." Vera rubbed her face as if to wash away the thoughts in her head. "No, I have to put my boots on."

In the early morning, they explored the forest, climbed over the giant roots, and munched on the wild berries they recognized. The cool morning air refreshed them as they walked —or rather stumbled—farther than they had planned to. The beauty and vitality of the rainforest beckoned them to continue, to never stop exploring. The morning melted into early afternoon, and the air grew thick with humidity. When they stopped at a stream, the crisp water woke their minds.

"We're lost," Vera said, splashing her face and hair.

"How?"

"You vent off zah path." Daisy hovered above them with a dismayed smile. "You are not supposed to do zat unless you are in view of your cabin, or vith a fairy."

"Have we broken some law?" Yateem looked mortified.

Daisy giggled and landed silently on her feet, the clovers covering her toes. "No. But zis is no ordinary rainforest. Zere is magic here that vill make you valk forever. Zee ground here can shift and change. Zah paths are vhat keep people from getting lost. Even ven flying, zey are like a map."

"So we could've walked until…" Vera rubbed her empty stomach.

"You died. Zat is vhy I have been looking for you since I brought lunch and found zah cabin empty."

"Well, that presented itself a lot sooner than I thought," Vera muttered.

"Lunch sounds great. Will you guide us back?" Yateem spoke fast to cut off the question that was resting on Daisy's lips.

"Yes, of course." With a smile, the fairy turned, and hovering just inches off the ground, she led the way back to the cabin.

Lunch revived them, although as the effects of the rainforest's magic wore off, both could feel the physical toll they had put on their bodies. They decided to rest for the remainder of the day and allow themselves to recover.

Yateem walked toward the hammock that was strung up between two medium-sized fern trees and slowly lowered himself into a reclined position, alternating between napping and reading a book that Manon had let him borrow.

Daisy asked to see Vera's drawings, partly so that she could make sure that they stayed at the cabin, but mostly as an excuse to spend more time with Vera before they left Feyerabend and Shifra. Lying in a bed of clovers, Vera doodled sketches of wild flowers, and Daisy flipped through the loose papers.

The drawings had decisive strokes and personality. The fairy was pleased to see the majority of the sketches were of nature—a charming nightingale, a blue-speckled gecko, a yellow-bellied flycatcher, a bull shark in a battle with a terrifying yagim, a condor, a spotted owl, and a wolf howling at the moon. She muffled a gasp, so as not to offend Vera with her reaction, as she set the wolf drawing aside and found the portrait of the two dead soldiers underneath. Quickly moving that drawing to the bottom of the pile, Daisy was relieved by a portrait of Yateem, his smile seeming to beam off the page. Next, she saw a sketch of an ornate ring, a dragon with outstretched wings and glittering eyes. The last couple of drawings were of people she did not recognize. The man was tall—taller even than Yateem—and had slate-blue eyes with dark blonde hair and high-set cheekbones. The woman looked very similar to Vera, with auburn hair and periwinkle eyes.

"My parents." Vera's voice was meek, almost shy.

Daisy tilted the thick paper to the side. "It saddens me zat he haunts even your memories of zem."

"What are you talking about?"

"Zere…" Daisy handed the drawing of Vera's mother to Vera and pointed. In the darkest part of the shading in the right pupil was a tiny outline of a raven's head, unnoticeable at first, but then undeniably there. "Zere is one in every drawing."

Chapter 17
Presage

The fairy that insisted on washing their laundry brought dinner back with their folded clean clothes. "It is blood orange braised beef stir-fried with broccoli, green carrots, vater almonds, hot peppers, and egg noodles." She flapped her small round wings proudly as she handed the large basket holding the cast-iron pot to Yateem with a bow.

"That sounds delectable. Thank you for your hard work."

"It vas nothing. I only vashed ze clothes and chopped vegetables. Mama made your dinner."

"Will you join us?" Vera smiled.

Her wings closed, and her cheeks blushed a bright red. "I could not, but sank you for ze honor of being of service to you both." Obviously embarrassed, even her deep-purple markings were being warmed by red tones. "I must go now." She bowed deeply and then quickly grabbed Vera's hand and kissed it. "Sank you for everysing." With that she flew away.

"Huh…interesting." Vera watched the silhouette of the fairy as she flew into the sunset.

"Vell, I must go as vell. I trust you two vill stay here tonight?" Daisy gave both of them a scolding smile.

"You're not staying for dinner?"

"No, my dear, I have just been summoned by za queen." Daisy bowed to Yateem and then kissed both of Vera's cheeks. "I am honored to know you." Her smile lacked the brightness of her disposition, and in a flash of bright yellow, she was gone.

Vera stared after her. *You might not think that soon.*

"Come on. This dinner smells too good to let it go cold." Yateem lightly bumped Vera on the shoulder as he turned to walk inside.

"I wonder if that fairy girl packed our bags when she put the clothes in our rooms," Vera playfully mused as she followed Yateem.

"I honestly would not be surprised."

The dinner was delicious and filling. Afterwards, Yateem brewed tea, and they both took their place in the rocking chairs on the cabin's front porch for the first—and last—time.

The illumiem seedpods were giving off a white light, as opposed to the soft green they naturally gave off. Vera and Yateem gazed at them with confused concern as the seedpods started to glow brighter and brighter. The light was so piercing that their eyelids slammed down defensively, and they were left blinking like newborns when it decreased.

The first thing their shocked eyes registered was Her Lady of La Luna, Queen Emmanuelle, standing barefoot on the clovers in front of the cabin, her ethereal wings settling with a few tiny flaps against her back.

"Your Majesty!" Vera squeaked, clumsily throwing her body out of the rocking chair to join Yateem, who was already kneeling on the porch. She silently grimaced as her startled actions caused her tea to splash over her knuckles and burn the flesh.

"Tis no need for dat. Please rise."

Vera and Yateem's eyes met as they slowly stood.

"Vera, my dear, if you have no prior engagements, I would like you to join me in a walk. Dah rainforest is lovely at dis time of night."

"A walk?"

"Indeed." The queen's crown of star markings brightened to celestial silver.

"Well, alright...Yateem?"

"Can wait here," said the queen. "Twill only be a stroll."

"Go on, Vera. There is nothing to be nervous about."

Vera muttered under her breath as she set her cup of tea on the table and made her way down to the majestic queen. "Just a night promenade with one of the oldest and most powerful beings on the planet, yeah, nothing to be nervous about. I might as well be dancing the tango with a hungry orca."

"From what I have seen, you prefer waltzing with an owl in dah forest, rather dan a tango in dah sea."

Vera fisted her right hand over her mouth, the red seared flesh of her knuckles matching the color of her cheeks.

Queen Emmanuelle glided over the clovers and took Vera's hand into her own, placing it on her left arm. "Let us walk."

The fairy queen was taller than Vera remembered from their first meeting. Each movement, every step, was the essence of grace. Since Vera's arm was linked with the queen's, she had to concentrate on matching her majesty's long, fluid stride. The Lady of La Luna's fair skin glistened in the moonlight, as if the soft rays falling through the branches were resting on her with a kiss. Vera was fighting the urge to shiver as the queen's left wing gently tapped against Vera's hair and back with the weightless touch of gossamer. Instead, she turned her attention to the illumiem pods that would turn from a green glow to a white light as soon as the queen neared.

"Where is Ierá Flóga?" the fairy asked as she laid her right hand over Vera's.

The cooling sensation against her raw burned skin made her suck in a loud gasp. "Oh, it's back on my nightstand. I like to think it watches over me when I sleep."

"Twould watch over you in dah day too if you let it." Emmanuelle stopped and turned Vera to face her, her gown flattering her svelte body. As the fabric flowed in the breeze that her wings created, the dress shifted in color, like the odd shapes and reflections the moon made on a lake. Her silver eyes also shifted, from sweet moonbeams to hard steel. "My dear, you must wear it always. Twill protect you from evil."

"No disrespect, Queen Emmanuelle, but how can a ring protect me?"

"With faith, everything can be transformed. A ring formed from a single drop of flame from Zakiyyah can be deh most powerful object in dah world...And a beautiful young lady can hold inside her the very strength to save all of Zerahlinda from the lurking of an evil menace."

"Why aren't you the Lavender Soul? You could have killed all evil just as the world was starting."

"I cannot explain why, but dat was not—and is not—my purpose."

"But you can see things no one else can!"

"Aye I can, and that is dah gift I must use to fulfill my purpose. Arivos gave you great talents dat your lack of faith has kept you from unlocking."

"When will these talents show themselves? When I'm dead?"

A jaguar appeared from behind one of the illumiem bushes. It stretched its body as if wanting to bow before them, and then ran off into the night. Vera stared in the direction the jaguar ran, wanting to call out after it.

"Twasn't him." Emmanuelle's eyes softened as she looked at Vera.

"How do you know?"

"No scar, and the energy he gives off is distinctive. Radov was punished for distressing you."

"Punished?"

The queen turned and motioned for Vera to join her in walking again. "He is being held in his quarters until you leave, so do not fret. You will be bothered no more."

"Don't you think you have punished him enough?" Vera's teeth were gritted in an attempt to strain the anger from her words.

"You find his sentence to be harsh?" Queen Emmanuelle's elegant demeanor was not affected by Vera's animosity.

"A hundred years for a crime he did not commit, but only witnessed."

"Dere are sections of his story dat you do not know, a purpose to his long sentence for which he held from you. It is not my story to tell, but I do ask dat you try to understand dat we have been merciful to him."

"Merciful? He didn't do anything but what he thought he had to, to save his family."

"Tell me, if a man is dah only one dat sees a tsunami on dah horizon and runs with his family without first warning de people of his coastal town, is he guilty for letting so many die? Or is it justified because he thought he could save his family?"

"That is different. He could've warned people as he ran. Radov had no choice."

"He had dah choice to warn Sinclair, a fairy dat could hear de voice of Arivos himself. You of all people should learn deh lesson of Radov's tale." The queen's voice was stern, her eyes full of pain.

"What is that, that if I don't live up to this vision that everyone has of me that I will be found and turned into a shape shifter?" Vera spit the words out with a poisonous insolence.

The fairy queen stopped, grabbed Vera by the shoulders, and spun her around with such speed that she nearly fell down. The illumiem seedpods started to flicker as all the light in the night seemed to draw itself to The Lady of La Luna, making her markings almost blinding with the amount of power Emmanuelle was giving off. "Dat each of us has a purpose, and to deny dat is to deny dah world a bit of love dat it desperately needs. Dat no matter what, twould be better to die your single life over all de lives in dah world. Dat making a little deal with evil to preserve your life is not worth dah deaths of many. Draven may be powerful, but he will always be alone, always be consumed by dah need for more, and will never stop until dah whole of Zerahlinda is poisoned into serving him. To serve evil is to spread evil."

Tears welled in Vera's eyes. "You saw me fail, didn't you?"

"Dah future can change with a single choice." She dimmed her power, wrapped her arms around Vera's shaking body, and hummed an ancient song until Vera's sobbing quelled.

Chapter 18
A Gift of Danger

"I've made breakfast," came Yateem's muffled voice from outside the cedar door, waking Vera. "It will be the last hot meal we have for a while, so please get dressed and come eat."

Vera groaned and threw the covers off herself. Sitting on the edge of the bed, she grabbed the lavender velvet bag off the nightstand, opened it, and slid Ierá Flóga onto her right index finger. Vera stroked the open wings and head of the dragon, the gold warm and smooth under her fingertip.

"Please protect me, Arivos," she whispered and then kissed both of the dragon's lavender eyes, got dressed in a pair of riding pants and a cotton shirt, and went to eat her last hot meal.

Leaning against Vera's doorway, Yateem asked, "You only packed what you absolutely need, right?"

Vera secured her sleeping sack to her backpack with a smile. "I don't know why you would think otherwise."

Yateem chuckled. "Right, no reason at all. Amaury is here."

She shrugged on her pack, took in a deep breath, and smiled at the golden dragon perched on her finger. "Ierá Flóga, can you protect me after death?"

Amaury led them down a soft, bouncy moss path that Vera had never seen before. It wove between the giant trees of Feyerabend, leading them away from the central hub of the Pixie Kingdom.

Vera looked back to see the early morning sun just barely peeking over and through the forest's low shrubbery, the illumiem pods still glowing slightly in the faint darkness of the dawn. As she turned back, she saw that Amaury was facing her, looking like he wanted to say something. When Vera took her next step, she felt like several steaming and frigid fists punched holes right through her.

"Ah! What?" She felt all over her torso, checking for the gaping wounds that she thought should be there.

"Sorry, I meant to varn you sooner. Crossing through Ze Great Enchantment vill cause some discomfort."

"Thanks for the warning!"

"Well, I'm awake." Yateem stood next to Vera, his hand rubbing his ribs.

"I am accustomed to it. I hope ze pain is not too great." Amaury put his hand over his heart, bowed his head, and brought his wings together in apology.

"It's starting to fade," Vera grumbled between her teeth.

They continued on through the Shifra rainforest. The trees were smaller than those in Feyerabend, but these had a wild nature about them. There was no path here, and as they went deeper and deeper into the forest, Amaury had to resort to walking because his wingspan was too large to fit between the crowding trees.

Vera put her leather hood over her head to keep the water dripping off the branches from snaking down her collar and back, and her eyes were on the ground, watching for the roots sticking out. These trees had no need to dig deep into the earth to find an ample supply of water.

"Did you say fairies live outside Feyerabend?"

Amaury turned sideways to maneuver through a tight group of trees. "Yes, zey are smaller in stature, vould look almost like a child to you. Zey can fly around here vith ease. Zey like the vild and can play vith even ze most dangerous anaconda or bear and not get hurt."

Snap.

Vera popped her head up, her eyes scanning for fur.

142

"I am sorry. Zey are curious who zey vere commissioned to build a canoe for."

"I don't see anyone," Vera said, trying to keep her footing as she raised her eyes again to look through the thick branches of the forest.

"I thought we were crossing over the river and going through the Rinan Rainforest?" Yateem said as he also looked for the unseen pixies.

"Yeah, our last excursion on a boat didn't go so well."

"Zere is no need to fret, and your eyes cannot see zah fairies zat are all around us because zey have zah ability to make zemselves invisible."

"Right you are, big fella," came a deep, robust voice from overhead.

Yateem drew his sword, and Vera jumped with fright.

"Oh, please don't do that!" Vera yelled back up in the direction of the voice.

Several different laughs erupted from the shaking branches of the trees. She glared up at them, and Yateem sheathed his sword but walked with his dagger in hand.

"I apologize zat zey are lacking in manners." Amaury aimed a cold, threatening look at the branches where the laughs came from. "Zeir only interaction vith humans is ze natives of ze Rinan Rainforest, who sometimes swim across ze Kallisto River and try and hunt zem."

"Humans hunting fairies?" Vera was shocked.

"Aye, they tell tale of little flying pixies whose blood is the key to invulnerability and invisibility!" The boisterous voice was so near Vera that it made her flinch.

"But the buggers seem to be both those things, so they're mighty hard to hunt." This sneer came from behind.

"Impossible more like it." The fae whispered in Yateem's ear.

"And I hear they like to play jokes on the poor human savages!" A chortle followed in the branches to the left of them.

"No, my source says that packs of scared wooly monkeys and hungry white panthers are their welcoming gifts." The threat roared from the tree to the right.

"Don't forget the anacondas!" Another fae sneered from behind the traveling party.

"Or the patches of man-eating flowers!"

The threats were circling around the humans. Yateem got closer to Vera as the baritone voices coming from the gregarious invisible mouths got closer and rowdier. Vera was getting worked up as her eyes tried to follow each new voice and catch any movement.

She balled up her fists, these fairies seemed cruel, and they enjoyed seeing her get stressed by their imperceptible presence. "Enough!" Branches groaned as they bent back under the force of Vera's command.

A small thud indicated one of the antagonistic fairies fell from the yielding trees and landed at Vera's feet. Yateem pushed Vera behind him and crouched down with his dagger ready to attack.

"Zere is no need for violence," Amaury said, keeping his voice calm.

The fairy uncloaked his appearance and brushed himself off in front of Yateem. "Who is this girl that can command my forest?" Standing in front of Yateem, the top of the fairy's bright-orange, wildly unkempt hair just barely reached the height of Yateem's hip. His eyes were hazelnut brown with curved strokes of deep green in them. The markings above his eyes were tight curlicues that spiraled up toward his wild hair, and they matched it in color. He snarled at Yateem. "Well?"

Amaury stepped up behind the slight fairy. "Enough, Yosef! King Benoit commissioned a canoe zat vill grant safe passage to Elspeth. Take us to it."

"This little girl threw all of us out of our trees with nothing but a word, and I am not allowed an inquiry?"

"Who are you calling little?" Vera fumed, stepping out from behind Yateem.

Compared to Vera, the fairy was eye level with her belly button. He was lanky, thin, and fair. His wings were skinny; the bottom point of them nearly touched the ground, and the top point was a foot above his head. The intricate pattern on his wings matched the bark of the trees around them. His face was beautiful like all fairies, and even smudged with dirt and stuck in a scowl, he would quicken a maiden's heartbeat. All fairies had the appearance of youth, but Yosef's features held the spirit of ageless, ancient wilderness that gave an authoritative edge to his young looks. He took in Vera, starting at her feet with a snarl and made his way up until they made eye contact. His jaw dropped in awe. He unclenched his fists. "Gents, her eyes."

"Are the color lavender, I know!" Vera's frustration rattled the trees in their immediate vicinity; she looked at them with a worried stare.

"The truth has unveiled my eyes, and I praise Arivos for the service we have done for you!" Yosef flapped his wings and hovered right next to Vera.

"What service?" Yateem was still on edge.

Yosef prompted Vera forward with his arm as he continued to fly next to her. "When His Majesty Benoit sent a message for us to make a secure canoe, it was with a frown that we cut down a robust, healthy laurel tree and fashioned a vessel for you."

"Thank you for cutting down your favorite tree for me."

"Do you not know of the power of the laurel? You will be victorious over any foe! We sealed the boat and oars with hot pitch we extracted from the tree. If there is an enemy in the water, his eyes will be cloaked and blind to your presence!"

"Will this enchantment only work in the waters of the Kallisto?" Yateem had sheathed his dagger in his boot.

"No, it should last as long as the canoe is in one piece."

They broke out of the forest and onto a beach that looked completely out of place. The wild vegetation seemed to fight to spill over the border of the coarse sand, but couldn't succeed. Vera sucked in a quick gasp when she saw at least thirty black caiman lying on the riverbank, sunning their large reptilian bodies around a honey-colored canoe. The coarse sand of the beach had clearly been smooth stones like the ones on the bank on the opposite side of Shifra, but the strong current of this part of the Kallisto River and the wear of the crocodiles' bodies over the years must have crushed them.

Yosef spun himself around with a theatrical arm gesture. "Oh, the cleverness of us!"

Small footprints were making indentations in the sand of the bank, and brusque "shoo" noises and light tapping sounds could be heard.

Yosef crossed his arms with a defiant yet victorious look on his face. "These black caiman travel as a bask, together with their newly hatched young'uns, to the abandoned shores of Elspeth, away from hunting savages, to live seasonally on the banks of Lake Kassiopeia, which is plentifully stocked with fish."

Vera nervously watched the fairies whose feet were making indentations next to the fifteen-to-sixteen foot long reptilian beasts. "The canoe will be invisible to them, right?" She looked back to Yosef with a hopeful smile.

"That would not be clever, little lavender princess."

"Why not?" She clasped Yateem's hand, trying to gain some of his strength to face the long rows of scales that led to sharper rows of teeth.

"Crocodiles are very protective of their young, but not all the babies make it out of the eggs. We took those unhatched eggs and painted the blood of the unborn caiman on the canoe. The entire bask of crocodiles will protect you as if you were one of the tiny babies floating down the river!"

"So they won't attack us?"

"Not while you are in the boat."

"Zat is clever, Yosef. I shall tell Zeir Majesties of your good verk."

Yosef bowed to Amaury, grabbed a stick off the beach, made himself and the stick invisible, and joined his kin in clearing a path through the groggy, snapping crocodiles.

Amaury turned and smiled at Yateem and Vera, his striped wings fluttering as he bent down on one knee. "It has been an honor. And since I can no longer be of any service, I must return to my post."

Yateem stuck out his hand and helped Amaury up to his feet. "Thank you."

As Vera wrapped her arms around his waist, the few beats of his wings to stabilize himself tickled the tops of her arms. "Thanks. I hope this trek didn't ruin your shoes."

Amaury awkwardly squeezed Vera's back. "Nosing a few hours of cleaning cannot fix." He unwrapped her arms from around his waist, picked her up, and placed her an arm's length away from him. He reached into a pocket in his pants made of woven fern and pulled out an envelope made from a banana leaf. "Daisy asked zat zis be given to you."

The envelope felt waxy smooth in her hands. "Tell her thank you, and sorry I didn't say goodbye." She slipped it into her pack.

"I vill."

"Oy! We've cleared a path—now use it!" Yosef's voice came from the direction of the beautifully made canoe.

It was twelve feet long, just big enough for Yateem and Vera and their packs. The sap sealant made the honey-colored planks shine in the morning sunlight, and if it were not for the smudges of dried blood on the canoe's side, or the beach covered with huge black caiman, the scene would have looked serene, and nearly recreational.

Yateem drew his sword. "If any go to attack, I will be right behind you."

Vera reached back to the sword hilt sticking out from under the top flap of her leather pack and pulled out her sheath. Each of her fingers shook with the intensity of her grip around the hardened leather. "Okay. Bye, Amaury."

"Arivos be vith you," Amaury said. Then he flew over the canopy and was almost instantly out of sight.

Vera looked at the small, crooked path through the giant reptiles and willed herself to walk over the small footprints in the sand. The constant chattering kept the crocodiles' attention off Vera and Yateem, but each time one of the caiman snapped out at the jesters, Vera froze, her sheath clutched to her chest and no strength to pull her sword out of it.

"Keep moving, girl," a gruff voice whispered in Vera's left ear, making her jump. "Sorry, didn't mean to scare, but you're only halfway, and the crocs grow tired of our pestering."

"Vera, I can carry you, but I will have to sheath my sword."

She closed her eyes and took in a few deep breaths. "You can do this. They are just lizards, they are just lizards, they are just lizards," she muttered to herself.

Exasperated sighs surrounded her, and Yosef's familiar, brusque voice called out, "Lads, lift her."

The gruff voice whispered in her ear again, "Don't move."

Vera laughed nervously. "I think I can handle that."

She kept her eyes clenched shut and bit her lip as she felt four pairs of hands grab onto her arms and legs. Her hair blew into her face with the wing-generated wind, and she felt her toes scrape along the sand before being lifted up. The abrupt chomp of a caiman's jaw made a high-pitched squeal escape Vera's lips. Her feet landed on a solid, teetering surface, and the light grips of unseen hands vanished.

Opening her eyes, Vera saw the bow of the canoe and kept from falling out of the boat by quickly sitting down on her seat as Yateem stepped in the boat. A caiman shifted to smell the vessel, and Vera gripped the hilt of her sword. Yateem slipped off his pack and placed it in the middle of the canoe, then sat down with his sword at his feet and both oars in his hands.

"Vera." Yateem tapped her shoulder with the round handle of the laurel oar.

She let out a shrill scream that got all the caimans' attention and caused them to start crowding the canoe.

"You alright?"

"Jumpy and embarrassed," Vera said as she shrugged off her pack and let it fall into the middle section of the boat before she snatched the oar from Yateem. It was carved from a solid piece of the laurel tree, most likely a large branch. The beauty of the oar mesmerized her so much that she forgot about the bask of protective crocodiles surrounding her. The shaft was about three feet long and had tiny carvings of vines leading down to the blade of the oar, which was a foot long and six inches in width, carved to resemble a laurel leaf.

Vera jerked back as the canoe was pushed forward. The grating of wood over sand was uncomfortable, and the hissing of the crocodiles that were being nudged, and the persistence of the fairies pushing it, was unsettling. As soon as the canoe was fully in the water, Vera and Yateem shifted their weight around and found their stability.

Vera went to paddle when she realized she was about to hit a very large black caiman that was on her right side. "How are we supposed to paddle?" she called back to Yateem.

"I went right next to the canoe," he replied. "It dragged along the side of one of them, but it made room for the paddle."

"And they aren't going to attack, right?"

"They may be cold-blooded, but they do take care of the littl'uns." Yosef's voice came out of the air over Vera's right shoulder. "Now we're going to try to keep the savages from noticing you. Arivos' blessing on your journey."

Vera closed her eyes as a blast of wind hit her face.

"What is it about the caimans that is scaring you so much?" asked Yateem.

"I've never seen them before. Even the little baby ones look capable of killing." Vera tentatively drew her paddle through the water and gently knocked it against the jawline of one of the aquatic creatures. The crocodile gave the canoe some space with an effortless grace she wouldn't have expected from such a bulky, armored body.

"I know you…it is more than that."

As Vera gingerly pulled the blade of the oar on the other side, a baby caiman chirped from its mother's back as the oar cut through the water next to it, making tiny wakes lap against the mother caiman. "I was just thinking…there's so many of them…I wouldn't have a body to come back to—just partially digested bits scattered among a whole bask of crocodiles."

Yateem directed the canoe toward the strong current that pushed the water along in the middle of the river. "I would not…when it is time for you…" He pushed the wooden leaf through the water with increased purpose, his movements strong and with a fluidity that matched the grace of the caimans' aquatic skill. "I will not let anything horrific happen to you."

"Death will find me. Queen Emmanuelle saw that much." The canoe lurched when Vera's strokes increased with a vigor that clashed with Yateem's. "There's nothing you can do about it. Just make sure I don't get torn to pieces when it happens."

Yateem breathed a heavy sigh, straightened the canoe in the fast-moving current of the Kallisto River, and then laid the oar across his lap. "This current will take us to the Cardea River in good time. No need to paddle. Rest and conserve your strength."

The water wasn't as clear as the section of Kallisto River that she first saw. The strong current made it look like the water was slowly boiling at some points, and it churned the silt on the riverbed, clouding the light-green water. Only fifty feet of river separated the canoe from the Rinan Rainforest on the right. The trees were smaller than the ones in Shifra, and while the forests mirrored each other to a degree, Vera didn't like the feeling of the trees on her right. The Rinan trees had the same sort of wildness about them, but there was no sense of vitality. The ground looked to be covered in a thick blanket of decay, and the branches of the trees intertwined and fought for sunlight. Briars grew up and over the trees, their thorns cutting into bark, their presence giving off the disturbing feeling that the forest was being overrun and choked from within.

Chapter 19
Solitary Survival

It was early morning yet when Vera twisted to put the oar in the space between Yateem's and her seats. She made sure to avoid eye contact with him as she slid the oar along the side of the canoe, the tip of the blade tapping Yateem's foot, the handle resting against her seat. Her hands were quick to unlatch the top flap of her pack and retrieve the banana-leaf envelope before tossing the flap closed again. She sat up straight, unfolded the waxy leaf envelope, and spread it out on her lap. Inside was a smaller paper envelope and a bright-yellow piece of paper. The sunny piece of paper felt thick and fibrous in Vera's hand, but the penmanship on it was small and elegant, the Bordeaux ink accentuating the beauty of the writing and the warmth of the paper.

My dearest Vera,

I guess I have lived a sheltered life because I have never had to say goodbye to a loved one before. I'm sorry I didn't have the strength to hug you and kiss you on the cheek this morning, but I fear I would've cried. Just know that my tears that fall at this moment of your departure are not because I believe we will never see each other again. They are from the knowledge that when I see you again, my dear friend, I will not be worthy to be your acquaintance. You will be saving the world from the destructive power of evil. What then could I ever offer you?

I was once told that some humans pluck the petals of daisies to ascertain if they are loved or not. I am your Daisy, and there is no need to pluck any part of me because I will be your chosen sister and true friend until the end of time.

Arivos' Blessing,
Daisy

Vera ran her hand over the sunny note and felt a warm smile stretch across her face as she eyed a crocodile passing by. The paper envelope was made with a smoother white paper that was smudged with dirt. Vera broke the spattered wax seal, and as she pulled out the folded letter, a small pin fell onto the banana leaf in her lap. Round like a coin, it had the depiction of a white raven's head on it. Vera immediately dropped the coin as if it had burnt her and cautiously unfolded the letter that accompanied the pin.

Vera,

There is little chance that this will find its way to you, but if it does, please know I didn't mean to hurt you. Forgive me. The pin is the only remnant I have of my old life. It is the totem I was allowed to keep to remind me of who I am after shifting for so long. Ravens were symbols of great fortune and wisdom in Elspeth, and their feathers used to be pure white. That is why Draven was named after them in the first place, but he corrupted my country's symbol of hope. As much as I want to be at your side, I don't want to bring any corruption with me. May Arivos' light guide, and this pin be the vow that I will be with you again. I know it may be of little consequence to you, but your sacrifice is my freedom.

Love,
Radov

"We will reach the Cardea River soon. You will want to put Daisy's letter away. The crossing of the two rivers is going to be bumpy." Yateem's voice was alert, yet distant.

Vera snapped out of the trance her letters had put her in and looked around at the bask surrounding the canoe and the trees on either side of them, passing swiftly as the river swept them toward the Cardea. The current of the Kallisto River picked up even more. The cloudy water mixed with the clear water that she had first noticed when entering the pixie kingdom. The two clarities of water mixing made a strange illusion, like drowning smoke. Vera squinted and took in a deep breath as she saw dark-black serrated teeth along raw white bone on the bottom of the riverbed as they crossed over the water border into the Cardea River with a splash. She spared a glance backwards to see the river-made island of Shifra fall away. Yateem steered them to the right, the land bent away from them, tall dry reeds blocked Vera's view of the tree trunks, and the dark canopy loomed over the reeds like a monster from a nightmare.

She quickly pinned Radov's token to the inside of her pants over her right hip, the wings of Ierá Flóga catching on the fabric and making it difficult, and then folded up the banana-leaf envelope.

"Uh…alright," she replied.

As she turned to put the envelope back in her pack, Ierá Flóga caught her eye; the amethyst eyes almost looked to be glaring up at her. She was trying to remember if the little gold dragon's head had always been tilted to the side, and if its mouth had always been open, as if it needed to say something.

Vera held out her hand toward Yateem. "Look at—"

The envelope was ripped from her hand as a spear made from a sharpened bamboo shoot pierced it and bounced off the back of a large crocodile, sinking the letters in the water.

"Get down!" Yateem yelled, paddling vigorously.

Vera threw herself over their packs and felt little vibrations from the ridges of a caiman's back rubbing against the bottom of the boat as she listened to deranged whoops and yells coming from the Rinan shoreline as well as the quick snaps of crocodile teeth. Spears whirred through the air overhead. As the canoe was rocked by a large wake, Vera watched one spear barely arch over her hand that was gripping the side of the canoe.

A scream came from the shoreline, followed by gruesome crunches and cracks. Vera felt sick to her stomach, but she noticed that the number of spears flying had dropped.

"One of the caimans got a native," said Yateem. "I think that drove most of them back. I need you to get up and start paddling. I can't get through these wakes fast enough on my own, and our lives depend on getting to the Zivan side of the Cardea River."

Vera flung her body to the side of the boat, trying to counterbalance the wakes of the two rivers meeting. A native broke from the tree line, his grass skirt smeared with mud and blood. He looked Vera in the eye with a crazed smile and raised his spear above his head. Gripping the side of the canoe, which was threatening to flip in the turbulent water, Vera made eye contact with her soon-to-be murderer. She was determined to die with dignity. A flicker of recognition caused the native's merciless expression to soften, and his hand to hesitate. A large caiman took the man's legs from under him with one charging bite, and as the man fell into the water with a scream, another caiman bit into his chest.

It all happened in half a moment. Vera was in such a state of terrified shock that when the canoe dropped between two wakes, she could no longer hold down the contents of her stomach.

"Vera!" Yateem's shout was as strained as his muscles.

She shot up in her seat, yanked her paddle out of the center of the canoe, and started to pull the blade through the wakes. The whistling of spears returned, but most sunk in the water or plunked off the armored hide of a caiman. Vera's arms burned as she hastened her strokes at the sight of the smooth waters ahead. Her body jerked back, and the canoe reverberated with the thunk of a spear driving through laurel planks.

"Yateem?" Vera would have looked back, but an extraordinarily large wave crashed on the bow, hitting her with a wall of water and nearly sinking them. She pushed the Kallisto River behind her with determined strokes and did not stop until they were in the middle of the smooth Cardea River. When she could finally look around, she saw that their bask had diminished. "Did we lose some of the crocodiles?"

"Some are probably fighting over the dead men. The rest are under water." His words came out through gritted teeth. "You cannot stop paddling until we reach Lake Kassiopeia."

"What? We're out of spear range. My arms need a break." She turned around so that Yateem could see she was soaked, as much with water as with exhaustion, and saw him grimacing as he sat there trying to work out a spear that had gone straight through his right leg and pinned itself to his seat.

Vera gasped.

Yateem tried not to gag as he tore his pant leg open and pulled at the spear. "Keep paddling. The water may look smooth, but the Cardea current is incredible, and we have to go upriver."

Vera looked back and noticed they were already twenty feet downstream from where they had emerged onto the Cardea. With renewed vigor, she gripped the handle of her oar and plunged it through the water.

Yateem let out a muffled groan. "I will help you as soon as I get this out and stop the bleeding."

"Don't worry. I can do this."

"I know you can. The current is not as strong along the Zivan shoreline."

Vera dug into the river with all her strength, fighting for every inch upstream she could gain. As the late morning sun started to beat down on their backs, the majority of the bask went on ahead of the canoe, clearing fishermen's boats out of the way and freeing Vera from the need to veil her eyes from curious onlookers. After two hours of strenuous paddling, the river started to narrow. Vera's arms felt as if jellyfish had wrapped their tentacles around them, making her muscles spasm between taut exertion and limp exhaustion. The noon sun beamed down on her, sucking her remaining energy, reminding her stomach that it was empty.

Yateem had yet to start paddling, but no matter how tired or hungry she grew, Vera wouldn't stop. She could feel the vibrations through the boat as he tried to work the spear out of the wood of his seat and his leg. A snap made Vera gag, and she began to panic as Yateem let out a wrenching yell. As a coppery scent clung to the air, the world around her seemed to fade. All Vera could think was that Yateem might lose his leg—or worse —if he couldn't stop the bleeding.

"Beach." Yateem's voice could barely be heard.

"What?"

"Beach the canoe." The words were breathy and forced.

"I can make it," she huffed.

"I can't."

Vera stopped paddling. Her chin brushed her shoulder, but she was afraid to look back at him. Instead, she brought the oar to the right side and headed to the nearest beach. Half the bask crawled onto the warm pebbles before the canoe plowed onto the beach, and the other half of the caiman made their way out of the water after Vera had gotten out and made sure the canoe was successfully beached.

"Help me." Yateem's face was pale, his teal eyes cloudy, his voice very faint.

Vera had never seen her handler hurt before, and as she gingerly placed her feet next to the head of a sunning crocodile and faced Yateem, she had to earnestly fight the urge to vomit and cry.

Yateem's skin had a sickly green-white hue to it. Blood, caked on in various hues of red-brown, covered his arms and legs. His face was smeared with blood where he tried to wipe away the pain that had settled on his brow. He'd managed to remove the spear from his right leg and broken it to use it as a tourniquet, but dark blood still seeped out the top of the wound and dripped out the bottom, creating a red puddle that sloshed and stained his leather boots.

"How do I help? Do you have medicine?"

"In pack, small silver cylinder, and grab shirt."

Her hands were shaking as she unlatched his pack that had bloody finger marks on it. Yateem had obviously tried—and failed—to open it. She frantically grabbed the cold silver cylinder and the first shirt she came to and then whipped around to hand them to Yateem.

"No." He coughed. "Help me lay down."

Vera stood next to the canoe and held it steady with her right hand as Yateem put his left arm over her shoulders. As soon as he was out of the boat, Vera let go and wrapped her arm around his waist, taking as much of his weight as she could without falling over. He hopped with his left leg and took a sharp breath if his right foot even tapped the ground. Vera nudged the caiman in their way with her foot to make the short journey easier for Yateem. When they got out of the water, Vera gently lowered him to a seated position, and he slowly laid his head down on the smooth pebbles.

"What do I do with these?" Vera held the cylinder and shirt in his line of sight.

"Go on bluff, dig until clay, bring clay."

"Will you be okay if I leave?"

"Hurry." Yateem was fighting to keep his eyelids open.

Vera laid the cylinder and shirt on Yateem's chest and then started to run toward the bluff, but she stopped when she heard the pebbles grating against scales. Looking back, she saw that the caiman surrounding Yateem were interested in their human companion.

Her tired hands ached as they balled into fists. "Don't touch him!"

The yell sent tiny ripples through the water, and all the caiman hunkered down to the ground and froze. Vera snatched up a sharp rock by her foot and continued to run up the nearest bluff. Ripping away a patch of grass at the top, she drove the rock into the soil. As she chucked the loose dirt out of the hole, she prayed that her homeland of Ziva would give her clay soon. Within a few more scoops of dirt, the rock hit a muddled-green substance. Vera took two big handfuls of the clay and sprinted to Yateem, not noticing that all the caiman hurried to get out of her way.

"I have clay!"

"Take off tourniquet, wash, put salve in cylinder on wound, seal with clay on both sides, bandage with shirt."

Vera set the handfuls of clay on top of the clean shirt on Yateem's chest, took a deep breath, and then followed his broken instructions. Her hands shook, and she could feel her stomach acid burning in her throat, but she worked as fast as she could.

The broken spear was easy enough to untwist, but the blood had adhered to the ripped piece of pant that created the tourniquet. Vera had to endure Yateem's silent grimaces and his back arching, causing his body to turn away from her—and from the pain caused by ripping the crusty fabric from his skin. Vera took river water by the handful, splashed it in the wound, and watched the crisp clear water enter in the top of the spear puncture and run red out the bottom of the perfectly hollowed flesh and muscle.

The salve was a clear beige color, cool to the touch, with a thick, silky texture and a heavy herbal smell. Two of her fingers could fit into the wound, and she tried to put the salve in it delicately, but she flinched when her soft fingers grated over exposed bone. Vera gagged at the sensation of Yateem's rapid pulse pushing his life force out of his ruptured muscles and veins. The amount of blood that he was still losing started to panic Vera. She lifted his leg up and rested it on her bent knee so that she could put the rest of the salve in the bottom of the wound. Then she grabbed one of the handfuls of clay and tried not to look up at Yateem as she pushed some of it in the wound and then smoothed the rest around it. Yateem held a hand over his mouth to try to muffle the screams that he could not contain.

She tilted his leg slightly to drain some of the blood before sealing the top with the rest of the clay, then she tightly wrapped his leg with the clean shirt and tied it off at the sleeves. A heavy sigh escaped them both as Vera returned his leg to the ground.

"Well done, Vera."

She crawled toward the water, pulled half her body over a fat caiman who seemed to be sleeping, and scrubbed the blood, clay, dirt, and salve from her hands. "Are you going to lose your leg?"

"No."

"Are you going to die?"

"Rest. Current only gets stronger."

Vera rested her cheek on the caiman's ridged back and watched Yateem's chest rise and fall as she enjoyed the coolness of the giant reptile's body seeping into her own.

"Wake up." Yateem's voice grated at Vera's ears like rocks being scraped against a stained-glass window. "The caiman are leaving."

Vera pushed herself off the giant lizard she had been using as a body pillow and watched as the sixteen foot crocodile slipped its body into the river and disappeared from sight. The sun wasn't overbearing with the heat of high noon, offering instead the warm embrace of late afternoon. Vera worried about how little time they had. "How's your leg?"

"I had to loosen the shirt due to swelling."

Vera squatted next to him and helped hoist him to his feet. "You're talking more like yourself. That makes me feel better."

They hobbled over to the canoe, and Vera helped Yateem lie down in the middle section. Her pack was his pillow, and she placed Yateem's bag under his right leg and his feet on the back seat.

"I can help…the current," Yateem said, trying to sit up.

Vera pushed down on his chest. "I got us this far." She walked back to the bow, shoved it into the river, jumped into her spot, sat, turned the canoe around, and followed after their scaly bodyguards.

After a half hour, the Zivan bluffs to the left were smashed under the roots of the first mountain where it pierced the sky like a burnt arrowhead, and Vera shuddered in the cold of its shadow. The briar vines reaching into the water from the Rinan Rainforest suddenly made her heart constrict. The river narrowed, and the water seethed from within, as if alive. The surface was chalk-white and frothed with sick yellow foam. Vera couldn't see the caiman as Yateem shifted erratically in his feverish sleep, threatening to drown them both. The dark rainforest was swallowed and pushed back by a sheer cliff that rose out of the river like a threatened cobra, while the mountain rose on the other side as if to challenge it. Vera saw a faint outline of a crocodile pop out of the water near the tip of a sharp rock cutting out of the churned surface of the river, and her arms throbbed as she paddled upstream against rapids. Each stroke felt like she was dragging the blade through a mountain. Every centimeter was like crossing an ocean. Just as she saw the mouth of Lake Kassiopeia, her muscles seized, she lost her grip, and the powerful current swept the paddle out of her hands as the canoe propelled down river. The bask seemed to have abandoned them.

Yateem was unconscious, and his paddle was wedged under his left leg, out of reach. Vera lacked the means and strength to fight the current.

In just thirty seconds the canoe had floated back past the beach where Vera bandaged Yateem's leg.

"No!" She wildly shook the boat as her arms flung through the water, her exhaustion making them as useful as a blade of seaweed. Vera could not stand to see how far they were drifting downstream, and her chin hit her chest in defeat.

"Help." It was the most honest word she had ever uttered.

The muscles in her arm spasmed so badly she hardly had control of them. The canoe started to rock, and Vera feared that if they tipped, neither of them would be able to swim to safety. Reverberations went through the laurel planks, and the canoe felt like it was being lifted in the air. She was sure that the enchantment had been washed off, and that they were about to be shredded by a voracious monster hiding in the tempestuous water.

Yet the canoe settled into a strange zigzag motion that propelled it back upstream. Vera slowly leaned forward, ready to jerk her body away from sharp teeth if necessary, and peered into the water in front of the bow for a clue as to what magic was pushing them in the right direction.

Charcoal-black scales covered the V-shaped jaw that stuck out from under the bow. Vera recognized the green-tipped, pointed eyelids of the caiman she had fallen asleep on.

She kissed her uncontrollably shaky hand and leaned precariously far over the front of the canoe to touch in between the crocodile's eyes. "Thank you."

The crocodile slowed a little, closed its clear eyelids to protect them from the splashing water at the narrowing of the river, and then sped up to meet back with the rest of the bask at the mouth of Lake Kassiopeia. What had taken Vera a half hour took this sixteen foot black caiman a minute. Within five minutes, the reptile caught up with the bask, got through the stretch of rapids that opened up to the lake, and slowed to a leisurely cruising speed in the placid waters of the great Lake Kassiopeia.

Vera massaged her arms and took in the landscape around her. From the middle of the lake, almost all the countries of the mainland of Zerahlinda could be seen. In the southeast was a small slice of the light-green bluffs of Ziva. In the south, the formidable Ruwaydah mountain range punctured the skyline, rising up like teeth in a predator's growling mouth, blocking a better view of Vera's homeland. In the northeast, the dark wild trees of the Rinan rainforest made up a large portion of the lake's border. The most western mountains, and the dunes of Elspeth, blocked the view of Yakootah, the country currently plagued by Draven. In the northwest was the dull beige-brown color of the desert that used to be the plentiful Elspeth; now it was nothing but an abandoned wasteland. The only illusion of life was the wind shifting the dunes, looking like a mole pushing the dirt up as it scavenged for worms.

The bask reached the shore of Elspeth as the sun set halfway behind one of the Ruwaydah mountains, its silhouette a soft orange-red. It looked like a defeated fortress, and the deep-purple sky that surrounded it tightened Vera's stomach for some reason. She jumped out and tackled the caiman that carried them on its back, embracing it in a hug. Being more than three times Vera's size, the crocodile easily slithered out from under the canoe—and out of her grasp—but it did bob its head and make a deep guttural croaking hiss with an open mouth that seemed to be smiling.

"What's wrong?" Yateem's hands slammed down on the sides of the canoe and groggily shoved his body upright as the canoe nearly flipped over due to the escaping crocodile.

"Nothing. We're on the shore of Elspeth," Vera told him, grunting as she pulled the canoe halfway onto the thick, dry sand.

"How?" He looked at the bask that was becoming hard to see in the increasing darkness.

Vera lifted Yateem's left leg to grab the remaining oar and slung her pack over her shoulder. "Don't you know? I'm as strong and fearsome as five gennadius!" She walked away from the waterline and up a dune, took out her sword, laid the oar on the ground, and started hacking it into smaller pieces with heavy strokes from her deadened arms. "Oh, and that giant lizard to your left—the one that woke you up—it carried us on its back after I lost my grip…and my oar."

"Fascinating." Yateem leaned over to his left to take a look at the cold-blooded creature that saved their lives—and their quest.

In the quickly fading light, Vera used her flint to light the small oar-fire. "You know what would fascinate me?" Vera asked, returning to help Yateem out of the canoe. She grabbed his pack before hobbling to the tiny fire. "If we could somehow make sure your leg isn't going to fall off, and if we could eat something before this fire dies."

"Eat first. If my leg is going to fall off, it is going to fall off." Yateem sat next to the fire and loosened the shirt bandage again with a grimace.

"Are you serious?" Vera threw Yateem's pack on the ground and knelt down to look at the green-stained shirt wrapped around his right leg, which was now twice the size of his left.

He leaned over to grab his pack. "I'm not going to lose my leg." He handed Vera a small bundle that held a miniature sourdough loaf, a large chunk of cheese, and a purple pear-plum. "Hebians are excellent healers."

They both tore off the ribbon holding the bundles together and ravaged their food.

"Hopefully I can keep that down," Vera muttered as she unwrapped the slimy shirt bandage from Yateem's red-blotched, swollen skin.

"Huh." Yateem gritted his teeth as he scraped aside some of the clay covering the top of the wound and looked inside.

"Huh? 'Huh' isn't good, is it?"

"Take my pack. At the bottom in a bronze case is my Sospitas canteen. Do you remember what it looks like?"

"It was the last thing I saw before my eyeballs felt like they were boiling in pitch. I couldn't forget if I wanted to."

"Get it out for me." Yateem started to scoot his body back toward the water.

"Where are you going?"

"You do not want to see—or smell—what's about to happen."

Vera shivered at the thought and started to rummage to the bottom of his pack.

Yateem scuttled down next to a caiman and took in a very deep breath before removing the clay seal from the bottom of the spear puncture. In the darkness he couldn't see the repugnant color created when the green clay residue mixed with the yellow-green pus and dried blood that drained out of his leg and slopped onto the ground. He could, however, feel his stomach flip as the smell of it singed the inside of his nostrils. Yateem moved to the side of the thick puddle so that he didn't drag his heels through it as he made his way back to the fire.

"Is it bad?" Vera asked, holding out the steel canteen.

His breaths were short and restrained. "The bleeding has stopped, but it seems the spear tip was poisoned. The salve sealed the toxin in my leg, thus the swelling. This wound is not going to heal without something to help accelerate my healing capacities."

"I thought this water was just for transforming appearance?" Vera said, twisting the top off the canteen.

"No. It's for everything. It's for safety while being off Aequitas." Yateem grabbed the two pieces of cloth that had held their meals, cursing under his breath and repressing a gag as he pushed one of them into the bottom of his wound. "Can you bring me my sleeping sack?"

Vera hurried to untie the rolled-up wool sleeping sack.

"Put it under my head, please." Yateem grabbed Vera's arm. "After this, plug your ears and get some sleep. The caimans will protect us tonight."

"Plug my ears?"

"I can handle this. Besides, I have lost so much blood today, I will most likely pass out from the pain."

"Are you sure this is going to work?"

"It worked on your eyes, did it not? Made it safe to travel in Dayo. Pour a little bit of the water in the wound, give the canteen to me, and then go to sleep."

Vera flinched as she let some of the Sospitas water trickle into the large wound, making Yateem wince loudly. She hesitated when Yateem tried to pull the canteen out of her hand. "Just remember, I'm supposed to be the dead weight here, okay?"

"I will be better in the morning." He pulled the canteen out of her hand and took a big gulp from it, stuffed the second piece of cloth in his mouth, and secured the lid back on the canteen. His teal eyes widened as the cloth dampened a scream. His eyes closed, and his body went limp.

Vera put her ear on his chest. When the rhythmic beats of his heart tickled her eardrum, she breathed a little easier. Then she pulled the cloth out of his mouth so that he wouldn't suffocate during the night. The desert air was hot and dry, but Vera's clothes stuck to the sweat on her body. Her fingertips skidded across the back of her clammy neck, sweeping the hair off it as she rested her head on her sleeping roll. In the last burning embers of the fire, she saw tears gliding down Yateem's cheeks.

Chapter 20
Control

When Vera woke, the sun was already high in the sky, and she flipped over to check on Yateem. He was examining his now normal-sized leg with a look of concern that turned to cautious optimism when he felt Vera's stare. Where there once was a hole straight through his leg, there was now pale pink-white scar tissue, and a healthy color had returned to his dark skin that relieved Vera.

His eye caught on Vera's face, and he flashed a smile. "The muscle is sore from the trauma of being sliced, poisoned, sealed, and then healed in so short a time span, but other than that, it feels alright."

"You looked worried just now." Vera leaned on her elbow.

"No, a little apprehensive, it should have healed completely, with no scar, especially not one this light. The poison must have been strong...it is fine. It *will* be fine."

"You had me worried. Carrying you the whole way wasn't an option."

"Here." Yateem handed her another mini-loaf and some dried huckleberries. "Eat. We should leave soon."

"Are you sure you can take walking on that all day?"

"I will limp for a few days, but the water helped heal it, the bone feels solid, so walking should not harm me. You are not the only one as strong and fearsome as five gennadius!" He stood and tested his injured leg before putting his full weight on it. Grabbing fresh clothes from his pack, he limped behind Vera, toward the lake.

When Vera had finished her breakfast, Yateem walked back and tossed his torn, bloodied clothes where the fire was the night before. He wore riding pants, a beige linen shirt, and a deerskin vest, with his bloodstained, stiff stingray leather boots.

"Can I bathe before we leave?" Vera asked, holding her change of clothes in her arms.

"Yes, of course."

"Aren't you going to tell me to make it quick?"

"I found that a whole shoreline of inquiring caiman eyes on your naked body makes the bathing process go fast."

Vera giggled and walked to the lake. She had grown to like the sight of the tough scales and blank stares, and the claws that slowly dragged across the shore to move out of her way.

The water felt cold as she scrubbed the grime and let the sleep rinse off her body. The dark water was as smooth as a glass table. Vera barely even noticed the ripples that hit her ankles as she walked out of the lake, and she didn't see the nostrils and peaked eyelids that emerged where she had stood just moments before. She didn't hear the shifting bodies as she slipped her feet into her clean, tan leather riding pants. When Vera raised up her arms and the cotton shirt fell over her head, an eruption of splashing, teeth snapping, and low, angry, resonating hissing broke out in front of her. A cold, slick, sharp surface swiped Vera's feet from under her. She tugged the shirt down in absolute panic and saw that the tail of the caiman that had carried the boat was inches from her face. The caiman had its mouth open and hissing. Four of the largest caiman of the bask snapped at Vera's protector, their hisses making acid rise into her throat.

"No!" Vera grabbed her stained deer leather boots and half-crawled, half-ran up the shore. Looking back, she saw the protective caiman stand its ground as at least five others attacked. Vera ran and didn't look back when she heard strange cracking sounds or the out-of-place chirping of the baby caiman that must have been watching the fight.

Yateem met her at the top of the dune in a dead sprint, his sword in hand. Vera ran into him, not even seeing what was in front of her. The question was on Yateem's lips, but at the sight of the sixteen foot caiman's blood soaking into Vera's abandoned clothes on the edge of the water, the answer was given. "Get your pack. We are leaving now."

Vera sprinted to her pack, fumbled the ties on the bottom around her sleeping bag—just barely securing it—wrestled her boots on, and kept her eyes on the top of the hill that crested down to the bloodied, hissing creatures.

"Are you alright?" Yateem asked, kneeling beside her, sword still in hand.

"What? Just...no." Vera stood and brushed herself off. "I'll be better when we start heading for the mountains."

Yateem pushed himself up off the ground, grabbed his readied pack, and placed his left hand on the back of Vera's neck. "The best way will be to make our way into Yakootah and then cut over to Ruwaydah. Is your hood on the top of your pack?"

"Who are we going to meet?" Vera asked, spreading her arms and looking over the desolate sand dunes that comprised Elspeth as she sped up her gait.

"I did not ask you to put it on, but I do want it accessible if we come across shepherds." Yateem sheathed his sword, feeling a safe distance from the lake. "Think about what just happened. Do you really want to take any chances?"

"Yes, because me whipping out and putting on a veiled hood at the sight of a shepherd wouldn't be suspicious."

"Vera."

"A veil over my eyes isn't going to stop me from dying! So let's get on with it already." Vera marched past Yateem and toward Yakootah, securing Radov's pin that she had been clutching under the collar of her shirt, so that Yateem wouldn't notice. She cursed under her breath at the opened wings of Ierá Flóga, which always made pinning her token from Radov difficult.

Yateem sighed and rubbed the back of his neck as he followed Vera with a slight limp and an almost imperceptible wince on his brow.

At midday they stopped and had a lunch of dried elk and walnuts on the border of Elspeth and Yakootah. They filled their canteens one more time in Lake Kassiopeia and then started to make their way through the rugged hills of Yakootah.

The border cut the land with severity as they stepped off the cursed sand of Draven's homeland and entered the country that he so brutally claimed. Yakootah opened up. Although it was similar to Ziva in its rolling plains, it had a palpable hostility. There were no groves of trees, no vitality in the air. The hills and plains were covered in blades of dry grass the color of rust, dusty green-blue sage bushes that gave off a rich scent, and tiny scattered dots of livestock. The land seemed to thrive on scarcity, the suffocating presence of drought and repression the fertilizer that kept this country running while under the menace of evil. The Ruwaydah mountains looked like a dangerous border meant to imprison the Yakootans in their own country. In the distance, large black cliffs protruded from the land, making Vera uneasy.

Before the sun sank behind the great mountain range, Yateem found a clear spot in the terrain to make camp and built a large fire to ward off any nocturnal predators, and to warm their bodies from the cool night breeze. Vera put on a lambskin vest and a jacket to keep her warm through the night.

"How am I supposed to sleep on this ground? It's like sleeping on barbs!"

"Just close your eyes. Your body needs the rest."

"My body also needs to not feel like the earth beneath it is purposely pricking it!"

"Enough."

"Please let me take the first watch."

"Are you sure?"

"Hello? What've I been saying? I can't sleep. You might as well get some first."

"Very well. Good night, wake me if you hear anything moving." Yateem's eyelids were heavy and seized their opportunity to close.

Vera leaned her back against her bundle and stared out over the black expanse of land. Because of the sage bushes covering it, the landscape looked like stationary black clouds. She imagined the faint flickering of distant fires of herders, the only people that would voluntarily sleep on the hard ground of Yakootah.

Sparks flew into Vera's face and startled her. "Stupid fire." Her mumbled complaint made the fire shrink down and hug the sage firewood as the rustic scent came into Vera's nose and calmed her grievance.

The hushed fire then started an intricate dance—twisting, lurching, rising, descending—demanding Vera watch. Her left hand reached over to stroke the ring on her right index finger. She must've been tired because the dragon perched there seemed to be glaring at the gorgeous choreography of the fire. Vera examined the ring closer, trying to remember if the dragon's wings were that spread when she put it on. She was about to kiss the metal face, when the fire stretched its brilliant orange fingers and almost caressed Vera's. She pulled back her hand and watched as the oranges brightened and the tips of the flames grew blood red. She couldn't move. She felt her body go limp and her vision black.

Vera woke up alone on top of a broad hill in Yakootah, the stiff red grass pricking her back. "Yateem!" Her call was lost in the empty hills. "What's going on?"

The question was answered by the awkward clicking of a raven, one that dropped from the bright sky and landed in front of the overwhelmed Vera.

She stood up. "Is this a test? Majlis, I know this isn't real. There's no sage here, and it's daytime. I'm not dumb." Vera waited for the fairy to respond. "Majlis, please! Where's Yateem?"

At the sound of Majlis' name, the raven flapped its wings in agitation and lifted its beak up to the sun, letting out a shrill scream that made Vera cover her ears. At the end of the horrible screeching, the sky grew dark with ravens. She tried to run, but the rust grass wrapped around her ankles, holding her in place. The ravens swooped over her head, smacking Vera with their wings anywhere they could. She tried not to panic as the black feathers whipped against her skin, her arms desperately trying to protect her face and ears.

The flock started to fight. The sound was deafening as they pecked and pushed each other, rising in the air, the aggressive tangle of birds intertwining tighter and tighter. Vera's eyes followed in terror as the mass plummeted to the ground in a heavy, writhing heap. The birds seemed to be falling toward her. She covered her face in horror, but the dreadful raucous stopped abruptly, leaving a vacuum of silence that made Vera drop her hands.

A man stood before her. He had maggot-white skin and tar-black, ragged, greasy hair, and he wore a dull black trench coat that fell rigidly to his ankles, making his tall stature even more intimidating. His emotionless raven eyes gave his harsh, square face a severity that drove fear with malicious cruelty. There was something about him that seemed familiar—maybe the vagueness of his age reminded her of the fairies—except this man did not look young, but rather like a well-crafted weapon, that the touch of blood and time may corrupt, but which would never lose its fatal gift.

"Do you know me?" His voice reminded her of the lurking mouth of a cave, hollow and calm.

While his words were tranquil, his body threw off an energy that ran through Vera. The current terrified, electrified, and strengthened her somehow. "Draven," she said, her voice shaking. She wasn't prepared for this.

"Vera Xochiquetzal of Adowa, I have been looking for you."

"What did you do with Yateem?" Vera struggled against the grass that bound her.

"You are both lazy kittens sleeping next to the fire." Draven looked at Vera's feet and the grass released her, but his gaze held a tighter grip. "You are gorgeous."

The words wrapped their way around Vera's neck and warmed her cheeks as they slid into her ears. She shook her head to refocus. "So Yateem is safe?"

Draven's smile revealed teeth that had been yellowed by years of bloodlust. "As safe as you can be on the Yakootah plains at night."

"If anything happens to him, I'll—"

"You'll what?" His voice hit her like an avalanche. "You have no power here, not yet. I can strip the flesh from your handler's bones and cook it for breakfast, and you wouldn't wake up. You might even have pleasant dreams of eating bacon."

His words drained Vera and left her feeling sick and helpless. "Please don't hurt him. He's all I have."

Draven sneered at her plea. "He is all that is holding you back."

Vera shook her head. "No."

He took a step closer. Every muscle in Vera's body flinched as Draven bent down and put his round, sunken raven eyes level with her lavender eyes. He was repulsive. A century of evil had rotted his looks, but the power that radiated out of his skin was disorienting. "It is a handler's job to restrict, not protect. You are weak, defenseless, and do you know why *Yateem* did this to you?"

Vera was trying her hardest to break eye contact, but she was paralyzed, rooted to the spot where she stood. Draven's energy surrounded her, nearly strangling her with anger and hatred.

"He made sure that you were this weak so that you wouldn't think twice about waking up Zakiyyah. Oh, look…" Draven reached down and grabbed Vera's right hand, holding it up to get a better look at the ring. "You even have this little token as a reminder of that burden. A ring I will be taking back soon."

Vera let in some of the intoxicating anger that was swirling around her head and ripped her hand out of his dry, cracked grasp. She no longer stared helplessly into his empty eyes, but held his gaze with force. "This ring was from my mother. You and your greed killed her and my father! This ring keeps that in my mind. I will destroy everything you are!" Her voice shook with the realization that she was yelling at the man that would set an entire village on fire just to warm his hands as he enjoyed the melody of screams.

Draven grabbed Vera's throat. "You are nothing compared to me." Her pulse hammered against his palm.

"I *will* pass through the White Gate." Her words slid past the vice of his icy fingers and escaped through her determined breath.

"That's impossible to know. You will be faced with the chance to break time's grasp on your life, to live forever with a power that is beyond any mortal's understanding. Even if you do choose the White Gate, until you awaken the dragon, the darkness could take you…I could have you."

"What…what are you talking about?" Her voice was barely audible.

He pulled her close, touching her elegant nose to his knife-sharp one. "Look into my eyes, little nightshade blossom. What do you see? You see nothing, because I absorb everything into my darkness. Not a glimmer of light is left in my path. If you pass through that gate, I will hunt you and drown you in my hopeless, cruel abyss. A small fragile blossom is no match for the lightless void I am."

Vera dug her fingers in between his fingers and her throat. The dragon ring scratched her chin, and her struggle only made his choking grasp tighten. "No, I wouldn't—never."

Draven's grip lessened, and his fingers drug down her neck and rested on her shoulder. "Darkness has such a negative connotation to it, but it is a sensation, an ecstasy to which nothing else can possibly compare. If you pass through that gate, you will receive your power, and you will start to wonder about all the freedom you could have…" he paused, brushing her cheek with the appearance of admiration, "away from your handler. Freedom to love and live as you wish."

With the rush of power pumped through each molecule in her body, she felt the exhilaration of complete control of everything around her. The enraptured Vera shuddered and furrowed her eyebrows. "Yateem has been with me my entire life."

"That Hebian has hid you your entire life! Your beauty and love from the world, from me." Draven lightly kissed Vera on the cheek. "I can love you like no one else can because no one understands you better than I do."

"What?" She rubbed her cheek to make sure there wasn't a burn.

Draven took Vera's hand with too much passion for a lover. "I understand that everyone treats you differently, and for you I will make the whole world blind so that no one will ever looked at you like a freak again."

Vera, after some effort, withdrew her hand. "That's not love! That's cruelty! You are a monster!"

Draven cupped Vera's face in his hands. "I could be good for you. Unite the whole of Zerahlinda under one rule. I will lay the world in your hands, and you can decide what to do with it. As long as you are happy, my life is at peace. Please think of it, my little blossom, for to be immortal is awfully lonely." His mouth was close to hers, and in his black eyes Vera could see the reflection of her confused expression.

She was becoming intoxicated with sweet fumes coming out of Draven's mouth as he talked. Her mind was vacant, but complying. She found herself smiling at those yellow teeth and black eyes.

Her right hand grew cold, and rhythmic bursts of air crashed against Vera's arm. It was not until she saw the concern in the darkening eyes that she had the will to look down.

The ring had come alive. The metal dragon beat its wings, getting bigger and bigger with each pulse of air. Draven's spell was shattered. He stepped back with frustration.

The tail that had wrapped around Vera's index finger slid down and tightened itself around her shaking wrist. With the tail in place, the dragon poised itself to attack Draven. Vera held her arm out straight, afraid of what was about to happen. It took a deep breath, and as it breathed silver flames at Draven, its wings wrapped around Vera's hand and solidified. The flames were blue with heat, and as they reached for Draven's throat, they smoothed and became the sharp blade of the Ierá Flóga sword, a treacherous weapon of the olden days.

Vera was more shocked than Draven as she stared at what she thought was an old relic. Draven glared at the sword, curling his lips and growling like a rabid dog that had been backed into a corner.

"Don't have any power, huh?" The sword acted as a shield for Vera's mind, making Draven's deceptions clear.

"What danger is there in a girl with a sword?" Draven said, maintaining his distance, staying a little more than the blade's length away from Vera.

"While hiding me from the world, and from *your love*, my handler taught me well. Try to kill me without the spells—I promise it won't be as easy as you thought."

Draven chuckled. "I wasn't going to kill you, Vera. I was merely showing you that Yateem is stifling you. Giving you no choices in your own life. I wanted to give you a taste of what it would be like to have your power with me."

Vera positioned herself to plunge the sword through Draven's throat.

"Careful, little lavender one, you don't know who you're attacking, or where you are."

Yateem didn't wake as the wind blew the hearty scent of sage in his nose, but he did force his body to roll over to warm his face by the fire's heat. Lazily he opened his eyes to check on Vera and was happy to see her alert and staring at the flames. A deep sleep came over him, and he couldn't stop his eyelids from dropping. All he could feel was the growing warmth of the fire. Yateem heard Vera stand, but he didn't stir, assuming she was stretching her legs to help keep herself awake. It wasn't until quick blasts of air made the fire lick Yateem's face that his eyes could open, and his mind woke up.

With great alarm, Yateem jumped up and away from the fire, grabbing his singed sheath. The threat of the reaching flames was diminishing as the brightness of the orange blended with the crimson, and then seemed to melt in the inferno as the fire shrank back toward the ground.

"The wind must have picked up the fire. Are you alright?" Yateem's relief switched to horror when he saw Vera's catatonic face and her dragon ring growing and breathing a strong silver blade out of its golden jaws. "How are you doing that?"

Her response was to get into battle position, ready to stab Yateem in the throat.

"Vera! Wake up!" Yateem had his sword drawn and planted his feet in anticipation of a battle he was unwilling to fight.

Vera blinked and finally saw who was in front of her. "What are you doing? Put that away!"

"You first."

She looked down at her right hand and saw that it was still encased in golden wings. She struggled to pull her hand out of the gold hand shield, but the dragon's tail and wings weren't budging. "I'm not attacking you. I...I met Draven and the ring changed. Yateem, what's happening? Why won't it change back?"

Yateem sheathed his sword, still keeping his distance from Vera and her weapon. "What do you mean, you *met* Draven?"

"I was sitting here, and the fire changed—"

"You were asleep."

"I know. That's how I met him."

"And he told you to kill me?"

"What? No! I was attacking Draven!"

"That ring changed around me. You were attacking me!"

Vera's eyes narrowed. "Why do you never believe me?"

"Vera that isn't..."

"I have more control," Vera said, pointing her sword at Yateem. "That makes you weak, doesn't it?"

The dry crunch of a sage branch stopped the conversation.

"Nyx." Yateem's face was stern as his ears strained for the next misstep of the approaching threat, but he knew there would be no more warnings. "Put your back against mine. They will come from all sides."

Vera did as Yateem told her. Her face had lost all its blood, and her right hand shook under the weight of the sword...and her fear.

"Yateem..." Vera's voice was raspy.

"Don't touch their skin," he ordered.

"I didn't think nyx were real." Vera stared out into the night, where the fire gave no help to her eyes.

Three nyx jumped over the tall sage bushes and aggressively circled Yateem and Vera. Gray-red foam seethed between their pointed teeth that jutted out horribly, with no jowls to cover them. The creatures' large squared heads were even with Vera's quivering heart, and their red eyes looked their prey up and down ravenously. They looked like large, black, slimy, deranged Great Danes.

A low growl came from the surrounding night and the nyx stopped, crouching down and letting out guttural snarls. Yateem and Vera held their breath and steadied their swords. The canines wanted to pounce, but something was holding them back, something big that moved around them in the darkness.

Suddenly, a quick bark came from the black night and the nyx attacked.

Two of them went for Yateem who, without losing his footing or composure, sliced one's head off and thrust his sword into the other's heart. Vera screamed as the third nyx jumped at her, but the dragon sword somehow made its way through the sticky throat. The finality of taking a life made Vera's stomach spasm and hastened her breathing as the metallic stench of blood filled the air, inflating Vera's fear.

"Well done."

"Are we going to die?"

"No."

"Because Draven said—"

"Remember your training and listen. That was only the first attack."

The firelight caught on the glimmer of translucent motion to Vera's right.

"What was that?"

"The alpha male. Get ready."

The black night that crowded around the ring of firelight was silent for what seemed like a week. Vera kept scanning the surrounding sage bushes, horrified by what might be in the darkness. Yateem's feet were firmly planted, and he closed his eyes to listen for any movement.

The sagebrush snapped like dried bones as five nyx stepped into the firelight. Two of the younger ones near Vera leaned down to smell the carcass of the nyx she had killed. When they saw her sword dripping with black blood, a slow growl began in their throats.

"Yateem, I can't do this."

"You have no choice. Steady yourself, and keep your back to mine."

Three nyx targeted Yateem, leaving no room for him to run. They got closer together, pushing on each other's sides, snapping at each other for the claim of being the first to attack.

"I don't want to have to die like this."

"Vera, control yourself."

A single tear made its way out of Vera's right eye and landed on her quivering lip. "Taken away from my home, following what some stupid fairies say…"

"Vera, focus!"

"…Having to always listen to your orders, forced to listen as Draven threatens me!" Vera's voice was like a gentle breeze that had suddenly become a furious torrent.

"Listen to me!"

"NO! I'm done listening!" She stepped away from Yateem. Hysterically screaming, she swung at one of the nyx in front of her, taking its snout off, and while she pulled the sword back to finish the creature off, the tip of her blade sliced through the top leg muscle of the other nyx. Tears blurred her sight. All she had the power to do now was to kill—or die a horrible death at the hands of a monster she didn't even believe in. The fire glinted on the silver blade as it fell in a heavy stroke into the mutilated nyx's skull and brain.

Fear and anger no longer weakened Vera. She was in control. She was powerful. The remaining nyx lunged toward Vera, but its sliced leg hindered its jump, making it lurch forward and hit the side of its body against Vera's leg. Her feet were unsteady, but she managed to jab her sword into the heart cavity before falling and realizing that the venom on the nyx's skin had started to eat through her riding trousers, and was about to devour her flesh.

"What's happening?!" Vera screamed.

The three nyx were large, crouched down, and ready for the race to Yateem's throat.

"Listen to me!" Yateem reached behind him with his free hand, trying to grab onto a piece of her clothing.

"NO! I'm done listening!" She screamed as she took a step away from Yateem, exposing both their backs.

One of the nyx in front of Yateem seized the opportunity and released all the pent-up energy in its muscles as he launched his body over Yateem. But before the creature got a chance at Vera, Yateem thrust his sword straight up through the nyx's chest and into its head. His movements were a violent dance as he dodged the dropping carcass and thrust his sword into the mouth of the oncoming nyx.

"What's happening?" Vera's scream was shrill with panic.

"I'm coming, Vera!" Yateem pulled back his sword and severed the last nyx's head that continued to snap its teeth as it fell to the ground.

"Yateem!" Vera's voice held pure agonized horror.

He turned and saw a huge translucent nyx dragging Vera by her feet through the sage. Grabbing a sage branch, Yateem lit it on fire and sprinted after them, but he didn't need the torch to find them, Vera's tormented cries led him to her and the monster.

"Help!"

Yateem came skidding around a large bush and found himself eye to eye with the translucent beast, the torch in his hand casting eerie, slick light on its body as its red eyes gleamed heartlessly at him.

"Arivos, please make this stop!" Vera helplessly writhed with pain.

Yateem pushed the flaming branch onto the nyx's throat, turning its skin charcoal gray. The canine yelped at the burn, and in an instant grabbed the branch with its teeth and yanked it from Yateem's grip, tossing it into a nearby bush that ignited immediately.

"Please, Yateem!" Vera cried out. "I can't take this… This…ARIVOS…Someone help me…" Her screams increased with every moment the nyx's venom devoured the skin on her leg.

The heady smell of burning sage steadied Yateem's hand as he jabbed at the alpha nyx with his sword, though none of his quick strokes were lethal because Yateem had to dodge the beast's needle-like teeth that were dripping with hungry saliva. When one such advance came quicker and closer than Yateem had anticipated, his feet slid on the dry land as if it were ice. He reached for something to keep him upright and ready for the next attack.

"Draven!" Vera screamed, "You were right!"

Yateem landed in a huge sage bush, where the branches seemed to hold him down.

"I'm not strong enough!" she screeched.

"Yes, you are, Vera! You can do this!"

"ARIVOS!"

The alpha nyx walked up slowly to Yateem and leaned over him, looking into its captive's teal eyes with his ferocious red ones. A drop of saliva hit and burned a hole in Yateem's vest. He fought to free his sword hand, but the curving sage fingers gripped all the tighter.

"NO! Yateem!" Vera reached toward him with her sword hand. In her weakness, the dragon's silver flame of a blade had become the size of a dagger.

Yateem pierced the night with a battle cry as he yanked his arm free, his sword flashing in the growing wildfire. The blood spatter from the beast's slit throat burned the grass with an acidic hiss.

The monster reeled backwards and staggered around, thick blood pouring freely from the widening slash in its throat. Dry snaps and the smoky scent of burning sage filled the air as Yateem struggled to free the rest of his body before the wildfire reached him.

"Get away!" Vera yelled, and her dagger grew slightly as she waved it at the lurching beast.

"Kill it!" Yateem ordered as he thrashed against the seemingly possessed bush.

Vera swung with little strength, and hit nothing.

The nyx, its red eyes glazing over and its translucent skin fading to a dull gray-black, looked toward Yateem. Blood dripped down its legs toward Vera's face, and with surprising speed it plunged down on Vera's throat, its sharp teeth cutting out any scream she might have given in response. The alpha male then stumbled backward until its lifeless legs gave out and it collapsed behind a nearby bush.

"NO!" Yateem's scream broke the sage's hold on him. The misery in it seemed to freeze the world and create a vacuum of despair that shook the night sky as he ran to Vera, and cradled her in his arms.

"Vera? VERA!" He swept the auburn strands away from her eyes to find not lavender, but sickly gray-white. "There was not supposed to be so much pain!" He rocked her in his arms, his tears mixing with the thick purple blood that pooled around her exposed spinal cord.

Raising his face to the stars, he cried, "Why this way?"

Damp smoke stung his eyes, choked his questions, and dimmed the wild firelight. Yateem looked around, his hand shaking with tense rage as he wrapped his fingers around the hilt of his sword. His jaw throbbed from gritting his teeth.

"You will not touch her, Draven!" he yelled, his voice wielding desperate wrath with every word.

"You knew this had to happen, Hebian." Majlis' swaying figure looked down at Vera. The smoke swirling around her gave a ghostly beauty to her gaze of empathetic sorrow.

Yateem clung to Vera as he rocked her slackened body back and forth.

Majlis' watery projection absorbed a tear off Yateem's cheek. "I will help. Get her out of the open," she instructed before dissolving her projection.

The resulting water raised a dense cloud of smoke as it extinguished the sage fire, leaving Yateem in the dark.

Chapter 21
Stolen Passage

Yateem could not afford tears or grief.

His despairing scream must have alerted other nocturnal predators that fresh meat was near. Placing his sullied sword on the rough ground, he tried to force the tears in his eyes to recede to a manageable distance from the present.

Although Yateem's hands shook with emotion, they were nonetheless graceful and efficient. Grimy fingertips ushered Vera's eyelids to close over the inanimate gray-white orbs beneath and gently wrestled her mouth out of the grotesque shape of her final, unreleased shriek. Lastly, he cut away Vera's soft lambskin vest from under her jacket and wrapped her neck to cover the gaping hole that caused stomach acid to rise up Yateem's throat.

"I am sorry. Vera, if you can still hear me, know that you are strong enough." One last tear was spent before the hard mask of a set jaw and glazed-over eyes replaced the deep-set lines of sorrow on Yateem's face.

He placed her over his shoulder and grabbed his sword to hack the smoldering fingers of the sage bushes away from them. Once Yateem made it past the burnt sage, he rubbed the remainder of smoke and desolation from his eyes with the back of his hand, making sure the blade did not come near Vera's body.

Their campfire was nearly burnt out, and it was just as well because the little light that it cast overwhelmed Yateem's senses that had grown accustomed to the bleak night.

He knew that it wasn't practical to take Vera's pack, but it also could not be left. Those nyx were undoubtedly led to their camp by Draven, and Wachiru would soon be scouting for the site, trying to get any scent of Vera they could find. They would then be looking for a traveler that fit Yateem's description.

There was only one thing to do. Yateem set Vera down next to the fire, as if she were a sleeping child that he didn't want getting cold. He then went to his pack and pulled out the Sospitas flask and breathed deeply before taking a long drag from it.

He had to stuff an entire corner of his sleeping bag into his mouth to keep from drawing the attention of any more predators with the cutting screams he fought to silence as the water's effects surged through his body. He punched the hard, dry ground until the skin on his knuckles split open and started to bleed. To keep from further hurting his sword hand, he lay on his back and crossed his arms, focusing on his true age and not on throwing himself into the embers of the failing fire.

Yateem, exhausted from both the torment of the Sospitas water and the prior events of the night, ate a ration of dried beef and roasted pine nuts. He then went to give Vera her share, but stopped when he saw her lying dead by the fire, and he ate her ration instead. After several gulps of spring water from his canteen, Yateem grabbed Vera's pack, searching for the ornate looking-glass he knew was there, even though he'd told her not to bring it. The mirror revealed that the pain he'd endured to conceal himself was not a waste.

His thick, wavy hair had thinned and turned white, his dark skin was now faded and leathery, and his teal eyes had dulled and sunk into his time-beaten face. He looked eighty-five. He looked his age.

In the cold of the dying fire, Yateem skirted around the strewn nyx corpses and gathered Vera's pack and sword and strapped it to his own. "I would not want you getting angry at me for leaving your things," he said, but the taste of bile filled his mouth as his attempt to cut the dead air between himself and Vera's limp body fell flat, like a spoiled plum falling out of a tree.

As Yateem went to wrap Vera's sleeping sack around her to prepare her for the long journey, he saw her leg in the shadowy light of the dying fire. The venom had eaten away a large portion of her thigh down to the bone and was making its way up to her hip. He cursed himself for letting the loss of Vera's spirit make him forget to take care of her body. The venom was at a point that was beyond Yateem's healing ability. At the most, he could only slow the effects, and if this was what it could do in an hour and a half, there would be little left of her flesh by the time he reached the mountains. Flashes of burning the alpha male gave him regretful hope, and his aged hands grasped a smoldering sage branch in the fire with the strength of a younger, determined man.

He had gently placed Vera's arms across her chest and lightly kissed her forehead. "Please forgive me for saying this, but I am glad you are not able to feel."

Yateem's throat muscles tightened as he held back vomit while he pressed and rolled the red-hot branch in the wound, burning Vera's infected flesh. He watched with disgusted relief as the slimy substance crackled and the flesh and bone turned a pallid gray.

Hoisting the packs onto his back, he used some of his canteen water to extinguish the fire and then lifted Vera into his arms. With her head resting on his shoulder, he could pretend she was breathing lightly in her sleep. Using the waxing moon for light, Yateem took his first steps into the darkness, weaving through the sage bushes and rugged hills, praying to Arivos to give him the strength to make the daylong journey to the mountains without tiring—and without Draven finding them. Yateem readjusted his sheath on his belt. Every time he took a step, the hilt hit his left hand, but the tactile security it brought him outweighed the pain.

Hours passed, their progress slower than Yateem's pounding head wanted it to be. Even though he'd had little sleep, had been in a fight with ferocious beasts, suffered through the double trauma of watching Vera die and now carrying her body, Yateem couldn't shake his head of the need to be out of the open lands.

With each noise—a breeze rustling a nearby bush, a rabbit tapping its foot on the ground—Yateem would freeze, his entire body tense. He would put Vera down at his feet and draw his sword. Yateem's chest rose and fell in heavy, silent pumps, his eyes scanning over the vague dark shapes of the night. He was an animal at bay, aware of the hunter, but ignorant as to when his demise would occur.

His instinct for survival pushed past the exhaustion and the pain that constricted his insides whenever he let himself process the fact that he was carrying the dead body of the one person he loved in this world. At the bottom of a particularly large hill, Yateem's heartbeat quickened as he noticed a soft light coming from the east that just brushed over the top of the hill. His feet felt like lead as he continued; for the first time in his life, Yateem felt his age.

When he finally crested the hill, he closed his eyes. "We need to get there today. You won't make it through another night."

"No disrespect, but I don't think she's going to make it through tonight."

Yateem's eyes shot open and took in his surroundings with a watchful eye. The light, which he thought was dawn, came from a raging fire. He assumed the worst about the voice, which he had yet to see the possessor of, and looked for a place to shelter Vera while he fought.

"Calm down, stranger. I want peace just as much as you do." A young shepherd, maybe a couple years older than Vera, stepped out from behind a bush with a crude spear tentatively pointed toward Yateem and Vera. His ashy blonde hair was coarsely cropped in tight, as if he had done it himself with a dull knife. His tattered clothes were made from a thick, rough material, his short boots were formed from an ill-tanned leather hide that had deep cracks, and his cloak and hood were made from sheepskin and lined with the wool. A hundred sheep were clustered at the base of the hill. The young man held his gaze, the cinnamon color of his eyes dark in the shadows the fire threw.

Yateem's stiff muscles and tired mind took in the sight of the fire and the pitifully armed shepherd. "I thought the light was dawn. I did not know. I apologize. I would have avoided…" Yateem usually only mumbled apologies after Vera had sassed a powerful fairy, but in his current situation, with Vera's body in his arms, everyone had more power.

"Are you one of the Dark One's Wachiru?" The shepherd lowered his spear only slightly, still ready to defend himself and his herd.

"No." Yateem's voice grated the air, the remembered stench of Vera's burning skin still clawing at his senses.

"How can I be sure?" The deep cinnamon eyes searched Yateem's suspiciously.

"You can't." Yateem walked past the shepherd slowly, gently laid Vera down next to the fire at the bottom of the hill, and brushed the hair away from her eyes. "She refused to become his pet, so he sent some of his slaves to hurt her." His voice was even and soothing as he looked at Vera, as if she were a child he didn't want to wake.

"Who?"

"Draven, you slow-witted worm!"

"Is she…?"

"Dead."

"How?"

"Nyx."

"Here, sit. A man of your age shouldn't be walking about in the middle of the night with such a burden. I'm Fenelle." The young man tried not to stare at her body, but he couldn't help but be a little curious and frightened. "What makes her so special that the Dark One would send nyx specifically for her? He usually just lets them roam."

Yateem sat on a rock that Fenelle had pointed out to him and looked the young man up and down. Could he be a spy, or was he just a man with understandable curiosities about strangers who stumbled upon him? "Draven fancied her."

Fenelle's eyes widened, reflecting the warmth of the fire and the coldness of Vera's body, as he tried to look past the queer color and grime to assess the beauty of the corpse next to his fire. "I always assumed he couldn't see beauty—or feel. Just darkness and destruction."

Yateem ran his leathery hands through his now-thin hair. He did not need to be reminded. "Is dawn close?"

"No, we still have hours yet till the new day."

"Good, I am making better time than I thought."

"Where are you going, stranger?"

"The southern mountain of Ruwaydah."

"The southern mountain of Ruwaydah?"

"Yes."

"That's too long a journey for a man of your age."

Yateem lightened a little. "I usually feel younger than I look."

"I don't care. That's more than a day's journey on horseback for a young, healthy man. For an elderly man with a hurt leg, carrying a limp, dead body…"

"Careful."

"That's suicide…sir."

Yateem looked up, ready to convince the shepherd that he knew more of journeys, when his eyes landed on a sturdy-looking horse whose tan body had broad shoulders and stocky muscular legs. "You are right."

"Obviously. I'm not without my wits. I can tell that you are well armed and have hands that still know how to wield your weapons with skill."

"I mean you no harm."

"I can see that you are wearied by the burden of your dead…companion."

"Granddaughter."

"Really?"

"You doubt me?" Yateem stood, his hand at his sword.

Fenelle dropped his spear and raised his hands. He was a few inches taller than Yateem, but by no means intimidating. His lanky limbs were covered in lean muscles, and the way his hands shook in this moment proved that the shepherd had probably only killed animals, and only out of necessity. "No. Your skin is darker than hers, but it may just be the color of death on her, or the night making you look…I didn't mean anything. I'm just…you came marching into my camp, and…"

"Calm down. Do not give me a reason to kill you, and I won't." Yateem sunk his body back down onto the rock.

Fenelle crouched down in front of Yateem and spoke through gritted teeth. "My home was on the edge of *his* lands. I was watering the sheep, heard the screams, smelt the smoke…" He looked over at Vera's body. "I am sorry for your loss, but these days it seems that the land itself craves blood." Fenelle stood and grabbed his spear as he walked away from Yateem. "I will let you sleep here a while, if you promise to defend my herd against the nyx that attacked you."

"None live."

"The alpha male will track you and bring more."

"I killed the alpha male."

"You?" Fenelle arched an eyebrow and assessed Yateem with renewed curiosity. *How could an old man kill a monster that has kept Yakootans up at night for generations?*

"I cannot sleep. I thank you, but I have to take her to South Ruwaydah before the next nightfall."

"I'm telling you, they'll find you. It would be best to bury her and try to disguise yourself as best you can."

"What is that horse worth to you?"

"My livelihood."

"I will give you this sword for it."

"Offloading a woman's sword on me?"

Light hit the eyes of the dragon ring so delicately perched on Vera's right index finger that lay limp at the base of her neck. It seemed to wink at Yateem with a contemptible confidence about its deadly secret.

That ring had woken him just hours ago. Those wings. That blue flame solidifying. The crazed look as Vera stood and faced him, her imprisoned hand ready to plunge the white-hot blade into Yateem's tightened neck. The horror of pulling his sword on her when she stepped closer. The hate and betrayal that boiled inside him as the dragon's blade shrunk when Vera most needed an enchanted weapon. He knew it had to happen, but he could not forgive Ierá Flóga, the ring that was supposed to protect Vera. Nor would he ever trust it.

Yateem's eyes went back to Fenelle's, which held a prideful disgust at the idea of being offered a woman's weapon. "I can kill you with one stroke if you wish to see its quality."

"Is that a threat?"

"It is a trader's courtesy."

"It's bad luck to take a sword that failed to keep its master safe."

"She wasn't fighting with this sword." The glint of the fire on the dragon's upraised wings halted his speech. "She had another weapon…" Yateem said, pausing to look over at Vera's right hand, where the jeweled eyes watched him, "…that failed her."

"It's a tragedy that she died, but most likely you'll encounter Wachiru on your journey, and then I'll have lost a good horse, and you your life. Stay here, rest in the warmth of the fire, and then leave in the morning, when you're refreshed and no longer feel the need for a horse."

Yateem grabbed the collar of Fenelle's hood with the swiftness of his younger-looking self and pulled the shepherd close to him. "I do not have time to rest. The longer she is dead —" He growled in the young man's face. "Death is hunting me, boy. Give me the horse, and you won't lose anything else." There was an animalistic quality in the desperate pain that strained Yateem's voice.

The threat was greeted by a shallow, warm smile. "I've already lost everything."

Yateem pushed the boy away from him with an exhausted sigh and thrust the sword into Fenelle's hand. "Take the sword, here is my sleeping sack for good measure. I am taking that horse."

Fenelle sighed as he grasped the hilt of the sword and threw the sleeping sack toward his own bedroll. "Aethon, approach."

The hearty steed stamped its hooves on the cold ground toward Yateem and the shepherd, his neck arched high with pride. His fuzzy nostrils flared as he got closer to Yateem.

"You've served me well. Now carry his little one to the gates of the afterlife. Follow whatever he commands." There was warmth in the young man's cinnamon eyes as he tried to make his voice strong and authoritative.

Aethon stamped his hoof again and shook his mane.

"My gratitude is beyond anything I can express."

"When you give her a proper burial, thank Arivos for my help, yeah?" Fenelle's lips formed a crooked smile, but his eyes were unable to mask the sadness of giving up his only living friend.

"May Arivos smile upon you in these dark days, and in the brighter ones to come."

"Thank you, stranger."

"If I can, I will send him back to you."

"My only hope is that he'll find a good home at the end of your road."

Yateem had no more time for idle chat and well wishes. He took Aethon's ropes and started to guide him toward Vera's body. Fenelle came over and placed the riding blanket, as Aethon started to shuffle his back feet when the he saw what they were walking toward.

"Will he carry her?"

"He will, if you make him."

Yateem stooped down and lifted Vera. He was thankful for Aethon—for bearing the burden and for not being as tall as Vulcan. Yateem went to place Vera facedown at the base of Aethon's neck, but at the moment he took his hands away, the horse abruptly shifted its body, causing Vera to slip off and land on her face.

"You ass!" Yateem rushed to Vera, flipping her and brushing the dirt from her cheeks. "Do you not know who she is?"

"Who is she, old man?" Fenelle stepped toward them, his voice raised with anxiety. "Who is she?"

Yateem ignored Fenelle and slowly stood up, making sure to calm himself so that the horse wouldn't stomp Vera. As he began to chant sacred words of his homeland, he looked into the horse's eyes. The words seemed to have a calming effect—

the skin twitching lessened, and the nostrils were no longer flaring as if he had just run from a nyx.

"You are a noble creature, Aethon. Please accept this weighty task. I have no one else I can depend on. I need you. *She* needs you." Yateem stroked Aethon's nose as he spoke in a voice that was both soft and demanding.

"Old man, who is my horse going to carry?"

"Fenelle, this is my horse now." Yateem first took their tied-together packs and slung them over Aethon's broad hips. Then he lifted Vera up in his arms and kissed her forehead. "Be gentle."

Aethon's skin twitched violently as Vera's body was placed across his shoulders, but he did not sway. He stamped his feet and pushed air out of his lips much like a small child trying not to throw a tantrum.

"They're going to kill me for helping you, aren't they?" Fenelle's voice shook.

"I would move your herd before dawn."

Chapter 22
Violent Desperation

The snowcapped mountains lost their warm, buttery complexion as the sun retreated behind them. Aethon's pace had lessened, his hooves stamping into the softening soil with dead thuds. Yateem walked beside him, trying fruitlessly to make his heavy feet silent, the increasing pain that exaggerated the limp in his right leg not helping the effort. He felt the talons of unease grip into his shoulders as they got closer to the roots of the mountains, and the hills became jagged and steep. Majlis had not appeared to help, and now ever present in Yateem's mind was the suspicion of a trap devised by Draven.

As they approached the mountain range, trees had started to intermingle with the sagebrush, and now the travelers were hiking alongside a river that flowed down the gradual slope of the foot of a mountain, into a thick forest that lurked in the ghostly shadow of the rock giant. The trees grew close together, healthy and tall with large branches covered with pine needles that blocked most of the light.

The faint bird songs and the chattering of squirrels twisted Yateem's nerves with anxiety as he wondered what could be lurking in the shadows growing all around him. His right hand rested on the hilt of his sword, while his left gripped the wool of Vera's sleeping sack.

Her body was cold.

Yateem had smiled at death many times. He had been in so many battles, covered in blood, with only enough strength to look into the eyes of the men who thought they would end his life, but he had never sensed danger so acutely as when he felt

Vera's cold body rising and falling on the horse's shoulder blades. As the light rapidly failed him, the trees became haunted silhouettes.

The river turned sharply, protected by pine trees that drooped down to the ground and created a wall of branches that blocked Yateem's view of the riverbank. At the sound of unnatural splashing, he drew his sword as he held the shocked Aethon's reins. Pushing back the branches, they followed the curve of the water.

Two men with bulging arm muscles were untying a small oar-less rowboat from the trunk of a tree and arranging aqua-colored pillows in it. Standing warily, they stared at Vera on Aethon's back and at Yateem, sword in hand. Two rusty lanterns stood a few feet away from the water on the bank, casting shadows on their faces.

One of the men stepped forward to more closely inspect the odd arrivals. His stature and presence were like that of a bull, and he had short, sandy-colored hair and eyes that offered no consolations. "She said you would be younger."

"What did you say?" Yateem pointed his sword at the bull-like man, making sure to hide Vera's body behind him.

The man turned and walked back to the boat, stepping into the water to help with the preparations.

His companion was a smaller, older man, but his large muscles suggested that he was just as strong. While he was wrapping the ropes into a neat coil in the boat, his evergreen eyes landed on Yateem's face. "Our mistress told us to prepare a boat for your charge there, and that you were a Hebian. Your appearance is not what we were told to expect."

"She said you looked like the girl's father, not her grandfather," the younger man said with his back to Yateem.

Yateem glanced around through the trees surrounding the river, looking for the black eyes. "Is it not enough that you killed Vera?" He turned his gaze on the two men standing in the river with the boat in their hands. "You will not take her, Draven!"

A disrespectful laugh escaped the sandy-eyed servant's mouth. "The journey must've been too much for him."

The man with the evergreen eyes scolded the other servant and slowly took a step toward Yateem, staying in the water to avoid the sword pointed at him. "Yateem Rukan Wulfgar of Xipili is your name. Our mistress is Majlis Lady of the seas, who sent us to escort you to her."

"Wachiru could have that information."

"She said he wouldn't trust us."

"You talked to our mistress the same night that she tested Vera by waking some trees in Ziva. She told you—"

"Draven has spies everywhere."

A small whirlpool began in the spot next to Yateem. The two men jumped out of the water and knelt on the bank, holding the boat. Majlis' voice emerged from the whirlpool. "Calm down, Hebian. I told you she would face worse things than moving aspen. Now let them put Vera in the boat. I have prepared a place for her."

The whirlpool caused the river to flow back on itself, to move unnaturally up and into the mountain. Yateem's arm went slack, his sword tip hitting the ground. "Be gentle with her." His eyes were on the brink of watering, his voice weak with resignation.

The older servant gave a nod to the other servant as he remained to hold the boat.

The other servant strolled up toward Yateem and the frazzled Aethon. "You know she's dead, right?"

Yateem's sword came up swiftly, stopping an inch away from the man's mouth. "You know who she is, right?"

The man's sand-colored eyes were wide and focused solely on the blade that promised to gag him if he chose his next words poorly. "She is the Lavender Soul. My deepest apologies, Master Yateem. I only want to help get her to a safe place out of Draven's reach."

The young man could breathe again as the sword found its home in Yateem's sheath, and Yateem's index finger took its place. "If that boat tips and she goes in, I will carve her name in your chest so that you never forget it," Yateem growled through bared teeth.

The servant made sure to keep eye contact as he placed his hand on top of Yateem's, grasped it, slowly returned it to Yateem's side, and tried to comfort the drained man. "I will treat her as if she were my daughter, Sophia."

"We must hurry. I don't think she can keep the river like this for long." The older servant's muscles strained to hold the boat in place against the unnatural flow of water.

The sand-eyed man was still standing in front of Yateem. "Do I have your permission to help put her in the boat?"

"Yes."

He then hoisted Vera off Aethon and placed her in the hand-carved wooden boat as if she were made of fine etched crystal. Yateem followed them and was about to step into the vessel when both men stopped him, and the river's unnatural current swiftly took Vera away and toward the heart of the mountain.

"Vera!" Yateem fought against the men, diving for the river, clawing and punching against their strong arms, but he was too exhausted and ended up on the edge of the bank, on his knees.

The older servant placed his hand on Yateem's shoulder. "We will escort you to our Lady Majlis now. She will take you to the girl."

Yateem's body shuddered as he cried over the water. The reflection of his grayed hair and aged face was distorted by the water's struggle to break from its natural direction. He only looked up at the servant when the bank nearly flooded as the flow of water returned to normal. "She has never been so far out of my sight."

The sand-eyed man rubbed his chest as he looked at Yateem and then took hold of Aethon's halter and grabbed one of the lanterns. "I will take the horse to get food and rest. Can you manage him alone?"

"Yes. Go."

Yateem's eyes glazed over as he stared at the river. "I have failed."

The man sat next to Yateem without saying anything, awkwardly patting Yateem's back and letting the handler cry, as a father would a son.

An hour passed, and the effects of the Sospitas water were gradually wearing off.

"Sir, it's dark." The servant finally stood and looked down at the Hebian's hunched-over body.

Yateem dug his fingers into the soft bank of the river. They were no longer leathery or wrinkled, but they ached as those of an old man.

"This isn't wise. The path to the fortress is difficult to follow in broad daylight. The lantern will light the path, but it will not stop ice from forming. This is becoming more dangerous by the minute for a man in your state—"

"What state is that?"

"Your appearance is changing, sir, and your heart is… uh…broken. I fear if we stay here any longer, you will not have the strength to stand, let alone navigate switchbacks in the woods."

Resting his forehead on the edge of the bank, Yateem took in a long sigh and ruthlessly punched the soft soil before picking himself up and standing face-to-face with the servant's compassionate evergreen eyes. "Lead."

The switchbacks were an ambitious task for a well-rested person, and near torture for an exhausted one. Stubborn trees grew from the cracks, as if willing themselves to live off water and the heart of the mountain alone. Their branches seemed to want to strike out at faces, and their roots, delicately curved over the roughly hewn stone walkway, itched to catch the toe of any boot that walked by.

Yateem brusquely wiped his nose and mouth with the back of his sleeve repeatedly throughout the somber march, trying to snuff out the smell of burning flesh and the taste of bile. The rock face of the mountain was weeping groundwater on them, and the cliff that led down to the river was slowly being engulfed in blackness.

He didn't notice when tree branches hit his numb limbs, Yateem only focused on making his feet mimic the servant's. His

wandering thoughts and exhaustion distracted him, his tired feet
betrayed his natural grace. His right foot caught under a tree
root, and a sharp pain went through his body as his knees hit the
solid rock beneath him.

The servant stepped out of the way to show Yateem the
clearing they had just entered and a small, run-down wooden
dwelling across the way built into the side of the mountain, with
broken windows and crooked side paneling.

"Don't worry, sir. There is plenty of room inside." When
the servant helped pull Yateem onto his feet, the limp was worse.

As they got closer to the house, some of the glint in
Yateem's eyes came back. "Where did she take the boat?"

"Only my mistress knows."

"Where?"

"There are parts of this place that are forbidden for
humans."

Yateem drew his sword, grabbed the servant's shoulder,
and turned him around. "Show me where she is."

His evergreen eyes darted toward the doorway fifteen
paces away. "I can't. There are enchantments on the banned
places that will confuse me, or make me walk backwards."

"Show me!" The sword tickled the servant's throat.

The servant looked Yateem in the eyes. "I will not, my
lord, even if I knew. My fealty is to my mistress, my protector."

"If you do not show me where Majlis has taken her, I
will—"

"Do it if it gives you some comfort in your sorrow, but I
will die before I break my promises to Lady Majlis."

"I will find her."

"Majlis will show you what I cannot."

"Not soon enough."

"Then Arivos' blessings on your quest, my lord."

With a growl of despair, Yateem took a heavy swing
toward the servant's neck. He stood with crazed eyes, his chest
rapidly rising and falling, his sword releasing drops of blood
onto the fallen servant's clothing.

Chapter 23
Icy Reception

"I am glad to see you looking youthful again. My servants tell me you cannot stop crying, Hebian." Majlis' words were as cold as the stone walls that surrounded them. Her dress of light-green Spanish moss hung down and brushed the tops of her bare feet.

Yateem bowed over Vera's blood-soaked lambskin that lay in his shaking hands.

"Yateem?"

"I feel ancient. Where is she? They refuse to show me. They just brought me this." He turned and shook the lambskin toward Majlis, the vest rigid with crusted blood.

"They do not know where she is, and I told them I should be the one to bring you to her. I do apologize for taking your weapons, but I really cannot have you hurting anyone else." Her face was spellbinding, heart-shaped with a fair complexion that brightened her ancient youth, her markings glowing with her jade eyes, as wild as a raging sea. Majlis looked to be about five foot eight, taller than Yateem would've thought from the water projections, but her wings made her look smaller, being about her height in wingspan, and four feet long.

"He wouldn't take me to Vera!" Yateem did not remember seeing the intricacies of her eye markings in the projections, or the tiny flecks of magenta in her jade irises.

"He's fine. You just grazed the collarbone." Her light-pink lips parted, revealing a mischievously sweet smile, with teeth as white as a freshly made pearl. The luminescent cresting waves of the markings above her eyes vacillated easily from a deep blue to the jade of her eyes, giving the illusion that they were made from the sea itself.

"Please, Majlis."

"Follow me." Her light-green dress shifted as a current in a river, smoothly flowing over the curves of her slender body. Her golden hair cascaded down over her back, moving like a school of fish with each movement of her wings, which dwarfed her slender body. They did not flutter so much as sway, as a sea anemone's tentacles sway with the currents of the water. They were an opalescent magenta with solid jade lines depicting a coral reef on the wings; the edges were not hard lines as the other fairies' wings were, but rather had tiny curvatures that resembled the edges of a beta fish's fins.

Following her out of the room that had been appointed to him, Yateem wiped every tear off his cheeks with stubborn pride, afraid of Majlis looking back and seeing his emotional state.

Majlis' fortress was vast indeed, a castle chiseled out of the inside of one of the great mountains. Hallways with arched ceilings were lined with doors and entrances to different passages. It was a maze of halls, bed chambers, servants' quarters, kitchens, storage rooms, dining halls, banquet halls, even a weapons vault—an entire city built within the gray rock of the mountain. The rock provided no heat, and even though Yateem could not understand the ventilation of it, there were grand fireplaces in almost every room.

The passageways were six feet wide, enough to accommodate foot traffic going either direction, or just enough room for Majlis to fully open her wings. She turned and glided down several halls, closing her wings to let people by—or rather to pass them as they stopped and bowed. Yateem noticed that the farther they went into the maze, the fewer people they came across. When they had not seen anyone for what seemed like a very long time, Majlis whispered a fairy spell and a hall opened out of the dark-gray stone walls without making a single sound.

The passage echoed with Yateem's hollow steps, his eyes were trained on her dress and wings.

Had she no words of comfort? No little jewels of ancient wisdom?
Her heart seemed as cold as the snowy mountains where she
lived, her apathy cutting Yateem to his core, chilling him. His
recovering limbs were regaining their stiffness, his breath turning
to fog. Wiping one last tear away before it crystallized in the
corner of his eye, he let his eyes focus on the wall next to him,
stopping short when he realized it was not Majlis' incivility that
caused the chill.

Frost.

"Where are you taking me?"

"Vera's quarters, of course."

"There is ice on the walls."

"Yes, it is about to get much thicker. I apologize for not
making you grab your cloak."

Yateem had to steady himself and control his weak leg as
they progressed and the entire hall and floor went from being
frost-covered to coated in several inches of ice. A light came
from the end of the corridor, bouncing off the walls and playing
in Majlis' blonde hair, which distracted Yateem so much that her
wings brushed his face. As he bumped into her, it felt like a
breeze blew fine silk across his cheek.

Majlis turned around, her lips nearly touching his, and
placed her hands on Yateem's shoulders, smirking as she gently
pushed him an arm's length away from her. "You cannot go in. I
put an enchantment that will kill anything that goes near her."

Majlis stepped aside, revealing a room of glacial ice with
a translucent dome in the center. Yateem raised his arms to
shield his eyes from the cool blue light that pierced them. After a
minute of dazed blinking, he dropped his arms and struggled to
look past the dome of light. He saw Vera in a simple white dress,
her wounds exposed. His body shook from the cold. He looked
at his hands, bright red in the frigidness, and then with a fire in
his eyes, he looked at Vera.

He leapt for the icy threshold, arms outstretched.

"No!" Majlis pushed Yateem against the doorway,
making the ice threshold wrap around his right side to hold him
in place.

"She will freeze to death!" he insisted, fighting against the grip of the ice.

"She is dead, Yateem." Majlis placed her hand on his shoulder and tried to catch his gaze.

Yateem blinked as he stared at Vera. "She looked me in the eye when it happened...I could not...why so horrible an end?"

"She will return."

"When?"

"You must give her time to make her choice."

"And when she gets through, will it be the Vera I helped raise?"

Majlis took her eyes and hand off Yateem. "You have to be ready..."

"I was not ready, Majlis. Not for that!" He just stared at Vera's gaping throat and the ice crystals that were forming in it.

"You have to be prepared if she chooses not to go through the gate." She stared at Vera, the markings above her eyes darkening, as a sea does during a storm.

Yateem looked at Majlis' liquid eyes, trying to will her to look at him. "What are you saying?"

A tear froze on Majlis' cheek. "I cried myself to sleep for months, haunted by those empty, black eyes."

"You never believed she would pass, did you?"

"If she does not pass through the gate, if her eyes come back as dark as the dank caves in which Draven dwells...you must kill her."

Yateem used his free hand to grab Majlis' delicate throat, his eyes narrowed with fury, his jaw clenched tight.

Majlis grabbed Yateem's hand, trying to put her fingers in between his grasp and her throat, straining to get free. "I lacked the strength to kill Draven when I should have...you cannot allow two bearers of evil to live." She struggled to get the words past Yateem's grip.

He pulled her in close, until their noses touched, and his snarl brushed against Majlis' lips. "She was born to pass through. Vera—my beautiful, brave Vera—will make it."

"I thought mine had a chance of making it too."

"*He* sent nyx. *He* made her almost attack me. *She* would never do that."

"You need to be ready." The magenta specks in her eyes grew and wrapped around her pupils until it looked like an anemone lived in the jade waters of her irises.

He tightened his hold on her neck. "I am ready for you to release me, siren."

Majlis' mouth gaped open and closed like a fish dangling on a hook out of water. "Swear to Arivos you will not go to her. She will need you when she returns." The words came out as a choked whisper.

"By the oath I took to protect Vera, I will turn around and leave this place, never to return until she has woken."

The ice loosened its grip on Yateem's body, as did Yateem's left hand from Majlis' throat.

She brushed a chunk of ice off his right shoulder and then stroked the side of his face, looking for common ground in his teal eyes. "I apologize, Hebian. I wanted you to hear the things I should have heard."

Yateem closed his eyes and could barely stop himself from leaning into her caress before brushing her hand off his face. He turned and headed back down the hall in a jilted marching stride, his limp causing a horrible scraping noise against the ice.

Majlis watched him from the doorway of Vera's chamber. "You and I live longer than the humans. To live with the regret of a single moment—a single decision—is agony." She sent her voice to echo down the hall after him.

Yateem kept walking, his vision blurred, his fists clenched as he trudged his way back to his quarters.

Majlis looked back at Vera. She was about to say something, but she hesitated with her face leaning against the threshold of the room. "We could have been friends," she whispered, and then turned and glided down the hall as gracefully as if she wore skates.

The protection enchantment over Vera glistened as her visitors left, and though to the naked eye small details were difficult to make out, a tear seemed to glisten on Vera's cheek.

Chapter 24
After Life

Darkness.

Silence.

The air has movement, a current that takes the deafening quiet out of my ears. The darkness envelops my head like a thick, scratchy blanket. I can feel light on my limbs but cannot see it, cannot reach up and move the intangible blindfold.

Afraid, I crawl on the floor, trying to find my way back to Yateem, back to the campfire. The surface feels wrong—cool to the touch and smooth like pillars of granite, but no seams, no crevices. Just endless smoothness in all directions.

"Hello?"

The darkness absorbs my question. Where am I? What happened? Should I be looking out for that nyx? Nyx. Nyx…was that a dream, or a nightmare? A horrible monster lunging at me, biting me, secreting its venom-rich saliva and pointed teeth into my screaming throat…

"Am I dead?" I claw at the darkness, wanting to see—to see Yateem healthy, to see anything. Anything that is not nothingness. I feel my hands against my face and my fingers pulling my hair, but see nothing.

"Do not hurt yourself my child." The voice is soft but authoritative, familiar from a time outside this.

"Please take this off my eyes." My hands reach in the direction of the voice as I pray to Arivos that he is a friend sent to rescue me from a trap.

"Your eyes are not used to this place. It will overwhelm, and possibly blind you." The voice is like fire, warm and comforting, but cautioning not to get too close.

"If I'm dead, what does it matter? Doesn't this prove it?! I'm not a person in a dumb story! I was blind to the truth then. Don't let me be blind now," I stand tall, readying myself for whatever horrors awaited me.

"I had so wished that would be true when you were born. I prayed so hard to switch places with you, knowing how people would treat you, that you would eventually end up here." He touched the darkness, and it started to fade from my eyes. "Just know that I would not have chosen this for you. Arivos knows what He is doing. Trust in Him. I love you, Vera."

"Father?" The darkness fades away in layers, and as it does, so does my father—those familiar slate-blue eyes, a cautious sorrowful smile. His arms reached out for me, and I try to run after him, but the colors catch my eyes, and disorient me.

The air is alive and bright. I freeze. Can I breathe this? Is this some kind of trick? My legs collapse onto the smooth surface on which I was crawling. It is an opalescent white, and it appears to move like liquid...but it's solid, or else how can I lie on it? The air—if that's the right name for it—starts to dance above my head.

The colors are so bright they are nearly white, but at the same time they keep their individual pigment. They have dimension, expanding and collapsing into each other like a breathing organism. I raise myself to watch as they start to weave. The blue, the same color as the northern sky, spins and twists like ocean waves in a storm. Auburn, yellow, and orange braid together and somehow make several images of falling leaves without breaking the strands of color. The red, pink, and purple leap with joy as they make a sunset. Greens intermingle, sowing everything together with glistening vines.

Then everything freezes. The air is no longer filled with colors; they all composed the tapestry. The white that remains makes me close my eyes. The purest white I have ever seen, it makes my very soul quake. I can feel the intensity of it as it seeks a way between my closed eyelids.

A sweet, fleecy breeze caresses my cheek, and the colors silently call me to look. I open my eyes. The tapestry of light rips in two with no sound but my gasp to acknowledge the destruction. A light more powerful and pure than that of the colorless one surrounding me bursts out of the wound. My heart is at peace as my eyes are transfixed… and somehow not blind.

A figure…the light is making a figure.

Arivos.

Not knowing what else to do when faced with the creator of the universe, I bow my head so low it hits the ground.

Chuckling. Is He laughing at me? I know He is the almighty one, but that's just rude.

"Vera, get up." It is a command, but it is virtue that gives the voice its gentle power. It consumes my soul with happiness, peace, love, and an overpowering sensation of being home.

"I don't think I can move in front of you."

"Vera Xochiquetzal of Adowa. You have nothing to fear. I made you. Now stand."

His presence energizes my limbs, and I stand to face Him. He is spirit, the image of purity and holiness, but underneath that light is a semi-human-looking form—probably for my benefit so that I don't go crazier than I obviously am—worrying about which part of the light to talk to. His smile fulfills in me any need for love and acceptance I ever wanted in life. All the times I was frustrated by the way I could never fit in simply melt away in his presence. Beauty beyond explanation, beyond comprehension. My vision blurs from the intensity of light, or possibly because of the tears building up behind the dam of my eyelids.

"So…um…" *Calm down and speak!* "I guess the fairies didn't make up those stories?"

Arivos' laugh skips around my soul and makes my heart giggle. "You never did like learning those stories, did you?"

"I was five when they told me I was the Lavender Soul. Everyone expected so much of me." *Can I even talk to Him like this? I mean, what happens if I get sassy with my creator?* "I just wanted to be a kid." I barely heard that; maybe He didn't hear it at all.

"I made you with this purpose in mind. I know it has not been easy, having a prophecy define how you live. I ask for a lot of trust and sacrifice from you, and you have to believe that I know all. My plan for your life is what's best."

Years of other people's expectations boiled inside me, despite Arivos' presence. "Then why did I die? Why didn't you swat away that nyx like a fly?" *Too much, too much, lower your voice.* "And where is Yateem? Is he okay? Or did he have to die too for this great prophecy?!"

Arivos steps back. The ground and air shake, and I fall to my knees.

"I made Draven and you so that I could see if man could truly believe. Not just pray, but *believe* that what I have planned is better than anything that could ever happen to you on your own. Draven failed, and now he spreads his evil like a virus. Thus, you were born." He steps closer to me, the nearness of His immense love making tears stream down my face. "You know the prophecy. You have to pass through the White Gate of Fire."

"I don't have a choice in this life, do I?" Sobs choke my question to my creator.

"Of course you do, my sweet Lavender Soul. Draven chose power above the needs of others. So can you. You can choose to have the power to rule all of Zerahlinda and live forever, or you can choose to be a servant to my will, suffer greatly, but save Zerahlinda."

Two teardrops hit my empty hands. Can I save everyone? Can I *free*…everyone? "I don't know if I have the strength."

Arivos wraps himself around me—love so overwhelming, so incomprehensibly healing that the years of pent-up tears no longer have an excuse to weigh down my life. A puddle should be forming at my feet, but the infinite compassion of Arivos absorbs all my sorrows. My pain shrinks, my anger diminishes, my despair lifts. He takes my burden.

"I made you for this purpose. I will give you the strength you need. All you have to do is believe." Arivos places a rough object in my hands. "This is the key. If you choose the path of immortal power as Draven did, you stab the ground on which you stand to break time's restraint on you. To wake Zakiyyah and fulfill your true purpose, touch the White Gate with this, and you shall pass through it. Reflect before making your decision, because only a resolute heart can survive passing through the gate."

"But how do I even find the White Gate?" I looked up to see that Arivos had disappeared. The tapestry of light that He had torn in His entrance stands before me, whole again. The colors burst into a white-hot flame that silently burns in the same gorgeous pattern the colors wove.

"Found it."

The purity of the white flame pierces my eyes, and as I look down, I remember the key. It's made from a dull, charcoal-colored crystal, but as I rock it between my palms and fingers, I see that it reflects bits of light, like stars in a stormy night sky. An odd-looking thing, like a crude dagger with no handle and only four inches long, the tip is tapered so thin, that I'm afraid to touch it, for fear of breaking it or pricking myself. My fingers and eyes grope over the jagged surface of the dagger with increasing interest. My little finger catches on the broad top of it, and I almost dismiss this as anything out of the ordinary because of the natural rough surface of the dagger, but this was smooth. My eyes struggle to find the hole on the rough black surface, but then I see, and realize that a column of light makes its way through the dagger when it is tipped the right way. My legs cross themselves as I sit and become mesmerized by the glittering, black funnel-dagger.

"Believe," It's going to take more than saying it out loud to believe in myself.

"She is dead, Yateem." Majlis' voice came from far off, like it traveled on the waves of a distant ocean to reach me.

"Majlis?" I look all around me, but see no one.

"She looked me in the eye when it happened." Yateem's voice sounded like the sad howl of a cold night wind.

I jump to my feet. "Yateem! You're alive! If you can hear me, I'm alright."

"Will it be the Vera I helped raise?"

"I've got the key." My hand reaches up in the air to show the dagger to Yateem's unseeing eyes. "The gate's right there. I'm just…reflecting. Arivos said—"

"You never believed she would pass, did you?"

"What are you saying?"

"You must kill her."

The bright air pricks my lungs as I gasp it in. Why is she saying that? "Don't listen to that nasty fairy, Yateem!"

"Vera—my beautiful, brave Vera—will make it."

"Believe. Believe. Believe." Yateem would never hurt me. I can do this.

The gate is so bright I have to shield my eyes with the black dagger. The air no longer pricks, but soothes my lungs as I take a step towards the silent white flame.

"I thought mine had a chance of making it too."

My heart and lungs tighten. The air no longer feels breathable, my head feels heavy with dizziness, and my feet can't move. Draven had been in this situation. He met Arivos and felt His love, and he still didn't pass. The gate now seems too bright and burns too furiously for a young girl to walk through. Only the resolute will pass through. What if I die all over again? What if I choose me? Arivos just said I would break time's restraint on me; either way I get powers, so who am I to say that I couldn't use them for good? Draven was raised poorly…I know better. I would be powerful enough to defeat Draven, and then free Radov, and I could protect Yateem for a change. Draven's eyes turned black because he was evil on the inside. I am not.

The dagger digs into my hand, breaking my spiraling thoughts.

"Vera, I will turn around and leave this place, never to return."

My shaking legs buckle, and my knees come down hard on the ground. "Yateem, don't leave! Please don't leave me! I was just thinking."

Majlis' voice changes direction and gains strength, as if it's a tidal wave heading straight for me. *"We could have been friends."*

"If this was a test, I think I failed." I had just experienced the complete love and peace of Arivos' presence, but Majlis' and Yateem's conversation, that somehow made its way to my afterlife, opened up fresh wounds of abandonment, distrust, and betrayal.

My hand tightens in a solid grip on the dagger, and my eyes glare at the single tear that escapes and becomes one with the opalescent floor. "Majlis," the name comes out as a growl, "we will never be friends."

Chapter 25
Uncivil Attentions

Yateem trudged his way as best he could back to his room. He slammed the door in the face of the man that had showed mercy and guided him to his bedchamber. The vaulted ceiling opened up the room, there were the appearance and smells of perfect hospitality and comfort, but the lack of windows made him feel even more trapped in his life, in this situation. Someone had started a fire for him, and a dinner was laid out on the small table, still steaming.

Vera's blood-soaked lambskin vest had been hung over the back of the chair, as if it were nothing more than a jacket a child carelessly left on the ground. Her death lingered on his shoulders. The memory of ice protruding from Vera's exposed throat made Yateem feel like his organs had been crushed under the weight of the mountain, and the accommodating warmth of the fire seemed to burn his flesh. Yateem balled up the crusted vest and rubbed his cheek against the stiff, clumped wool that would no longer swaddle anyone in its warmth.

"No more."

Yateem threw the vest on the fire. Sparks flew. The flames winced and cracked, almost extinguished, and then burst out with a ravenous appetite.

He sat down on the end of the bed, his elbows digging into his knees as his knuckles ached under the strength with which he grasped his hands together.

The wool turned black and curled into itself as the blood liquefied and dripped muddy red on the hissing embers and settled ashes, as the flames lapped over the last possession that felt Vera's heart beating.

The cedar door gently creaked, and Yateem woke as if the noise were a battle cry. A woman stood in the doorway, the tray of food in her hand just barely shaking. A man peeked his head over her shoulder.

"I will not hurt you," Yateem said as he rubbed his eyes and sat up on the side of the bed. His clothes felt stiff from being slept in, his body cold from sleeping on top of the many comforters.

The man urged the woman through the door. He carried a basketful of firewood and started to bring life back to the low-burning embers, awakening a coppery smell in Yateem's nostrils.

The woman sat the breakfast tray on the table and noticed the untouched dinner. "Was is not to your liking, sir?"

Yateem's smile was shallow and only accentuated the blank look in his eyes. "I have no appetite. Please do not waste the time, or the food. When I am hungry, I will ask for a meal. Thank you for the fire. If you leave the rest of the wood, I can stoke the flame myself."

Both bowed, and before the man could walk off with the dinner tray, the woman snatched the little water carafe. She did likewise with the breakfast tray, leaving the two carafes and a cup on the table. Her steps decisive, her pale hands grabbed the handles of the breakfast tray, and her thick skirt rustled as she knelt in front of Yateem, set the hot porridge next to his feet, and bravely stared directly into his eyes.

"I cannot eat."

"I know." Her warm hands were a solace to Yateem's cold, worn knuckles as she placed a mug of aromatic, gray-blue tea in his hands. "This will warm your heart." She looked up at him with her deep-brown eyes that spoke of years of great nurturing love, and of tremendous loss. With a quick smile she grabbed the tray of food and left him.

At each mealtime she returned, with a full water carafe, a fresh mug of spiced tea, and an invitation of company in Lady Majlis' personal parlor. The fourth time the gentle, stern woman came in, Yateem agreed to have dinner with Majlis out of hungry resignation.

"I will tell M'Lady at once. She will be delighted!"

"I doubt very much she knows how to be delighted."

A scolding look escaped the woman's eye before she left to deliver the message.

Yateem nodded his thanks to the woman who had sustained him with tea and who led him to the large cedar door of Majlis' parlor. He smiled at the bronze sea-urchin doorknob, gently turned it, and pushed open the heavy door.

Majlis sat with her legs tucked under her on a low chair that resembled a black bean, her wings barely beating against the chair that scooped across her low back. As Yateem leaned against the doorway, all the anger he held toward this woman began to dissolve as he became enamored by the porcelain beauty before him.

"Will you please come in? You are distracting me." Majlis did not lift her gaze to meet Yateem's, but a smirk lay on her lips as her eyes concentrated more on the army of words that marched between her hands.

"I am flattered." Yateem nonchalantly pushed away from the threshold, crossed his arms, and stood tall, putting himself on display.

"The draft from the hall is the distraction."

Yateem let out a loud breath that deflated his chest as he stepped into the room and leaned his back against the door until he felt it click closed.

The parlor was not extravagantly large, looking to be about fifteen feet wide and forty-five feet long. The furnishings were situated in such a way that easily divided the room into three equal sections, but which still flowed together as one cohesive space. The ceiling was vaulted over the three sections.

The door on which Yateem leaned was in between two bookcases, and there was another on the wall to his left. In the middle of the section were two black leather chairs and the bean-shaped one that Majlis currently occupied. Small tea tables stood next to the chairs, and a large evergreen woven-silk rug covering the stone floor in the sitting area gave this part of the room a very warm atmosphere, perfect for the avid reader.

A massive fireplace was hewn out of the center of the right wall. It was ten feet long and four feet tall, the rock in front of it blackened from the very heat of the enormous fire raging inside of it. There were two red velvet armchairs, the backs of which were short—presumably so that Majlis could choose which she wanted to sit in—and a wooden-framed, brocaded couch in this second section. They all sat together five feet away from the fire on top of another evergreen rug. Across from the fireplace on the left wall hung a tapestry with a strange design, the subject of which was abstract and difficult to discern, but Yateem assumed it was something to do with fairies. The ornate Elmwood coffee table and the cocktail trolley to the left of the tapestry gave this second section of the room the air of aristocratic leisure.

What perplexed Yateem about this room was not the strange furnishings or the enormous fire, but the lack of candles or lanterns. By all reasonable logic, the fire would light up the middle section of the room, but leave the rest of the space in the dark. Majlis' parlor apparently resided outside the laws of nature because the full room was illuminated. Majlis was not straining her eyes to read a book by candlelight, but rather reading as if she were sitting under a midday sun. Yateem examined the room again, looking for any signs of enchantments, which was when he noticed the large circular window high up on the far wall. It shone a very bright bluish light that had started to bleach the mahogany dining table beneath it.

"It is an iceberg portal to the side of the mountain, thus the rather large fire to fight the cold."

Yateem had not noticed that Majlis had been watching him study the room, and now wished for bad lighting to hide his embarrassment in shadow. "No doubt bound by one of your enchantments to enlighten the room without ever melting. Very clever." He was anxious to seem her equal, but he over-annunciated the words in a deep baritone voice that sounded like he was imitating the gimmick of a street magician.

Majlis laughed at him, the sound a splash of crisp mountain spring water during the heat of the day. "Yes, I do have an enchantment to keep the warmth of the room from melting the glacier. But I believe that the magic source of my parlor's *enlightenment*, as you say, is the refraction of sunlight through the ice." Majlis placed a seaweed bookmark on the page she was reading, closed the book, and set it on the tea table next to her chair. Her dress, made from pressed and sewn Columbine flowers, escaped from underneath her bent legs, and the skirt swished as it fell down to the ground, just brushing the tops of Majlis' wiggling toes. She brushed a blonde lock out of her face and smirked at Yateem. "You really never relax, do you?"

"Excuse me?"

"You came in here, gawked at me and the whole parlor, tried and failed at an act of patronizing flattery, and yet you still stand with your back against the door as if you are a soldier at his post." Majlis crossed her arms and tilted her head, as if the exaggerated stare at her guest would loosen him up.

"I can relax. I just cannot seem to around you." Yateem took a few steps into the room, forcing his arms to rest at his sides instead of crossing them behind his back.

"I can fix you a drink if that will help." Majlis gave the mischievously sweet smile as she glided toward the cocktail trolley, the firelight flashing off the crystal carafes.

"No, that may make matters worse."

Majlis raised a carafe of amber-colored spirits toward the glacier window, nodded her head at the color, lifted out the crystal stopper, and poured a very generous serving of the liquor into two tumblers. "The housekeepers here are husband and wife, descendants of Elspethians that I chose to save. In their gratitude, they gave me all the barrels of the finest spirits that their family brought to Yakootah in the exodus caravan. I only serve it on special occasions."

"Such as harboring the dead Lavender Soul and her handler from Draven?" Yateem walked over to the middle section of the room, the anger from the sight of Vera's crystallizing body two nights ago making his thoughts burn.

"I was hoping that your refusal to see me yesterday, and the fact that it took you until dinner to join me today, meant that you were coming to terms with the current state of affairs." Majlis offered the glass of liquor to Yateem with a genuine look of empathy.

He grabbed it and took a long draw, flinching as the strong substance stung his throat. "My anger is not unwarranted. You took Vera out of my sight, hid her from me—"

"Hid Vera's *body* from Draven." Majlis sat in one of the velvet chairs, her wings looking like an ornate back piece until they fluttered and sent shimmering movement through her hair —and a shiver down Yateem's spine.

"And you suggested that I would soon have to kill her!" Yateem threw back his head as he guzzled the rest of his drink and clanked the tumbler onto the drink trolley.

"I was merely pointing out the unbearable things that need to be sorted." Majlis ran one of her long fingers around the rim of her glass, making a low-pitch resonance.

Sitting down in the armchair across from her, Yateem hunched over and rubbed his eyes with the palm of his hands. "I helped raise her, held her in my arms when she cried, scolded her, and taught her. Now I just feel as if I brought a lamb to the slaughterhouse."

"Oh, that is awkward." Majlis guzzled her drink as well.

Yateem glared at Majlis' insensitive response to his open emotional exhaustion and confusion.

Seeing his look, she said, "No, not what you were saying just then—that was touching, really." There was a quiet knock at the door, and Majlis called elegantly, "You may enter." The door opened, and their dinner was brought in. "I thought since you refused to eat yesterday, and showed no signs of eating all day, that your body needed a hearty meal."

Yateem watched as a small cauldron of soup, a large platter of rice, baked potatoes, and all the appropriate condiments were carefully displayed around the roasted lamb that had been put in the middle of the dining table.

"We rarely eat livestock here in Elea. It would be cruel to make them live inside the mountain during the winter. If you prefer, I can send a message to my cook to take the lamb away and grill some trout for us."

One attendant remained at the door when he heard this, waiting to be given the order.

Yateem stared at the lamb for a moment and then burst into laughter. "Look who is pandering now."

Majlis dismissed the attendant with a wave of her hand and a sigh. "Please join me at the table, and I think silence will make this most enjoyable."

Yateem tried to chuckle quietly as he followed Majlis to the dining table, sat on the opposite end, and ate more than his fill of the scrumptious meal. They did not speak a word to each other, but their gazes would occasionally rise above their silverware and food, meeting each other like two seas crashing together.

When they were both done eating, Majlis stood and walked back to the middle section of the parlor. "Care for a nightcap and conversation by the fire?"

Yateem smiled as he pushed back his chair, straightening his shirt as he stood. "No, I believe we have offended each other enough. More alcohol may loosen our lips and cause real injury."

"Well then, thank you for your company. However tempestuous it might have seemed, I did very much enjoy our time together." Majlis gave a slight curtsey, and the fire and glacial light danced and swayed in her loose, blonde, wavy curls. Her skin seemed to glow, and the magenta in her eyes brightened, making her jade stare seem even more haunted.

Yateem bowed formally to her. "Thank you for the invitation. I am honored with your presence." He started to march out of the room, caught himself at the first leather chair, turned around, and marched back to Majlis.

"You may go, if you are looking for a dismissal, soldier." Majlis took a step back from Yateem's determined stride.

"I am only going to say this once, and I expect you to take my next statement into consideration the next time you... judge my behavior." Yateem took in a deep breath and shook his head. "You are infuriatingly gorgeous. In most cases, an impossible and highly implausible infatuation comes to a withered end because...because the subject-of-adoration's merits were grossly exaggerated in the lover's mind." His hands waved about as if that would help convey his emotions through his frustrated stammering.

"The memory of your projections would cause my mind to wander, and I came here tonight...I came here tonight to...or in the hope of proving to myself I had exaggerated your beauty beyond the realm of reality." Yateem brushed back the hair from Majlis' cheeks, cradling her face in his hands. "Your astral-projections did not show your wings, or the tiny flecks of magenta in your eyes." Yateem softly drew his thumb across the markings over her right eye. "Your beauty, your body...is maddening. It is like a sea that has stripped me bare of my senses and control and left me with nothing but useless, raw emotion." He looked into Majlis' eyes, his mouth open like a beached fish, gasping for words. "I cannot lose focus of the quest at hand. Please release me from this enchantment. Choose some other fool to be your plaything." Yateem pulled Majlis toward him. Just before their lips met, he sucked in a breath as if waking from troubled sleep, released his hold on her, and stepped back as if she were a green mamba.

The magenta had grown and consumed the jade in her eyes as he spoke those last words. Her mouth was set in a dignified glower, and she pushed Yateem's hands away from her as he released his grip and backed away. "The wisest words you have spoken thus were the ones that called for no more offense, but I see you have leapt across the boundary you set and aimed at injury.

"I have made no enchantment, especially not on a man so above love and 'raw emotion.' What you are feeling, Hebian soldier, is mutual attraction. I am not one to use men as my 'playthings,' as you so delicately called it. Love is something pure. Arivos told my late husband, Sinclair, that as long as love remains pure and selfless, there is hope for this world. To surrender to love is the bravest act a person can accomplish.

"For the sake of Zerahlinda, I pray Vera was taught what real love is by someone other than you, or else it is certain she will choose the same selfish path Draven did."

Majlis whipped Yateem's face with her wing as she flew to the door and stormed out of her parlor.

Chapter 26
Healing

The two serving trays clanked on the dining table in front of Majlis, who was so immersed in the journal in her hand that she had not noticed Yateem walk into the room.

"Thank you." Majlis raised her eyes, and her markings slightly darkened. "Why are there—" Her eyes caught on the teal of Yateem's.

"I am sorry." His hand gently pushed down on the alpaca shawl that covered her shoulder to dissuade her from standing. "If my presence makes you uncomfortable, I will leave, but please allow me to try to make amends."

Majlis closed the leather-bound journal in her hand and reached for her breakfast, which Yateem quickly placed in front of her. "Sit."

He bowed in gratitude, and they ate their porridge in silence. Once breakfast was eaten and the reviving tea drank, Majlis pushed the tray aside and opened the journal to read.

"I *am* sorry for what I said last night." Yateem looked at Majlis and then stared at his hands. "Accusing you of being some conceited enchantress…was moronic."

Majlis stared at the thick pages and elegant calligraphy with great earnestness.

"The truth is, I have no idea how to let someone love me. As an orphan on Aequitas, I was raised by scholars and then grew into a man while becoming a soldier. Logic and fighting are all I know. I met Zivan royalty due to my skill in battle. My knowledge was what singled me out to be the Lavender Soul's handler. During her infancy and early childhood, I was barely more than a guard to Vera…then her parents died." Yateem closed his eyes and let the light from the glacial window hit his face. "In an instant, I became everything to this little girl. There was nothing but the bond of being orphans, and my oath, to guarantee that we would never part." Yateem paused and traced the lines in his palms.

Majlis closed the journal and focused intently on Yateem and the words he was willing to share.

"Before that day, I had only held her once, when she was just a baby. When I told her the news of her parents, I went to cautiously hold her hand, and Vera jumped into my arms. Tears streamed down her little face, and those lavender eyes looked at me with all the sorrow of the world and yet with complete trust that I would love, protect, and nurture her without reserve—me, this rigid soldier who had stood at attention his whole life…You were wrong." Yateem looked up at Majlis, a little taken aback that her eyes were searching his. "I did not teach Vera what love is because I did not know that love could be anything more than a young man's passing fancy. She forced her way into my heart, taught me how to love…I just hope I showed her enough of that."

Majlis grasped his hand and kissed it. "I am certain you did."

Yateem ran his calloused thumb over her soft skin. "Do you not remember the warning you gave me?"

"I only said that *if* she came back dark, you should be prepared. I do not think she will choose that way."

"How can you say that?" Yateem stood up, suddenly feeling claustrophobic.

"It took Draven only a couple days to make his choice. If she is taking this long, it must mean…"

Yateem paced next to the table, his limp worse than the day before. "Is there a chance—I cannot believe I am about to say this—is there a chance that she could choose not to come back?"

Majlis ran her hand over the soft cracks of the leather cover of what she had been reading. "There is no way to know. I have been looking through all of Sinclair's journals, but he never goes into detail about what the Lavender Soul truly faces after death. He must not have known."

Yateem ran his fingers through his hair, trying to remain composed in front of the gorgeous fairy. "Nearly six days…I am going mad waiting like this."

"How long have you been limping?" Majlis stood to better assess Yateem's health.

"Seven days ago, the day before Vera was killed, we were attacked by natives of the Rinan Rainforest. A spear went through my leg."

"How did you heal it?" Majlis pointed toward the couch in the center of the room, ushering Yateem toward it.

"I had blessed salve made by the monks of Aminia. What the contents are, I do not know, but it sealed it, stopping the bleeding."

"And trapping the poison." Majlis gestured for Yateem to recline himself on the couch.

"Yes, but I drank some Sospitas water to accelerate my healing abilities, and I woke the next morning with a mostly healed leg." Yateem had to pick up his right leg and pull it onto the couch; the pain was starting to alarm him.

"You had no time to worry why it did not fully heal, or if some of the poison was still in you." Majlis walked over to the drink cart and poured Yateem a glass of water.

"One of the effects of the Sospitas water is to circulate through the blood and alleviate some of the long-term pain. I drank nearly all my canteen in a matter of thirty hours. First with this," Yateem held back a wince as he readjusted himself to drink the water that Majlis gave him, "and then when I needed to change my appearance."

"Save your Hebian water. I have something stronger. Are you attached to these pants?"

Yateem choked on the last gulp of water.

Majlis giggled lightly as she approached him with a knife. "I need to cut the pant to examine the wound."

"Of course." Yateem laid his head back on the velvet pillow behind him, crossing his arm over his flushed cheeks.

The cotton pant easily ripped apart under Majlis' precise touch and the sharp blade in her hand. Yateem's dark skin pulled tight toward the light scar tissue, which sagged down past the top of the leg, as if deflating. The veins that were visible around the wound were starting to spread a thick, black substance into Yateem's body.

"I thought Hebians were extraordinary healers. Have you not looked at this?" Majlis' eyes were wide, her tone scolding, and her wings gently beat to give herself fresh air.

When Yateem leaned forward, his mouth gaped open in confusion. "That is not possible. The poison is—"

"Liquefying your newly healed tissue and muscle and opening up the wound again. Those spears were not tipped with frog poison for hunting. They were enchanted with an evil meant to assassinate." Majlis hovered up and over the couch, heading toward the door, leaving Yateem with no explanation as to where she was going.

After a few moments, the heavy door opened again. Yateem lifted himself up enough to see the parade of servants scurrying in with towels, a heavy iron teapot with steam coming from its spout, a few basins, a tray of shiny blades, a small basket of dried sage, and Majlis holding a small parcel in her hands. The noble fairy excused everyone from the parlor.

"I am going to fix you." Majlis placed the wrapped parcel on the coffee table, gently lifted Yateem's right leg, and laid down several towels and an empty, carved wood basin underneath his bent knee.

Yateem grabbed her hand that was gently massaging the skin around the wound. "Thank you."

Majlis shook her head. "That is a bit premature. This is going to hurt. I would like to say I can take the pain away from you, but I cannot. I can only make you sleep so deeply that you will not thrash." She unwrapped the parcel on the coffee table, revealing a small wooden chest containing tiny luminescent pearls of every color imaginable.

"What are those?" Yateem looked curiously at the pearls.

"Have you not heard of pixie dust?" Majlis picked out a light-blue pearl with grace, shut the chest, and leaned over

Yateem. Pinching her fingers together, she crushed the glowing pearl and sprinkled it over his face.

Yateem blinked in a daze, and his eyelids grew heavy, his thoughts mystified. Majlis kissed each of his closed eyelids and then got to work.

With the dexterity of a surgeon, she used the scalpel to cut away the dying tissue and muscle and let it slop onto the wood beneath. Then she drained what had already liquefied into the wooden basin, rinsed the wound thoroughly with warm water, and wiped away all the drippings from the surface of his skin. Majlis took a few sprigs of sage and shoved them into the wound, watching with satisfaction as the blackness in the veins surrounding the opening receded, and the frosty green of the sage leaves started to darken. As the last of the poison was absorbed into the sage, Majlis pushed it through the wound and heard it splat into the basin. Yateem started to toss.

"No." Majlis looked at the large wooden bowl full of diseased flesh and poisoned blood, and then saw how much pain Yateem was in. She took the bowl, removed the protective grate from in front of the fireplace, and gingerly put the vessel on top of the fire. The basin exploded, and the rancid flesh and blood blew up into the chimney, a black cloud of smoke forcing Majlis back.

Yateem started convulsing, gasping for air.

"No, no, no, no, no!" Majlis flew over to the chest and grabbed a dark-purple pearl and a bright-orange one. Flying over to the iron teapot, she crushed the pixie dust into the hot water, threw a basin underneath Yateem's leg, pushed down on his chest with her left foot to try to control his convulsions, and poured the steaming water through the wound. Majlis held her breath, waiting for the potion to take effect, for Yateem to stop convulsing, for her world to stop cracking at its fragile edges.

As it surged through the opening, the hot potion loosened the muscle ligaments from where they had been sealed. The muscles started to rebuild, the cracked femur solidified into one piece, and the skin on either side grew back as darker, stronger scar tissue. Majlis could breathe again, but not calmly. Yateem still struggled to inhale, and she had already given him too much pixie dust; any more would mean certain death. With shaking hands, she removed the tin basin and poured it over the flames that consumed the poisoned wood. The dark-red fire was extinguished for a second and then returned, burning a bright purple for several minutes before returning to a natural flame.

Majlis sat on the floor and stroked Yateem's right hand. Kissing it, she laid her head against his rib cage so that she would know the proper time to say goodbye. "I will take care of her."

Chapter 27
Diversion

A soft substance tickled the inside of Yateem's elbow and woke him from his troubled sleep. Majlis lay with her head against his side, her golden hair draped over his arm, her markings dark in her sleep. His left hand reached over to feel the source of throbbing in his right leg. Majlis stirred as the door to the parlor clicked open.

The same woman who had brought Yateem tea walked on her toes until she could see that both Majlis and Yateem were awake. "Oh, pardon me, I thought I would come to pick up the dishes from lunch, but I see you haven't touch it yet."

Majlis stretched her hands out over Yateem's chest, feeling for his heartbeat. "Thank you, Persephone. You can take the solid food away. I believe both of us will do much better with broth and bread." She never once took her eyes off him.

"Yes, of course, M'Lady. Would you also like incense to burn the smell of blood out of the room?" Persephone walked straight to the dining table, stacked the plates, cups, utensils, and trays, while purposely not looking toward the couch.

Yateem smiled as he ran his fingers through Majlis' hair. "Does it smell like blood?"

"It's quite repulsive, sir." Persephone turned and started toward the door.

"We still have plenty of sage. I will burn it before you return." Majlis kissed Yateem's hand.

"Thank you, M'Lady, I will bring the broth as soon as I can." Persephone rushed out of the parlor.

Yateem softly chuckled once the door was shut. "Sorry I have been so troubling to such a dedicated woman."

"She will recover. As will you, thankfully." Majlis stood, gently pulling her hand from Yateem's grasp as she walked to get the sage and throw it on the fire.

"I never doubted I would." Yateem cocked his head to the side when he saw the blackened tin basin that was upside down on top of the roaring fire.

"You should have. The poison was more potent than I anticipated, and the amount of pixie dust I used would have killed most humans." Majlis turned and faced Yateem with shame.

"I did not expect that much pain, or having dreams of drowning in the deep, but now all I have is a throbbing." Yateem rubbed the scar tissue. "It feels whole again."

The hearty smell of burning sage brought flashbacks of Vera's death, and Yateem rubbed the back of his neck while staring at the tin basin.

"Sage was burning that night—I am so sorry!" Majlis grabbed the fire stoker to try to flick the sprigs off the firewood.

"I am fine. I would like it if…" Yateem paused when he heard the door open.

Persephone and a young girl walked in with the food. They set the small cauldron of broth, the bowls, some tea, and what smelled like freshly made soda bread on the table. "Anything else, M'Lady?"

"No, that is all."

When Persephone and the girl had excused themselves swiftly from the room, Yateem started to hoist himself up to a seated position.

"Stay there. You cannot walk on that leg today." Majlis strolled over to the table, ladled the thick broth made from lamb bones into a bowl, and tore a hunk of bread off the loaf.

"So I am supposed to sleep here?"

"I will help you get back to your room tonight." Majlis handed him the bowl of broth with the hunk of bread sticking out of it. "But until then, you are under my care."

Yateem smiled as he bit off a small piece of the soaked soda bread and slowly chewed, trying to gently introduce food to his traumatized body. "A scary prospect indeed."

The hours passed. Majlis was determined to distract Yateem's burdened mind with conversation and moments of comfortable silence, and by sharing with him whatever book he wanted to see in her library. She even started to teach him the ancient language of the fairies so that one day Yateem could read Sinclair's original writings. When Majlis saw Yateem fighting to keep his eyes open, she helped him hobble back to his room and bid him good night, promising that the next day would be equally diverting.

The next day was full of laughter, with only a tinge of sadness. When Vera was spoken of, it was as if she was in the other room, alive and well. At one point in the day, the furniture was rearranged so that Yateem could teach Majlis traditional Hebian dances. Her smile made his heart skip.

They sat close on the couch after dinner, content to do nothing but stare at one another.

"Are fairies allowed to love humans?" Yateem asked, stroking Majlis' hand.

"It is not recommended, but I have always had a problem following the rules others try to enforce upon me." Majlis' coy smile was radiant.

"It is a wonder why you and Vera did not become immediate friends."

Majlis traced her elegant finger over the curves of Yateem's face and leaned in toward him. Their lips collided as a gale meets a tsunami, with a desperate harmonic violence that burst from their passion.

"Wait." Yateem feebly pushed Majlis' torso away from his. "Wait."

"What?" Majlis' breath was sweet against Yateem's face.

"This is not fair to you." Yateem rested his forehead against hers, trying to distance their lips as far as he could. "I cannot give you my heart, not like this, not when it is broken and lying on the floor at Vera's icy feet."

"When will you let yourself be happy?"

"When this is over, when my task is done." Yateem held onto Majlis' hands with an anxiety that pleaded for love and acceptance…and forgiveness.

"Your life should not be ruled by tasks." Majlis leaned away from Yateem so that she could look into his eyes.

"Please understand, I am only thinking of you…"

"No. You are thinking of *her*. Will I ever come before her in your mind?"

"Can we talk of something else? I feel as if I am about to lose you, and that is something that I will not tolerate thinking about."

Majlis breathed out a heavy sigh and brushed the hair out of her face. "Yes, if you promise me one thing."

"Anything."

"When Vera comes back, be careful. That poison connected itself to your nervous system. There is no way to know if it somehow planted something in you, something meant to corrupt her."

Yateem rested his head in his hands, gripping his dark hair with his tightly curled fingers.

"When I told you that everything would seem to be against Vera, I never thought it would be…I never thought Draven would think to do *this*…and I am not certain of anything, but I thought it right to tell you."

Restraining himself from slamming a closed fist down on the coffee table in front of the couch, Yateem looked at Majlis. "How can I protect her? How can I, when I might be…"

Majlis reached her hand out for his. "I have yet to tell you of my childhood, and what a terror I was for my parents."

Stories that had happened before the evil of Draven were told with great charisma and enthusiasm. Yateem was swept away from his present fears, burdens, and worries by the bewitching nature of the pixie that sat, legs akimbo, on the couch, as if she were a child again. What should have felt like days in Yateem's darkened thoughts were but minutes in her presence, until weariness and the day's activities took their toll, and both fell asleep.

Chapter 28
Rise

Majlis lay on top of Yateem, listening to the lullaby of his steady heartbeat, her wings closed so that they would not wake him with a breeze.

Yateem lay with one arm behind his head and the other wrapped over Majlis' shoulders. She looked up and smoothly reached her hand to brush a dark wave of Yateem's hair away from his handsome face. He woke with a start, nearly knocking her off the couch.

"Sorry, I did not want to wake you so early." Majlis flapped her wings and gripped his shirt to keep from falling on the floor.

The breeze from her wings made Yateem more alert. "What time is it?"

"Just about dawn." Majlis folded her arms on his chest and smiled. "Our conversation must have been thrilling if we both fell asleep."

"Sorry, but that was the best sleep I have had since Vera died." Yateem lightly caressed Majlis' cheek.

"She will pass through soon."

"Not soon enough."

Talitha Koum. A whisper shivered through the room, barely audible, but it hit Yateem and Majlis like a lead spear to the heart, to hear words from a language so ancient and holy that no one dared to speak it out loud.

Majlis hovered above the couch, and Yateem jumped up.

"Draven?" Yateem looked around for a weapon.

"It is not possible. That language would choke him if he tried to utter it." Majlis flew to the door and opened it. The sound of running feet and hushed murmurs filtered into the parlor from the hall.

"We don't know that. He could have poisoned one of the residents here." Yateem joined her at the doorway with the fire stoker.

"I am the protector of Elea. All who live here are loyal to me."

"Everything is corruptible." Yateem slid by Majlis with the wrought-iron fire stoker in his hand, looking up and down the hallway, trying to sense a threat.

Talitha Koum. The voice was a spoken command that filled the heart with terrified wonder. Screams could be heard down the hallway.

"Vera." Yateem sprinted, a flash of hope in his eyes.

"This way." Majlis' wings beat so fast that they were only a blur of jade and magenta as she flew down a corridor to their right.

Yateem ran as fast as he could to keep up with Majlis' turns and tried not to collide with the frantic people pressed against the stone walls to make way for the lady of the castle and the stranger running after her.

"We cannot let him get to her," Yateem huffed out.

"This cannot be Draven. We would have been alerted," Majlis called back over her shoulder as she turned another corner and stopped in front of the enchanted stone wall that was the entrance to the icy passage.

Yateem clung to the fire stoker and panted next to Majlis. "Then why am I so afraid?"

"There is power beyond our imagining at work here." Majlis placed her hand on Yateem's shoulder. "We have no control over what is about to happen."

He could hear the rapid footsteps and panicked cries echoing throughout the halls. "Hold the enchantment. If Draven is coming, I want Vera to be as safe as possible." Yateem gripped the cold, wrought-iron stoker as he would a sword and turned toward the direction from which they had come.

Majlis looked at Yateem's tense body, his flexed back muscles pushing against the cotton fabric of his shirt. She leaned forward and lightly kissed the enchanted passageway and then backed away from the wall to watch the other direction, her wings barely brushing against Yateem's back.

TALITHA KOUM. This time the voice was a calm, clear declaration that sent a shock of exhilarated fear through all Elea. There was a moment of pure silence, then a wave of light shattered the enchantment to the icy passageway, knocking Yateem and Majlis into a jumbled heap of crushed rock and ice.

It all happened so fast that Yateem could do nothing except shield his face from the shards of ice, so completely caught off guard that he did not notice the flying debris was avoiding him. As both Majlis and he hit the ground with the rest of the flying ice and rock, the wave of pulsing light bounced and surged down the slick passageway.

"No!" Yateem scrambled to his feet, grabbed the fire stoker from under a chunk of rock on the floor, and raced clumsily toward Vera's frigid chamber. Slipping and stumbling on the thickening ice, the stoker held high, suddenly he lost all power and froze.

Vera stood in front of Yateem, the black tourmaline dagger Arivos gave her gripped in her hand. Her throat was no longer a gaping hole, but red and white mottled scar tissue, and the white dress Majlis had put on her showed the pallid gray scar that covered where the nyx venom ate the flesh of her left leg.

She simply stared at Yateem. "Do you really think you could kill me?"

Chapter 29
The Call

Majlis melted the ice blocks that pinned her wings to the ground, kicked the broken rocks off her legs, and was forced to run after Yateem because of her damp wings. She saw Yateem stop and fall to his knees, revealing Vera standing before him with a dagger in her hand and an emotionless expression on her face. Flashbacks came to her mind of Draven waking and laughing at the pain and heartache that throbbed out of the porcelain fairy's body, his black eyes piercing through any hope Majlis had had for his future. The images made her run faster, fearing what Vera might do to Yateem. "Do not dare hurt him!"

Yateem turned to look at Majlis with tears in his eyes. Cold water splashed on her legs as she sprinted toward them, melting the ice with every step. Yateem held his hand out toward Majlis. She reached for him, and just as their fingertips were about to touch, she hit an invisible wall. Majlis crashed into the force field like a wave hitting the face of a cliff, her body slamming down with a splash on the hard rock ground.

"Vera!" Yateem's voice echoed against the inside of Majlis' skull.

"She put me in an ice block!" Vera accused Majlis, hammering the fairy down with her words.

Although her head pounded, through the dizziness of her fall, Majlis commanded the water around her to help her stand. With a cloak of water around her, she turned the water around her head into lethal icicles, ready to plunge through Vera's black eyes.

"I'm going to be honest, I expected a little more hospitality, even from you, Majlis."

When Majlis looked into Vera's eyes and saw the shifting shades of lavender, the icicles and liquid cloak fell to her feet in a silent waterfall. The powerful fairy dropped down to her knees, closed her wings, and bowed her head.

"Forgive me," she said. "Wounds from my past made my eyes blind to the glorious truth of the present."

Yateem threw a cautious look of reproach to Vera, who sighed and reached her hand out to help Majlis stand.

"I was dead. What do I care if I was in a glacier for a day."

"A week."

"What?"

Yateem stood, lightly touched the scar tissue that composed Vera's throat, and then embraced her tightly. "You were gone seven days."

Vera pulled away from the hug just far enough to be able to look in his eyes. "And now I've returned."

"Triumphant!" Yateem tried to tell himself that the unsettling shift of Vera's once-familiar eyes was caused by the tears building up in his own.

Majlis took an awkward step back, her natural grace lost in the feeling of intruding on the reunion. "My apologizes again for your accommodations. I wanted you to be safe, and I did not know how long you would take to make your decision. A decayed body would not be of use to you."

"Speaking of, may I have a hot bath?" Vera asked, resting her head on Yateem's chest.

Majlis' eyes slightly narrowed as she watched Yateem holding Vera, but she managed to regain her composure. "Of course. I will have my attendants ready a room close to Yateem's and draw a bath with hot oil for you. Are you hungry?"

"Yes, who knew dying and coming back would be so famishing."

"I will have a breakfast made up for you." Majlis stared at Yateem's enraptured face, hesitating to leave the two of them.

Vera gave Majlis a confused look. "I didn't know you're telepathic like your king and queen."

Majlis snapped to attention as if being awakened. "What? Oh, right, I shall go and prepare for you."

Vera tightened her embrace around Yateem's waist before releasing him and taking a step away. "I do appreciate it. Death doesn't smell good on anyone."

Majlis gave a quick smile, then turned and walked away with rigid shoulders, stiff wings...and a seemingly bruised ego.

Yateem looked at Vera's scars with veiled shame. "How does walking feel?"

Vera's eyebrows furrowed. "What do you mean?" Her eyes followed Yateem's distracted gaze to her scar. "That wasn't a nightmare?"

Yateem found it easier to look at the ground when he shook his head. "I had to burn you to keep the venom from spreading any farther."

Vera placed her hand on his cheek. "It feels a bit tight, a little out of place, but I am alive and can walk—and apparently throw force fields. I may have to play with that one a little bit." She grinned smartly at him and then felt her throat. "I must be quite the terror to see."

Yateem kissed her hand. "You are the most beautiful sight I have ever seen."

Vera started to walk down her private hall, the icy water quietly sloshing under her bare feet. "I will feel more beautiful after I get clean."

Yateem joined her and showed her the way through the stone maze.

"I meant to ask before Majlis left us...what happened between you two while I was dead?"

"What do you mean?"

"Majlis was very jealous...and a little bit angry at me for hugging you."

"Majlis probably seemed that way to you—"

"No, I felt her energy swirling around us, wanting to be between us. Just as I feel your feelings for her rising in your chest...dare I say love?"

"Vera, I drove myself mad with worry while you were gone."

"Mad enough to fall in love with an immortal?"

Yateem stopped in front of the door to his chamber. "Vera..."

"Your Majesty?" A young maid bowed before them, her face stuck in a look of regret at the possibility of being an interruption. "Your bath is ready."

Vera smiled at her. "Thank you. I will see you at breakfast, Yateem."

He leaned against the wall and watched her walk a couple doors down, her head held high.

They sat at Majlis' table eating breakfast—or rather Vera ate anything she could get her hands on, Yateem pushed his food around his plate as he ogled Vera, and Majlis sat with an empty plate in front of her, staring at both her guests.

Majlis looked at Vera as if she were a poisonous scorpion whose venom was about to cure an epidemic. "Have you any clue as to where Zakiyyah sleeps?"

Vera set down her fork and looked up at Majlis with a conflicted look. "No." Her body tensed and froze, the lavender of her eyes intensifying and shining, like light glinting off amethyst.

"Vera?" Yateem reached over to touch her rigid hand that gripped a silver butter knife.

She sucked in a deep breath, as if just surfacing after being trapped in an underwater cave. Vera released the knife, pulled her hand out from under Yateem's, and stood. "We have to go." She immediately headed for the door.

Both Majlis and Yateem pushed their chairs away from the table, stood, and turned to watch Vera's determined march.

"Where are you going?" Yateem's voice tried to come off as inquisitive, but his furrowed brow just confirmed the tenor of concern in his question.

"Do you have my clothes? A dress won't work." Vera reached the door and looked over her shoulder at them.

"Yes, but you need to rest, recuperate." Yateem paced toward her.

"I was dead. I don't need any more rest." She put her hand on the bronze sea urchin.

Majlis flew over close to Vera. "Might I suggest you delay, get accustomed to the changes."

"Might I suggest that I have my clothes." Vera was reaching the point of detached anxiety. "It is calling, and I have no time to be instructed."

"Zakiyyah is calling out to you?" Majlis' face lit up with hope.

"Darkness is beckoning. I can't stay here." Vera's eyes grew wild.

Yateem put his hand over Vera's and pulled open the door, motioning for her to continue into the hall. "Do you know where we must go?" His voice was shaky, but urgently formal.

"The sea, I saw us on the sea." Vera got into the hall and let Majlis fly in front of her so that she could get to her clothes and chamber without getting lost.

A gentle tap on the door paused Vera's frantic rush to get changed into her tan riding pants and periwinkle cotton button-down shirt. Her bare feet smacked loudly against the stone floor as she jogged to the door. When she opened it, she found Majlis standing there with a serious expression on her face. The fairy closed her wings and walked past Vera into the room.

"Please, do come in." Vera gave an exaggerated bow.

"Sorry, I know you are preparing for your journey, but I need a private audience."

Vera closed the door and started to tuck her shirt into the waistband of her pants. "Let me dismiss the masses," she said as she swept her gaze around the empty room and then looked at Majlis. "Private audience granted."

The Lady of the seas breathed a heavy sigh. "I found something on your body that deeply alarmed me when you first came here."

"Was it that most of my throat and the flesh on my leg were missing, or that I was dead?" Vera strode over to the vanity and sat on the stool to put on her socks and journey-stained leather boots.

"Vera, stop and listen to me."

"Will you please get to the point because I'm in a hurry to do some pretty big things." She pulled on her second boot, purposely not looking at the fairy.

Majlis chucked the small round object in her hand at Vera's feet.

Vera bent down and picked up Radov's pin, smoothly caressing it with a small smile on her lips.

"I did not show Yateem," Majlis said. "He had enough to worry about."

"Like whether or not to kill me as soon as I woke?" Vera glared up at Majlis.

"How did you...I only meant that if you did not pass through the gate."

"Which you were so sure I wouldn't!"

"Do you know what that is?" Majlis pointed at the pin as if it was going to explode.

"A token from a man I care for."

"Care for?" She was horrified.

"Yes, a man I care for. A man that you helped sentence to an eternity in prison!"

"Vera, you do not know what you are saying. If I had had the strength, I would have killed him and saved him from what he is now!"

Vera unbuttoned the top of her shirt and pinned the white raven-crest pendant over her heart. "I will free him."

"He is in a prison of his own choosing!"

"Who would choose a hundred years of shape-shifting!" Vera stood up, outraged.

"Shape-shifting?" Majlis' eyes widened with a spark of recognition, and she grabbed Vera's hands. "You do not know him. I beg you…throw it in the fire."

"Do not touch me!" Vera ripped her hands out of Majlis' grip.

"Darkness is not calling to you. You are calling out to it, and the frightening thing is that you don't even recognize that."

"Get out." Vera growled as she pointed to the door.

"Vera, please listen to me."

"No, you listen to me now. I am the Lavender Soul. Arivos chose me, not you. Just as He chose your late husband to hear His voice, and not you. You have not been chosen to act a part in this. You have no say. *You* have but to watch as *I* save Zerahlinda."

Majlis' slapped Vera's cheek. "If you will not listen to me, listen to yourself. It is disgusting!"

Vera lashed out and grabbed a handful of Majlis' beautiful blonde curls. "You are the disgusting one, always testing others, never having faith in anyone. I can feel your fear of me. If you say anything to make Yateem doubt me again, I will prove to you how right you are to be afraid." Vera threw Majlis' face away from her own.

Majlis smoothed her hair away from her cheeks to show a livid smile. "I want to have faith in you, but cannot bring myself to be so impossibly optimistic. Know this—I will not allow another Dark One in this world. If you decide to continue on this path toward Draven, I will kill you."

"You dare threaten me?"

"It is not a threat. It is a vow." Majlis strode over to the door and was out of the room before Vera could respond.

Vera turned to the vanity to give herself a victorious smile in the mirror when she saw that her eyes were no longer lavender, but a light violet color. Her smile vanished. "Who am I?" she whispered.

Sinking down on the velvet cushioned stool, she looked at her reflection, running her hands over the smooth ripples of the scar that covered her neck, avoiding eye contact with herself. Vera closed her eyes. "You are strong, you are beautiful, and you passed through death to do what you were made to do. So why are you fighting?"

"Ready?" Yateem stood at the door with his pack secured on his back and his sword at his side.

Vera opened her eyes and let out a relieved sigh as she stared into the lavender irises that looked back at her from the mirror. "Majlis talk to you?"

"Yes, she said we need to leave now. Did you two fight?"

"Overall, I have to say she has been the most gracious of hosts, and I simply recognized that." Vera pet the dragon that still perched on her right index finger.

"Grab your pack."

"Do you love her?"

"My feeling is that we are running out of time."

Vera looked away from the mirror and toward Yateem. "When will duty be put aside?"

"When our purpose is fulfilled."

"Is that when we will have a choice in life?" She walked over and picked up the deerskin vest that lay on her pack. Lined with soft alpaca wool, it was every bit as warm as her old lambskin vest, but less comforting.

"There is always a choice. You made the biggest decision of your life when you passed through that gate."

"Why didn't you tell me I can choose to become evil after passing through the gate?" Vera shoved her arms through the straps of her pack.

"Is that what you and Majlis talked about?" Yateem rubbed the back of his neck.

"No. Draven told me before I died. Why did you keep that from me?"

"I could not risk you doubting yourself."

"I feel like every moment is a test, and with every breath I can feel darkness creeping in around me. If I could feel you doubt me, like I can feel Majlis does…" She walked over and grabbed the tourmaline dagger off the vanity counter, the jagged stone cold against her skin as she rolled it in her palm, the dragon ring making an unsettling scratching noise each time the ancient weapons met.

"I will never stop believing in you."

Vera did not respond as she pushed past Yateem and walked into the hallway.

Majlis stood at the end of the hall talking to one of her attendants in what appeared to be a franticly heated conversation. When Majlis saw Yateem and Vera, she dismissed the attendant and flew over to them.

"What's wrong?" Yateem stepped closer to Majlis and resisted grabbing her hand.

Her jade and magenta eyes flitted to Vera's eyes for the smallest of moments before she gave a forced smile to Yateem. "Nothing."

Yateem stroked his hand along Majlis' jawline. "I am no fool."

As his lips gently pressed against her fair cheek, Majlis looked at Vera. "One can always hope."

He stepped back, cocked his head to the side, and furrowed his brow, waiting for an explanation.

"I cannot accompany you to my boat, but I can show you the tunnel that will lead you to it."

"Why?" Yateem's question was warm and concerned.

"Elea is under attack. Draven has found Vera." Majlis gave Vera a knowing look when she saw the Lavender Soul bring her hand up over her heart. "Vera was right to say that darkness is seeking her."

Yateem drew his sword. "Tunnel. Now."

Majlis turned and flew down the hall, Yateem and Vera had to sprint to keep up with her. The farther they went, the fewer doors and turns, and then it was just one dank hall with no doors. Only the torches Majlis and Yateem had grabbed from the inhabited halls shed light on the uneven ground on which they were running. It felt like they were in the core of the mountain, and only the heat of the blood rushing through their veins as they sprinted kept them from stopping to put on heavy jackets. Soon the floor of the hall was a stream that Yateem and Vera were trying to quickly slosh through.

The tunnel seemed to dead-end into an impenetrable stone wall. Majlis turned and looked at them as both stood catching their breath. "Once I open this passage, you have to hurry. The tunnel was built as an escape route for me and will gradually collapse behind you."

"How long?"

"Once dusk hits the other opening, the tunnel will be destroyed."

"I'm sorry…I'm not used to…living in a rock prison… how long do we have until the tunnel crashes down on us?" Vera huffed.

Majlis rolled her eyes. "About eight hours."

"And how far north in Ruwaydah are we?"

"More than a day's walk by way of the hills of Yakootah. The tunnel should make it faster." Yateem lightened his tone so as not to distress Vera.

As Vera leaned against the cool gray stone of the hallway, she started to take in deep breaths. "There has to be a better way."

"Unless one of your new given powers is teleportation, this is your option. Take it, or face Draven before he tries to take the mountain down." Majlis' voice was carefully controlled, her stare frigid.

Vera glared back.

"The hall is wide enough to allow me to fly, but the ground was not manipulated much." Majlis held out a thin, broken bluish-silver chain to Vera and looked at the black dagger. "You will need both hands."

Grabbing the chain with a quick fist, Vera cautiously let it go through the handle end of the funnel and was slightly shocked when she saw the chain was thin enough to go through the tiny hole at the end of the dagger.

"It is made from osmium, the strongest substance on Zerahlinda. It came from the cooled magma of an underwater volcano. It will not corrupt the dagger in any way, and once the ends of the chain touch together, it will not break unless the owner of it wills it to."

Vera put the chain around her neck and brushed her auburn hair out of the way so that she could touch the ends together. They fused with a warm snap, and the dagger lay like a big heavy pendant on her chest. She shoved it underneath her shirt for safekeeping. "Thank you," she muttered with reluctant gratitude.

"*Arivos* be with you." The magenta in Majlis' irises grew into thin spindles.

"And you."

Majlis turned to Yateem. "I beg you, never falter. Know that if I could—"

Yateem cut off her goodbye with a kiss. "As certain as Vera is the true Lavender Soul, I will see you again."

Majlis wrapped her arms around Yateem's waist. "Nothing is certain these days." She lightly pressed her lips against his and then strode over to the stone wall. A silver dust fell to the ground as her hand swept over it. With a few mumbled words, the wall turned into silver water that fell to join the stream and rush down the hallway.

"Hurry." Majlis flew off without looking back.

Yateem held up the torch in his hand and started to walk forward in the ankle-deep stream, running his hand along the left wall to help him stay upright. Vera kept her right hand on the wall and held her left hand out for balance. The torch did provide light but little help, because it only reflected off the moving water. They both had to keep up a steady pace while trying to feel for the smooth parts in the ground with their feet.

"What did you mean when you said you 'saw us on the sea'?" Yateem asked as he nearly tripped in an unseen divot.

"Is now really the time for a chat?" Vera replied, successfully avoiding the divot.

"Do you have a better idea of how to pass the time in this place?"

"Yeah, with a little more light, my eyes are hurting."

The flame of the torch in Yateem's hand doubled in size. He stopped and looked at it, and then stared at Vera. "Did you?"

"No…I don't think so." She looked as confused as Yateem.

Rocks crashing together in the distance demanded both of their attentions.

"How much longer do we have?"

"Impossible to say, we must keep moving." Yateem snuck a quick glance at Vera and then the flame before he continued with increased speed.

"If I could've seen this piece of the future, I wouldn't have eaten so much!" Vera grabbed at either side of the hall, bouncing from side to side in an attempt to run down the stream without falling on her face.

For hours they ran, slipped, nearly extinguished the torch, and beat their hands raw on the stone walls that, from all indications of the volume of crushing rocks behind them, were collapsing at a faster rate than they had anticipated.

Finally, dim, natural light shone in front of them.

"Nearly there!" Yateem had to shout above the sound of the latest collapse.

The rocks came down so close that they knocked Vera on her hands and knees, her feet just inches from being trapped. "Go faster!" She pushed herself up and ran into Yateem, nudging him along.

They were ten feet from the exit when the rock above their heads started to crack.

"We're not going to make it!"

"Throw a force field!"

"What?"

"Throw a force field against the rocks! We'll make it!"

Vera held onto the back of Yateem's collar, closed her eyes, and then let a concentrated burst of energy hit the now-falling rocks. It was like setting off a bomb. The rocks were blown back, and the two of them were propelled out of the hall and thrown over the ramp that led to a dock. They hit the dock like cannonballs with no time to recover. When they looked up, they saw the rain of boulders that was falling directly toward them.

Yateem grabbed Vera by the waist and hoisted her to her feet. "Come on!" He ran toward the sloop tied onto the end of the dock.

"Wait!" Vera raised her hands up in the sky and whispered, "We need time."

The boulders slowed, as if gravity had little effect on them.

Yateem took his sword and slashed through the thick ropes that held the small ship secure. "Vera, there is no time!" He held onto the railing of the boat and looked back toward the girl…and lost all sense of authority and control at the sight of the slothful avalanche of rock.

Vera jogged to the end of the dock and jumped on board Majlis' ship. "We need to go. They'll drop soon."

Yateem pushed off from the dock as he boarded the vessel with ease. "How?" He made himself busy with unfurling the sails and looking at the bright oranges and reds of the sunset instead of the wavering color of Vera's eyes.

"I asked the rocks for more time."

"You knew that was going to work? Like the torch?" As the two triangular sails lightly flapped in the breeze, Yateem jogged to the aft of the sloop, placing himself behind the steering wheel. His hands gripped two of the handles, but his eyes were staring at the boulders.

"No, but I figured it was worth a try." Vera tentatively walked around the cabin of the sloop, her fingers gliding across the mast as she passed it to grip the wooden railing at the bow. "Brace yourself."

The boulders ended their lazy descent and fell into the sea with a monstrous roar, sending a large wave that propelled the sloop out of the little mountainous cliff bay and into the open water.

During the night a storm rolled in.

Yateem struggled to aimlessly steer against the wind that beat a torrent of rain on the ship. "Where are we going?" he yelled out to Vera.

She stumbled toward the wheel, trying to maintain her footing. "I don't know."

"You said you saw us on the sea!"

"I don't know if you've noticed, but the sea is a big place. I could've seen us anywhere!"

"Can you not look and see where we are supposed to go now?"

"The vision just hit me. I don't know if I can control them!"

"Well, I need a heading. We cannot get lost in a storm at night! Either ask the rain to stop falling, or ask for a vision."

"Oh wow, brilliant, I hadn't thought of that!" She grabbed at anything she could get her hands on to steady herself, and to make herself feel less like the storm had originated in her stomach.

"I have to trust your navigation. The least you could do is try!"

Vera walked over to the railing of the schooner, closed her eyes, and breathed in the heavy storm air. She reached out with her energy, trying to feel for a spark of light. Her energy swirled around her, one big cloud of anxious desperation and hope pounding on her brain. As much as she wanted certainty, she could not find it. "We keep to our current course," Vera shouted over the wind at Yateem. "When my vision changes, I'll let you know."

Yateem kicked a coiled rope over to himself, and while holding the wheel, he tied a small loop in the rope that he put over one of the handles of the steering wheel, and then secured the line to the pilothouse, the part of the ship that protects the wheel and pilot from harm, thus anchoring the steering wheel on its current course.

They sailed through the night. Yateem sat on the deck and leaned against the wheel, nodding off every once in a while. At his request, Vera went below into the cabin and slept in Majlis' sleeping quarters for the rest of the night.

As the dawn feebly shone through a break in the storm clouds on the horizon, Vera opened the hatch and crawled onto the deck. The new day seemed to have invigorated the storm; the winds picked up, and the waves with them.

"Did you sleep?" Yateem shouted.

"Did you?"

"As much as I needed."

"When is this going to get easier?" Vera clung onto the side railing of the ship, fighting the urge to vomit as the storm violently rocked the vessel.

"When the storm eases," Yateem yelled back at her as he fought the wheel to turn.

Vera screamed over the wind, "If this is what I'm supposed to be doing, why does everything in our path have to fight us?" She staggered over and looked at Yateem through the spokes of the wheel.

She shrieked, her eyes shone like amethyst, and her blank stare pierced through him as she gripped one of the spokes and pulled down with incredible strength, turning the rudder with ease against the resistance of the storm. Yateem let go of the handles and let the wheel spin until Vera stopped it, and became present in her body again.

"We have to go that way." Vera pointed in the direction her vision told her.

Yateem curled his fingers around two of the handles of the wheel, wiped the rain off his face with his upper arm, and let out the breath he had been holding during her trance. "You just steered the ship that way."

"Oh. Sorry."

"Is Zakiyyah on Aequitas, because that is where you just changed our course to." Yateem's exasperated yell was nearly swallowed up by the roar of the storm.

"I've told you, I don't know where It is. I only see the next step." The last half of her screamed response seemed far too loud for the suddenly placid sea and calm sky.

Yateem and Vera looked around them in wonder. The sun hurt their eyes, which had been so used to the clouds pouring rain on them, and their ears felt the suction of silence in the absence of wind and crashing waves.

"See, have faith. We must be on the right course." Vera's whisper filled up the silence as if she had still been yelling.

"Be careful." Yateem placed the loop on one of the handles to keep the ship on course and walked up beside Vera to look at the calm water.

"Yes, because calm waters kill so many." She rested her hand on the railing of the ship and breathed in the crisp after-storm air.

"The road that welcomes you with smooth tread is rarely the pathway to good."

"That doesn't make sense. If Arivos wants people to be good, why does He make it hard?"

Five light-pink flukes breached the water one hundred feet west of the sloop.

"Tie me to the mast." Yateem's face was flushed as he jumped on top of the cabin's roof and stood next to the mast.

"What?" Vera examined Yateem's face to look for signs of sleep deprivation.

"Quick, before I fight you." Yateem kicked a coiled-up rope toward Vera, tore two strips off the bottom of his shirt, and started shoving them in his ears.

"I don't understand. Is this a joke?" She hoisted the coiled rope over her shoulder.

"Just hurry!" Yateem's voice was awkwardly loud due to his ears being plugged.

"Fine, fine." Vera started to wrap the rope around the mast that Yateem was holding onto with his eyes clenched shut.

A breeze fluttered the end of the strip in Yateem's left ear and started to loosen it. "Vera, push the strip—" The piece of cloth fell out and blew off in the wind. "No!"

"What's the matter?" Vera stopped wrapping the rope around Yateem. "Are those pink dolphins?"

The pink flukes surfaced next to the boat, and a smooth, hypnotic melody rose out of the water with them. Yateem started screaming to try to drown the sound. Vera walked over to the side of the boat in a catatonic state and gazed upon the strangest—and most enchantingly gorgeous—creatures she had ever seen.

Their hair was luscious, spiraled sea grass that beautifully floated and swayed in the calm waters. From the hip down, the mermaids had the slick, rubbery tail and fluke of a pink dolphin, while the top half of their bodies looked human. Their skin matched the color of the sea, vacillating with the many shades of blue in the water. Soft-pink coral stemmed from their tails; the pale, cord-like trunk of the coral wrapped around their seductively toned waists and then branched off into two plumes of thousands of tiny feathery tentacles that covered their breasts. Their eyes intently stared at Vera, and time felt slow as the deep-black of their pupils started to branch out into tiny reef designs within their rich, red coral irises. The mermaids' stares wrapped themselves around Vera as they batted their white eyelashes and curled their navy-blue lips into sadistic smiles.

Vera could not move. All she could do was adore the terrible beauty before her. Not even Yateem's incessant yelling could distract Vera's reverence.

"Yateem, how can anything be so beautiful? Come look."

"Finish tying me tight, and tie yourself!" Yateem's voice cracked from desperate exertion.

The mermaids swam around the ship with devious smiles on their faces. Their arms slowly and peacefully flowed through the water, their three-inch long nails gleaming like the inside of an abalone shell.

"They want to help us." The dragon ring was trying to beat its wings and grow, but Vera put a force field around it that kept it dormant to the evil surrounding the ship.

"Vera, please!"

"Yateem." The mermaids' voices harmonized and made his name sound like the sweetest melody ever created.

"No!" Yateem started to thrash against the coils of rope that held his hands against the mast.

The little gold dragon broke the force field around it and flapped its wings a few beats. "What's happening?" Vera had power over her mind again, and ran to Yateem.

"Untie me. I need to cover my ears!"

The mermaids stopped circling, gathered on the port side of the boat, and sang a soft, melodic song that swept through the air and wrapped itself around Yateem's neck and mind.

"I can cover your ears!" Vera went to cover his ears with her hands.

He snapped his teeth at her like a caged animal. "No. You must untie me."

The song's volume and intensity increased, and tears started to well in Vera's eyes as she involuntarily started to untie and uncoil the rope. When it was down to the last few coils, Yateem brutishly pushed the rope to the deck and then shoved Vera aside as he rushed to the port side. Recovering quickly, Vera ran and threw her arms around his waist, and planted her feet against the railing of the boat to stop him from jumping into the water.

"Fight it! You're strong! Fight it!" Her muscles were pushing past their limits to resist Yateem's desires.

The mermaids smiled up at him, each one motioning for him to come into the water, their long nails glittering in the sunshine, the song beckoning sensually to him.

Yateem ripped the piece of cloth that was still plugging his right ear, breathed in the spellbinding notes, and elbowed Vera in the chest. He turned and smiled sweetly at Vera as she lay on the deck. "I *want* to give in," he said before he dove in the middle of the mermaids.

They surged on him. One grabbed his head as the others each grabbed a limb. Yateem beamed up at Vera as the mermaids pushed him underwater. Vera pulled herself up in horror.

"Stop!" Vera screamed.

"Stop?" The mermaids spoke in a harmonized musical snarl as they pulled Yateem up to take in a euphoric breath of air. "Who are you to order us?"

"Someone who has recently died and would like her handler back!" she shouted angrily.

The sea creatures' laughter sent electric shivers up Vera's spine. They each started to kiss Yateem's skin, which made him fight—not to be free, but to dive into the water. "You see…" their voices were staggered, echoing one after another, all a beautiful lyric that made Vera dizzy, "…he wants to go to our home. He does not care for the duties of a nurse any longer."

"What do you want?" Vera gripped the side of the ship, her nails making indents in the sturdy wood plank.

"It's not what we want." Their cannon of hypnotic voices made Yateem dunk his head under the water again. "It's what you desire most, Lavender Soul."

"Just tell me what I have to do to get Yateem!"

The black reef designs in their irises flared and then contracted back to the pupil, like a squid descending into the deep. "Give in."

"Give in?" Vera stood up straight.

"To the dark. See how happy Yateem is now?"

"Give in to the dark."

"Become our queen."

"Queen of all Zerahlinda."

"Save all that you love."

"Command and smite all who displease you."

"Give in to the comforting cold of the dark."

"Save him. Save him. Save your precious Yateem."

Their voices swelled, the phrases flowing in and out of each other, repeating over the others, somehow changing with each echo, like a song reverberating off the rocks and water in a cave. It curled its tentacles around Vera, the melodic words stroking the inside of her ears. Vera's legs grew weak, her mind feeble. She could do nothing but focus on the hands that gripped Yateem so tightly.

"He loves you. Why will you not join him?" The song of their voices mellowed to a sweet, cooing inquiry.

"He would tell me to fight if he could." Vera was dazed. "He would want me to fulfill my purpose."

The mermaid that cradled Yateem's head in her blue hands glared at Vera and gave her a contemptuous smile. Grabbing a fistful of his hair, she lifted his face up so that their cheeks touched. Yateem stared with awe at her as if she were the incarnation of love. "Not him." The mermaid stroked the right side of Yateem's jawline, leaving a dark-green liquid to seep into the cut her nail left. "Draven will make you the ruler of the world. He will do all that you bid."

As the green poison of the mermaid's nail sank into the cut along his jaw, Yateem woke from the mermaids' spell. He looked at the creatures that gripped him tightly and started to thrash against them. "Vera, go! Pray for wind and leave!"

Vera stared down at Yateem in despair, and then looked back at the mermaid gripping the base of his head, trying to hold him steady. "Draven is a disease." Vera pointed at Yateem and said, "If you release him, I promise I will make Draven's death quick."

"You dare refuse and threaten our master!" All the mermaids shrieked at Vera and then shoved and held Yateem underwater. "For that, you will watch him die!"

Vera had no voice to let the scream that ripped her insides out. She had no tears as she looked each mermaid in the eye. She could feel her horrified rage pulsing around her. It intoxicated her mind as she focused on Yateem's weakening body, his flailing slowing.

Vera closed her eyes and gathered all her rage close to her with a deep breath. When she opened her eyes, the lavender seemed to be on fire. Even her pupils had changed from black to deep purple. "Let him go!"

It was a command rather than a yell, and would have only made the mermaids laugh had Vera not released all her rage at them in an energy force field that lit the temptresses on fire. Their screams were a mixture of tortured harmonies as their nails stuck into Yateem and their bodies sank to the depths of the sea, seared by a fire that all the water in Zerahlinda would not extinguish.

As Yateem's anguished screams mingled with the diminishing ones of the sinking mermaids, Vera looked on with horror at the scene she just caused.

Yateem struggled to swim to the side of the ship, each movement accompanied by a yell of pain. He reached up a very shaky arm that had ten long abalone nails jutting out of it.

Snapping out of her shock, Vera truly saw Yateem and his need. Behind her was the tangled rope at the bottom of the mast. She hurried to grab an end and run it over to Yateem. He grasped on to it and tried his best to help Vera hoist him over the railing. He came down on the deck with a crack.

The nails turned from the beautiful iridescence to the jagged, flaky, rigid gray of the outside of the abalone shell. The dark-green poison seeped into each puncture wound. Vera leapt down and started to rip the nails out with both her hands, ignoring Yateem's screams and the wind that started to raise the waves that slapped against the ship. Once Vera got ten nails out of Yateem's right leg, she frantically remembered the poisoned nails that were sticking out of his neck. Slipping around him, she wrapped her scraped fingers around one of the nails.

Yateem grabbed her hand in spastic panic. "No. It is done." He took a labored breath. "You made the right choice. Let me go so you can…" His eyes rolled back as he passed out.

Vera looked at her hands, bloodied by her efforts to save Yateem. The waves threw the sloop, knocking it off the course that the line attached to the wheel tried so hard to keep it on. Spray from the ferocious sea blurred her vision and stung the small cuts on her hands as she smeared blood all over her face, attempting to clear the water out of her eyes. As she stared at Yateem's limp body and watched blood ooze out the ten puncture wounds on his leg, she noticed the green tinge to his skin around the forty shell-nails still stuck into his dark skin. Her throat burned as the stomach acid rose. She fought the familiar urge to vomit as she realized that he would bleed out in minutes if she pulled out the rest of the mermaids' parting gifts. As the small sloop rocked, Vera grabbed the collar of Yateem's shirt and dragged him in front of the pilothouse, assuring herself that he could not roll off the sloop there.

She had no choice but to let him lie on the deck and get slowly poisoned to death as she struggled to navigate the sloop by herself. Vera closed her eyes, took a deep breath, and said a silent prayer over Yateem. At that moment, a wave crested over the ship and crashed down on the two of them. He screamed as the salt water reacted with the poison in his skin, causing the shells to sink even farther. Vera opened her eyes, the color in them ignited, the expression blank. She looked through Yateem, deaf to his agony.

In her trance she stood and walked with grace to the steering wheel, like she was gliding across a ballroom. The gale and waves had no effect on her as she removed the rope that was at its breaking point. Spinning the wheel against the pull of the storm, she held it with unwavering strength.

For hours, she went in and out of her trance state, and each time she came out of it, she was more drained; it got harder to hold the wheel on its course. The storm was so fierce that she could not tell if it was day or night. The dark, gloomy tempest beat down on her, but no matter how tired and hungry she was, or how horrible Yateem's condition, the only choice she had was to stay at the wheel, or let the sea swallow them.

Vera felt rigid, her body stuck in its position at the wheel. Yateem went in and out of consciousness with fits of tortured screaming as waves crashed on him, sinking the shells deeper and deeper each time.

A light directly in front of the ship alarmed Vera, until she realized that it was a lantern hanging from the last post on a dock. Steering the ship so that the dock was on the starboard side, Vera sloppily jumped onto the dock, her legs halfway collapsing under her weight, and tied the sloop to it with two lines.

Another light moved out of the fog that surrounded the dock and hid the land to which it was connected. Sounds of footsteps followed it. Vera looked at Ierá Flóga, its lack of agitation reflecting in her countenance as she watched two men dressed in royal blue uniforms march toward her.

"Who wishes for harbor at this late hour?" spoke the man that held the lamp in a stern, formal voice. His partner had a hand on the hilt of his sword.

"Where am I?" Vera's head was held high, her voice hoarse.

"The port of Sanctimonia." The guard's look of suspicion turned to one of concern when he took in the blood-smeared adolescent that had been seemingly lost on the sea. "Aequitas?"

"Where have you come from?" The guard came closer and lifted the lantern to shine on Vera's face. Upon seeing her eyes, both men fell to their knees. "What can we do?"

"Do you know Yateem Rukan Wulfgar of Xipili?"

"We trained together. But he no longer resides on the island."

"Get off your knees. I need you to get him out of the boat and to an expert healer."

Their faces paled as they stood and peered over the railing. "What happened to him?"

"Mermaids. When I killed them, they detached their nails into him, and every time seawater touched them, they sank deeper into his skin. You can barely see them now, but make sure to tell the healer they are inches into him, and poisonous."

One of the guards handed Vera the light and then motioned for his companion to join him on the ship. They lowered the gangplank so that they could walk Yateem off easily. As he was lifted up in his former comrades' arms, Yateem groaned before they gently conveyed him down to the dock.

The guard who had been silent until now stared at Yateem in distress, the light from the lantern gleaming in his turquoise eyes as he took it from Vera and looked at his partner. "I will go wake the healer, and get a cart to deliver him in." He bowed quickly toward Vera and then ran with the lantern into the fog.

As Vera stared at Yateem, the color in her eyes shifted like amethyst; her stare was miles away, which the guard took as a sign that she was in a state of shock.

"Our healer is one of the best in Zerahlinda. He will be able to help Yateem. You will be permitted to stay with him, of course."

Vera snapped to attention. "No." She kneeled down and pressed her forehead against Yateem's. "I can't." Tears welled in her eyes, and her hands balled up into fists as she gripped the fabric of Yateem's shirt, as if it was a lifeline that kept her from dropping into an abyss.

"Then you can stay in my house tonight."

She kissed Yateem on the forehead and whispered in his ear, "I'll save us." She untied the boat with quick, jerky motions, as if afraid that if she stopped moving, she would not have the strength to leave. She ran up the gangplank, unfastened it, and used the wooden ramp to push off the dock.

The guard stood next to Yateem in the pool of light that the hanging lantern cast, his handsome face distorted with scorn. "What?" he sneered. "He is of no further use to you, so you abandon him on a dock as he dies?"

"I have to do this alone," Vera choked out in a whisper, one that she very much doubted the guard could hear.

"Is this the thanks that he gets for his sacrifices for you?!" He ran to the very end of the dock, wanting to reach out and stop the boat.

Vera spun the ship around so that she was facing east from the dock and called back with a hoarse, choked yell, "I love him! When I come back, there had better be a warrior's monument for him! Or I'll—"

Wind picked up the sails and pushed her into the fog that mingled with the black night sky. Seasickness wasn't the only reason that Vera felt her stomach flip. She stubbornly pushed away the tears that wanted to fall and swallowed the acid and bile that rose up her throat. *Could he hear me? His chest was barely rising. His last screams were so weak...I...can I save him? What if he wakes just long enough to hear those guards tell him I left without a second thought? Are those going to be the last words he hears? If I make it out of this...will they even let me visit his grave?*

There was no moon or stars to guide her, and even if there were, she didn't know where she was going. All Vera knew was that her visions were leading her to light, though all she saw and felt was darkness, and the winds carried voices to confuse and dissuade her.

"I am responsible for your well-being, for your safety and happiness." Yateem's weak voice accused her of negligence.

Vera threw the wheel to turn into a wave that threatened to capsize the ship. "I've never thought about your happiness, Yateem. I'm so sorry."

As the bow collided with the rising water, Radov's voice sang out in the melody that first drew her in. His voice grew desperate. "Vera, you are my only hope of freedom from the pain of this life."

The collision with the wave knocked her down onto the deck, the wheel spun uncontrollably in the storm, and the boat began to sway precariously. Vera was beyond fatigued. Between the physical and emotional strain of her sea voyage and the visions, she could take no more.

"Rise." A whisper traveled across the sea, slithered up her spine, and coiled inside her ears. "Feel the power in your veins. Soon you will be my queen."

Vera felt a dark fire burst in her chest and ignite her muscles with energy. Reaching up and grabbing a spoke of the wheel to stop the erratic motion of the ship, she pulled herself up.

"We will be the most powerful force on earth, my lavender princess. Join me."

Vera stared out into the night sky, the empty void of blackness a calm, welcoming sight compared to the tumultuous sea. Ierá Flóga grew cold on her finger, the amethyst stone eyes seeming to inquire about her decision. She stroked the dragon's head, assuring it that she would not restrict it with a force field again. Her eyes darkened, and she raised them again to the black night sky with an incredulous smile on her face. "No one will share in my power."

"Then you shall have none!" Draven's voice screamed.

The waves rose up twenty feet above the ship and crashed down on all sides, casting Vera into the angry waters.

Chapter 30
Inferno

Air seared into her lungs as Vera coughed up briny water mixed with blood onto a shore of white, crushed shells. The sunlight reflecting off the glossy white ground made her blink dazedly. The sea was a beautiful light turquoise, and as smooth as the finest blown glass. The whole scene felt so peaceful, and if she had not woken coughing up water and blood, Vera could have easily convinced herself that her entire life had been nothing but a vivid dream.

She lay on her stomach, heaving brisk oxygen into her sore chest. The dagger was still on the chain and felt as if it had fused itself to the skin over her collarbone. Her body, while fatigued, was somehow rested. Vera's hands sunk lightly into the warm sand as she pushed her body up to take in her surroundings.

The white beach diminished into a dark forest only five feet in front of her. The water lapped at her legs, and as she squirmed to look to the side, she saw the land curve away in the distance, making her feel as if she were floating on a drifting island. And while she might not have been the most attentive student when studying the geography of the Seija Sea, Vera knew this island would not be found on any map.

She could feel the rhythmic, overwhelming pulsing of energy from the land, like a kitten sleeping on her stomach whose purring reverberates through her soul. Revived by this, Vera jumped to her feet in realization.

"Zakiyyah!" The excited whisper escaped her lips as her body braced itself to meet a very large mythological fire-breathing creature.

The silence was dishearteningly maddening. There was not a creature in sight, not even a fly to swat away from her damp, salt-encrusted, sweaty body. She felt a gentle tug from her soul to enter the forest.

"Wake up!" Vera yelled as she started to tramp into the dark forest, the sea water sloshing in her boots as she pushed past the hemlocks, pines, cedars, redwoods, and other large trees that she had never seen before. "Zakiyyah! Enough beauty sleep, time to go save the world!" Her calls echoed off the trees as she hiked deeper and deeper into the heart of the island.

She was sure in her footing, the soft ground, rocks, and roots presenting no obstacle, although the land grew steeper as Vera approached the center of the island. The high sun grew hot as it filtered through the leaves and pine needles of the forest, and Vera struggled to peel the wet deer-leather and alpaca-wool vest off her body, dropping it to the ground with a splat as she continued up the graduated mountain. The trees started to thin, and as she reached the summit of the lazy mountain, she leaned against a tree to try to calm her galloping heart.

The center of the island was a clear blue lake in a crater that looked to be the aftermath of a volcanic eruption that took half the mountain with it. In the middle of this lake was a small rock island, whose natural formation resembled a domed temple. The walls of the crater were sheer cliffs of lava rock. Vera tried to see if there was another way to the temple island, where she was sure that Zakiyyah lay, but could not see a carved path to the water in any of the cliffs. The shortest drop she could find looked to be about sixty feet to the water.

She mumbled a nervous prayer, took a couple steps back, and jumped. Her body was momentarily suspended over the water, and then was pulled back to the rim of the crater.

"What are you doing?" Yateem examined Vera for wounds.

An immense heat made her lightheaded. She saw that the crater was full of lava, and that Yateem was unharmed before her. His eyes seemed blurred, or maybe that was the effect of the heat on Vera's brain. "How are you here?"

"Vera, I have been with you the whole time. You went into a trance, called out to Zakiyyah, and went to dive to your death."

"No, no, *you* were dying...I left you." Vera's eyes welled from the heat and remorse in the air.

"You hallucinated it all. I had to tie you to the ship." His face was too scrunched up, his hair moved in an unnatural way as he gripped Vera tighter, and the color in his eyes smeared a little into his pupil as he looked toward the ring on Vera's right hand.

"You're lying."

Yateem's familiar face was touched ever so slightly with viciousness. "Then jump."

As Ierá Flóga started to grow and lightly beat its wings, Vera's eyes shifted to deep lavender, their focus as sharp as the dagger the dragon ring had turned into. She put it to Yateem's throat. "Why are you here? Nothing is going to change my mind."

Draven shed the guise and leaned toward Vera, drawing blood from his throat. "Smell the blood. Do you feel that yearning? That hunger? Do it."

Vera gritted her teeth, but could not bring herself to act on her deepest desires of revenge. The heat made sweat drip down her face.

Draven rolled his eyes, snarled, and grabbed the collar of Vera's shirt. "I killed everyone you loved, gave them slow, painful deaths. Are you so devoid of feeling, so self-righteous, that you refuse to avenge them?"

"I'm smart enough to know that you are too much of a coward to actually be here."

He growled and shook Vera, exposing the dagger and the raven pin Radov had given her. A gruesome smile spread over his cracked lips, his yellow teeth in full view. "In all my darkest hopes I did not dare expect this. Wearing my family crest over your heart. Oh, well done, my little pet."

"Family crest?"

"Oh, he did not tell you? Little Radov claimed it as his own, did he?"

"You miserable liar!"

"Were you cold after the enchanted song made you dance into the fountain at Lolani?" Draven asked, wrapping the fingers of his left hand around the dagger.

"How?"

"We are linked, he and I, and when he is outside the cage of Shifra, I can hear his every thought. How else would I know to send a creature that could rival a large bull shark? Or be able to track you on your journey, and find the entrance to Elea?" He brushed the pin with his right thumb.

"No."

"Well, this is the only piece he has left of his original life. It has a part of his heart, so I can sense it once it is out of the reach of any fairy who dares enchant it."

"It can't be…"

"True? What? Your beloved one not as honorable as you wished? He is only using you to get free. In the end, that is what you are to everyone, a tool to be used and then discarded."

"Your jealousy is pathetic." Vera bit down on the words.

Draven tightened his grip on the dagger and pulled her in close. "What did you say?"

"People adore me, but have nothing but disgust and hatred toward you. They bow at my feet and wish to stomp you out with their own." Her eyes deepened in color.

"Those people do not bow out of praise and adoration, but out of fear for what you could do if you stopped listening to their prayed requests and started giving out orders. They used to bow at my feet, but now they throw themselves down and grovel, begging to do my every command."

Vera's glare faltered, her mouth opened, but no words escaped. She tried to push away from Draven. His body felt wrong, like flimsy metal under her hands, yet she was tethered to him by his grip on the tourmaline dagger.

"You know I speak the truth. Everyone who has ever seen your eyes has met you with a terror in their hearts that could only be quelled by encouraging your goodness, affirming in their mind, and yours, that your destiny—your future—is one of blind servitude. Nothing strikes fear into a master more than an unbreakable workhorse that threatens to buck and lash out instead of using its strength to plow the fields for which it will never taste the harvest." Draven pulled on the stone weapon, a growl catching in his throat as the chain held strong.

"What am I to do?" Vera looked at the lava that bubbled and snapped as the air shimmered with unfathomable heat.

Draven reluctantly let go of the dagger and smoothed his hands down on her shoulders. "Reap what others sow, live in the peaceful shadow of your power, and never have the burden of other people's hopes on you." He slid his hands down her arms and grasped her left hand, making sure to keep away from her right hand, which was still encompassed by the wings of Ierá Flóga and had a dagger coming out of its mouth. "Come away from this infernal place, and let us find somewhere you can rest and gather your thoughts. This obligation you feel will drive you to death."

Vera let him lead her away from the lake of lava, her body complacent with the idea of resting in a cool place. Her eyelids grew heavy, and when she went to wipe the sweat from her face with her free hand, she was shocked by the coolness of Ierá Flóga's golden wings against her forehead. "It already drove me to death. I don't want to go through that again."

"Do not worry. I will help you relinquish all hold of time and humanity on you." Draven's crazed raven eyes coveted the dagger hanging from Vera's neck.

"I have one concern." Vera forced her voice to be casual, wanting every advantage in this moment.

"What is that, little nightshade blossom?" His black eyes could not stray from the jagged black edges of the tourmaline dagger.

When tree roots came out of the ground and gripped Draven's legs, Vera ripped her hand out of his grasp. "That life would be a living death."

She turned and sprinted toward the crater wall, and jumped feet first toward the magma.

The hot air whipped at her face, making the seconds it took to plummet the sixty feet feel like she was falling through a thick cloud of torrid gas that slowed down time. As the tips of her toes cracked through the lava, Vera took in a deep breath. The heat sent panic through her entire body, a feeling that could only be overcome by her confusion at the cold that swirled around her. Vera surfaced to find the elaborate hallucination Draven had made was gone, and that Ierá Flóga had returned to a ring. All that was left of the illusion was the steam rising off the lake. She stirred the water around her, mixing the cool water from beneath with the hot surface water so that she didn't get burned.

The water dropped down to a deep blue. The rock outcropping looked to be only a short swim away, but Vera knew that was a hopeless mirage. She swam over to the chalky gray cliff to catch her breath, but found that the lake had worn the rock smooth, so she moved along the water's edge to see if she could find any holds or outcroppings to rest on. The waste of her precious energy made her want to abandon this search, but then she saw a small ledge about three feet under the surface.

Her body wobbled in the water as she placed her feet on the five inches of protruding rock and clumsily pushed her body against the cliff as she straightened her legs. The wet cotton of her shirt made an awkward slapping noise against the rock as she quickly turned around and leaned her back against the slight outward slope of the cliff, her auburn hair making tiny, dark-gray waterfalls on the rock's surface. Vera's heart thudded against the warm cliff so hard that she would swear the whole lake was shaking, and that her chest jabbed the air in front of her body.

Spreading her arms out to the sides, she flattened her hands on the igneous wall she perched against, wishing she had suction cups for fingertips. The shelf under her feet felt like it dropped to the end of the world as she slowly slid her right foot to the edge and started to drag the heel of her boot against it. Once her ankle and heel got loose, she gently shook her leg until the boot came off. Leaning forward ever so slightly, Vera watched as her blood-, mud-, and sea-salt-stained boot sunk down from the clear blue water to the graduated darkness of the lake, finally losing sight of it about fifty feet down, where the water turned to a cold midnight blue.

Confident in her balance and the imaginary suction cups, Vera dragged, wiggled, and kicked her left boot off in a considerably shorter time, and then there was an awkward balancing dance as she reached down and removed her socks. With that done, she let out a breath that felt like it held all her pent-up energy, and she placed her head against the cliff again to breathe and relax her galloping heart as she spread her toes on the slick roughness of the lava rock shelf.

The gray domed rock stood out of the water like a healthy palm tree stands out in the middle of the desert, something in its nature making it exceptional and awe-inspiring, despite its ordinary appearance.

"What were you thinking?" she scolded herself. "Do dragons even like water? And even if it is sleeping inside that hunk of rock, how are you going to get there? How are you going to get inside a hunk of rock?"

Vera closed her eyes so she didn't have to look at the long swim she would eventually have to make. "You are strong. You are brave. You are a beautiful creation of Arivos." She filled her lungs with the crisp warm air, opened her eyes, and stared at the island with a toothy, confident smile. "I'm going to make it to that lump of rock and wake up a snoring dragon!"

She stepped off the ledge. The cool water swished in between her toes, swirled around her body, and wrapped her auburn waves around her head. The blue water fell away from Vera's face, sweeping the hair out of her eyes as she surfaced, exhilarated. The backs of her hands came together as she reached in front of her and pushed the water away in a wide arching motion that looked like the graceful flapping of a phoenix rising.

Slowly Vera made her way toward the temple rock. She should have drowned—she would have given up—if it had not been for the energy that invigorated the lake. Each atom of water that touched her skin filled her with the urge to continue, reminding her that she could not quit now.

As she got within a manageable distance, smooth rolling waves rippled out from the island. When the first wave picked Vera up, she grimaced at the thought of fighting against waves pulling her toward the cliffs, but she was forced to look around her as she felt her body being pushed in the direction of the small island. The waves pulsed out from the center of the lake, but their motion somehow propelled Vera's swimming toward it.

Vera panted as she smacked her hands against the warm lava rock and pulled herself onto the small island. Her hair, shirt, and pants clung to her saturated body, and a puddle formed around her knees as Vera let her legs fold underneath her and her body slump into a seated position. Wiping the hair out of her face, she gazed up toward the domed rock formation above her.

Different from the smoothed cliffs surrounding the crater lake, the rigid walls of the stone structure rose up out of a ragged slope of bric-a-brac lava columns. From far away, the dome had looked perfectly round, but this close Vera could see the graduated stone columns that created the temple façade.

As she sat there, the dagger on her chest started resonating with the same low electric current that had sent the waves out to her. The chain rattled against the back of her neck and made her groggy brain alert, and her eyelids felt like they would never close again. Water dripped on the warm stone as Vera crouched, took in a deep breath, pushed off the ground, and stood. She searched her mind for a sarcastic quip to prep herself for the slope that looked like a drunken staircase, a climb that in its nature would be the easiest Vera had to make so far, but the feeling coursing through her body, the whole lake that surrounded her, and the entire island that she had found herself shipwrecked on hours ago, made her mind clear and determined. The dagger sent pulses through her chest, and her bare feet struck hard against the stone as she started her ascent.

She stumbled around the structure, trying to find a door before the sun dipped behind the tall cliffs of the crater and made her search impossible. Stopping to catch her breath, Vera realized her feet were raw; they felt like they might be burned from walking on the black stones. Vera thwacked her hand on the stone and huffed, frustrated by her fruitless efforts. The pads of her sweaty fingers wiggled around in an attempt to not slip and cause her to collapse. Two fingers found strange dips and small peaks to grip, but the other fingers and thumb rested on a slippery-smooth rock. Vera's hair whipped her in the face as she stared at her hand and straightened out of her hunched stance.

The smooth surface was four feet wide and ten feet tall and looked like the beginnings of a door that had never been carved out. There were no seams around the edges, just the abrupt change from perfectly smoothed, charcoal-black rock, to the naturally uneven surface of the lava rock. In the failing light, her eyes were drawn to the center of the would-be door. Bulging from the center was hard, shiny lava rock, as if a mini lava flow had exploded and branched out of the slab. Vera ran her fingers along this slick substance, the flow of it reminiscent of tree roots. The two middle fingers of her right hand slipped into a hole at the center of the door. She held her breath and looked around, as if a child who has broken a priceless heirloom. Her cheek instantly chilled as Vera leaned against the stone and tried to see what her fingers had encountered. The sun was halfway gone behind the cliffs, and her nose was practically in the hole, yet it was invisible against the black lava.

The dagger pulsed energy through her body at an uncomfortable frequency, she grabbed it off her chest to try to relieve the agitating sensation. All sight of the dagger nearly vanished against the darkness of the lava.

Vera's eyebrows rose up in epiphany. "How many doors are you going to make me open with a dagger, Arivos?"

The sun had nearly deserted her as her fingers groped for the hole that was literally in front of her nose. She pulled at the dagger in her hand, seriously doubting that the chain was going to break as Majlis had promised, but with a clink it released. Vera tucked the broken necklace into the small pocket of her pants and brought the dagger's point up to her left index finger that was marking the center of the door. She pushed the dagger into the opening.

As the earth began to quake, Vera desperately held onto the tourmaline dagger that was still in the assumed keyhole. The miniature lava flow glowed red and dripped down to Vera's feet, the searing heat increasing the rhythm of the spastic dance her body had started the moment the earthquake hit.

Panic-stricken that she had just played further into one of Draven's illusions, she closed her eyes and shook her head, attempting to return to reality. She felt as if her insides were grasped in a great eagle's talons and being pulled forward and out of her body. Quite suddenly, the earth became still, and Vera could feel light shining on her clenched eyelids.

Her teeth showed white in her smile. "When you open your eyes, you will see your chamber, your comforter, and your windows with a gorgeous view of the sun on the sea."

Vera's fingers cramped from the grip she had on the dagger. She opened her eyes—not to an ocean view from a fluffy mattress, but to the warm sight of torches that lined either side of the black hall in which she stood. Only the two closest to her were lit. Vera turned around, or tried to as her shoulder skidded against smooth rock. It was only after she took a few steps back, being cautious of the flames, that she noticed the wall had the same root-lava-flow design in the middle of it, except it looked like it was pressed in the rock, and its stark white color was a slightly overwhelming sight in a black hallway.

Vera looked at the dagger in her hand and stepped up to the wall, feeling over the familiar lines, the only difference being the size of the hole in the center. It was nearly imperceptible, like a tiny, ignorable imperfection when a finger ran over it.

Her mouth hung open, and her brained wheeled in shock. She felt along the edges of the wall but could not find any evidence to prove to her mind that the hallway she stood in was not somehow carved out of a solid piece of rock, and that there was a reasonable explanation as to how she just traveled through a solid stone wall. Vera's lips mouthed awestruck questions without making a sound, and then she let out a nervous laugh. "I was just…then…this isn't…what?"

Vera turned around to investigate the hallway she had just been inexplicably teleported into. The corridor was jagged, as if it had been done with a simple pickax, nothing like the smooth wall to her back. When Vera went to grab the torch on the left side of the hall, the simple silver torch felt cold as her fingers easily wrapped around it. It looked as if it had just been made and polished. A very plain, organic design that even an apprentice could have easily made, the only adornment the torches had was a small etching of a dragon's head at the very brim. There was no pin or latch securing the torches into their rock sconces; rather, they looked as if they were formed with the rock.

Vera tried to blame her exhaustion, the fact that she was using one hand, and the awkwardly high height of the torch to explain why she could not even wiggle the torch out of its place. With a huff, she let her left hand rest, resigned to the impossibility of having a guiding flame. Looking down the hall, all she could see was the glint of light off the next unlit torches that were five feet away. She shoved the dagger into the waistline of her pants and then shot up both her hands, as if to surprise attack the torch. Vera jumped, grunted, and pulled with all her might, but the torch was as unyielding as a mountain.

Throwing her arms down in exasperation, she grabbed the dagger and looked down the hall. "Well, it's not like I can go anywhere else." Vera walked forward and paused at the border between dim light and complete darkness, then she took the first step into the unknown.

The unlit torches just in front of her ignited with a burst of hot orange flame, and the twin flames that had first shown light on the door were extinguished. So Vera went onward down the hall, able to see only five feet in front of her, leaving where she was just steps before in the silence of dark.

Only after six pairs of extinguished flames lay behind her did she find a single lantern hanging at the threshold of a tight spiral staircase. Vera switched the dagger to her left hand and grabbed the warm handle of the rusted lamp. It came off the rock-hook easily, and she started her descent. One would suppose that her feet would be numb from the cold this far into an enclosed rocky cavern, but on the contrary, as she continued her way, the dryness and warmth around her increased. She was not afraid of slipping on damp stairs, but rather that the sweat on her feet would cause her to crash to the bottom and that the lantern would be thrown from her hand, leaving her lost in the unrelenting darkness of this grand mausoleum.

When her right foot stepped off the last stair, her toes slightly kissed the hot ground just before the pads of her feet rocked against the distinct sensation of carved stone. Vera lowered the lantern so that she could see the ancient art she was unintentionally standing on. Engraved in the lava was a message surrounded by a border of intricately carved flames.

It read:

> *Blood will boil*
> *in the crucible*
> *of the Holy Dragon.*
> *His light will sear the fallen,*
> *and cleanse the misled.*
> *Relinquish the flame.*
> *Greet Fate.*

There was a musty smell for which Vera was suddenly afraid to find its origin. The color of her eyes glinted and vacillated like an amethyst in the light of the lantern. Her entire body felt as if it would escape to the farthest reaches of the sky if she did not get a hold of the energy she felt around her. There was nothing to be seen but the deep, thick dark that only a cavern can wrap around a person, shrinking even the strongest rays of light.

It was by far the loneliest—and longest—moment of her life. Vera felt that ages must have passed as she went from reading the carving over and over, to staring into the dark.

Then she saw.

The years of anger, doubt, and bitterness were barely even a memory in the presence of the absolute love that she was becoming more and more aware of, that she was allowing to enter her heart.

The engraved flames led her a few feet away and wrapped around a huge beige-brown stalagmite that had an odd branch-like outshoot at face level. Securing the tourmaline dagger in her waistband, she clenched the handle of the lamp in her trembling left hand. She rested the handle on the hooked end of the branch, and immediately thirty stalagmites, reaching up seventy feet, burst into flames around the great cavern that reached all the way up to the domed top of the structure.

Vera could barely jump a safe distance away from the burning pillar that consumed the guiding lantern. Her knees cracked against the hard stone floor, and her lavender eyes were sparkling, brimming with overwhelming tears of belief and joy.

"Zakiyyah."

Chapter 31
The Task

The cold bit at his cheeks as Fenelle tried to warm his hands by a fire that was more embers than actual flame. He had sold his flock for the best price he could find, which was barely equal to the price for ten sheep, let alone a hundred. The poor shepherd rued the day that he let an old man and a dead girl take his horse unchallenged.

"I probably would've died in a fight with that blood-crusty man, but at least that'd be better than freezing to death," he muttered to fading embers and the dark.

Snap.

The nearby branch might as well have been Fenelle's back, the way horror and the anticipation of pain washed over him. Vera's sword lay on the ground by his side, and he slid it silently out of its leather sheath. Fenelle stood, holding the sword as a drunkard would hold an empty bottle in a pub brawl.

An angry huff made the young man flinch as Aethon's fuzzy face emerged out of the night. The horse's soft fur scratched Fenelle's face.

"How?"

The weary horse lay down, nearly extinguishing the tiny flame. It intently smelled the ground, started to lick at the dry red grass, and a puddle seeped up through the cracked dirt for him to drink.

"What!" Fenelle's fear of being discovered was lost amidst his complete shock.

It was only when Aethon started to shift uncomfortably that Fenelle noticed the packs strapped on the horse. Fenelle awkwardly wrestled to relieve Aethon of his burden as the stubborn beast refused to stand on its fatigued legs. The packs were made from treated sheepskin that was soft to the touch, but completely sealed and weatherproof. Fenelle fell to the ground with the final yank to free the packs, and the horse fell immediately to sleep. In the packs were all the provisions he could possibly need, and a little bit more.

"Good boy! I don't know how you made it to me without being ransacked, but thank you. You might not wish you'd found me!" Fenelle stuffed half a soft roll in his mouth. "The Wachiru are searching for me, and no inn will allow any strangers, particularly shepherds. Dark times, Aethon, dark times." Fenelle shoved the rest of the roll into his mouth and plunged his hand into the saddlebag to see what else he could find.

His fingers happened upon the abrupt edges of an envelope. Pulling it out, he broke the wax star seal and lay down next to the sad excuse of a fire to read its contents.

> *These provisions will last through your task. Let the horse rest, but as soon as it is able, you must start. Aethon knows where to go. Do not give any of your water to him; he will be provided from the earth whenever he has need of it. Sleep, Fenelle, and do not underestimate the importance of your task. You are needed. Stay close to your steed; he has already carried death and has an instinct for avoiding danger.*
> *Queen Emmanuelle*

"Queen? Aethon, you make better friends than I."

Chapter 32
Awakening

The dragon's scales had the dull sheen and texture of a tempered golden shield and overlapped so smoothly that, from fifty feet away, Vera wondered at the seemingly delicate flesh of the impenetrably armored creature. Its tail curled around It, and Its wings lay wrapped at Its side.

Zakiyyah's eyes shot open after Vera's salutation, and she was unable to make an utterance after that.

Pure white. Not the muddled gray-white of a death-clouded eye, or the white of royal marble pillars that have cracks of imperfections and remnants of other substances. Its pupil-less eyes were the white of untainted sunlight bursting through freshly made clouds, the white of the flaming gate that Vera passed through death to find. A wave of terrified delight gripped Vera by the shoulders as the dragon shifted Its head and stared at her. Zakiyyah's eye showed no reflection of the cracking flamed pillars, but rather shone a pure light on all that It looked on. They were a perfect sphere, two feet in diameter, but seemed to take up Vera's entire world. These eyes knew all, saw all, conveyed all.

As the dragon rose up, blocking the view of most of the stalagmites but diminishing none of the light in the cavern, Vera understood the risks she was about to take. She had never felt so terrified as she stood, so unworthy and unequipped as she took that first step, and Vera had never felt so strong as when the wind from the unfurling of Zakiyyah's massive wings knocked her on her back.

Chapter 33
Lethal Escort

"Alright, time to rest." Fenelle slumped his pack onto the ground. Vera's old sword hung around his waist.

The mountain horse stomped its feet, shook its head, and kept walking through the sagebrush, which was getting shorter and scarcer the farther they went.

"Aethon." Fenelle's whisper was urgent. "Aethon!" He stood and watched as his horse continued on, then finally grabbed his small bag and ran to catch up with it.

"My dear fellow, you may have been told you need to do something in The Vanished Lands, but you are mistaken." Grabbing the top cross strap of the packs on Aethon, Fenelle tried to pull the horse back.

Aethon's strength made Fenelle's attempt to stop the stubborn animal embarrassing. The holes in his leather boots were filling up with hard, cracked dirt as the horse walked on, as if the shepherd whose arms and legs were shaking from exertion was nothing more than a fly gnawing on the horse's flank. Aethon whacked Fenelle in the back of the head with his thick tail to try to release the prideful youth's grip on the pack straps.

The ground beneath their feet grew harder with each step, and the bushes suddenly ended as they reached the border of the land that Yakootans called The Vanished Lands— sweeping hills covered in rust-colored grass, with large black rock outcroppings sticking out in the distance, tall leering cliffs staring at the two intruders. The smell of dusty decay clung to the air.

"This is not our home anymore," Fenelle said, throwing his hands up in the air as Aethon leaned down and drank from a puddle that had suddenly appeared at his feet. As he looked off in the distance, the young man couldn't hear the horse's slurping, not above the buzzing in his ears.

A half mile, that was it. He could run and be there in minutes. *Has the red grass grown tall over their graves yet?* His fingers gripped the hilt of Vera's sword, rubbing the smooth ivory of the handle as he turned a glare to the looming black cliffs that punctured the skyline. "*He* made sure of that. *He* turned my home into The Vanished Lands."

Aethon lifted his head and sprayed a watery sneeze all over Fenelle's torso.

"Thank you, just what I wanted." He released his grip on the weapon, brushed his hands down his rough shirt, and then rubbed in between the horse's eyes.

Crack. Snap.

Fenelle whipped around to watch his death come at him through the last small sage bushes. Quickly he pulled the sword out of the sheath and waited. Three Wachiru were thrown out from behind the bushes with as much vigor and ease as a puppy throws a pinecone. Looking at the full-grown men that lay dead before him, Fenelle shook with the thought of what could possibly do that with so little effort as Aethon dug shallow holes in the ground with his back feet, preparing to charge.

In a flash of black, orange, and white, Vulcan and Minerva pounced over the sage and landed on top of the bodies they had thrown, their teeth set in a snarl, growls rumbling in their throats.

"Well, at least I'll be close to my family's graves." Fenelle's fingers let the sword drop to the ground. "Please, Arivos make it quick."

Minerva prowled up to the sword, smelling it intently. She then smelled the shepherd, making her way up from his feet, pausing at the sleeping roll attached to his pack and ending with her cold, wet nostrils touching the sweat that dripped off Fenelle's nose. Her fangs gleamed in the sunset, dark blood caught in the tiny grooves of her canines. He closed his eyes and flexed every muscle, expecting the end, when the warm, rough sensation of a giant cat's tongue drew itself from chin to hairline.

"Oh, come on! You just killed people! You think I want your saliva on me?" Fenelle gently pushed on Minerva's neck to try to get the purring animal to back up.

She hesitated and then licked the other side of Fenelle's face before going over to Aethon and nuzzling him in an animal sandwich between herself and Vulcan. The horse was rigid with confused tension as the large predators cuddled him. He then leaned down and started to lick the ground to get the gennadius some water. Both of them drank in excitement, their thick, heavy tails thumping against their flanks.

Fenelle slowly picked up the sword and returned it to the sheath, bewildered beyond comprehension by what was happening. "Can we rest now?"

All three animals looked over at the young man with knowing looks and then exchanged agitated huffs and head tosses, with some stomping mixed in. Vulcan's ears perked; his nose smelled something on the night air, and he trotted off in the direction that Aethon had been heading before. Both Aethon and Minerva looked back at Fenelle.

"I'm the human here. Aren't you supposed to listen to me?"

Aethon walked up beside the shepherd and started to swing its head toward where Vulcan was running.

Fenelle sighed. "Some random queen gives you enchanted supplies, and now you're in charge?" He stared at the horse, willing the animal to understand him, and then saw a flicker of something in the horse's eyes that made Fenelle start. Purpose. He looked at Minerva, who was watching after Vulcan as he ran off. "I suppose it would be faster." Fenelle grabbed onto the horse's packs and pulled himself onto Aethon's back.

The horse shot after Vulcan, and Minerva followed. The horse looked to be just a foal compared to the great gennadius, but it matched their speed, probably because of its stubborn nature.

Into The Vanished Lands, into the night they ran with renewed vigor for the task that would change the fate of the world.

Chapter 34
Ethereal Fire

Vera woke to the sound of talons clinking against stone. She had passed out after her head hit the warm stone ground. As she picked herself up, the golden wings folded against Zakiyyah's side. The dragon swerved Its head back and forth slowly, and with a swift grace that she would have never expected from a creature that size, It took a closer look at Vera.

She shook, on the brink of hyperventilation. Her body could barely handle the storm of love, inspiration, and power that pressed upon her in the form of dragon's breath, which smelt like freshly fallen snow, and not decay. The humongous nostrils flared just inches in front of her face, and Vera was conflicted between the urge to run and the desire kiss the dragon's snout.

It looked similar to the drawings she had seen in the older books Yateem made her read, but she highly doubted that ink and parchment could capture Its beauty. The dragon was two hundred fifty feet long from Its snout to the razor-sharp edge of Its tail, with a wingspan of two hundred feet. Zakiyyah's whip-like tail wrapped around Its body as It silently lowered back down into a lying position. The energy that filled the room was of comfort, courage, and understanding. The dragon did not want Vera to fear It, but fear was understandable when facing a creature that could kill an elephant with as little effort as a human could kill a baby ant.

Although she had seen depictions of great dragons with gnarled horns and teeth that dripped with blood, Zakiyyah lacked both. Instead, It had a golden mane, reminiscent of a lion's, but infinitely more majestic. The mane looked like a golden ethereal fire.

"What…" The word barely scratched its way out of her throat. "What do I do now?" The words piled one on top of the other as the question quickly tumbled out of her mouth.

The dragon shifted so that one of Its eyes was directly in front of the teenager. She had never felt so small. Zakiyyah's head was taller than her—at least six feet in height and twice that in length, with a jawline of about seven feet. Vera couldn't help but think that she could fit comfortably inside the great creature's mouth. Ashamed of her panicked, distracted thoughts, she could only stare at her bare feet. A hot puff of smoke made Vera look up again and pay attention to the reflection that Zakiyyah's light was casting on her.

She was no longer in her torn, bloodied, stiff clothing, but in thick, dark-brown leather pants, much like the ones in which she would practice swordsmanship. A breathable, soft, long-sleeve, white shirt lay beneath a double-breasted leather vest with a large hood, which held the dagger and chain that were now around her neck again, secure in a pocket underneath the front flap. Her feet felt agile and secure in short leather boots. Radov's pin had vanished.

Vera touched the vest and was taken aback when she realized that what she thought was a reflection cast on her was her new reality. The vest felt smooth and durable, and both the vest and pants were a heavier leather than she was used to, meant to protect.

Her hand lingered in the air as she tried to confidently touch the golden scales before her—almost unbearably hot, but somehow soothing. Her palm lay on the ancient creature, next to Its eye. She could feel the faint lines of the scales, but could not perceive any change of height or texture between them. The eye never faltered. Its purity looked on Vera with incomprehensible love.

She leaned in and lightly kissed Zakiyyah. "Lead, and I will follow."

Zakiyyah laid Its head on the ground in front of her, and as she walked to the base of the dragon's skull to climb onto Its neck, she was taken aback by the mane. Like gold fire, the mane moved and flowed all on its own. Its ethereal appearance made Vera cautious to touch it, but once she grabbed onto a single strand, the mane seemed more solid and alive, and possessed more power than any worldly army. She climbed up and swung her leg over Zakiyyah's neck, trying not to pull the pieces of mane to which she clung.

The dragon raised Its body up, opening Its wings again. Vera was filled with giddy fright as she pulled her hood over her eyes and hunkered down against the base of Zakiyyah's head, the mane brushing warmth against her cheek. The dragon beat Its wings and pushed off the stone. At an alarming speed, they flew toward the solid rock dome ceiling of the cavern. Vera's heart skipped a few beats as Zakiyyah closed Its wings and spun through the dome, blasting the rock out into the crater lake.

As they rose, Vera looked down at the island on which she had somehow been shipwrecked to see that it was sinking into the vast ocean. The lake in the middle of the volcanic island could be clearly seen, as could the tiny black island from which they had just burst out, where she found the dragon of myths.

Vera thought it was strange, but the tiny black island in the crater lake, in the middle of the big sinking island, looked like an eye within an eye dropping into the deep expanse of the sea. It made her wonder how much Zakiyyah could see in his sleep, or if the big island was merely an image of Arivos' eye.

Chapter 35
Familiar Stranger

"That's disgusting!" Fenelle shook his head at the gennadius as he shoved a chunk of cheese and smoked salmon into his mouth.

The two great predators had gotten a nyx in the last minutes of daylight, before the cover of night allowed the beast's skin to produce the flesh-eating poison. They feasted, ravenous after the nearly twenty-four hours they had run. Aethon was content lying down and grazing.

"If the meat is poisonous, I won't grieve a bit for the loss of you two." He stoked a fire—nothing grand, but certainly a more confident flame than he ever would've constructed in The Vanished Lands if he didn't have two very large, very efficient killers gorging themselves a few feet away.

"No, you would not have time to lament, such an unaware young man as yourself could easily be attacked within minutes of those creatures' deaths." The voice was stern and came from behind Fenelle, where the darkness had settled down to the earth.

Fenelle gagged on the food in his throat, but wanting to die with some semblance of honor, he swallowed it. He looked over at Vulcan and Minerva, who seemed to be standing at attention to whomever was lurking in the night.

"I would introduce myself," Fenelle said, reaching for the hilt of the sword in his pack, "but my big cats are about to make you dessert."

A large hand reached out and drew Fenelle's sword before the young man could grab it. "The gennadius will not hurt me. I have had my doubts about the female one, but in times like these, trust is what is going to keep you alive." The man strutted in front of Fenelle, and the fire hissed at his feet.

The young shepherd remained seated, refusing to anxiously exert himself before he was murdered. "What do you want from me? Just get on with it!"

The man looked down the blade. "I would first like to share a well-earned meal with you, rest through the night, and then take back my steed."

"Oh, Arivos in the sky! No. Aethon is mine!"

The man placed the sword on top of Fenelle's pack, crouched down and smiled at the lost shepherd. Fenelle wondered at the crescent-shaped scars on the man's dark skin, the fresh scar along his right jaw, and the oddly familiar young facial features.

The stranger's teal eyes sparkled in the firelight. "I am not talking about the horse."

Chapter 36
Cruel Encounter

The rust grass crunched beneath the giant eagle-like feet of Zakiyyah, and dry dirt cracked under the digging pressure of the opalescent talons. Vera kicked up a small dust cloud when her feet hit the ground. When she swept the hood back, her auburn waves rippled with the slight breeze.

Closing her eyes, she reached out with her energy for any approaching threats. An evil that sucked all vitality out of its surroundings came from the south. Unseen by Vera's eyes but as sure as storm clouds bring rain, this force was bringing destruction to all it touched.

"He's coming for us."

Immense pressure shoved down on Vera's shoulders, dirt crammed under her nails as she tried to stop her fall by gripping the dry grass. Her hair swirled around her face, and surges of pounding air made her ears feel like they would burst. Vera turned around to see that the dragon was hovering.

"Are you going to kill him?"

Zakiyyah arched Its neck, opened Its mouth, and brought Its gleaming teeth down to Vera. She shook again in the majesty of the holy creature's power and feared that It was hungry. It breathed white smoke over Vera, which stabbed her heart with a spark of heat and filled her with a sense of power and purpose.

"I have to do this without you, huh?"

The dragon gave what almost seemed like a smile, and before Vera could process what was happening, It flew straight up into the clouds and disappeared from sight. Vera watched, and even though the humungous creature wasn't going to be standing behind her, she could feel Its power, strength, courage, and hope within her. She would not be fighting alone.

The Athanaric Cliffs broke through the landscape like a dark blade. *That's where Draven died, and lives.* Vera looked down at Ierá Flóga, its wings outspread and ready. She looked back at the cliffs and crunched the dry grass in front of her in a determined step.

High above her came the cry of a peregrine falcon. Her hand blocked the sun from her eyes as she watched the great predator dive. She could not bring herself to think that Draven could create an illusion that beautiful. The blue-gray feathers on its back glistened as its wings folded in, and the tear-shaped body dove at a graceful-lethal speed of two hundred miles per hour, directly at Vera. Ierá Flóga's wings flapped once when the falcon was eye level with Vera, but the bird vanished, and in front of her crouched a young man with disheveled black hair.

She opened and closed her mouth, words refusing to escape her lips.

He looked up with his ice-blue eyes and smiled as he stood in one fluid motion. "I saw Zakiyyah!"

"How?" She was breathless but kept glancing down at her ring, which had not shrunk down yet.

"It's flying around up there, hovering over you really. I dove out of fear that it was hungry." Radov dug his hands into the pockets of his tan cotton pants.

"No, I mean, how are you here? Are you real?"

"Queen Emmanuelle released me." He took a step closer, ran his hand down her arm, and kissed the golden head of Ierá Flóga.

A smile spread through her lips. "And you came to me?"

He wrapped his arms around her. "Where else would I go?"

Radov leaned down and kissed her, soft at first, but then passionately, like it was the last kiss he would ever get.

Vera's eyebrows furrowed when a thought crossed through her feverish mind, and she pulled away from Radov's embrace. "Draven said you two are connected." She untangled herself from his arms. "That pin you gave me, he was able to track it. Did you know?"

"Yes." The word was contrite, and full of shame. "We are connected, but I didn't know that he could track the pin."

She stepped back in horror and held up Ierá Flóga, waiting for it to breathe out a blade. "I don't understand."

Radov wiped his hand across his lips, as if trying to get the taste of Vera off him before he spoke again. "Do you have the dagger?"

"You've just been using me this whole time!" Vera yelled.

"No! No, not the whole time. I care for you, deeply and truly, but right now I need to know that you have the dagger with you. It's the only way to kill him. Shove it in his heart. I'm so sorry, Vera. You can't imagine how much I want us—but after what I have done…" The words spilled out of his mouth in a desperate confession, he grabbed her dragon wielding hand frantically. "I pushed him to it. I resented him…I wanted him to fail."

Vera pulled her hand back and felt the edge of a wing catch and tear Radov's skin. "So you know Draven."

"Yes, he was…is—" His body froze, but his eyes were present. They shot around wildly, as if looking for a cure to his sudden paralysis. He turned, not by stepping, but as if he were a wooden soldier being twisted around on a play battlefield.

Vera turned to see what he was being forced to look at.

A tall silhouette cloaked in black appeared on the horizon, almost imperceptible against the backdrop of the tall cliffs that were darker than the night sky. The high sun soon revealed the pack of creatures that flanked the sinister threat.

"Hello, little nightshade blossom. Where is your flying lizard?"

Vera flinched with the shock of watching Draven approach and having his toxic voice hiss in her ear at the same time. "Clever trick, but one I've experienced before. Remember the island?"

He snaked his face in front of Vera, his black raven eyes sneering at her. "Oh, how victorious you are!" Draven twitched the fingers of his left hand, twisting Radov around again so that he could watch. "I quake at your newfound power, your army that inspires great fear in all its enemies, and especially in your beauty, that not even evil would dare to ruin." Draven double-stroked the mottled red and white skin on Vera's throat with an icy sensation. "Oh, pardon me, I had you confused with someone who may actually present a threat to me." The snicker that emanated from his chest put a vice around Vera's stomach, and his smile sadistically tightened that grip. "I am eager to be able to touch you for real, to feel your blood drip from my fingers."

Radov made a clicking sound, as if he was trying to speak, but the air got trapped in his throat.

Draven cocked his head and smiled. "My pet found you sooner than I thought. We shall have fun once I arrive. For now, I would like you to sit…" Draven pointed to the ground, and Radov's legs collapsed, sending him down to the dry earth with a thud, "…and watch."

While Draven spoke, Ierá Flóga had grown into a short sword, and Vera brought the tip up against the inside of Draven's eye. "See you soon then?"

As she dragged the blade down his cheek, black-red blood trickled down with it. Draven sneered, and the illusion vanished, leaving Vera to clean the edge of her blade.

She walked over to Radov and knelt beside him. His eyes had the look of someone who was resigned to be crushed by the weight that lay on his shoulders.

"When you said 'freedom,' you weren't talking about shape-shifting, were you?"

The muscles in his neck flexed, his mouth opened, but only air broke out. His eyes seemed to be memorizing her features, and then they flitted in Draven's direction.

Vera turned and stood with the sword Ierá Flóga at her side, its golden wings wrapped around her right hand. Her eyes didn't falter from the approaching threat. "I'll find a way to save you."

As Draven approached in a leisurely manner with his battalion of minions, he bi-located to Vera. When his threats produced only stronger resolve in her, he resorted to wrapping hallucinations around her. She struggled to hold her ground, to ignore the ravens that pecked at her, the wolves that circled with foam dripping from their bared teeth, the sensation that the air around her could no longer fill her lungs.

Radov could do nothing for her. His limbs were deaf to his commands, his tongue mute.

Falling to her knees, Vera's left fist beat the grass flat as an illusion of her mother, on her knees weeping, appeared.

"Oh, my beautiful child, run." Her periwinkle eyes beckoned and her words begged. "You will join me today. You will fail!" She ripped out clumps of her auburn hair as she petitioned her daughter. "This is why I prayed every day that you had never been born!"

Vera bit down on her left hand, choking in a scream. With difficulty, she stood and looked down on the hallucination of her mother. "I will be glad to see you, Mama, the real you. Be gone from me."

Vera's mother screamed as her body ignited on fire and evaporated. Vera gritted her teeth and shook her arms to slough off the weight of that last hallucination. Ierá Flóga felt less like a sword and more like an extension of her right arm, and Vera could feel an intense connection to the silver blade as another illusion curled itself around her.

The sky grew dark with clouds, lightning struck where she supposed Draven truly was, huge raindrops started to pound the dry ground, and a veil of falling water approached. Vera's fear grew as she saw the deluge was burning the grass and earth in its path, tingeing the air with a coppery, acidic smell.

"It's not real. It's not real," Vera muttered to herself.

"Oh, it isn't?" Draven's voice boomed like thunder. "Why don't we see…I'm excited to watch that pretty face of yours melt."

She could barely control her breathing as she tried to gather the courage not to step back as the grass a foot in front of her turned black and withered into the dark smoke that rose from the ground. Radov's eyes were wide with horror as the burnt, acidic smell choked the air around them.

Vera could feel Draven's sadistic joy very near to her, within striking range. She took in a deep breath and closed her eyes as a line of smoke erupted in front of her toes.

"Enough!" She let a burst of energy explode from her chest. The white-lavender light rolled through the hallucination, evaporating the rain, drying out the clouds, and revealing Draven and his pack of nyx and Wachiru standing twenty feet away.

Draven tried to hide his shocked expression with a big smile and gestured to the minions surrounding him. "Why are you even trying?"

"Scared to fight your nightshade blossom the old-fashioned way?"

Draven's smile got a touch of acid in it that burned through some of Vera's confidence. "Yes, of course, you want a shot at a fair fight, do you?" He snapped his fingers, and a cloaked Wachiru came out carrying an iron scabbard that was almost the same height as the shaking man. As Draven drew his sword, the four-foot blade made the nauseating screech of wet bones being dragged on hard dry stone.

Draven's tall body looked even more formidable with his blade, which looked like it was carved from sun-bleached bone. The hilt was a stark black with large black thorns reaching up toward his wrist. His yellow teeth bared like a rabid dog, Draven sliced through the air with agile movements, as if the enormous blade weighed nothing. With a dramatic flourish and a flick of his wrist, he held the sword out to the side, and with the scratching of fortified steel against fortified steel, huge black thorns emerged on both edges of the blade.

"If you wanted a fair fight, you should have found a wounded rabbit, instead of tripping into my lair."

Vera readied her sword. "I flew here."

"And yet, you stand without the mighty reptile." He swept his sword over the land in front of him, and then raised it to the sky.

Vera had to regain her balance as the earth between them shook, and a hundred rocks the size of large watermelons burst out of the dry earth and loomed overhead. With the movement of a general, Draven motioned toward Vera with his sword, and a volley of the rocks came crashing down on her.

Squinting into the sun, Vera tried to assess the situation. The air pressure changed as the large rocks were upon her. She quickly wrapped a force field around them and chucked it back at Draven. The stones catapulted through the air and crushed down on the right side of the pack, smashing ten Wachiru and three nyx with muffled, excruciating screams.

Her knees almost buckled from the exertion.

"Well now, if you wanted to have fun, you just had to ask." Draven brushed the dust off his black trench coat and snapped his fingers at Radov.

The young man sucked in a deep breath and slumped to the ground.

"Radov!" Vera ran over and knelt beside him.

He looked up, his face twisted in pain. His hand shook as he reached up to cup Vera's face. "Thank you, for trusting in my goodness. I'm sure Arivos will smile on me because of that."

Vera brought her left hand up to hold his hand against her face. "Don't talk like that. I'm going to free you, remember?"

Draven's pasty left hand was outstretched, his fingers curled as if he had just caught an invisible orange. "I grow tired of your useless babbling…big brother."

"Brother?" Vera withdrew her left hand, looking to Radov to refute it.

With tears in his eyes, he let his quaking hand drop. "Forgive me." Radov vanished, and almost instantly a bright-white raven appeared in front of Vera, flapping its wings wildly, but progressing nowhere.

"How nostalgic." Draven closed his left fingers into a tight fist and pulled it to his chest.

The white raven gave out a high-pitched cry, somersaulted in the air, and then went limp on the ground as some unseen force dragged it toward Draven. The raven changed back to Radov, screaming and grasping the burnt grass and mounds of broken dirt, vainly trying to stop himself. In the ten feet he was drug, Radov was but a blur of shifting animals, all in a panic to stop the inevitable. A bull rutting the burnt dirt, a charging elephant, a red Kodiak bear digging in with four-inch claws, a rhinoceros with nostrils flaring, and finally a wondering albatross, beating its thirteen-foot wingspan as if it were flying into hurricane winds.

Draven punched the air downwards with his fist, and the great bird crashed to the ground at his feet with the severity of an iron spike being driven into stone. The bird evaporated, and Radov lay curled up, shaking like a sick dog at its master's feet.

Vera stood, her shock and horror beyond words, beyond all thought. Her fingernails made indents in her cheek as she tried not to vomit.

"Oh, you poor thing," Draven mocked. "The truth given you a bit of a start, has it? You thought the whimpering fool was an innocent? How embarrassing." He hooked the toe of his boot under Radov's chin and lifted it so that he could see into his older brother's frightened blue eyes. "I did not expect my brother to be checking in on me, so he must have really been released." Draven held eye contact with Radov while he talked. "You are a fool to come running to her. Did you think she could protect you? Did you forget that I own you?" Draven maliciously cooed at his brother.

"You didn't keep your end of the bargain. Release me." Radov choked the words past the tip of Draven's boot.

"Oh, but you kept your side! And that is all I cared about. Besides, that was so long ago, it does not matter now. But since we are family, I will let you spend more time with my soon-to-be withered blossom over there." Draven kicked Radov in the throat. "Get up."

Vera's exhaustion, hunger, shock, and bewilderment made her helpless. She had tunnel vision. Reality hit her with such severity that she could not move; she could do nothing but watch the brothers.

"No." Radov spat up blood.

"Come now, brother, do not make me embarrass you in front of your special lady friend," Draven smirked.

"I won't do what you want me to do any longer!" Radov clenched the withered black grass in his fists and stared at Vera with a look of dread.

Draven stepped in between them, his black coattails blocking any possible view of Vera. He crouched down and looked at the crumpled, hunched figure with his cold, emotionless black stare. Then he leaned closer and hissed a breath of fear in Radov's face. "Whatever gave you the impression that you had a choice?"

Brushing the hair out of his older brother's face, Draven watched the veins in the whites of Radov's eyes turn black, then he stood and pointed at a Wachiru, who brought forward a sword. Radov stood, his face devoid of expression, thought, and life.

"I do believe you have been wanting to dance with my brother again…" Draven handed the already bloodied sword to Radov.

"No!" Vera muttered as she dropped her left hand from her face and lifted Ierá Flóga to defend against Radov's catatonic attack.

His advance was one of calculated fear. Each strike came in fast and skillfully, and yet there was a reckless abandon to it all. His feet navigated the disrupted earth with ease as Vera deflected and dodged the blows. The sun cast a haze over the battle, the eerie light making her squint. Her body was becoming too weak to be careful about how close her blade was getting to seriously injuring Radov. He struck the dragon sword down, the tip biting into the dirt. The dented and bloodied iron blade fell to the ground with a muffled clang, and his rough hands grasped Vera's scarred throat.

No recognition even flickered in the glazed-over blue eyes, but the black in the veins receded slightly from his irises, and Radov started to plead. "Vera, kill me. Please, I can't stop. I've tried. Please kill me!"

The edges of Vera's sight were growing fuzzy and dark. She couldn't speak, and her right bicep quaked as she used the last of the air in her lungs to raise her right hand. Ierá Flóga's blade glinted red in the sun's light before she drove her hand down, cracking the golden-wing hand-guard against Radov's temple. His grip loosened, and Vera sucked in air as his body went slack on the ground.

Draven looked at his brother's limp body with a detached apathy, and then sighed, "I am bored." He looked back at the pack of followers that cowered behind him, and then nodded his head toward Vera.

She tried not to reach for her throat when she saw a large nyx emerge from behind Draven. The monster was a sickly gray. Its skin looked cracked and slightly burned as it lazily prowled toward her. When the dog-like creature got a few feet away, it growled and charged. Ierá Flóga came down quick and effortlessly before Vera could even think to have a flashback. She stepped around the limp carcass and shortened the distance between her and Draven, trying her best to walk in a straight line over the erupted earth. With just ten feet between her and the core of evil, Vera prepared herself for what was sure to be the longest hours of her life.

"Did you like the kill?" Draven's emotionless smile gave her chills.

"No, but I have a feeling I'm going to enjoy your death."

"Kill her."

Four Wachiru sprinted toward her. Two carried axes, one a scythe, and the other a spear. The sun descended in the sky while Vera fought against the crazed men, who were undeterred by the blows of her sword, the fear that Draven drove them with making them senseless to pain. Hours passed, and Vera's potency was limited.

Finally, with the last of her strength and a hopeful prayer, she looked to the ground and felt into the ruptured earth, felt the empty space where the flying rocks had come from, and she breathed out a sigh of relief. All four severely injured Wachiru swung toward her in a lethal advance. Vera closed her eyes and breathed in. She was knocked to the ground as the dirt around her opened up and swallowed the Wachiru before they could get to her. When she opened her eyes, four round spots in the ground looked oddly smooth compared to the rest of the disrupted earth around her.

Vera turned in a circle. The nyx corpse already had flies swarming on it, Radov's seemingly dead body lay behind her, and she stood on the ground in which she buried four nearly alive men. She stared at Radov's body; sunset made him look pallid. Draven looked on with an eager smile.

"No more," she croaked.

"Well, to be honest, I did not think you would make it this far." He signaled to the Wachiru, and several started to advance toward her.

"No more, for tonight."

"How adorable. You think the night will bring you rest?" Draven raised his sword and slowly walked toward the weary girl. The nyx growled.

Two Wachiru grabbed Radov by the arms and started to drag him away. Six other Wachiru surrounded Vera. Draven had cut off any escape she could have had. The nyx started to circle around the Wachiru who encircled her, their skin already exhibiting a slight sheen—the beginnings of the venom in the failing light of day.

Ierá Flóga had shrunk to a short sword, yet Vera's arm could barely hold that up. There was only a sliver of light left on the horizon, and she could feel a noose of evil trying to tangle itself through her hair and around her neck.

Vera could not remember the feeling of food on her tongue, her throat scratched for water, and her body felt like the bones were liquefying. Her clothing and body were splattered with blood from the day of fighting, her cheeks flushed from exertion and anger at Draven's cruelty.

Ierá Flóga grew cold against her hand as she lifted it up and pointed the shortening sword at Draven. Vera collected all the energy she could, and with a white-lavender-red surge of light from the little dragon's mouth, she hit Draven with the only defense she had left. As the ray of light hit him, Draven started clawing at his chest, snarling and growling at Vera. She balled the light energy in his chest and exploded it out, making it reach over all Draven's minions like a pyroclastic flow. The Wachiru around her were knocked unconscious, some seizing up, and the nyx started yelping and sprinted off as if their paws had been lit on fire. Draven lay on the ground, spasms running through his entire body, dark gray foam oozing from his mouth.

Vera swayed over him. "Like I said, enough."

Chapter 37
Belief in the Impossible

She glared down at Draven, whose black eyes rolled back and closed as he lay on the burnt ground like a dried-out worm. Her knees collapsed, and her left hand landed on Draven's chest. She could feel his erratic heartbeat. Ierá Flóga breathed in the blade and returned to her finger so that she could unbuckle her vest and pull the tourmaline dagger from the chain around her neck. His power tingled against her fingertips; her right hand shook as she brought it up. It glinted like the far-off stars as she drove it down...and then hesitated. Her grip failed, and the dagger slipped through her slack fingers, hit Draven in the chest with a light thud, and rolled down his arm, almost making it into his open hand.

His eyelids shot open, and he growled, "You lack the will." He was still immobilized, but even without the ability to move, he held more strength than Vera.

Retrieving the dagger, she clutched it and crawled backwards on all fours, nearly hyperventilating. Vera fell over the body of a Wachiru, but she couldn't take her eyes away from the knowing smile on Draven's face. With some effort, she pushed off the body she tripped over, stood, and backed into the night, away from the bottomless pit of Draven's black eyes.

A spark of light in the distance caught her eye, but the only concern on her mind was somehow finding food, water, and a safe place to stay. She didn't know where the dragon was, although she did know that It was the only reason she made it this far.

The toes of her boots scraped the ground with every step toward the supposed fire. Vera stretched her cramped fingers. The camp was undoubtedly for some Wachiru, but she could stand to fight for sustenance.

For twenty minutes she forced her feet one in front of the other to get close enough to see two hooded silhouettes in the light of a small fire. Vera ran the osmium chain through the dagger and returned it to its place around her throat. She approached with caution, trying to drag her leather boots across the cracked dirt as quietly as possible.

Vera still hid in the dark when the bigger of the two men stood and drew a sword that seemed familiar. The tall, skinny one got flustered and clumsily unsheathed his sword that definitely brought some confused memories to Vera's mind. She looked down at her right hand and saw that the dragon was still resting on her finger, so she confidently stepped into the ring of light.

A smile broke out on the bigger man's face. His bright teeth and a scar on his right jawline were all the hood allowed Vera to see.

"Not possible." Vera rubbed her eyes.

The man laughed, swept his hood back, and shook his head at Vera. "I would think you of all people would have started to believe in the impossible by now."

"Yateem!" The realization gave life back to Vera as she ran and wrapped her arms around the man she thought she had left to die on a dock. His heartbeat drummed against her ear, and tears streamed through the dirt and dried blood on her face.

Yateem stroked Vera's messy hair and tried to hold on to the feeling of old times. "Are you hungry?"

Vera vigorously nodded her head up and down.

Yateem held her at arm's length and tried not to notice the cuts and dried blood all over her. "Let me get you some food, and then you should rest." As he walked over toward the saddlebags on the other side of the fire, Yateem didn't know what to say, how to ask the questions he wanted answered, and if he should even try. "Where is Zakiyyah?"

"I don't know. Flying around."

Yateem looked up, only a hint of suspicion in his features.

Fenelle had set down the sword on his pack and stood awkwardly awaiting his introduction to The Lavender Soul. He removed his hood and brushed some of the dirt from his clothes.

Vera eyed him up and down. "Hello."

"Wow, you're a lot prettier when you're not dead." Fenelle gave her a smile.

"Excuse me?"

"Even with all the blood and stuff." Fenelle gave a half-assed bow. "The name's Fenelle." He looked up and winked at her.

Vera looked at Yateem for an explanation as Aethon strutted up and nuzzled Vera's hair with his forehead.

Yateem walked up to her with water, smoked salmon, and bread. "Fenelle gave me Aethon to carry you to Elea."

Vera grabbed the water canteen and guzzled half of it down, then started to devour the food. She looked at her sword on the shepherd's pack, and then at the horse, who was standing right next to her, acting like Vera was an old friend.

"More like you *took* him and off-loaded some items on me, but when Aethon returned to me with untouched saddlebags full of provisions, I was intrigued."

Vera stumbled closer to the fire and then collapsed, hugging the food and water to her chest.

"Queen Emmanuelle sent Aethon to Fenelle, and then Fenelle to me, along with some others." Yateem's voice was soft, a balm to Vera's obviously strained nerves.

"Others?" Vera talked with her mouth full.

Yateem whistled, and Vulcan and Minerva came into the light and ran over to Vera. As their soft fur brushed either side of her head, the vibrations of their purrs made Vera dizzy.

"Mini. Vulkey." Vera placed the food in her lap and scratched under their chins with both her aching hands.

"I am not sure whether Arivos or Emmanuelle sent them to find me, but I feel safer, and am glad they found Fenelle."

"They shaved a couple years off my life before I was glad the big cats were around!" Fenelle quipped.

"Queen Emmanuelle released Radov from Shifra." Vera stared blindly into the fire as she gave the last bite of smoked salmon to Minerva, who had lay down to provide a backrest for Vera.

"You saw him? When?" Yateem was weary of the look in Vera's eye as he crouched down close to her.

"Today." Vera leaned her head against Mini's side, calmed by the steady rising and falling of her ribcage. "I fought him."

"I'm sorry, who are we talking about?" Fenelle resumed his spot by the fire.

"Draven's older brother."

"What?" Yateem stood and started to pace.

"He's been imprisoned by the fairies as a shape-shifter. He was freed recently…I killed him, before he could kill me." The words left a bitter taste in her mouth as she glared at the fire, trying not to cry.

"Are you okay?" Yateem crouched down again, this time craning his neck to make eye contact with her.

She shook her head from side to side as she stared at her hands. Because of the hand-guard of Ierá Flóga, her right hand was clean, but her left was caked with dirt and blood.

"What was that purple-reddish horizontal lightning about?" Fenelle muttered the question, not sure if she actually wanted to answer any questions.

"Me, putting Draven and his *pets* to bed for the night."

"Why didn't you just kill Draven while he was down?" Fenelle's cinnamon eyes drove a look of accusation at Vera.

Vera's glare shifted to Fenelle's face. "I lacked the will." Her hands shook, and her voice came out as a shaky growl.

Fenelle looked at the sword that lay on top of his pack, as if wondering if he could have killed Draven.

"Vera, what can I do?" Yateem wanted to reach out to her, but feared the quick shift of color in her eyes.

"Tell me how you're alive." She looked with tears in her eyes at the crescent-shaped scars that lined his neck.

"You delivered me to the best healer in Zerahlinda. I almost died from blood loss when all the nails were removed, but when I woke, I felt both renewed and an urgent need to get to The Vanished Lands. I took a small ship, and once I landed, I followed my instinct, which led us here." Yateem placed his hand on top of Vera's.

She drew away and lay against Minerva. "Too much has happened today." She closed her eyes. "I'm happy you're alive," she murmured.

Yateem pinched the bridge of his nose, trying not to cry as he watched Vera's body go limp.

"So, *she's* supposed to rid the world of evil? Seems unlikely." Fenelle pondered Vera. The way the firelight glinted off her auburn hair brought out conflicted feelings in him.

"It is certain—as certain as you breathing your last breath if you ever utter anything close to that sentiment again." Yateem lay down on the hard ground, sleeping sack under his head, his feet near Minerva's head, his line of sight to Vera unobstructed.

"Not a word out of me from now on." Fenelle lay next to the fire and stared at Vera, who looked so small and helpless curled up against the huge gennadius. "So why are we going to sleep right after dark?"

"Come daybreak, boy, we will be fighting to the death for Zerahlinda's future." Yateem didn't open his eyes to see the young shepherd's reaction.

"Well, that's a lullaby for you."

Chapter 38
Freedom

The earth shuddered. The air hung with electricity. Eyes focused on the immediate enemy, the inevitable danger. Blood ran cold as the battle grew ever closer.

Vera's breathing was labored as the two sides collided with the ferocity of injured animals recklessly abandoning their will to live. Like the morbid sight of falling ash being swept away by black smoke, Draven and his minions rode on nyx, all with a dreadful look of unbridled bloodlust in their eyes. Fear reflected in varying degrees in the eyes of Vera, Yateem, and Fenelle, who rode their animals also, meeting the evil threat which was at least ten times their number.

Sword met sword with spine-cracking screeches. The nyx and gennadius bared their teeth and sunk them into as much soft flesh as they could. Vera and Yateem jumped from Minerva and Vulcan when the animals pounced onto the first line of nyx, the nauseating sound of rabid dogs fighting over a scrap of decayed meat erupting from the attack. Fenelle was launched onto the back of a Wachiru when Aethon started to buck and kick anything that came near him.

Terrorized pandemonium.

Yateem struck down all Wachiru that dared to get within a blade's distance of him, his eyes glazing over in the heat of battle. Fenelle swung wildly at man and beast alike, angry tears streaking through the caked-on blood and grime on his cheeks.

Vera terminated Draven's hallucinations by trapping them in a force field around him. After a globe of flame engulfed him and ravens picked at his flesh, Draven ceased using that weapon, and with pecked skin and smoke rising from his clothing, he showed his teeth in a hostile smile. Radov approached, with an unmanned stare, a nyx also stalking the same prey.

Draven hissed, drew his sword, and cut the nyx in half. "She is mine! Cut the shepherd into tasty bits." The black eyes held Fenelle in their gaze, the flashing of the panic-stricken swinging of the blade reflecting off the obsidian-like globes.

Radov sprinted toward the wincing young man with animosity, and Fenelle turned around just in time to block a fatal blow. Their fight looked like a tiger and an antelope, one obviously more dangerous, more malicious with the blows, but the other still fighting with the helpless hope that there might be an escape to life.

Vera faltered, watching, not wanting either of them to die. Ierá Flóga grew hot around her hand, returning her attention to Draven where he stood with an expression of anticipated carnage.

"At last, time to taste your blood." He flew at her with the rage of a Fury.

Vera raised her dragon sword and fought. With every iota of belief she had in her body, she fought. The black spikes of the fiend's blade got very close to her scarred throat, and Ierá Flóga got to bite into his flesh a few times, but no real damage was accomplished.

Yateem ferociously cut down all foes around him, making his way through the mutilated bodies toward Vera's side. Fenelle and Radov's fight was also nearing the dueling pair of light and dark, as if some type of magnetism was pulling them in.

Draven's fervor was revolting. The black of his eyes grew darker the closer he was to accomplishing his evil goal. Vera was near panic. Her strength couldn't match his, her determination flinched with every blow, and her faith hesitated. There was nothing else than this moment. His cloud of hatred, anger, and cruelty was suffocating Vera's light. With a repugnant scream, Draven drove his sword down, snapping Ierá Flóga's blade in two, and then drew it upwards, spraying Vera's blood in her face.

As a deep gash opened from her right hip to her left shoulder, the metallic taste of her own life seeped into Vera's mouth. She looked at Draven, tears in her fading eyes. All she could feel was pity and despair. Ierá Flóga returned to a ring on her index finger, and Vera brought her hands to her chest, trying to close the wound, trying to grip the exposed dagger. Her hands fell lifeless to her side, and the ring slipped off with the blood that dripped from her fingers. As the heavy ring hit the ground with a dreadful thud, a wind rose. Brightness shone in Vera's eyes, and a bit of strength returned. "I forgive you." Her voice was meek, but the words were not.

Draven frowned. "Save your forgiveness. I plan on tasting your flesh."

Yateem lunged at Draven. The Dark One grabbed Yateem by the throat, crushed his windpipe, and dropped him like a rotten potato. Radov had struck Fenelle down with a cracking punch, but both were too petrified to continue the fight. They could only watch Yateem's body fall to the ground, Vera trying to put pressure on her wound, trying not to bleed out, and Draven looming over her as a cliff looms over a calm sea. The two young men could do nothing but watch, as the hope of the world faded.

"I forgive you."

Draven let out a venomous hiss and charged at Vera. Breaking out of his fearful obligation, Radov sprinted and jumped in front of Vera. Draven pierced his blade through Radov's stomach, twisted it, and then pulled out the dripping blade from the hole it created with a nauseating wet, tearing sound. Radov shook, fell to his knees, and looked up at his little brother with tears in his eyes before collapsing on the hard, dry land.

As he lay there, his gaze turned to Vera. Dirt crammed underneath his nails as his fingers crawled across the dirt and grass, through the growing puddle of her blood, and rested on her boot. Dark blood pumped out of his wound at a grotesque rate, his eyes were already clouding over, but the corners of his mouth turned slightly up. With his last breath he mouthed the words, "I'm free." His eyelids slammed down, and the feeble pressure his fingers put on Vera's boot was gone.

A purely reptilian animalistic roar rumbled from above the clouds. A swift wind swept over them, breathing life into Vera, and doubt into Draven.

His black eyes looked up to the sky, concerned and despairing. With self-loathing, he looked at his hands, dripping with the blood of his older brother. The anger in his heart rising, his breathing on the verge of hyperventilation, Draven looked down on Vera, who had a trusting, sad smile on her face as she looked at the destruction around her. He gritted his teeth, stepped over Radov, threw his sword down, clutched the chain around Vera's neck, and pulled her up to his face.

"I have taken everything, everyone you love. I will drown everyone in my hatred, hack them to pieces until I am declared the lord and master of this world!" He still could not break the chain that held the dagger, so he wrapped the illusion of flames around it, heated it till it was radiating an orange-red color, and pulled it so that it burned into the back of Vera's neck.

She tried not to scream as she looked into Draven's eyes, which were a void. That which she could blame for all the pain in her life—the death of her parents, the obligation to give up any sense of normalcy or belonging, the reason she had to experience such trials as no one should ever have to face—was staring her right in the eyes. And yet, Vera could not feel hatred, could not taste the familiar bitterness on her tongue. Even as her flesh burned and blood drained from her body, she could see that she was the one that was free. Vera's suffering was but a drop of water in a desert compared to the excruciating enslavement that Draven had put himself through.

Her trembling, bloodstained fingers wrapped around the broad end of the dagger, and in a movement too swift to be stopped, she yanked the chain apart and plunged the tourmaline weapon into Draven's heart.

"I forgive you, for everything." She let go of the dagger and dropped down to the ground, her legs too weak to hold her up.

Draven tried to pull the dagger out, but had no power over it. His eyes faded from black to red, to gray. He fell to his knees and shrieked as he pulled out his hair.

Zakiyyah broke through the clouds and inhaled the black tornado that was escaping through the dagger into the sky. As Its mane whipped and undulated like golden fire in a strong wind, the tourmaline dagger was swept up in the ending of the dark life force that Zakiyyah breathed in. Draven's lifeless body hit the ground, and the mighty dragon hovered over the scene of mutilated destruction.

Zakiyyah looked to be a smudge of pure golden light in the growing darkness of Vera's blurring sight.

"Thank...you...for...strength." Vera could barely hear the words that came out with her forced breaths.

Her eyelids grew heavy, and for less than a moment she looked at Yateem's limp body, saw the downed gennadius' rib cages rising and falling feverishly, and made eye contact with Fenelle, who was silently crying and trying to crawl over to Vera.

The last thing that Vera was aware of was all the air around her being sucked away as Zakiyyah took in a breath. The last sight her lavender eyes saw was a bright and pure white flame descending upon the land. She smelt the burning of bodies and felt the searing touch of holy flame on her as she closed her eyes, and welcomed her end.

Chapter 39
Zakiyyah's Flight

The sound was tremendous. The young shepherd raised his arms to the sky, the dragon's flame reflected off his cinnamon eyes. The scourging fire hit with the beauty and force of an avalanche. The golden wings brought a gale that swept the flames up and blazed them across the land.

The rusty grass erupted, the white flame consuming all destruction in its path. The dragon landed among the flames, Its enormous claws nearly crushing the golden dragon ring into the smoldering dirt. It took in the sight of Vera, Yateem, Fenelle, and even their animals, all that had sacrificed their lives for Zerahlinda. Unable to cry for lack of tear ducts, the ancient, holy draconem breathed in the ashes of Draven and his unfortunate minions and unfurled Its wings. The flame was such a pure white that human eyes for miles around would be clenched shut and covered for fear of going blind from the brilliance. Zakiyyah spiraled upward as It breathed more holy fire down on the gruesome remnants of the destined battle.

It then looked onward. The crucible of Zakiyyah's flame would reach every dark crack, deep canyon, thick forest, and high plateau. No one would be spared the sight of the terrible beauty of the holy dragon of legend, and the purifying light It brought.

Every Wachiru, nyx, yagim, mermaid, stone, tree, and grain that had been poisoned against Arivos was devoured in a flash of white heat. All those that had let hatred, rage, envy, greed, selfishness, and impurity burrow their way into their hearts felt the searing burst from their chest, and when the smoke cleared, felt reborn.

Zerahlinda was renewed. All that burdened it, all that invited darkness into the lives of the people was eliminated. People no longer feared what the dark of night held for them, but rejoiced in the rest that was given them by Arivos. Many could not sleep that first night.

Many feared it had all been an impossible dream; the huge golden dragon, with Its panic-striking majesty, Its purity that shone through Its white eyes, Its mane that wavered like liquid gold, Its wings that fueled the holocaust of evil, and Its breath that at once took in the ashes of malevolence and gave out the gift of life.

In Its shadow there was light, in Its light a promise, and in that promise a new hope of a beautiful dawn.

Epilogue

Robins, wrens, chaffinches, warblers, and song thrushes mingled their gentle waking song in a dawn chorus. The delicate smell of lavender and calla lilies mingled in the sunlight that streamed into the warm bedroom.

Vera stirred and opened her eyes slowly, expecting the overwhelming light that she had endured after she died the first time. Fenelle lay on a big couch, his left arm and leg hanging off the edge, a stream of drool spilling from his mouth.

She delicately pushed her body up into a seated position and looked around at the room that was full of the flowers that had woken her with their aroma.

Fenelle lazily opened his eyes to check on Vera. On seeing her up and sitting, he shot upright on the couch. "You're awake!"

She looked down and felt where there should have been a fatal wound on her torso. "I'm alive?"

"I have to go wake up the king and queen! They'll be so excited!" Fenelle ran toward the glass French doors that opened up to a garden.

"Wait! Where are we? How did I get here? And where is Yateem?"

"Well, if you look out the doors, you will see we are in Lolani. When I woke, after getting holy dragon fire breathed on me, I saw that Vulcan and Minerva were lying near their unconscious masters, and that Aethon was anxious to be on our way." Fenelle walked over to the bed. "Yateem had mentioned some Wachiru you guys came across in Ziva, so I left you guys with the gennadius and rode Aethon as fast as he would go to the nearest village to see if there were any shepherds or merchants that could show me the caravan trail through the Ruwaydah mountains, to Ziva." Fenelle tried not to seem hesitant or shy when he sat on the bed next to her.

Vera scooted over so that he had room to sit comfortably. "And both of us couldn't wake?"

"I figured that your wounds were too severe to recover right away. Your scars were gone, so I knew you would be alright. I explained my situation to a merchant, who was still so mystified by Zakiyyah's appearance that he agreed to do whatever it took to get you home."

"Where did the flowers come from?"

"They sprouted from the earth where Draven, Radov, and all the other nasties fell. The merchant, really the whole village, picked them and lay them around you and Yateem in the wagon that we put you in for the journey."

"Radov?" Vera stared at her fingers.

"Turned to ash." Fenelle put his hand over hers. "Arivos and Zakiyyah saw his last act. All the others were black ash; his was white." He scrunched his face, frustrated by the casual manner with which he blurted that out. "Sorry, that's morbid. I'm just saying, I think he's free with Arivos right now."

Vera gave Fenelle a faint smile and squeezed his hand to get him to look up at her. "Yateem?"

"Oh, right! He's fine, in a room down the hall. He just woke up yesterday, so don't feel too lazy. By the way, I didn't realize that you're related to the king and queen of Ziva. When the caravan came to the palace, the rumor of the Lavender Soul apparently made it up to the throne because they came to the wagon that I had been guarding with my life a little over two days straight, and next thing I'm aware of, I'm being hugged by royalty! And I was a few days—or weeks—shy of a good cleaning!"

"Fenelle." Vera put her hand on his shoulder as a broad smile broke on her face. "I would like to see all of them, before your babbling puts me back to sleep."

"Sorry, I've been talking to you while you slept. I guess I'm not used to accounting for someone actually listening."

"Fenelle…"

"Right! Going to go wake up royalty like a rooster...or maybe I'll let Yateem wake them up." Fenelle jumped up and ran to the glass doors, flung them open, and leaped into the early morning air. "Pray I don't get beheaded!" He yelled back to her with a jolly air.

Vera smiled at herself in the mirror. Her eyes were a soft lavender and no longer shifted color, but they did have tiny flecks of gold in them. Her fingers glided over the satin straps just off her shoulder. The ball gown was lavender satin, with a deep-purple sash around her waist that had teal swirls sown on with silver thread. The satin was draped away from the front of the medium-bodied skirt, revealing a deep-purple organza underneath embellished with larger versions of the teal swirls.

"One last touch." Daisy pulled Vera's loose hair away from her neck and clasped a necklace in place. "I know zat it is not like zah jewels zat zee queen presented to you, but I have been holding on to it since you vere in Feyerabend."

"Daisy, you already made this gown. You didn't have to do this!" Vera's eyes sparkled as she leaned in close to the mirror to admire the necklace. It was a lavender orchid, delicate and regal, whose shape was reminiscent of a butterfly. In place of a chain was a thin vine with heart-shaped leaves, its gentle waves adding a whimsy to the necklace that suited Vera well.

"I could not help myself. I do not like vorrying about presents at zee last minute. I dipped it in zee pitch of a laurel tree. It vill not corrode." She beamed at Vera, her yellow wings fluttering nervously.

Vera grabbed Daisy's hand. "You always believed in me, didn't you?"

Daisy's lips lightly pressed against the top of Vera's hand, the wings of Ierá Flóga gently kissing the fairy's chin in return. "Of course."

A swift knock came at the door. "They are about to announce you." Yateem stood in the doorway of the waiting room, breathless as he looked at the strong young woman before him.

"I've been dreaming about going to a ball my whole life. I always thought I'd have to sneak into one, not be the guest of honor." Vera turned and smiled, trying to choke down a nervous giggle.

Majlis' wings were clearly visible behind Yateem. She stuck her head out, her golden hair resembling a waterfall, and smiled at Vera. "You are gorgeous!" she said, nudging Yateem in the ribs.

"Ow! Yes, I am not quite ready for you to be such a stunning young woman. Are you sure there is not a less becoming dress that you could wear?" Yateem looked at Daisy with a playful scolding glance, and then offered his arm to Vera.

"The radius of this skirt should keep everyone at an acceptable distance." Vera looped her arm with his.

"I doubt that. I was a young man once." Yateem shook his head as he led Vera, Majlis, and Daisy to the grand staircase that opened up into a magnificent ballroom. He kissed her cheek once they were at the top of the stair. "You deserve this. You deserve all the love in the world. So keep your chin up, and show everyone that charming smile that has frustrated and delighted me through the years." Yateem winked at the teenager, grabbed Majlis' hand, and started to descend the red-velvet lined staircase.

Daisy, unaccustomed to human interaction, flew to the ballroom floor, sending a flurry of gasps and laughs through the room.

The ballroom was full of laughter, chatter, colorful fabrics, and happiness. King Koios and Queen Prudencia stood when they saw Vera alone at the top of the stairs. Both wore brilliant smiles as they looked up at her.

"Ladies and gentlemen," King Koios projected with an eloquence and grace that sent a hush over the entire room, "it is by far the greatest honor of my life to present your guest of honor, my beloved niece, Vera Xochiquetzal of Adowa, The Lavender Soul!"

Cheers erupted from the crowd amid applause, screams, and tears of gratitude. Vera was humbled and touched. She smiled and tried not to cry as she picked up her skirt and descended the stairs with the air of royalty.

Vera was elated the entire evening. She met and socialized with people that, for the most part, treated her like any other young lady. There were no gasps directed at her, excepting reactions to her dress and her stories. Vera graciously answered questions about her life without any tinge of bitterness, regret, or anger. She felt blessed—extremely blessed—to be alive and was proud to tell of the ways Arivos moved her life.

Vera asked questions of her own, of the world outside that which she had experienced through her journey and through her prior studies. She was entertained by newfound friends' stories and was taught the newer dances. King Benoit, Queen Emmanuelle, Amaury, and Daisy entertained Vera—and most everyone else for that matter—with their presence.

As Daisy and Vera were giggling and talking on the outskirts of the dance floor, Fenelle, who looked slightly out of place in a finely tailored suit, strolled up to them, trying not to stare at either of the ladies as he did so.

"I must say you look ravishing, Lavender Soul." Fenelle gave a formal bow.

"Better than when I was dead, or covered in blood and stuff?" Vera returned a curtsey with a coy smile.

"Well, I am but a poor country shepherd and completely ignorant of the ways of noble people, and fairies as well." He gave a little nod to Daisy. "So it may just be the grandeur of the occasion that makes your beauty so completely intoxicating. And yes, your skin tone is a much nicer hue when blood is coursing through your body instead of out of it."

Daisy covered her mouth with her hand, holding in the laugh that was trying to escape.

"Compliments from you always feel like a trick."

"That's my charm."

Vera smiled and returned her gaze to the ballroom floor covered with the smiling, twirling, leaping, bowing, sashaying, and occasionally bumbling crowd of colorfully dressed guests dancing to the festive music.

Fenelle observed her in wonder. "What will you do now?"

"That's the beauty of it, I guess. I found out what I was made for. I think I'll travel. It should be more enjoyable without a threat lingering over me. I want to meet people, really get to know them, and try things I've never even heard of yet. Help rebuild Elspeth. In general, I want to spread love wherever I can. Basically, I've got the rest of my life to find out *who* I was made to be." Vera rambled with excitement as she looked at the party guests.

"Wow. I was talking about what you were going to do at this ball. You just laid some heavy thoughts on me."

Vera shook her head and smiled. "I think I'll start with a dance with you, if that's alright."

Daisy stepped aside with a big smile.

Fenelle blushed. "I would be honored, Lavender Soul." He bowed deep.

Vera lifted his chin. "The name's Vera." With a mischievous flash from her golden-specked lavender eyes, she winked.

The End.

Character Name Meanings and Origins:

People:

Vera Xochiquetzal of Adowa {VE-rah Sho-chi-KET-sal of Ah-DOH-ah}: Truth (*Latin*)—Precious feather flower (*Nahuati*)—Noble (*African*)

Yateem Rukan Wulfgar of Xipili {Yah-TEEM Roo-Kon Wolf-gar of Zee-peel-ee}: Orphan (*Arabic*)—Steady/Confident (*Arabic*)—Wolf Spear (*Ancient Germanic*)—Jeweled Prince (*Nahuati*)

Majlis {Mih-less}: Pearl (*Swedish*, but more importantly it is the middle name of a friend who asked to be a part of one of my stories)

King Koios {k-EE-aw-s}: From a Titan god of intelligence

Queen Prudencia {proo-DHEN-sya}: Prudence, good judgment (*Spanish*)

Radov {rah-DOH-veh}: anagram of Croatian name Davor, meaning expression of joy and sorrow

Draven: I cannot stand ravens, they have always symbolized darkness and trouble to me

Wachiru {wah-CHEER-oo}: lawmaker's son (*Kenyan*)

Amaury {A-MAW-REE}: work, labor, power (*French*)

Manon {Mae-noh}: bitter (*French*) (He didn't get Majlis)

King Benoit {bEH-n-w ah }: Blessed (*French*)

Queen Emanuelle {Ee-man-U-elle}: Faithful (*French*)

Fenelle {Feh-nell}: White shoulder (*Gaelic*)

Daisy: The flower

Arivos {Ar-ee-voh-s}: Anagram of savior

Zakiyyah {Zah-key-ah}: Pure (*Arabic*)

Hebians {He-bee-ans}: From the Greek god of youth Hebe

Gennadius {jeh-NA-dee-US}: Latinized form of Greek name Gennadas meaning noble, generous

Lands:

Zerahlinda {Zare-ah-lin-dah}: From Hebrew name Zarahlinda meaning beautiful dawn

Ziva {Zee-vah}: bright, radiant *(Hebrew)*

Rinan {Ree-nan}: Rain *(Anglo)*

Shifra {sh-ih-f-rah}: Beautiful *(Hebrew)*

Elspeth {ELS-peth}: "Chosen by God" *(Scottish)*

Yakootah {Yah-koo-tah}: Emerald *(Arabic)*

Ruwaydah {Roo-wa-duh}: Walking gently *(Arabic)*

Aequitas {eh-qui-toss}: Justice, equality *(Latin)*

Towns and Estates:

Saman {Sah-mah-n}: Beautiful, elegant *(Persian)*

Kuno {KOO-no}: Clan, family *(Ancient Germanic)*

Dayo {Day-oh}: "Joy arrives" *(Western African)*

Lolani {Lo-law-nee}: Royal hawk *(Hawaiian)*

Feyerabend {Feh-YAIR-ah-bend}: A famous philosopher

Athanaric {Ah-th-ann-ah-rick}: Power, ruler *(Ancient Germanic)*

Elea {A-la-ah}: An Italian village known as the home of the philosopher Parmenides

Sanctimonia {Sah-n-c-teh-moh-nee-ah}: Virtue, purity, sanctity *(Latin)*

Bodies of water:

Cardea {Car-dee-ah}: "hinge, axis" from Roman goddess of thresholds, and change

Kallisto {Kah-list-OH}: "most beautiful" the nymph that was loved by Zeus, and changed into a bear.

Kassiopeia {Kass-ee-oh-pea-ah}: Mother of Andromeda, changed into constellation after death.

Ireneus {I-ray-nee-oos}: Peaceful *(Greek)*

Seija Sea {Say-jah}: tranquil, serene *(Finnish)*